PASSION'S DAWNING

Tohave frowned. "Do you want to go back?"

She looked down. "I don't know anymore. There was a time when I would have given anything to go back. Now . . . I'm not sure I want to leave."

"Because you are learning to love the land?"

Katie turned and met his eyes. "You know that's not the reason. It isn't the land I'm learning to love."

He came closer again, and she could not take her eyes from the dark shadowy man who hovered over her.

"It is Tohave you love."

She could not deny it. He bent closer and she did not resist. Warm, beautiful lips gently caressed her mouth with loving little kisses until she felt limp with desire. He pulled her close then, crushing her against his powerful chest. Never did she dream she could feel this way in a man's arms, this alive, on fire, with urges she had never known surging deep within her. . . .

PRAIRIE EMBRACE

F. Rosanne Bittner

ZEBRA BOOKS
KENSINGTON PUBLISHING CORP.

ZEBRA BOOKS

are published by

Kensington Publishing Corp.
475 Park Avenue South
New York, NY 10016

Third printing: February, 1990

Printed in the United States of America

*To that inland sea of tall grass and lonely emptiness,
and to the only humans who fit that wide, wild land . . .
to the now-vanished wild prairies
and to the now-vanished wild Indians.
Both are lost and will never be found again.*

From the Author

The name of my character, Tohave, is pronounced Tow-ha'-vee with the accent on ha, and the letter *a* is like the *a* in spa. The name means wilderness in Cheyenne. Some other Sioux and Cheyenne words are used in this story, in which their meanings are made clear, but these words are also listed at the back of this book for your convenience.

This story takes place in northern Nebraska and southwest South Dakota, during the last days of the Sioux. The incidents that deal with the Ghost Dance religion and the final massacre at Wounded Knee are factual, except for the involvement of my fictitious characters. The source of factual material is *Bury My Heart at Wounded Knee*, by Dee Brown (Holt, Rinehart & Winston, Inc.). The main characters and events of this novel are purely the product of the author's imagination.

F. Rosanne Bittner

He moved like the gentle sway of tall prairie grass,
Brushed past her in the endless wind.
His skin was brown as the parched earth;
His smile bright as the prairie sun.
He was her only joy, her only hope.
Tohave.
He turned her lonely prairie life . . .
    Into a song.
She was the instrument.
When he touched her . . .
    The music began.

Chapter One

Katie watched the little black spot disappear and reappear as the wagon wheel made its monotonous circular movement, creaking over an endless land under an endless sky. It was early May but already hot, so very hot! The huge brim of her bonnet did little to relieve her, though it did keep the sun off her delicate skin and thick, auburn hair. The wagon jolted over a clump of bunch grass, startling her from a kind of trance brought on by the heat and the constant groaning of the wagon wheels. There was no other sound except the wind, the never-ending dry wind that seemed to penetrate her pores and drink up all the moisture in her.

"You could talk a little more, woman," her husband grunted.

She turned to look at him, squinting her normally large, vivid blue eyes, tired now from too much bright sun. What was there for a nineteen-year-old girl to say to a man twenty years her senior, a cruel and not-so-handsome man she did not love, even though he was her husband? And to make matters worse, he was bringing her into a strange, barren land, a land she already hated. She was sure it would soon shrivel her into early old age and ruin her pretty, soft skin. Only a few weeks earlier

11

her father had told her she would be marrying Ezra Russell, his best friend and a widower who needed a woman to take west with him to homestead. Objections had only brought a whipping with the familiar belt, and she'd been too frightened of the outside world to try to run away.

"Most girls your age have been married three, four years!" her father had ranted. "You've been too fussy, girl. It's time you were hitched and having babies—and out of this house. You'll marry Ezra, and you'll find it's not so bad. It's time for you to quit being a child, to start being a woman and doing what God intended."

If this is what God intended, she thought, then God is cruel. She could not forget her sick fear that first night: fear of the unknown things husbands expected of wives; fear of being the property of a man she didn't even like, a man who had cruelty in his eyes as well as a strange hunger when he looked at her. It did not take long to find out what was expected, what that hunger meant, and how cruel he could be. *Rape* was the only word that aptly described his treatment of her on her wedding night, and his attacks on her since. But she was his wife; she had no choice now. Her only hope was to get pregnant. Perhaps a baby would ease the lonely agony of her loveless marriage.

She said nothing. She only turned to watch the black dot go round and round again. Why would any man want to come to this land? They had left behind the big trees of Illinois—the shade, the water, the green. There were none of those things here, only barren emptiness and yellow grass. No neighbors, no friends. Back home on the farm, in spite of her unhappy marriage, there had at least been friends and a few relatives nearby, people to visit, to talk to—people with whom she could pretend life was good. There she could sometimes get away from Ezra, and he in turn had to put on some pretense of being a good husband.

But out here it would be different. There was no one to see, no one to care. He could treat her however he chose, and no one would chide him, nor was there anyone to whom she could turn for friendship and comfort. Why? Why had he come out here? She should have run away. Now she couldn't even do that, for where would she go in this naked land? She'd surely die of hunger and thirst before reaching safety and shelter. And there was not even a place to hide from Ezra while she ran. He would find her and beat her, and if he didn't, she'd probably be found by Indians and face horrible humiliation and death.

Yes, in this barren and lonely land Indians skulked about, or so she'd been told. They were supposed to be on reservations, but they didn't always stay there. The ones who didn't—wild ones, the untamed ones—sometimes raided farms and raped the womenfolk. The picture her friends and Ezra had painted was gruesome indeed; yet her "loving" husband had chosen to expose her to such dangers.

"Northwest Nebraska," Ezra had told them in a loud, bragging voice. She remembered that night, sitting around a huge table with her father and six brothers, and Ezra. They'd been married one week when her husband had announced that they would leave a week later. She'd hoped that he'd change his mind, but the land on his own farm was used up and useless. Nothing would grow there anymore. The soil was spent while out in Nebraska lay new, untouched land—cheap. Only a few weeks earlier the government had announced that land was available. The acreage was formerly reservation land, now cut away from the ever-shrinking section set aside for the Sioux. Ezra Russell wanted some of that land, to start a new farm. And he wanted a woman to work it with him. A man needed a woman on the lonely prairie, but none was

13

willing until Katie's father suggested Ezra marry Katie and take her along.

Ezra Russell! She'd never liked the short, dark, ugly man who'd been their neighbor. When her father had said they would marry she had not really believed he'd meant it. But he had, and two days later, Cathryn Elaine Williams had become Cathryn Elaine Russell. Shortly thereafter she'd learned through one quick, cruel lesson what her husband expected of his new wife. The memory of her pain still lingered, and she could not imagine how women could find such a thing enjoyable, though she knew some did.

"Good land," Ezra had bragged that night around the table. "Untouched. Indian land. The Indians aren't much for farming, you know. Most of that earth has never been turned. A good part of the prairie is settled now, but this is reservation land; it hasn't met the plow yet. I'm leaving this worthless farm of mine behind and going out where the soil is still virgin."

He'd laughed a deep, throaty laugh then, the ugly laugh she'd quickly learned to hate. "I've broke in a new woman, and now I'll break in new land," he'd added.

Her father and brothers had snickered while she'd blushed in humiliation. None of them had understood her terror and hurt. She was a woman. She'd done what was expected of a woman. She had no room to complain. She should be happy. She had a new husband and was headed for a new land. She should be grateful.

"What about the Indians?" one of her brothers had asked.

"What about them?" Ezra had retorted. "They're supposed to stay on their reservations. I'm not afraid of those red bastards. They've been whipped good and told to stay put. If they give me any trouble, I'll just send the soldiers after them, or shoot them myself. This is 1888, son. The day of the Indian is over."

14

Katie could not help feeling somewhat sorry for the Indians, even though the thought of running into one of them terrified her. It seemed they'd been pushed around a lot. How would her father feel if someone came and told him his land no longer belonged to him, that someone else was taking it? She did not really blame the Indians for fighting back. But that fight was over. The whites had come in great numbers and with far superior weapons, and the wild men of the prairies and mountains had been squashed by the white man's greed. The survivors had been herded onto small pieces of land and told to stay there. Now she and Ezra were on their way to claim some of the land that had once belonged to the Indians. She was one of those who were shoving the red man aside, and that made her feel guilty, though she feared the plains Indians. She'd never even seen one, but she pictured them as dirty and savage, though she thought they must be people, like Ezra and her father and brothers.

She watched the black spot. Behind them a cow and a bull plodded, while in front six mules pulled the heavily loaded wagon. There was no going back, no going home. They had traveled a good eight hundred miles, across Illinois and Iowa and across half of Nebraska. Still she'd seen no sign of Indians, and for the last several hundred miles no sign of any human being, white or red. Occasionally she heard the whistle of a distant train. They could have come west by train, but Ezra was a thrifty man and he would not pay the cost of a more comfortable trip. No. Ezra chose the old way—covered wagon—as did many others.

Katie's back ached from the hours she'd spent on the uncomfortable, bouncing seat. There was no room inside, not even for sleeping. That was done outside, beneath the wagon, while fighting insects. But the insects didn't bother Katie so much. The nights Ezra drank and felt he needed a woman did. How she hated those nights!

15

And how she hated this land! Her only hope was that things would be better once they settled in one place.

They rode through the tall prairie grass. There were six of them, all young and strong and itching for some excitement, searching for a few of the dwindling, nearly extinct buffalo. In their hearts they knew their own fate was the same, dwindling, nearly extinct.

"Someone will send soldiers after us, Tohave," one of the young braves called out to their leader.

"Let them come! This is our land!" the tall proud Indian replied. "To fight again would make this a fine day, would it not, Two Moons?"

Two Moons laughed then. "*Ai!* This is true."

"I will race you!" Tohave shouted, kicking the sides of his spotted pony, and his mount thundered away, Two Moons racing after. Their manes and tails flying straight out in the wind, the horses panted rhythmically, their muscles rippling as they ran, the animals sensing the excitement of their riders.

The one called Tohave wore only a loincloth. He had little use for the white man's clothing they were now expected to wear. He liked the feel of the sun on his skin, the feel of a horse's flesh against his legs, of the wind against his bare chest. A bone hairpipe necklace adorned his throat, and his hair, long and black and loose, was decorated at one side with a round, deerskin ornament, painted and beaded, and wound into one skinny braid at the side of his head. Only Indian blood throbbed in his veins, half-Cheyenne and half-Sioux.

These two young men rode far ahead of the others, finally coming to a halt at the top of a ridge that provided a view south across the prairie.

"I beat you again!" Tohave told Two Moons.

"Only because you never start even." Two Moons

laughed. "You always ride off before I realize we are racing. Start even and I will bet you my best blanket and finest bow."

The horses pranced and snorted, shaking their heads and breathing heavily.

"I will think about it," Tohave answered. "But now Runs Fast must rest a day or two before I race him again."

Two Moons nodded, and then both men looked out over the immense empty land.

"I see no buffalo," Two Moons said soberly.

Tohave just stared for a long, quiet moment, while the others rode up the ridge. "Nor do I." There was a hint of sadness in his voice. He turned to the other four, signaling them with a motion of his arm to ride west and see what they could find. He turned to Two Moons then. "They will find nothing there either, do you think?"

Their eyes held in understanding. "I think you are right."

Tohave nodded. "And so were you right, when you said we should not even be here. I know the men in Washington have opened this land, that it is no longer part of the reservation, but I do not like it. And Sitting Bull does not like it either. He refused to sign. It was the others, the cowards among our own people, who signed; those who bow to the agency and to the soldiers, who hold out their hands for food and fancy white man's trinkets."

"But it cannot be changed, Tohave. To fight it only brings hardship and sometimes death."

A bitterness came into Tohave's eyes. "I am not old, yet I remember the days when the Sioux and Cheyenne fought for their land. I was sixteen summers when my mother fled with Sitting Bull and others to the north. I remember a terrible winter, when many horses froze to death in a blizzard, and the government of that land

17

would not help us." He swallowed. "It is lonely to know no one wants you, Two Moons—not in that new land, and not in your own land. Yet many of us longed for our own country, so we returned with Sitting Bull." A cold hatred came into his eyes then. "And the white soldiers broke their promise that Sitting Bull could return to his land at Standing Rock. They put him in prison instead!" He spit on the ground. "Such worth there is to the white man's word!"

"It does no good to go over it again and again, Tohave," Two Moons told him. "That changes nothing. Sitting Bull is free now."

Tohave looked out over the horizon again. "For how long? The Great White Father does not like the way he is always advising our people not to sign away more land; the way he fights anything that is bad for us. He is still too much a leader. The Great White Father in Washington would like it if our people did not look to him so much. The white men tried to tame him. They thought when they took him along in that Wild West Show, with the one called Buffalo Bill, that it would change him. But Sitting Bull remains true to his people. He never forgot what is important, and now he is with us again. Everytime I talk to him I am proud to be Indian, and it angers me that we have lost so much more land against our will."

"Our leaders and most of the people signed the new treaty, Tohave."

"Of course they signed!" Tohave barked, turning sneering eyes to his friend. "They knew if they did not the white man would come and take the land anyway, without permission, and they might have lost much more. There is no longer any choice, Two Moons! Sitting Bull knows this. He refused to sign! I only wish we could still fight. I am not so young that I forget what it was like. You are only eighteen summers now. I am twenty-six. I

18

am old enough to remember—was old enough to be a warrior myself. I was at the Little Big Horn! I was only thirteen summers then, but I remember!"

Two Moons smiled. "Tell me again, Tohave. Tell me what you remember from that day."

Tohave stared at the gently waving prairie grass while his horse lowered its head to nibble at buffalo grass nearby. The soft wind blew Tohave's dark hair about his face as he spoke. It was a handsome face, with high cheekbones and a straight, prominent nose. His lips were full and finely etched, and his even white teeth made him even more handsome when he smiled. Now his dark, fiery eyes glittered when he spoke of his warrior days, of riding after deer or buffalo, of preparing to play a trick on one of his friends. Finally he spoke of the Little Big Horn, something of which Two Moons never tired of hearing.

"I will never forget that day," Tohave said quietly but proudly. "Hundreds of us, thousands. Both of my people—Cheyenne and Sioux. Circling. Circling. Shouting in victory. I rode with them, my first experience of warring against the bluecoats."

Two Moons closed his eyes, trying to picture that battle and wishing he, too, had been there.

"I can still hear the shouts, the Bluecoats yelling back and forth. I remember the desperation in their eyes. Now when I think of it, I know how afraid they were. But that day it did not matter. They had dared to ride into the heart of our camps. So foolish Long Hair Custer must have been. Surely he did not listen to his scouts that day. And our people—so afraid by then of the bluecoats and the terrible things they had done to our people—saw them in the midst of us. We were sure they had come to attack again, to murder the women and children. We knew only that we must prevent that, and when we saw that there were few of them and many of us, our blood was hot for revenge. The more we circled, knowing we could kill them all, the more we were determined to do so." His voice trailed off to a near whisper.

"And which one killed Custer, Tohave? Are you sure you do not know?"

Tohave shook his head. "There were many bullets and arrows flying that day. All of us killed him, I suppose. I killed one soldier all by myself, then rode in and killed two more who were already wounded. It was the first time I had killed men, and it felt good, for I was thinking of my mother, raped and killed by white men. And I was thinking of her again, not long after the Little Big Horn, when I sank my knife into two buffalo hunters. They were the ones who killed her. I remembered them." Tohave turned watery eyes to Two Moons. "No one knows I did that except you. I do not even know if their bodies were ever found, and I do not care. It is done, and it was good and right that it was done."

Two Moons nodded. "With your father dead of the white man's disease, you have been on your own for a long time, Tohave. I still have a mother and father, and my uncles. You have no one."

Tohave shrugged. "It does not matter. I need no one."

Two Moons grinned then. "Not even a woman?"

Some humor finally came back to Tohave's eyes. "Now and then, a widow grateful when I bring fresh meat, a loose squaw here and there."

"Many of the chaste young girls watch you. You please their eyes, and they steal looks at you when you do not look back. Surely you know this. You should take a wife, Tohave. You should have sons."

Tohave tossed his head, pulling hair out of his face. "Why? They would not be free. They would never know warrior ways. We cannot even find buffalo anymore. Our food is handed to us by the agency men. What reason is there now for sons?"

Wise for his years, Two Moons frowned. "To carry on,

Tohave. Sons keep the blood flowing—the blood of our people. Sons make sure our people never truly die away, no matter how they must live. We cannot just give up. And maybe some of the things the white man teaches us are good. Maybe we should listen to some of them and try to make certain that the Sioux and Cheyenne live on forever. To fight will get us nowhere."

Tohave looked long and hard at his friend. "I see. What should I do? Should I put on the white man's baggy, hot pants, then stand behind a plow and push it through the dirt while my children watch, thumbs in their mouths, because they are bored? Should I plant seed and reap the harvest like a woman?" He sniffled. "I want none of that, and neither should you."

"I don't want it. But I see no choice if we wish to survive on our own, Tohave. If we do not plow and grow cows for meat, we will spend the rest of our days waiting for handouts from the Great White Father."

Tohave smiled bitterly, blinking back tears. "You speak too much truth today, Two Moons. You are too wise for your years."

"I only speak what I see. I need no wisdom for that." Two Moons sighed. "Perhaps you do not need to push a plow. White visitors paid you for the wooden carving of a horse that you made—remember?—when they came to the reservation to see the agent?"

Tohave shrugged again. "I remember."

"You make beautiful things with wood and knife. If you made enough, perhaps you could sell them for money. Then you would not have to farm. And it would give you something to do. You would not be bored."

Tohave shifted his position on the flat, Indian saddle. "Perhaps. But I would rather be out here, riding free, feeling the wind." He straightened then, pointing. "Look—out there. One wagon."

They both stared for a few minutes. "They are brave,"

21

Two Moons muttered.

"They are stupid, these whites who come out here thinking they own this land and can just take it." Tohave sneered. "If it were not for the treaty and the soldiers, I would show them how stupid they are!"

The other four men rode up behind them, one of them holding a rabbit by the hind feet. "This is all we found, Tohave," one declared.

"Small game is all we ever find!" Tohave sputtered. "Tie him to your gear. We are going to put a scare in some stupid whites down there."

The other man looked, then grinned as he quickly tied the rabbit to his saddle strap. "Let's have some fun!" he said excitedly.

Tohave led the way, letting out a blood-curdling yelp as he rode down the wide, gently sloped ridge toward the lonely wagon, which was a good mile away, if not more. Distance was a tricky thing to judge on the vast prairie. Something miles away could look close, and something close often looked far away.

Katie continued to watch the black dot. The day had been long and hot and dreary, with few words spoken by herself and Ezra. She wondered if there would be any human inhabitants near where they would settle, and feared she'd go mad if there were not.

She heard a shrill cry then, and she raised blue eyes to see men riding hard down a ridge toward them. She counted six of them, and her heart pounded fiercely.

"Ezra!" she cried. "I think it's Indians!"

Ezra frowned as he pulled the wagon to a halt. "Goddamned redskins!" He gave her a shove. "Get inside! Hurry up! The bastards probably already saw you!"

Katie hurriedly climbed over the seat, half-falling into

the wagon, crawling over packed items in order to get all the way under the canvas, where it was dreadfully hot. Between the heat and her pounding heart, she wondered how much longer she'd be able to manage to breathe.

Ezra pulled a rifle from the back of the wagon and she gasped. "Ezra, there are six of them! Don't shoot! You can't get them all, and those who are left will kill you and me!"

"Shut up!" he growled, cocking the rifle.

Katie's eyes widened as the yipping and yelping came closer, and she could hear thundering horses. They were circling now, she could tell, circling, circling. Her chest hurt so badly she wondered if she was already dying.

"What do you want!" she heard Ezra growl. "Speak your piece or get the hell away from my wagon!"

She heard laughter, and she frowned. She had thought Indians capable only of cruel laughter. But this was not a wicked laugh. It was prompted by genuine amusement.

"It is bad enough that white men come into our land"—the voice was mellow, that of a young man— "but why is it the ugly ones come? Are there no handsome white men?"

There was more laughter.

"Get your red asses away from my wagon or I'll shoot you down from those horses!" Ezra roared.

"Go ahead, white man. Shoot me if you will. My friends will make you regret it."

Silence followed that threat, and Katie peeked through a space between two boxes to see Ezra lowering his rifle.

"What the hell do you want?" he asked in a more subdued voice. "I have supplies. You want tobacco? Flour? Just tell me what you want and let me go on."

"You speak as though you are alone, white man."

"I am!"

"Few white men travel without a woman, and I saw something in a skirt get into the back of that wagon as we

23

rode down. What do you carry back there besides supplies, my friend?"

"None of your business!"

"I think I will look and see."

"You stay away from this wagon!"

"Use your gun then, if you are willing to die. Are you willing to die for your woman, white man? Indian men die for their women. How about you?"

Katie could see that Ezra was breathing heavily. Then he laid the rifle aside. "You wouldn't dare hurt her. If you hurt her, the soldiers will find out and you'll all be found and hanged!"

The Indian snickered. "Just as I thought."

Katie heard a horse come closer, and she ducked down as someone ripped open the canvas at the back of the wagon. "Come out." It was a gentle command, but she stayed huddled behind the boxes. "I said come out, or I will rip every box and dish from this wagon and destroy it all! Do not make me come in after you, woman!"

Katie said a quick prayer and slowly rose.

"Is she as ugly as her husband, Tohave?" one of the young men called.

Tohave stared. Katie stared. Both were surprised at what they saw. She had expected a dirty, ugly savage. He had expected a plain, aging plump white woman. Their eyes held for a moment, his dark and hypnotizing, hers brilliantly blue and fascinating. He drank in her beauty: the fair skin, the full young breasts beneath the high-necked calico dress, the strands of reddish-brown hair tumbling from beneath her bonnet. His nostrils flared slightly as he breathed deeply in response to her beauty. Then her blue eyes teared.

"Please don't hurt me," she said in a near whisper. "I haven't done anything to you."

His jaw flexed in great satisfaction at what he saw. "Crawl over here to the back of the wagon . . . and re-

24

move your bonnet," he told her.

"But I—"

"Do it!" he commanded.

She fought more tears and tried to control her shaking as she crawled over boxes and crates to the back of the wagon, but she could not take her eyes from him. She was seeing an Indian for the first time, and he was tall and powerful and handsome—and to her amazement, clean. Furthermore, in spite of his commands, there was a gentleness in his eyes. A tear slipped down her cheek as she slowly removed her bonnet.

"Take the pins from your hair," he told her.

She reached up with shaking hands to undo an untidy bun, letting her hair tumble in thick waves over her shoulders. Then she closed her eyes and held her breath as he reached out and grasped a lock, fingering it gently.

"Tohave, what are you doing?" one of the men called out, and there were a few snickers.

"She is not ugly like her husband!" he called out, startling Katie, whose eyes were still closed. "He has a young wife." He lowered his voice. "Or are you his daughter?"

Katie swallowed. "I'm . . . his wife." She gasped and opened her eyes when she felt his fingers gently wiping the tears from her cheeks.

"By choice?" he asked.

Their eyes held. "What does it matter to you?" she said in a shaking voice. "If you do what you're thinking, it will be just horrible for me whether or not I am happily married."

He flashed her a sudden and provocative grin. "And how do you know what I am thinking?"

She reddened deeply. "I've heard . . . about Indian men."

He laughed lightly. "You whites are so stupid! You believe everything others tell you, without finding out

25

for yourselves. Your books and newspapers print all kinds of stories about Indians, most of them untrue." He looked her over carefully, making her feel naked. "But in this case, if I did what you think I would, I would surely have a fine time."

He dismounted, then reached up and suddenly grasped her arms, and she gave out a little scream as he jerked her out of the wagon and set her on her feet. Holding her by one arm, he pulled her in front of the others while Ezra just watched, saying nothing.

"Can you believe this pretty thing belongs to that ugly man?" he shouted to his friends in the Sioux tongue.

They all laughed, and some moved closer to look her over, hooting and howling. Katie cringed and tried to pull away from Tohave.

"Please! Please go away!" she whimpered, her tears flowing now.

Suddenly, he let go of her. Moving to stand in front of her, he commanded in English, "Look up at me!" She raised blue eyes to meet his dark ones, which were now angry. "Tohave does not rape women! Tohave's friends do not rape women! It is the white man who is good at those things—good at raping Indian women, like my mother! You have much to learn, woman. Believe what you will, but find out for yourself first!"

His eyes flashed as they moved over her once more. Then he backed away. "I am called Tohave. I do not care if you know this. I am not afraid of agency men or soldiers! Tohave will do as he wishes, and if he wishes to ride over your land to hunt, he will do it. Remember that." He removed a huge knife from his weapons belt and came closer again, reaching behind Katie's neck. Her eyes widened as he grasped a lock of hair and whisked his knife through it, then held up the tress. "See? I cut it from where it will not show and ruin your pretty hair. But Tohave has taken it because he wants it." He looked

26

at Ezra. "When you see me again remember that we are many and you are one. Tohave can take what he wants, white man, including the hair from your own wife's head. So think twice before you shoot at Tohave." He shoved his knife back into its sheath, and Katie wondered how she'd kept from fainting for she'd thought he was going to slit her throat.

Tohave walked back to the wagon then, and picking up the bonnet, he brought it around to her and plopped it on her head. "The prairie sun is bad for such fair skin," he told her, holding her eyes. His voice was again gentle, actually concerned. "Tohave would not want to spoil such softness as he felt when he wiped the tears from your cheeks. Do not cry when you see Tohave again. There is no need."

He tied a knot in the end of the lock of her hair before shoving it into his belt. He looked at Ezra then. "Where is the tobacco?"

Ezra swallowed. "I'll get it."

"Never mind! Tohave only wanted to see if you would crawl for him. And what if Tohave rode off with your wife, my friend? Would you try to shoot Tohave or come after him?"

Ezra reddened. "I'd have the soldiers on your ass so—"

"Just as I thought." Tohave looked back at Katie. "If she were my woman, I would come for her myself, and die, if necessary, to save her." He turned quickly then and mounted his horse with ease. His eyes roved over Katie again, as the others stared at her with pleasure. "What are you called, white woman?" Tohave spoke up.

"None of your business!" Ezra growled.

"I did not ask you!" Tohave barked, his eyes still on Katie.

Katie swallowed. "Katie," she answered in an almost inaudible voice. "Katie Russell."

27

Tohave grinned. "Katie."

"It's short . . . for Cathryn."

"Shut up!" Ezra fumed. "Don't talk to that red bastard! You'll give him ideas!"

Tohave looked at Ezra, contempt in his eyes. "It is white men who are quick to get such ideas," he hissed. Then he looked back at Katie. "I think we will meet again, Katie Russell," he told her, his eyes gentle.

"I hope not!" Katie retorted, at last finding some courage. "If your intention was merely to frighten us to death, you did. It was cruel and unnecessary! We've done you no harm!"

She could not stop her angry tears, and he just stared at her a moment, then rode close to her so that he and his horse were between Katie and Ezra. "You are right. I am sorry, Katie Russell, but because of you and your kind, Tohave's mother is dead, his father is dead, his relatives are dead, and sometimes Tohave feels dead inside."

He whirled his horse then and rode off with the others. Katie watched him, deep within her feeling some pity as well as a strange urging at the thought of his powerful, near-naked body, his gentle eyes, the brush of his fingers against her cheeks.

"Get up here in the wagon!" Ezra shouted. "We can make a few miles yet tonight. We've a way to go to get to our own land."

She turned and stared at him, realizing that if Tohave and the others had raped her, Ezra Russell would not have stopped them. She felt sick inside as she walked around and climbed back onto the seat, while Tohave and his companions disappeared over the rise. Ezra grasped her throat then, gripping it until she started to choke.

"What's the idea of talking to that heathen!"

"I . . . had to!" she choked out. "I was afraid! I only . . . answered his questions!"

"White women don't talk to Indians!" He let go of her,

28

shoving her away. "Don't you realize what he had in mind?"

She held her throat, gasping. "I didn't see you . . . trying to stop him!" she managed to get out.

He grabbed her hair and pulled. "I had no choice!"

"Neither did I!" she screamed at him. "What was I supposed to do!"

As he turned and picked up the reins, muttering about damned stupid women, she covered her face with her hands and wept. If ever she'd needed her husband to simply hold her and tell her everything was all right, it was that moment. But Ezra Russell knew nothing of compassion and understanding. She was an object to him, to be used as he saw fit, something without feelings. And it struck her that, in one look, the Indian called Tohave had seen that and had understood. In their brief encounter she had seen compassion in the eyes of someone who was supposed to be wild and savage, and she wondered which man truly was the savage. Tohave had not hurt her.

The wagon started rolling again. The prairie was quiet. She wiped at her eyes and rubbed her throat, turning again to watch the black spot go round and round.

Chapter Two

The rest of the day's journey was more bearable for Katie because something very different had happened to her, giving her something to occupy her thoughts. Tohave. She pronounced the name over and over in her head, wondering what it meant. The man had angered her, but not truly frightened her, not after he'd touched her cheeks and asked her with all-knowing eyes if she was married to Ezra Russell by choice. How did he know so quickly how unhappy she was? And why had he and those with him ridden down on the wagon at all? Apparently they'd wanted only to tease and frighten them, and once the incident was over, Katie could not help smiling at the thought of it.

The entire event had been nothing more than an adventure to the young Indian men, and for a moment she'd seen a sparkle of humor in Tohave's eyes, a humanness she'd not expected to find in Indians. She remembered his smile, quick and bright, and she realized with a secret guilt that his form was magnificent. She had never before been struck by such thoughts. Her rude and ugly awakening with Ezra Russell had left her hating men in general, hating her father for forcing her to marry and her brothers for not defending her. Yet when Tohave had asked her if she'd been married by choice, the gentle understanding in his voice had made her wonder if a man could be gentle, if a woman could give herself willingly after all, if it was possible to "choose" a man out of love and to enjoy being with him. It was not that she imagined being with Tohave; it was just that his behavior had made her wonder.

Or was it Tohave she was thinking of? she wondered. No. That was wrong! Very, very wrong! She was married, and Tohave was an Indian. No white woman should ever have thoughts about Indian men. That was out of the question. No. The man had simply awakened questions in her mind.

These questions became more prevalent the night following the incident, when Ezra Russell rudely pushed up her skirts and gruffly reminded her she was a married woman and should not have spoken to the Indian. It seemed to matter little to him how frightened she'd been at the time, how wise it probably was to quietly answer Tohave's questions, how confused she was as to what she should do. And it mattered little that her own person and life might have been in danger. She did not remind him that he had done nothing to defend her, but she would never forget that, nor would she forget Tohave's statement that Indian men are quick to defend their women to the death. And all the while Ezra grunted over her, bringing the usual humiliation and pain, she wondered how nice it would be to have a man who was kind and gentle, one who would readily defend her. Was there such a man?

Her life seemed doomed. She watched the black spot again the next day, thinking about home and how much nicer it was there, in spite of her cruel father and useless brothers. At least in Illinois there were trees, people, friends, and an aunt who was reasonably kind. How would she bear the agony of this hot, desolate land when she was alone with a man she did not love? She thought about her mother, long dead now. She didn't remember much about the woman, except that she'd been kind and quiet, a victim of her hard, unfeeling husband, Katie was certain. Poor Mother, she thought. She probably never knew real happiness, real love. Will that be my lot, too?

It was late that second day when she saw him, a lone Indian on the distant horizon to her right. She watched him quietly, saying nothing to Ezra. Why, she wasn't sure, but she wasn't afraid. She knew who the lone figure was. Tohave. There was, strangely, no doubt in her mind. As the endless wind picked up slightly and seemed to sing over the prairie grass, she realized how much a part of this land he was. Tohave belonged out here. Ezra Russell did not, nor did a fair-skinned girl like herself.

She continued to watch silently, goosebumps rising on her arms and back. Why did he follow? Where had he come from? Did he live on the nearby reservation, or just roam and live off the land? There was so much she didn't know about Indians, and now one was watching her quietly, like a sentinel. Or was he not guarding her, but gauging the best time to ride down and take her? Perhaps she was counting too much on his being kind and good. He was, after all, an Indian, a wild untamed man who could smile at one moment and plant a knife in a man's belly the next. Wasn't that what she'd heard? But Tohave had told her she should not believe those tales, that she should find out for herself. Yet how was she to find out anything. She was lost forever in this vast land and probably wouldn't see another human being for months.

She looked away for just a moment, not wanting to draw Ezra's attention by staring too long, and when she looked back again, the figure was gone. Her heart seemed to fall a little in disappointment, to her own surprise. And the goosebumps chilled her more, yet she was amazed at how easily the man could appear and disappear. Had the wind actually died down a little now, or was it her imagination? Did he move with the wind, direct the wind?

Night came again, and to her relief Ezra did not seek her out. Her back still hurt from the night before, and from other nights, when she'd lain on the hard earth while Ezra Russell had taken care of his manly needs. This night he slept soundly beside her, snoring and oblivious to whatever dangers might beset them. But Katie could not sleep. Her mind raced with thoughts of what it would be like to live out here forever, to have babies with no one around to help, to see no one but Ezra Russell day in and day out. The night frightened her, especially since she'd seen how hesitant Ezra had been to defend her two days earlier.

Then the wind suddenly picked up again, and the little night creatures suddenly quieted. Katie glanced at Ezra, still sleeping soundly in the dim light of their dwindling fire, and she carefully slipped out of her bedroll and crawled from beneath the wagon. The mules, and the cow and bull were all curled on the ground, asleep, but Katie felt a presence, a silent presence that didn't even disturb the animals.

Then he rode into the firelight, quiet as the wind! Tohave! She gasped and stepped back.

He sat grandly on his spotted horse, wearing buckskins this time, the bone hairpipe necklace at his throat, the beaded ornament in his long, black hair. He stared at her with handsome dark eyes, and she stared back, speechless but not afraid. He smiled teasingly then and quickly disappeared into the darkness, as though simply to show her that he could ride down on them at any time he chose to surprise them. She put a hand to her mouth and smiled. He was playing games, that was all. It was a teasing trick played by a young man who probably had nothing better to do. Yes, he was human. He was very human. It surprised her.

She crawled back into her bedroll then. No longer afraid, she quickly fell into deep, much-needed sleep. She would not tell Ezra what she had seen.

The day grew hot, hotter. Katie put on a dress with short sleeves, but it helped little. She could not help wondering if someone like Tohave liked this kind of weather. She searched the horizon all that morning as they traveled, but there was no sign of the Indian, and the only thing that made the morning bearable was her secret. Yes, now she had a secret from Ezra. Tohave had ridden right into their camp the night before and Ezra didn't even know it! She had to smile at the thought of it, yet she still wondered if Tohave could be trusted. Perhaps in her loneliness she was building the encounters with Tohave into something exciting, using them to break the monotony of her loveless life. How could she be sure Tohave and his friends would not ride down on them again, kill Ezra, and humiliate her before taking her life. She continued to remind herself that these men were Indians and should not be trusted.

They came upon a gently flowing stream by midafternoon, and Ezra halted the wagon. "This is it," he told her bluntly. "We'll build a dugout in the side of that hill and live there till we can have us a house. A dugout will be cooler anyway."

Katie slowly climbed down. When she removed her bonnet, the wind blew her auburn hair into her blue eyes and she pushed it back from her face. She stared out over a sea of yellow grass, broken here and there by rock-studded hills on the far horizon. There was no sign of human life.

"Let's unload the wagon. We need shovels," Ezra declared.

"Ezra, I'm so hot."

"You think I'm not? Go over to the stream there and splash some water on your face. Then get a shovel and come with me."

He walked toward a steep rise several yards from the stream and started digging. Katie watched him, discouraged. She had imagined some sort of grand announcement that they were "home"; had thought Ezra would be a little more excited, perhaps happier and therefore kinder to her, once he got to his land.

She walked to the stream and knelt, cupping her hands and filling them with water. As she rinsed her face she said a short prayer for strength to keep going, yet she wondered why she prayed to a God who had been so cruel to her. She watched the stream for a moment, wondering how long it would be before this awful heat dried it up. She could see marks along the banks that indicated how much the water had diminished.

She rose and started to climb into the wagon to look for another shovel. "What about the animals?" she shouted to Ezra. "They must be thirsty."

"Unhitch and hobble them and let them drink," the man shouted back.

She took strips of rope from the side of the wagon and went to the mules, bending down to hobble their front feet so they could not easily run away. The thirsty, skittish animals brayed and tossed their heads impatiently, and as she knelt before one, another kicked out, catching her in the shoulder. Katie grunted with pain and fell over. Then she scowled at the animal as she rubbed a painful shoulder and wondered if any bones had been cracked or broken.

"Hurry it up!" Ezra shouted.

36

Katie blinked back tears and started to finish hobbling the mules, but her pain was increasing. Though it was difficult to unhitch the harness she kept going for Ezra did not like complaining women. As each animal was freed, it made its way in stumbling fashion to the stream and began to drink. Katie then turned to the cow and the bull, hobbling them before untying them. She wondered if hobbles were necessary. It was so hot, she was certain the animals would stay by the stream and have no interest in wandering.

Her shoulder hurt fiercely, but she climbed inside the wagon, retrieved a shovel, and headed toward Ezra. For a moment she stopped and looked around. The constant wind was dry and hot, and the millions of tiny, unseen creatures in the grass were singing their little songs. But there was no music in Katie's heart.

So, this was to be home. There would be no visiting, unless one cared to visit with grasshoppers. There would be no dancing, for there was no music. And in her marriage, there would be no love. She studied the horizon again, watching. For what? For a wild Indian man who could not be trusted? That was stupid and foolish. Besides, Tohave, tired of his game, had probably returned to the reservation, to his family. Family! Did he have family? He'd said his mother was raped and killed by white men. How sad for him. But perhaps he had a wife, or someone he loved and would soon marry.

She was astonished to realize that an Indian had loved ones just like whites. And at the moment, she didn't doubt that an Indian on a reservation, surrounded by family, was better off than she was at the moment. She didn't care that she'd be living in a dirt house. She could bear anything if she were with someone who really cared about her. But she could not look at this land without hating it, for she hated the man who had brought her here. People like Tohave had known only the prairie, and

37

at least he was with friends and family.

She jumped when Ezra shouted at her to get moving, and as she walked toward the dugout, she decided to amuse herself by wondering how Tohave lived, whether he had family. It was not that she had an interest in Tohave as a man, but simply as an Indian, a thing of curiosity and wonder, a thing of this land, like the grasshopper, sometimes close but unseen. She told herself it was all right to think about him, for to think about her present predicament was too much to bear. She had no wrong thoughts about the young Indian man. She was only curious. Yes, that was it. Only curious.

She began shoveling away beside Ezra. Her shoulder ached fiercely, but she knew she dared not say anything. He'd only tell her she'd been stupid to let the animal kick her in the first place. Every shovelful of dirt made her shoulder throb more. The rich smell of earth invaded her nostrils, and she hoped the smell would eventually diminish once they were living in the "hole." Still, a dirt house was not so bad. There would certainly be little to clean. And Ezra mentioned earlier that as soon as they got settled they'd go to the nearest supply post and start buying up wood to frame a real house.

He'd said the closest place was Fort Robinson, where he would be signing the final papers on his land—two hundred and fifty acres. Katie didn't know how he'd recognized his spread, and she didn't really care. She only wondered if they would see Tohave at Fort Robinson, which was supposed to be near the Red Cloud Indian agency and the Pine Ridge Reservation. She looked forward to going to the fort. People! They would see people. She couldn't wait, and she dug faster in spite of her painful shoulder. The sooner they got settled, the sooner they would go to the fort. Yes, she would think of the visit to the fort and of the mysterious Tohave in order to ease her troubled mind and to forget about the unrelenting heat.

She shoveled until her hands blistered and the sun began to set.

"That's big enough for shelter tonight," Ezra announced, throwing down his shovel as the sun fell behind the western horizon. "Tomorrow we'll make it bigger yet. We'll fit our bed in here, use crates for table and chairs. I'll set you up a cookstove and run the pipe right up through the ground." His voice was muffled in the cool, dark hole. "Once we've got it opened up good on the inside, we'll take some sod and build walls up the front so there's only door space left to come in by."

"Won't it be awfully dark?"

"Of course it will. We'll use lanterns. You can't exactly have windows in a place like this, now, can you? We could have built a sod house, above ground, but that's just as much work, if not more, and not as cool. We'll dig another hole in this hill when we're through with this. It will be smaller. We'll use it to keep food cool. And we'll have to dig another shelter for the animals. That will have to be pretty big. The sooner we get all that done, the better. Then we'll have to get some fencing up for grazing, and of course there's soil to be turned and planted."

Her heart fell. The work he had lined up, and the thought of doing it in the wretched heat, made her want to scream. She looked down at her blistered hands, aware that her shoulder was throbbing.

"Ezra, can't we take one day to rest, tomorrow perhaps? We have shelter here at least, and—"

"What kind of a lazy bitch did I marry?" he growled. "Your pa said you were a good worker. I'm beginning to wonder, woman."

"I am. But it's so hot . . . and one of the mules kicked me."

He frowned. "Where?"

39

She blinked back tears and rubbed at her shoulder. "Here. It hurts bad, Ezra, especially after all that shoveling."

He rudely unbuttoned her dress and yanked it over her shoulder. The skin was discolored to red and purple. Katie let out a scream as he fingered the area.

"I don't think anything is broke," he announced. He stood before her quietly for a moment, then pulled the dress off her other shoulder. Her stomach squirmed and her heart filled with dread as he ran the back of his hand over the whites of her breasts, revealed above the lace of her undergarment. "Let's break in our new home the right way," he said in a husky voice.

"It . . . it's not big enough yet for our bed, Ezra," she replied, hoping to discourage him. "And I'm hungry and tired, and my shoulder hurts so bad—"

He grasped her chin in a strong hand, squeezing her jaw. "Quit making excuses. You've got a lot to learn about wifely duties, Katie Russell." As he kissed her with cold lips, she averted her eyes from the face she hated—a face with pitted skin covered by stinging stubble. His dark, piercing eyes were overshadowed by too-thick eyebrows, and his hair was thick, dark, and unkempt. They both smelled of sweat and dirt, but that didn't seem to bother Ezra Russell.

"You know when I get inside you you'll forget your aches and pains, Katie girl," he told her, deluding himself about his ability to please her. "You just relax. I know you're young and still learning. Someday you'll learn to like it, and you'll be panting after ol' Ezra like a she-cat in heat. And maybe you'll have a baby. Wouldn't you like to have a baby?"

She nodded, blinking back tears.

"That's better, Katie girl. Now you get your clothes off, and I'll get the bedrolls. I haven't seen you all the way naked in a long time."

"Ezra, you know I feel funny doing that."

"Well, get used to it! Now let's get to it and then get some sleep. We have a lot of work cut out for us tomorrow, woman!" He was angry again, and she knew if she protested much more he'd hit her.

"Could we . . . could we at least go to the stream first and wash a little?"

Ezra sighed. "I reckon. I could stand to cool off myself. And there sure as hell isn't anybody to see us."

As he walked out, her chest tightened. She hadn't thought of that—Tohave! One never knew when he might appear. What if she washed naked in the stream and he appeared on a nearby rise and saw her! Why had she even mentioned washing! She walked outside and looked around, breathing a little easier, for there was no one in sight and, besides, it was nearly dark. But she reminded herself that she must be very careful about things like bathing. If Tohave ever saw her unclothed, his wild instincts might be uncontrollable.

To her own shame and dismay, she found herself wondering what it would be like to be touched that way by the one called Tohave. She was consumed with guilt for even considering such a thought, for she belonged to Ezra Russell, whether she hated him or not. So far her experience with "man" had been horrible. Why would another be any different? And Tohave was an Indian. She wanted to cry, she felt so ashamed. It seemed that everything was wrong, including her own thoughts.

She hurried to the stream, where Ezra was shouting for her to get undressed and join him. He lay in the shallows splashing water over himself, a stocky man with more middle than shoulders. Her stomach felt queasy at the sight of the dark hair all over his body. How long could she continue being this man's wife without going insane? The only comfort she could find would be in having a baby. She only hoped it would not be as ugly as its father.

She looked around again. Was Tohave watching? She shivered in spite of the warm evening. If she didn't bathe now she'd face a beating. She had no choice. She took off her clothes, partly because she was desperately eager to cool off and to bathe her sore shoulder and blistered hands, and partly because she felt guilty about her brief speculation about being with Tohave sexually. She was a married woman and had a duty to her husband, although she'd been forced to marry him and did not love him, and although everytime he touched her she felt only pain and revulsion.

She hurried into the stream then, slipping into it and letting the cool water soothe her. But her peace lasted only a moment for Ezra was soon grasping at her. Ignoring her sore shoulder, he pushed her back against the pebbled streambed and lay on top of her.

"How about right here in the water?" he said excitedly, grasping her hips. "It's cooler."

"Ezra, my shoulder—"

"The hell with your shoulder!" he yelled. He jerked her up suddenly and slapped her, making her fall back into the stream. Then he stood over her, naked and beastly, studying her slender, young body hungrily. "How many men can say they had their woman in a stream, naked to the world!" he said with a gruff laugh. "You might be useless in most ways, girl, but that body makes up for most of it. Your pa didn't short me there." He knelt down over her again, putting a hand to her face where he'd hit her. "If you'd just cooperate, I wouldn't have to do that, Katie girl."

The wind picked up then, in the mysterious way it did when Tohave was nearby. Ezra Russell would never notice, but Katie did, and she looked around frantically. Then she saw him, on a rise not so far away. Her heart pounded with dread and humiliation.

"Ezra, please. Let's go inside the dugout! I don't want

42

to do this!"

"Well, I'll be damned! Don't you ever learn, girl?" He jerked her forward and began squeezing her shoulder until she cried out. "I swear you don't enjoy this unless I beat you first. Well that's fine with me. I like my woman crying and whimpering when I'm planting myself inside her."

He pushed her down then, and the pain he'd brought to her shoulder left her too weak to fight him. She tried to pretend Tohave was not nearby, was not watching, but she did not succeed and felt humiliated as her husband used her. However, her weeping went unheeded by the night wind.

Finally it was over, and Ezra got up and ordered her to get into her nightgown while he put the bedrolls down inside their new "home." Katie curled up in shame, wondering how she'd get out of the stream and walk naked to her clothes with Tohave looking at her. But when she dared to raise her eyes to the rise where he'd been sitting, she saw that he was gone. The wind had died down a little.

How much had he seen? Katie wondered. And did Indian men treat their women this way? She hadn't told Ezra she'd seen him. She knew why. Ezra might shoot him, and then the mysterious Tohave would be gone. He was her only diversion, her only means of escaping the horrible reality of her hopeless situation. Having Tohave around was like having a special secret all her own. It made her feel like the innocent child she was before the nightmare of her wedding night with Ezra Russell. Wondering when Tohave might appear gave her something to think about, a game she could play in her mind. She could only hope it wasn't a dangerous game, that Tohave could be trusted not to murder them both some day. Yet what did it matter? Death might be better than the life she now led. And what did Tohave think of her

43

now? How could she ever look at him, knowing what he'd seen? But he couldn't have seen much of her, not in the near darkness. Surely he knew what was happening though. The shame of it made her cry. At least he'd seen Ezra hurt her. He surely knew she'd been forced and would never have done such a thing openly and willingly.

She tried to control her sobbing as she crawled out of the stream and walked to her clothes, pulling on just her dress to cover herself before going to her trunk to get her cotton nightgown. She quickly changed, not even drying herself off first. She wanted to be wet. Wet was cool.

Ezra was already sprawled out on a bedroll in the dugout, a lantern burning low at his side. Katie wiped her eyes, and as she turned to go to the dugout the wind picked up again. She hesitated, then looked at the rise. He was there! She walked out a ways, staring, the wind blowing wet strands of auburn hair. All her shame was gone suddenly. He knew. Surely he knew she hadn't wanted to give herself to Ezra Russell, that she'd been forced. Yet it was humiliating to realize someone was privy to the ugliness of her marriage, to know a stranger had seen a hideous act committed right out in the open. Why, then, could she look back at him now so boldly? How did she know the one called Tohave understood her loneliness and shame and sorrow? The question. He'd asked if she was married by choice. Yes, he knew. Tohave knew. Again she wondered if there was a beautiful side to what her husband had been doing to her. It was difficult to think there could be. Yet whenever she saw Tohave, she wondered. Perhaps that was more shameful than knowing what he'd seen. An Indian man she didn't even know should not make her wonder about such things.

His horse turned and he was gone again. Katie walked to the dugout and lay down on her bedroll to sleep for the first time in her new home on the Nebraska plains.

Chapter Three

The next morning found Katie hardly able to move her arms, so sore were they from shoveling; and her shoulder was even worse. Because of it she could not lift her left arm so Ezra grudgingly shoveled alone, while Katie unloaded the wagon as best she could, mostly with one arm, cringing against the pain as she did so. The memory of the previous evening haunted her. A stranger, an Indian man, had seen her husband rooting over her like an animal. He could not have seen her nakedness very well, but he surely knew what was happening, knew what an ugly marriage she had. Why did that bother her and what did Tohave think of what he had seen? She'd heard that Indian couples made little attempt to hide their lovemaking from the children or parents inside their tipis, and that they did such things in the out of doors often, but in sweet, quiet, private places.

She sat down on a crate and frowned. Why had it come to her that way? A sweet, quiet, private place. Somehow she could not envision Tohave mating in the cruel, open way Ezra had taken her last night. Yes, Tohave would choose a sweet, quiet, private place. She covered her face. She should not be dwelling on such a thing. Her shame was only compounded by thoughts of Tohave.

What was happening to her? She still had no idea what Tohave was really like, nor did she have any right to wonder about that. Married women did not wonder about such things, even those married to animals.

She rose and continued unpacking, disgusted with herself, somewhat angry with Tohave. Why did he continue to just appear out of nowhere? What did he want? Was he truly just playing games and making fun, or were his intentions more serious? She still could not help smiling at the humorous side of it. She thought about the times she had seen him without Ezra even knowing it. Why didn't she tell Ezra? Why was she so sure Tohave meant no harm? Perhaps she was just a young fool, desperate for any diversion that might keep her from going crazy in this desolate land, for her cruel husband brought her only pain and misery. Was her situation so bad that she had allowed an Indian man to occupy her thoughts because he brought some small bit of excitement to her dreary life?

She scowled and set down a box of clothing. She would quit thinking of Tohave and think about visiting Fort Robinson. The other forts where they had stopped on the way west had been pleasant diversions, refreshing chances to see people, to rest. Now they were only two days' ride from Fort Robinson, according to Ezra's calculations. That wasn't so bad. Just forty miles. She could get there all by herself, once she knew which direction to take. It was comforting to know that, in case of some kind of emergency. But she'd have to worry about Tohave and his friends. Perhaps they would find out more about Tohave from the soldiers at the fort.

She returned to unpacking. She had to get that done and set up housekeeping, if that was possible in the rude underground hut her husband was digging. Then the shelters for the food and for the animals had to be dug. The sooner that was done, the better; then they could leave for the fort. At least it was cooler. If the pain would just go away in her arms and shoulder, it wouldn't be such a bad day. But then because of the pain she didn't have to shovel. Yes. It was cool, and she didn't have to shovel; and she had Tohave and the fort to occupy her thoughts. Perhaps in small ways God was beginning to be good to her. But the things she wanted to pray for seemed impossible. She wanted to go back to Illinois, she wanted to be free of Ezra Russell's cruelty, and she wanted to know true happiness and love. Those things could never be now. There was no use praying for them.

They rode northwest. Ezra explained that not many miles north of them lay South Dakota, rumored to be officially a state within the year, and to the west of them, perhaps an additional two or three days' ride, lay Wyoming Territory, where the place called Yellowstone lay.

"I've been told the Indians used to go there to bathe in the warm waters. They say you can bathe there even in the middle of winter. The waters are warm all the time, and in places the ground bubbles and steams."

Katie frowned and stared west. Could such a thing be? Had Tohave ever been there, perhaps bathed there with his wife? Did he have a wife? She could see him laughing and splashing with a beautiful young Indian maiden, and somehow it hurt to think about it. Weren't all young Indian girls supposed to be pretty, surely prettier than she, with their smooth, dark skin and long, loose hair. She strained her eyes to see the Rocky Mountains, but they were simply too far away. They would have to remain objects of wonder and curiosity. She'd heard so much about those mighty mountains, but it was doubtful Ezra Russell would ever take her to see them. This would be her world now—hot, miserable work in the summers;

long, lonely winters; occasional visits to the fort that might keep her from going mad. How could there be such desolate, lonely land? Miles and miles and miles of nothingness—nothing but constantly swaying grass, endless wind and sun, the loud singing of crickets and grasshoppers, and no shade, unless a person wanted to walk a mile to the nearest tree. But in one way at least, the land had helped her. It had quickly turned miserably hot again, and Ezra was so tired from digging out their dwelling place and the shelter for the animals that for the past few days he had left her alone in the night. Sometimes it seemed that one good point made up for all the bad. She'd put up with anything that kept Ezra Russell's rudely searching hands off her body, his cold lips off her mouth and breasts, his ugly man part from humiliatingly and painfully invading her body. Perhaps, if she had known what to expect in the first place, her first experience would not have been quite so bad, but it could have been a lot better in spite of that if Ezra Russell had one ounce of compassion and understanding in his soul. Yet she'd known only rough treatment from the very beginning, pain and beatings, harsh words and grunts from an ugly man she didn't even like, nor love.

She swallowed back the lump in her throat. To dwell on her fate was useless. She must take one day at a time and hope for the best. But she dreaded the coming night, when they would stop to rest before going on to the fort the next day. Ezra was rested, and the wagon was empty for now, with only a feather mattress in back. She had no doubt, after a few days of not mating her, what Ezra Russell would expect that night. She decided she would not fight him. Perhaps that way he'd get it over with quickly and not beat her.

To Katie's delight, Fort Robinson was bustling with

activity when they arrived. Several other wagons sat about, and outside the fort were several tipis. She gawked at them in wonder. She'd never seen a tipi. The Indians were long gone from the forts where they'd stopped on their way west, and it was rumored those forts would soon be closing. But Fort Robinson was near the heart of several Sioux reservations and still garrisoned. It was rumored that the Sioux were still not totally peaceful, and the one called Sitting Bull still lived, a man who, it was said, could stir his people into war again at any moment.

As they rolled into the fort, Katie caught sight of only a few Indians, mostly old ones and a few middle-aged men. They were wearing white man's clothing and were not nearly as naked as Tohave had been. She was struck by their sad, long faces and stooped shoulders. These men were not spirited and lively like Tohave and his friends. Her heart was pained. They looked the way she felt— beaten, giving in to their fate, hopeless. Yes, there were all kinds of imprisonment, all kinds of slavery, all kinds of defeat. One could be dead while still walking. That was how she sometimes felt and how these people looked to her.

Soldiers walked and rode about; some marched to shouted orders on the parade ground.

"You keep your eyes front and don't be looking twice at any of them men," Ezra muttered to her. "I catch you making eyes at anybody and I'll beat you from here all the way home."

Some of Katie's initial excitement left her. She wanted this visit to be pleasant and fun, but anything Ezra Russell could spoil, he would. How could he think she'd have eyes for any man, considering what she knew now about them? Did he really think after the way he treated her that she would go panting after others? She felt like saying it aloud, but that would only bring a beating upon her so she said nothing as he reined the wagon toward the officers' quarters and then braked. He climbed down to tie the mules, as usual not offering to help her alight. After she climbed down, Ezra grasped her arm and half-pulled her along with him toward one of the buildings. A young lieutenant stepped out of it and stopped short at the sight of Katie, a most pleasant picture for a man too long in a lonely land. Today she wore a yellow flowered dress and a yellow bonnet, and so far her fair skin had not been ruined, although it was more red than usual. The lieutenant smiled and nodded, then glanced at the young girl's scowling escort, who he supposed was her father.

"Can I help you, sir?"

Ezra half-shoved Katie behind him. "You can keep your eyes off my wife, for one thing," he grumbled, to Katie's embarrassment. "And you can tell me where I can find the commanding officer."

The lieutenant's smile faded, and he felt sorry for the pretty young girl standing before him. He cleared his throat. "My apologies, sir. I . . . didn't know. But you should be proud, sir, that your wife is such a very pretty lady." He turned and nodded toward a building across the parade ground. "The largest building, in the center there. Our commander is Lieutenant-Colonel Ronald McBain."

"Thanks." Ezra turned and shoved Katie along with him. She glanced at the young lieutenant briefly, trying to apologize with her eyes for her husband's rudeness. The man nodded back, again feeling sorry for her.

"Nice meeting you," he muttered. He donned his hat and walked off to tend to his own affairs.

As Ezra headed across the parade ground with Katie half running to keep up, several men stared at the pretty girl in the yellow dress. Then Ezra barged into the command post and removed his worn hat, motioning for Katie to sit down in a wooden chair nearby as he eyed the sergeant behind the desk.

"I'm looking for Lieutenant-Colonel McBain," he said.

The sergeant looked from Ezra to Katie and then back to Ezra. "I'll get him for you." The young man rose, glancing at Katie again.

"She's my wife so there's nothing to look at," Ezra growled.

Katie reddened deeply and looked at her lap, while the sergeant reddened a little himself. He then turned and went into another room, and moments later a middle-aged, graying man appeared. He was tall but a little heavy around the middle, with brown eyes and a pleasant smile despite his stern face. He nodded to Katie and put his hand out to Ezra.

"I'm Lieutenant-Colonel McBain," he declared. "And you, sir?"

Ezra shook the man's hand. "I'm Ezra Russell. I wrote I'd be coming to sign some final government papers on the land I'm claiming southeast of here."

McBain released his hand and went behind the desk. "Yes. I remember. Have a seat, Mr. Russell. And the lady? The sergeant tells me she is your wife."

"Her name is Cathryn—Katie," Ezra begrudgingly told the man.

The commander smiled at her. "Welcome to Nebraska, ma'am. I know it's a hard life for a young girl from the East." He looked at Ezra, silently wondering what it was like for a poor young girl out on the prairie with this much older and apparently gruff man. "My own wife chooses to live in Denver," he added. "Not enough comforts and excitement here for her, I'm afraid, and of course there are the Indians to worry about. But in about a year I'll be retired and we can be together."

He reached into a drawer and took out some papers. "What do you mean about the Indians?" Ezra asked. Katie had been hoping he would ask, for she was curious herself. "We were told the Indians are settled on the reservations now. According to the government, there's a new treaty. That's why this land came open."

McBain grinned a little. "The word treaty has different meanings for the government and the Indians. The Indians are fully aware by now, Mr. Russell, that whites break treaties whenever there is something more they want. I'm sure you're aware that Sitting Bull is still among the Sioux, and his power and influence cannot be ignored. He didn't sign the latest treaty, and there are plenty of young, restless warriors whose blood rises at any small incident that irritates them. Things are not quite as settled as the government makes them out to be. But we've made a lot of progress. The important thing now is not to make a big deal out of a minor incident. It's amazing how the smallest misunderstanding can lead to a large-scale war. We want no more large-scale wars." He looked at Ezra warningly, as if to tell the man to watch his own behavior around the Indians. "Have you had any problems since you arrived?"

"We sure have," Ezra grumbled. "A few days ago a wild pack of young warriors rode down on our wagon like a bunch of wolves. There we were, me and my woman, all alone. I considered shooting at them, but I was afraid it would start something big and figured maybe we could get through it with no trouble. I offered the bastards tobacco, whatever they wanted, but instead they dragged my woman out of the wagon."

McBain's eyebrows arched and Katie reddened again, looking at the floor. The man's face darkened. "I certainly hope they didn't harm you, Mrs. Russell."

She shook her head. "I think they were just . . . playing games . . . trying to frighten us," she replied quietly.

"Well they did a good job of that, nearly scared the poor girl to death," Ezra declared quickly. He did not mention how frightened he had been for his own skin, how little he had done to defend her. "The bastards had no right doing it, seemed to have no purpose in riding down on us except to show off and let us know they could kill us and do worse to my woman if they wanted."

McBain grinned a little and then leaned back in his chair. "I don't suppose you caught a name?"

"We sure did, and I want to file a formal complaint. Their leader was called Tohave."

As Katie watched the lieutenant colonel, she had to struggle to keep from smiling. She could see that McBain was verifying what she'd already suspected: Tohave liked to play games and he'd probably meant them no harm. She wished she could tell the commander that Tohave had sneaked up on them several times since, without her husband even being aware of it.

"I had a feeling he'd be among them," McBain told Ezra. "He's young and restless, Mr. Russell. So are his friends. Sometimes they get bored and go riding. They've caused no real trouble so far, but you have to remember that a tiny spark can ignite big fires, so be a little patient and think about their side. Those people have been forced to—"

"I don't really give a damn." As Ezra interrupted, McBain sobered, anger apparent in his eyes. "They're on reservations now, and should stay there, isn't that right?"

"Keeping the young ones there is not an easy job, Mr. Russell."

"But it is your job, so try a little harder."

The commander sighed. "We're here in case of big trouble, Mr. Russell. Keeping the Indians on the reservation is the job of the agents on the various reservation sites. When they stray, we're told about it and we ride patrol, check on settlers, things like that. There's nothing much we can do unless there's real trouble."

"Well, the one called Tohave has eyes for my woman, no doubt about it."

McBain glanced at Katie and smiled, running a hand through his hair. "Mr. Russell, any young man would look appreciatively at your wife. You married a young, pretty girl. You can't expect men not to look twice at her. I don't mean to be rude. I'm simply stating a fact. Surely you don't expect men not to look."

Ezra darkened. "Of course I don't! But Tohave is an Indian—a dirty Indian! He's got no right looking at a young white girl or touching one! He dragged her right out of the wagon, made her take off her bonnet and loose her hair! Does that sound harmless to you?"

McBain frowned upon seeing Ezra Russell's ugly anger and Katie Russell's humiliation. He studied her a moment, sensing she wasn't nearly as upset by the incident as her husband. He knew Tohave, was fully aware of the young man's unusual good looks and strong build. How must he look to this pretty young girl, compared to her ugly, obviously rude, and unfeeling husband? "Did he harm you in any way, Mrs. Russell?" he asked.

Katie shook her head. "He just wanted to see if he could frighten me," she answered. "And he did . . . at first. But I don't think he'd have done us any harm."

Ezra scowled at her and she said no more. "My wife is a stupid child who don't know what she's about," he said sharply. "I'm telling you I don't trust that Tohave and his friends, and I want it recorded that he bothered us and threatened my wife."

McBain sighed and took out another piece of paper. "I'll record it, Mr. Russell. But I want you to remember to be patient. Show a little kindness and Tohave will do you no harm. Look at their side of it. To them, we've literally stolen their land, their home. There are some Indians who still think there's hope of getting some of that land back. They're young and strong, and many, like Tohave, remember the days of victory. Tohave was at the Little Big Horn."

Katie's eyes widened with curiosity. The Little Big Horn! Custer and all his men had been killed there! It was a famous battle, talked about in the East for a long time. She was a very young girl when it had occurred, but she remembered.

"He was just a young warrior then. I don't doubt the Little Big Horn was his first battle. He couldn't have been more than thirteen at the time. But he remembers, and his spirit is still hot. The young ones are the hardest to control. His father died when he was quite small. Then a couple of years ago his mother was raped and killed. Not long afterward we found two buffalo hunters dead, and you wouldn't want to know what all was done to them. We suspect there's a connection but can't prove it. Some things are better left alone. If they were the ones who killed Tohave's mother, let justice prevail. It's better than starting another war. You wouldn't want to see what happens to settlers when the Indians are on the warpath, Mr. Russell."

Ezra scowled. "So, they can get away with a murder here, a murder there."

"Not necessarily, Mr. Russell. But a commanding officer has to use a little tact and common sense. You can't deal with Indians in quite the same way as your own kind."

Ezra continued to grumble as McBain wrote down his complaint, but Katie did not hear. Her thoughts were on Tohave. She was trying to picture him as nothing more than a boy at the Little Big Horn. She didn't blame him for killing the buffalo hunters, if he truly had done it, and if they were the ones who had done such a terrible thing to his mother. It did not frighten her that he had killed men. It only fascinated her. He'd killed for a reason, not wantonly. Still, she could not help but wonder if that meant they might be in danger out on the prairie. Was it true that once a man killed he hungered to kill again? She could not imagine Tohave killing indiscriminately, but the possible danger could not be ignored. One tiny spark, McBain had said. Ezra would certainly be good at igniting that.

The complaint was written, papers were signed for the land, and soon they were outside again, heading for the supply store. To Katie's surprise, Ezra left her alone for several minutes while he drove the wagon to the blacksmith to get some work done on the iron wheel rims. For the first time since her marriage she was actually alone among others, and her heart lifted a little. She went down her list of needs, piling things on the counter: potatoes, seed, Epsom salts, witch hazel, a bolt of blue cotton. Maybe she would have time to sew. She reached for some thread at the same time another woman reached for some. They looked at each other and smiled. The other woman was older, but not old, and her stomach was obviously swollen with child.

"Hello," she said, seeming as eager to talk as Katie was. Katie nodded.

"Hello. I'm Katie Russell." She blushed. "I guess I said that rather quickly. You probably don't care who I am."

They both laughed. "I certainly do care. One doesn't get to visit much in these parts."

"You're homesteading around here, too?"

The woman's eyes changed suddenly. Bright eagerness became discouragement. "Yes. Several miles west of here. But I don't know if we'll stay if this summer's crops don't turn out better than the last couple of years. It's a hard land, and now I'm expecting." She put out her hand. "I'm Dora Brown."

Katie took Dora's hand and squeezed it. "It's so good

56

to meet another woman. I'm so lonely." Her eyes actually teared, and her newfound friend squeezed her hand in return.

"I know the feeling. And you're so very young. Have you just arrived?"

"Yes. My husband claimed some former reservation land southeast of here. We came to the fort to sign some final papers and get supplies. My husband is at the blacksmith's now."

"Well, he'll have to talk to my Jacob. He can certainly give your husband some pointers on survival in this land. I wish the best for you, Katie."

A tall, blond man came up to them then, and put an arm lovingly around Dora's shoulders. "And who do we have here?"

"Jacob, this is Katie Russell. She and her husband just got here—claimed some land southeast of here to homestead. Katie, this is my husband."

Katie nodded and Jacob nodded back. "Nice to meet you, Katie Russell. Where is your husband? There are a few dos and don'ts he might like to hear from a man who's been through hell already out here." He smiled when he said it, but Katie saw the tired look about his eyes. She also saw the loving way he squeezed his wife. Jacob bent down then to kiss Dora's cheek. "I'm not sure I'll make my wife stay out here another winter." He patted her stomach. "We'll see how things go with the baby."

Katie smiled, feeling a pain in her heart, as she watched Dora gaze lovingly at her husband. Was Dora one of those women who enjoyed giving her man pleasure? But how could she? Jacob was huge. Surely he could hurt her easily. But love shone vividly in the couple's eyes.

"I . . . my husband . . . is at the blacksmith's," she told Jacob Brown. "He'll be along in a while. I'm picking up supplies while he gets some work done on the wagon wheels."

"Well, we'll be around all day, either here or at the livery. I'm taking my wife to the camp doctor, although I'm not sure how much an army doctor knows about women and babies."

Katie smiled as she glanced at Dora's stomach. "When are you due?"

"In August. But I feel fine. I'm sure everything will be fine."

The women's eyes met. "Aren't you afraid? Is this your first?"

Dora smiled. "It's my first." She put an arm around Jacob. "But I'm not afraid, not as long as I have my Jacob at my side."

Looking at Jacob, Katie was surprised by the gentle countenance of this huge man. He was not extremely handsome, nor was Dora especially pretty, but the two of them were obviously very much in love and they enjoyed being together. Their happiness was the kind she'd often wondered about, and she felt an aching longing to be so happy with a man. She would never know that kind of happiness with Ezra Russell. She forced a smile.

"I hope all goes well for you, Dora." Katie twisted a spool of thread in her fingers as she spoke. "Have you had any trouble with the Indians?"

Jacob laughed lightly. "We've been visited a few times, sometimes by old begging ones, sometimes by young teasing ones. There is one called Tohave who's been hard to tame. He's visited a few times, and I don't doubt he'll pay you a visit, too. He and his friends are wild and seem frightening at first, but if you treat them fairly and in a friendly fashion, they'll do no harm. Usually I have a smoke with them, and they like Dora's pies. For the most part, if you befriend an Indian and let him know you've put your trust in him, he won't betray that trust, unless you betray it first."

58

Katie smiled nervously. "He already visited us, rode down on us before we were even settled. He frightened me to death, pulled me right out of the wagon and said suggestive things. After a while I began to see he was playing games and meant me no harm."

Jacob frowned. "That doesn't sound like Tohave. Did your husband make him mad?"

Katie looked down. "My husband has no use for Indians. I think Tohave could see that and it angered him."

"Well, I'm not saying Tohave and his wild bunch are totally harmless, but they react to kindness the same as anyone. Tohave did not hesitate to tell us that he was at the Little Big Horn and killed soldiers. And he once hinted that he's killed other white men. I don't underestimate his capabilities, but neither am I afraid of him. I would fear him only if I betrayed or angered him. I've left my wife alone before and she's never come to harm, though a couple of times Tohave and his bunch rode to the farm and asked for pie."

"They come right inside and sit at the table," Dora added. "I don't bother with forks and plates. I just cut it and they all grab a piece and practically swallow it whole. And they always leave me some trinket in gratitude. I'm getting quite a collection of hair ornaments and necklaces and the like."

Katie put a hand to her chest. "I'd faint if Indian men came into my house and I was alone!"

Dora smiled. "That's the time when you must show no fear at all, Katie. Reveal only kindness and trust. They honor that. Remember it."

"As far as I'm concerned, the real danger out here is the land itself," Jacob put in. "The elements. The heat sometimes makes you want to die; the streams dry up; the singing insects make your ears ring and they often eat your crops; the wind never stops blowing; and there's little chance to socialize. If you aren't careful, the land will get you long before the Indians do."

"I'm afraid it's almost got us," Dora added sadly. "We've not had much luck since we came here from Ohio, and we're thinking about going back east if this summer isn't any better. The only thing that's made it bearable for me is having Jacob's support and love. I want so much for it to work. We had big dreams, as I'm sure you and your husband have. Maybe you'll have better luck than we did. I pray that you do. But a good husband can be a big help."

"And a good wife," Jacob replied.

The Browns looked at each other again, and Katie felt like crying at the love in their eyes. If Ezra would only once touch her lovingly, speak proudly about her, show some affection rather than just animal desire. Ezra came into the store then, and after grudgingly accepting Katie's introduction to the Browns, he rudely announced to Jacob that he needed no help. He'd do fine on his own. Katie was embarrassed, even more so when he told her loudly to put back the bolt of cloth and the thread.

"There'll be no time for such silly things, woman. We have work to do, lots of it. Maybe next fall you can buy some, so you'll have something to do in the winter when we're snowed in."

Katie put back the cloth, struggling not to cry, while Jacob and Dora watched pityingly. Katie wanted desperately to talk more with Dora but she knew Ezra would not allow it. They finished stocking up on supplies, and Ezra paid for them, telling the clerk to hold them until his wagon was ready and he could bring it over. "Let's go around back. There's some lumber there I want to buy so I can start framing a house." He glanced at Jacob Brown. "Nice to meet you."

Katie was surprised he even said that much. "There will be some Indian games here this afternoon." Jacob spoke up quickly. The soldiers are competing with some of the Sioux—a few games for goodwill purposes. Will the two of you stay?"

Katie's heart swelled with hope. "We might," Ezra answered. He then pulled her out the door. At least she had a slim hope of seeing Dora again that night and of doing a little more socializing before going back to the lonely dugout.

As they stepped off the boardwalk and started across the parade ground they heard yipping and calling and laughter, and several spotted ponies thundered past the marching soldiers, their riders nearly naked, feathers in their hair. A few emigrants stepped back, and Katie saw two women run and hide. She and Ezra stopped to let the riders by, and Katie's heart pounded, her face reddened. Tohave!

He stopped and whirled his horse around, looking down proudly at her. It was the first time she'd seen him in full daylight since he and his friends had surrounded her wagon, the first time she had met his gaze in full light since the shameful night when her husband had attacked her.

"So, we meet again, just as I said," he told her.

"Get your red ass away from me and my wife!" Ezra growled.

Katie looked up then, blinking back tears. Tohave only smiled at her, with a gentle kindness. He understood. They shared a secret, didn't they? He knew she'd never told her husband about the times he'd been nearby.

"One cannot see things well at night," he commented.

As he turned and rode off, Ezra Russell frowned. "What the hell did he mean by that?" he asked absently.

"I'm sure I don't know," Katie replied quietly, wiping at tears but smiling inside. Tohave was kindly trying to tell her not to be embarrassed about the night he'd seen Ezra hurt and humiliate her in the water.

61

Chapter Four

There could be no leaving until the wagon wheels were ready. Ezra fussed and fumed, wanting to get started back that same night, angry because of the wait for the wagon and because of the other wagons that had arrived on the same afternoon, swamping the blacksmith. To make matters worse, he had hoped to buy plow horses, but there were none to be had at the fort.

They spent the better part of the day sitting on a bench near one of the buildings, Ezra drinking from a bottle of whiskey he had brought along, Katie with nothing to do but watch the goings-on inside the fort and keep an eye out for Tohave. But he had ridden out again, and she did not doubt that he was just outside, somewhere amid the tipis nearby. Did he have a woman there? The lieutenant colonel had not mentioned whether or not Tohave was married, if that was what Indians called it. But Katie's womanly instincts, marred though they were by her ugly marriage, told her what a fine specimen of a man Tohave was. Surely the young Indian girls were pleased with what they saw.

To Ezra's irritation but Katie's delight, the Browns walked by in the late afternoon, Dora smiling pleasantly at Katie, Jacob frowning at Ezra, who wiped at his lips after slugging down more whiskey.

"Have you decided to stay the night at the fort?" Jacob asked.

"If that blacksmith doesn't get done soon, it's decided for us," Ezra grumbled. "I wanted to be on my way."

Jacob folded his arms and walked closer, while Dora sat down beside Katie. "Take my advice and stay the night," Jacob told Ezra. "There's no sense in going out tonight. You'll have a good rest before starting out in the morning, and the diversion will be good for your wife. You'll be spending enough days out there all alone, believe me. Take advantage of your chance to visit. Besides, there will be Indian games tonight."

Ezra sighed, but Katie's eyes lit up. "What kind of games?"

Jacob grinned. "Didn't you see Tohave and the others ride in? Before dark there will be a horse race between the Sioux and the soldiers. You came at a good time if you want to have a little fun before going back. There will be shooting contests, wrestling matches, and wrist wrestling. Anyone can join in. Once I managed to beat an Indian at wrist wrestling." He looked at Ezra. "But don't ever try body wrestling. They're damned good. And they're almost never beat at horse racing."

"I don't care about any of that." Ezra waved the man off. "But speaking of horses, how can I get my hands on a couple?"

Jacob looked around. "For some reason there are no traders around today, and the soldiers are short, so they won't have any stock to sell. Stay until tomorrow and maybe some horse traders will ride in, or you'll have to come back and try again. Just watch out for the traders. They're not the most reputable people."

"I'll buy anything they've got. I need a couple of good plow horses."

"Well, I wish you luck there, Mr. Russell."

"Be sure you keep plenty of creams on hand," Dora was telling Katie. "You have such lovely skin."

"And keep plenty of water stored up," Jacob added, looking again at Ezra and feeling sorry for the man's young wife. "If you have a stream nearby, you can't be sure it will last the summer. It probably won't, and rain is often scarce. Store up as much as you can in barrels and containers."

"I intended to," Ezra replied in an irritated voice.

Jacob ran a hand through his hair. "Mr. Russell, I'm not trying to act as though I know it all. It's just that we've been out here a couple of years now and we've learned a lot of things the hard way. I like to help newcomers as much as I can. I'm sorry if that offends you."

Katie looked at her lap, and Dora patted her hand as Ezra rose and met Jacob Brown's eyes. "I've been a farmer a long time, Mr. Brown. I know what I'm doing."

"Your wife said you were from Illinois. Farming in Illinois and farming in Nebraska, especially western Nebraska, are two different things, Mr. Russell, believe me. Why don't you and I go for a walk and a smoke, and we'll talk about it."

Ezra sighed again, then grudgingly obliged, pulling a tobacco pouch from his pants pocket. "I heard Crazy Horse was killed at this very fort. You ever hear that?"

Jacob grinned and nodded, pointing to a guardhouse. "Right over there. Come on. I'll show you around so you'll know where everything is the next time you come in. We might not see each other again."

The two of them walked off, and Katie sighed in relief.

"I think Jacob knew you might want to be alone for a while to talk," Dora told the girl.

Katie looked at her in surprise. "How?"

Dora squeezed her hand. "Your unhappiness is rather evident, Katie." Katie reddened slightly and looked down. "It's all right," Dora went on. "Is there anything I can do?"

Katie shook her head. "It will work out. I just . . . have to get used to being married . . . and to this new place." She swallowed. "I hate it here, Dora! It's not just that my husband isn't kind—I think if I have a baby he'll be better to me—but I hate this place . . . the heat . . . the loneliness."

The woman put an arm around her shoulders. "I know it's hard. It's been bearable for me because I have Jacob. I do hope things will get better for you, Katie. I know it seems we're intruding, but out here friendships must be made quickly. They're very precious."

"You aren't intruding. I appreciate your concern, Dora." She pushed a wisp of damp hair behind her ear. "And I truly appreciate your husband diverting Ezra for a while to allow us some time alone. It must be so nice . . . being married to someone so understanding."

"Jacob is wonderful."

Katie looked at her, her own eyes filling with tears. "Tell me true, Dora, do you mind . . . I mean, is it enjoyable being with . . ." She reddened deeply and looked away. "My God!" she whispered. "I hardly know you!"

Dora frowned. "What is it, Katie? It's all right, I assure you."

Katie shook her head. "It's too personal."

Dora squeezed the girl's shoulder. "You want to know if I mind being a woman to my Jacob," she said quietly. "Is your husband cruel to you, Katie?"

Katie sniffed and struggled to hold back tears. "I just . . . have to know . . . if sometimes it's good."

Dora ran a hand over her own swollen belly. "With a man like Jacob it's always good. In time perhaps, if the crops go well and you have a child, it will be good for you, too, Katie. Perhaps your husband is only irritated and impatient because of coming out here to start life over."

Katie shook her head. "You don't understand. There is no love . . . no—"

Just then there was shouting, and horses thundered by, cutting off her words.

"Katie Russell. Where is that black-hearted husband of yours?" someone shouted.

Katie looked up in surprise at Tohave, who proudly sat his mount, looking down at her, his eyes revealing his anger at the thought of Ezra Russell and what he had seen several nights before.

"Jacob took him walking." Dora answered for Katie.

Tohave nodded to Dora. "The white woman who bakes pies has befriended the young white girl with the sad heart," he said. He looked at Katie, and their eyes held. "You are coming to the races, the Indian games?"

Katie swallowed, quickly wiping at her tears, her heart pounding so hard it almost hurt. "I . . . don't know."

He removed a feather from the band around his forehead and handed it down to her. She frowned questioningly as she took it, being careful not to touch his hand, not because he was Indian, but because she was afraid of the emotions that might run through her if she touched him.

"I will be riding for you, Katie Russell," he told her. He flashed her a bright smile then and, turning his horse, rode off. Katie stared after him while Dora watched in wonder. When she looked back at Katie, the girl's sad blue eyes still watched the place where Tohave had disappeared from view. Were the girl's tears shed for more than a cruel husband and a lonely land? She took the feather from Katie's fingers.

"Do you have a pocket?" she asked.

Katie blinked and turned to Dora. "What?"

"A pocket. Your husband is coming. What do you want to do with this feather?"

67

Katie looked down at it, then quickly grabbed it. Much as she hated to do it, she broke the feather in the center and quickly put it into the pocket of her dress. She met Dora's eyes, and knew the woman understood.

"What am I to do?" she whispered.

Dora squeezed her arm. "Pray, and follow your heart, Katie. That's all you can do. God will bring things about in the right way somehow. I don't know how you ended up with Ezra Russell, and I can only guess at the meaning of the look Tohave just gave you, but be careful, Katie. Remember that you're a married woman—and that Tohave is an Indian. An unhappy heart can make a person do foolish things."

"But . . . it isn't like you think. I haven't the faintest idea why he gave me the feather, why he said what he said. And I . . . oh, please don't think me bad, Dora. I wish we had more time to talk!"

"I don't think you bad at all. Now take heart. Here come Jacob and your husband, and they seem to be getting along better. Everything will be fine."

They both looked at the approaching men. "I've talked Ezra into staying for the races and games," Jacob announced. Katie was relieved that the men were on a first-name basis. Perhaps making a new friend would put Ezra Russell in a better mood, and somehow Jacob had gotten hold of the whiskey bottle, sensing it would be easier for Katie if Ezra consumed no more. How he had managed that, she could not guess, but she liked Jacob Brown and she silently thanked God that they had met the couple. When the Browns offered to share their evening meal with the Russells, to Katie's surprise and delight, Ezra accepted. As they walked to the Brown's wagon, Katie put a hand in her pocket, fingering the feather.

*　　　*　　　*

68

Katie stood in the long line of soldiers and civilians along the route for the horse race, watching. The finest Army horse, a thoroughbred called Prince, was pitted against the finest Indian mount, a nearly black Appaloosa with brown, gray, and white coloring on his rump. Katie now knew the meaning of the feather. Tohave rode the Appaloosa, and Jacob had explained that he must have a special young girl in camp for whom he rode, for seldom did young Indian men ride in a race without such a purpose to spur them. Dora said nothing, and Katie reddened and her heart beat harder again, though only Dora knew Tohave had given her the feather, that he'd told her he'd be riding for her. She'd never seen him on the Appaloosa before, but Jacob answered her silent question by explaining that an Indian often had several horses, for different purposes—for the hunt, for making war, for races such as this, and for carrying supplies and pulling the travois. This horse had apparently been saved just for this race. Whether it belonged to Tohave or he had simply been chosen to ride it, Jacob could not be sure.

Katie was sure it belonged to him. The way he sat the restless mount, spoke to it; the confidence he showed. It surely was his own.

Bets had been heavily laid on both sides, the Indians wagering fine robes and blankets, some of their own finest mounts, and even money, though most had little. The soldiers bet money and tobacco. Tohave and the soldier racing him lined up, side by side. This was the last and best race. A private stood near them, raised a pistol, and fired. Katie jumped, and the riders were off. As the two mounts flew past, sod flying from beneath hooves, Katie put a hand to her chest, inwardly rooting for Tohave, while beside her Ezra backed the soldier.

The two mounts thundered across the flat prairie, over a half mile from the fort, while soldiers and Indians stood

69

along their path to be sure the race was fair. The crowd quieted as the two riders became small dots on the horizon, then seemed to grow larger again as they started the return. Soon it was evident that Tohave was in the lead. It was all Katie could do to keep from crying out in delight, but she feigned disappointment as Ezra stood nearby screaming for the soldier to get moving. The two animals thundered by them again, Tohave's a full neck in front of the thoroughbred.

Shouts and war cries sprang from the lips of the Indian men, while their women made eerie trilling sounds. As bettors gathered to collect their winnings or pay up, others held back, realizing such moments were tense, tempers high. Tohave rode back to his Indian friends, who whooped and yelped again, while Tohave laughed, raising his arms and giving out a shrill war cry of his own. When he glanced over at Katie, smiling, she looked down and Ezra grumbled about the "damned redskins" who probably fed their horses some secret concoction from weeds to make them go faster.

"No one breeds horses better or knows horseflesh better than the Indians, Ezra," Jacob told him. "They need no secret concoctions. It was fair, believe me. Stay around. It's nearly dusk. The young ones will show you some damned fancy riding before it's too dark. Then the soldiers will build a big bonfire and there'll be wrestling."

"Sounds like trouble to me," Ezra mumbled.

"It's an effort to stave off trouble," Jacob told him. "The government is doing all it can to keep this latest peace, to keep things quiet. Contests like this help. When the Indians win, they feel victorious without having fought a real battle. They know those days are over, but life on a reservation makes them restless. So the military holds little gatherings like this all over Indian territory, to keep them active and out of trouble."

"It hasn't kept that Tohave out of trouble," Ezra

70

grumbled. "I'm not about to forget how he threatened us, especially my wife. I don't trust that devil."

"Tohave's no devil," Dora reassured him. "He's young and restless, and I think perhaps very unhappy most of the time, in spite of his teasing and laughing and playing tricks. He's one of those caught between. The old ones know they will die soon, so it doesn't matter anymore what they have lost. The little ones don't even know what's been lost. But those of Tohave's age remember the old days, battles like the Little Big Horn, where they were victorious. Now they have to swallow defeat. It's humiliating for them, and they still believe this is their land, that we have no right to be here."

"Well, what's done is done," Ezra barked. "It can't be changed so they might as well accept it. And they'd better stay off my land or they'll be tasting lead."

The four of them stopped walking, as Jacob turned to face Ezra. "I would think twice before pulling a trigger, Ezra. It doesn't take much to start something that might be long and bloody. Be a little patient. Try to understand them."

"I've got no time to be worrying about what's happening to the Indians. I've got a farm to work, the sooner the better!"

"Well, there will be time enough for that when you leave tomorrow. You certainly can't do anything about it tonight," Jacob answered. "Let's go to the parade ground. You'll see some trick riding you won't soon forget."

Ezra scowled and followed after him. Katie realized then that she couldn't remember the last time she'd seen Ezra Russell smile, if she ever had. She recalled only the throaty, dirty laugh that came up from him when he was abusing her, but no genuine, kind smile. They walked to the parade ground, where people were gathering and where young Indian men were sitting on restless ponies

71

that tossed their heads and pranced nervously. Tohave soon joined them, now mounted on the Pinto Katie had seen him on the day he and his friends had surrounded their wagon, and the other times she had seen him without telling Ezra. The horse was almost but not quite as big as the Appaloosa, a beautifully formed animal, mostly white, with black and brown spots, a white mane and tail. Beads were braided into its mane and tail, and a sun was painted on one large white portion of its rump.

Tohave sat astride the animal wearing only buckskin pants, his bronze chest bare and glistening with sweat from his recent race; his dark eyes dancing wildly due to his recent victory were accented by the streaks of white paint on his high cheekbones. He pranced his pinto up to where Ezra and Katie stood with Jacob and Dora and some of the other spectators, and his eyes lit on Ezra.

"And did you lose money betting against Tohave?" he asked proudly. "That Appaloosa is the fastest in these parts, my finest horse."

"I didn't bet on anybody," Ezra growled back, holding the Indian's eyes steadily. "But you can bet that you and I are going to have at it one day, redskin. Nobody threatens me and my wife like you did, and you'd better know I reported it!"

Tohave just looked down his nose sneeringly, and Katie's eyes widened when the young man pulled out a knife. He tossed it so that it stuck in the ground between Ezra's boots. Bystanders gasped, and Indians and soldiers alike tensed. A sergeant ran for Lieutenant-Colonel McBain, while Tohave and Ezra glared at each other.

"You look like a strong man." Tohave sneered at Ezra. "I think perhaps you try too hard to show your wife how strong you are. Using strength against a woman is no proof of it, white eyes! Why not try a man? I challenge you to the wrist wrestling. Are you man enough to accept?"

He did not look at Katie, only at Ezra Russell, who had enough whiskey in him to be bold. "And if I win?"

"You will have proven that you are as strong as your mouth brags and as strong as the stink of firewater on your breath. If Tohave wins, we make a truce. You will remove your complaint to the soldiers so that Tohave does not look bad in their eyes."

Their eyes held a long, tense moment, while McBain came walking toward the scene. "Agreed," Ezra hissed.

"What's going on here?" McBain marched into the crowd.

"It's all right," Jacob spoke up quickly. "A little challenge has been made, that's all."

McBain looked from Ezra to Tohave and back to Ezra. "I want no unnecessary trouble," he told Ezra. "I told you that. A friendly attitude can make all the difference."

"Well I'm not in a friendly mood!" Ezra snapped. "And give some of that advice to Tohave there. He's the one who rode up here and challenged me."

McBain looked up at the Indian. "What are you up to, Tohave?"

The proud young warrior shifted his dark eyes to the commander. "You do not understand, and I do not choose to explain. My reasons are my own, and I have done no harm. I simply challenged this man to the wrist wrestling. No one will be harmed. You have my word."

McBain looked back at Ezra. "Did you accept?"

"I accepted."

The commander sighed. "Well there's no going back on it then. Make sure you both keep it to wrist wrestling. I don't know what put burrs under both your saddles and I don't care, so long as it doesn't lead to more trouble."

The officer turned and walked away, and Tohave's Indian friends started shouting for him to join them for the riding demonstration. Tohave stared a moment

73

longer at Ezra Russell, then his eyes swung to Katie before he turned his mount and rode off.

Moments later twelve Indian men, one after the other, rode hard around the parade ground, performing amazing riding techniques, many used in war. Each man, including Tohave, could do them all—hang on the side of his mount to avoid bullets; slip an arm through a leather loop while hanging over the side, so that both hands were free to shoot a bow—and to everyone's amazement these riders shot at haystack targets and hit their marks while hanging precariously from the side of a galloping pony.

Each rode standing on the back of his mount; turned around and rode backward while the horse never stopped running; jumped off a running horse, jumped back on; picked up an Indian man standing on the ground, hoisting him up quickly behind as in a rescue; hung completely under the horse's belly; changed from one mount to another. Through many of the tricks, guns were fired or arrows were shot at targets.

Through it all, Katie could only think of the challenge and wonder at it. What did Tohave want? What did he expect? Did the feather he'd given her mean he had no Indian lover for whom to ride? And if so, was he saying he did all of these things for her, to prove something to her? It made no sense. No situation could be more hopeless than that of a married white woman and an untamed Indian man, two people who barely knew the other. Why did he do these things? Why did he stir in her feelings she'd never known before, thoughts she'd never considered, questions she'd never asked? It almost angered her, and she didn't know whether to hate him or like him. His teasing of Ezra would only make her own life more miserable, for whenever Ezra was upset he took it out on her. She wished she could talk to Tohave, find out what he wanted, find out more about him. Never had she dreamed that such strange things would happen to her

74

upon coming to Nebraska. The worst part was that she could not quell the way her heart beat when she watched Tohave or when his dark eyes met her blue ones. She looked at Dora.

"I feel ill," she said quietly.

Dora looked up at Ezra. "I'll take her for a walk."

"It's that damned Indian! He's got her all scared and upset again," he growled. "He'll tame down when I put him down in the wrist wrestling. I used to be damned good at that."

The two women walked away, Katie putting a hand to her head. "Why did he do that, Dora?" she said quietly to the woman when they got away from the others. "If Ezra loses, he'll be so angry."

"Relax, Katie." She put her hands on the girl's shoulders and faced her. "I think you know why he did it. When Tohave looks at you he sees a beautiful girl, and it angers him that she is married to a man who does not appreciate her. He's decided to show Ezra Russell up, if he can. No doubt he has some special feeling for you, and surely you do for him. You're so shaken by his presence that you're ill."

"It's ridiculous! It's all ridiculous. He has no right to look at me in any special way. And you're wrong about my own feelings! Ezra was right. Tohave frightens me. I don't understand what he wants."

Dora let go of her. "I'm sorry. I had no right to say what I said. It's not my business, and I'm probably wrong."

Katie blinked back tears as she touched her friend's arm. "No, Dora. Don't be sorry. You're only trying to help. It's just . . . so many things are happening to me, and I feel so alone. I dread leaving tomorrow, not being able to see you again for weeks, maybe months. There is so much we could talk about . . . so much I want to ask you . . . about men and marriage and such." She breathed deeply. "I'll be all right," she said, but her heart tightened. "Look. Everyone is heading for another area. Your husband and Ezra are motioning for us to follow."

They hurried forward, slowed somewhat by Dora's swollen belly, and joined the men who'd formed a circle around a soldier and an Indian who were on the ground, the Indian wearing only a loincloth, the soldier only his trousers. Indians and soldiers were rooting for their own; the wrestling matches were underway. Katie looked away most of the time, blushing at the near-naked bodies of the Indian participants. Tohave did not take part in the wrestling, but stood at the side rooting for his friends, still wearing buckskin pants but no shirt. For Katie the matches were over too soon, for the next event was the wrist wrestling. Several pairs of men took their turn at the challenge, held always in the same area, the participants using a specially built table that suited an average man's height. The winners of each contest would face one another until only one man was left.

Suddenly it was Ezra and Tohave's turn. Soldiers and spectators shoved Ezra forward. Tohave came forward on his own, his eyes cold and menacing as he glared at Ezra. Only Katie knew what the man had seen, what he was thinking. Perhaps, if Ezra had proven himself a good and kind husband, Tohave would not have allowed himself further thoughts about Katie; he would not have shown himself to her again after that initial frivolity around their wagon. But now there was a determination in his eyes as he stepped up to the table, and it was in Ezra Russell's eyes. Ezra was shorter and older, too thick in the middle. But he'd been a very strong man in his youth, and he still had much of that strength. It would be a good match, and pure will would have as much to do with winning as strength.

The two men gripped hands, twisting, adjusting, getting a feel of one another until the soldier who

76

supervised the matches said the grip was good and they could begin. As men moved in closer, it was difficult for Katie to see. Tohave had challenged his opponent so this match was more exciting.

Katie left Dora behind and with Jacob's help, forced her way forward. For a few seconds the two men held equally; then Ezra's arm started going down under the more youthful Tohave's strength. Every muscle in the Indian's arms and shoulders was tense and bulging, his form magnificent as he touched Ezra's hand to the table. The Indians hooted and howled as Tohave rose and put up his arms in victory.

Katie's eyes widened when she noticed Ezra turn and eye a soldier's rifle while the Indians celebrated, but Lieutenant-Colonel McBain stepped close to Ezra and said something in his ear. The commander had a warning look in his eyes. Tohave turned and drew nearer himself then, unaware of the sudden thought that had gone through Ezra's mind. He actually put out his hand white man's style, and Katie knew in that moment that Tohave understood that if Ezra left angry he might harm Katie.

"Now you will remove your complaint, Ezra Russell, and we will begin anew. When you see me you will know who I am and know I mean you no harm."

The crowd quieted and Ezra hesitated, then stepped back, refusing Tohave's hand. "I'll remove the complaint—on paper," he told the Indian. "But not on the inside. You stay away from me, my wife and my farm, Tohave. You belong on the reservation. You might be able to beat me at wrist wrestling, but don't try beating me at anything else, Indian!"

Katie reddened as her husband turned and stormed off, embarrassing her in front of the others by grabbing her and dragging her along. Tohave watched, and while the winners of previous challenges gathered for playoff matches some of the people gathered about eyed Ezra and

77

Katie as they went off into the darkness, headed for their now-mended wagon. A few of the men spoke quietly about the belligerent Ezra Russell and the trouble he'd nearly caused.

"I'm sorry about that, Tohave," McBain said. "Don't let him bother you, and don't be starting something bad so that I have to arrest you. Understand?"

Tohave turned to sneer at him. "Tohave is tired of being told what to do. But he will do as you say, for the sake of his people and for no other reason."

He left the soldier to hurry up to Jacob and Dora Brown. "Jacob!" he called out.

The Browns turned. "What is it?" Jacob asked.

Tohave suddenly looked like a lost boy. "Go with them, please. Keep that man talking, stay around them until he falls asleep from the whiskey. If he is alone with her in his mood, he will hurt her."

Dora frowned. "I see something in your eyes that should not be there, Tohave," she said sternly. "Remember who you are—and who she is. We will go and stay with them as you say, but you go your way, and leave them alone for the rest of their stay here. You're upsetting the girl for wrong and hopeless reasons. You know that, don't you?"

He swallowed, his jaws flexing as a strange hurt came into his eyes. "Tohave knows who he is," he answered quietly. Then he turned and walked away.

"What the hell?" Jacob commented in wonder.

"Hell is exactly the word for it," Dora declared. "Right now we'd better go keep Ezra Russell busy until he can no longer keep his eyes open. Things will look better in the morning."

Chapter Five

There was no sleep for Katie that night. To her relief, Ezra fell asleep while Jacob and Dora were with them, something for which she would be forever grateful to her new friends. Ezra had drunk more, bragging that he could have taken Tohave if he hadn't been afraid trouble with the Indians would be the result, but Katie remembered the look on his face when he had eyed the soldier's rifle. If the fort commander had not made a move to stop him, Ezra Russell would have started the worst kind of Indian trouble, and Tohave, unarmed, would have been dead.

Tohave dead . . . It was not Ezra Russell's beating or rape that kept Katie awake that night. Thoughts of Tohave did. In her nineteen years, Cathryn Williams Russell had never been particularly stirred by any man, which was why at nineteen she'd been unmarried until her father had ordered her to marry Ezra. She had known nothing but hard work and brutality, even as a child. Now a man seemed to want to defend her, an Indian man. Why, she could not fathom, nor could she totally admit her own feelings—dangerous, unwanted, shameful feelings. It was not right. None of it was right. Since she'd married Ezra Russell and come to this new land, it seemed she'd lost her sense, her direction. She wished she could go back to Illinois and get control of herself again, shed Ezra Russell and be the old Cathryn Williams, at home on the farm with her brothers, wicked and wild though they were, be at home among old friends and her aunt.

But there was no going back, and seemingly no future here but a brutal and lonely one. To add to her misery, an Indian called Tohave had ridden into her mind. Worse, into her heart, for didn't it pound painfully when he was near? Didn't she wonder shameful things when she watched him? Hadn't he awakened feelings within her she'd never before experienced? The worst part was that even if she were a free woman, such a friendship could never be pursued, for such an alliance was simply unheard of. White women did not befriend Indian men. Who could she talk to? Who would understand? Today they would part from Dora and Jacob, and that tore at her heart. If they lived closer together and could visit more, Dora could help her. She would know what to tell her. But today the Browns were leaving.

Katie stared out the opening at the back of the wagon at a gray sky slowly turning pink with the rising sun. She had slept no more than two hours, and she knew this would be a miserable day because she'd be so tired. She rose from the feather mattress inside the wagon. At least they did not have so many supplies that they could not sleep in the wagon. The lumber was tied to the sides and bottom, and the other supplies only took up one end.

She crawled out and climbed down. She had not even removed her dress the night before. She brushed at it now, and then, pulling the pins from her hair, she reached into the corner of the wagon for her brush. After running it through her long, full, auburn tresses, she pulled them back and fixed them at her neck with a large comb.

Then she began to prepare breakfast, having decided

she would be as kind and loving as possible to Ezra today because of her guilty feelings about Tohave. She would forget about Tohave. Perhaps if she were more submissive to Ezra, more willing in the night, difficult as that would be, he would be more kind to her, more loving. Maybe it was just that he knew she did not love him and it irritated him. Yes, she would try harder to be a good wife in that respect.

If only he would show a little love and compassion, she could love him back, accept his manly desires, she was sure. She must accept her fate, for that was reality. To envision a friendship with an Indian man, to suppose she could have a man one day out of sheer love and desire, these were wild imaginings. She must face the fact that there would be little passion and joy in her life, but she would try to create those things. There was nothing more she could do, and if she did not stop fighting the ugliness in her life, she would go crazy. Today. There was only today.

She had the coffee ready and a pan of bacon frying when Ezra finally stirred and coughed. Her chest tightened and she prayed he'd be in a decent mood. Moments later he stuck his head out of the wagon and looked at her with scowling dark eyes.

"Good morning!" she said brightly. "I've started breakfast."

He grumbled something and climbed down. He was still shirtless, and she averted her eyes from the ugly dark hair that covered his body, making him look like a bear. He came closer, and she could smell the lingering odor of whiskey as he bent down to get himself a cup of coffee. She looked at him then, trying not to be repulsed by the pockets of sleep evident in his bloodshot eyes, and he hungrily returned her gaze.

"I hope you know I could have beat that red bastard last night and why I let him win."

81

She knew it was a lie. "Of course you could have beat him," she answered. "It's all ridiculous anyway, but now it's over. I just want to go home and get away from here, Ezra."

"Do you?"

She poured her own coffee. "Of course I do."

He knocked the coffee from her hand, some of it spilling onto her fingers and burning them. All her good thoughts about trying to love him vanished. "I know you deliberately waited for me to fall asleep last night, woman! It won't be that way tonight, you can bet on that. We'll be alone out there, and those damned Browns won't be around."

She blinked back tears and picked up her cup with a shaking hand. "They're nice people."

"They're too nice as far as I'm concerned. Anybody that shows hospitality to Indians ought to have their heads examined." He straightened. "We'll leave soon as we're through eating."

She wiped at her eyes. "We should tell the Browns goodbye at least."

"There's no point to it. We won't see them again for a long time, and you did your talking last night. Besides, it's not good for you to be getting too friendly with another woman. It'll make you too uppity, put thoughts in your head you don't need to be thinking. You don't need anybody but ol' Ezra. Now put some of that bacon and a biscuit on a plate so I can eat."

She quietly obeyed, and as soon as he turned away, she took the broken feather from her pocket and put it in the fire. It quickly flamed and disappeared.

All too soon they were rolling out of the fort, away from the Browns, away from people and life. Desperate loneliness grasped at Katie's heart. The anticipation of going to the fort had been wonderful. Now there was nothing to look forward to but heat and work and being alone with Ezra Russell. She knew he'd keep his promise about the coming night and already she felt sick. But in spite of his ornery mood, she decided to try her best to be more obliging, to act as though she took pleasure in his lovemaking, if it could even be called that. It was really much more like animal mating, no feelings involved, simply a release for Ezra Russell.

Their wagon rattled out of the fort without a goodbye to anyone, not the lieutenant colonel, the Browns . . . or Tohave. Where was he? Sleeping at this very moment in a tipi with an Indian girl? And what was it like, sleeping with a man like Tohave?

She sucked in her breath. There! She had allowed the thought to arise again, like a fool! Like a stupid, shameful fool! She shook away the thought and studied the rutted road ahead.

Tohave stirred as the high morning sun warmed the tipi he shared with Rosebud. A childless Sioux woman twice widowed, she took in any man who would provide meat for her, repaying him with sexual favors and cooking and shelter. Tohave turned and gently rubbed his naked body against her own to wake her, and she stirred with a smile. Rosebud was older than he, but her body was still firm for she had never borne children. She was certainly not the fairest of the Indian maidens, but she was a good friend and she satisfied Tohave's needs. To take out those needs on one of the young virgins or even to look at one hungrily without intending marriage could result in severe punishment or even banishment from the tribe. Tohave was not ready to think of marriage, and now someone else occupied his thoughts so that he hardly noticed the young available maidens.

"Why are you not already up and cooking for me?" he asked Rosebud.

She laughed lightly and kissed his broad chest. "Because once I am in your bed, I never want to leave it, Tohave," she answered. "You know you are my favorite. There is no other like you."

Tohave grinned and rolled on top of her. "We must head back for Pine Ridge today. There is not a lot of time. Already the sun is high."

"I do not like the reservation any more than you, Tohave." She spread her slender legs. "And there is always time for pleasure, is there not?"

He moved one hand gently over her full, firm breasts. "A man should make time for such things."

She closed her eyes and breathed deeply, never tiring of the handsome, hard man who hovered over her, yet fully realizing he might leave her at any time. But she accepted that. She gasped as he entered her, so much man he was, and for the next few moments they moved rythmically, in glorious satisfaction and pleasure, until his life spilled into her and he groaned out a name at the same time—Hemene, Mourning Dove in Cheyenne. When he moved off of Rosebud, he sighed deeply and ran a hand over his eyes.

She sat up and looked down at him then as she ran a hand over his chest. "Sometimes you speak in Sioux, sometimes in Cheyenne, my handsome lover. But either way I have twice heard you whisper a name, and behind those smiling eyes I see sorrow. What bothers you, Tohave?"

He rolled onto his side. "Nothing."

Rosebud rose and walked to a pan of water, intending to wash while he lay staring at the dead coals from their fire of the night before. Then she pulled on a tunic and walked to the coals, stirring them.

"Two Moons tells me you challenged a white man last

night to the wrist wrestling. He said you did it because you have eyes for the man's wife."

Tohave sat up and scowled. "Two Moons talks too much and doesn't know what he's talking about most of the time. He's too young."

Rosebud put some kindling on the coals. "When you make love to me, you pretend I am someone else. I know this, Tohave. I have been with many men, and I know when a man cries for someone. Who is Mourning Dove, and why does she have such a sad name?"

"It is a name I gave her, and it is none of your business who she is."

"It is if she is that white woman. It is bad enough she is white, but she is married. You walk dangerous ground, Tohave, if your thoughts are of that one."

"Shut up!" he barked.

The color rose in Rosebud's face, and she stirred the coals more, her lips pressed together. Tohave rose and tied on his loincloth; then he stood beside her, reaching down and patting her hair. "I am sorry. It is a personal thing and I do not choose to talk about it. I must deal with it alone. I will find a good man to help you back to Pine Ridge. I am not returning just yet."

She reached up and touched his hand. "Be careful, Tohave."

He walked outside without saying more. Three men from Pine Ridge rode into the small camp just then, and they greeted Tohave, who nodded back to them. "We are preparing to return to the reservation. The games are over," he said. "What brings you here now?"

The three dismounted, the one called Stiff Leg looking angry. "We came to report stolen horses to the soldiers. The stinking white traders have hit the reservation again, taking some of our best mounts. My roan mare and black gelding are gone. They were my best, strongest horses."

Tohave frowned. "Do you really think the soldiers will

do anything about it? Even if they find the animals and return them, nothing will be done to the thieves."

"Ah, but when an Indian steals a horse, he is quickly hung," one of the men grumbled.

"The treaty obliges the soldiers to defend us as they do the white man," Stiff Leg declared. "They must find our horses and the thieves must be punished."

"I hope you find them, Stiff Leg, and I hope you are right about the punishment," Tohave answered. "But I hold no high hopes for it. Will you return to Pine Ridge soon?"

Stiff Leg nodded.

"I would be grateful if you would keep an eye on Rosebud then. I am not going back right away. She will do your work for you, cook for you."

Stiff Leg grinned. "When will you take a real wife, Tohave? The young girls whisper about you."

Tohave laughed lightly. "I need no nagging wife or the old mother-in-law who comes with one. A man's life is not his own when he takes a wife. Rosebud suits my needs."

"Rosebud is getting old, and she can have no children. A man needs sons," Stiff Leg replied. "I have four sons. My heart is proud."

"And what is there for them on the reservation besides flies and bad meat, sickness and boredom? If my sons cannot be free, I want no sons. Your own wife is dead from the white man's disease, and your sons have no mother."

"We must learn a new way now," the one called Old Smoke put in. "It is hard for us old ones, but easier for young men like you, Tohave. And it will be even easier for your sons."

"Too soon you forget how it once was for us, Old Smoke," Tohave answered. "And I smell more death in the air. It is not over yet. I had a dream not long ago about

86

more of our people screaming and dying under soldiers' guns."

They all sobered. Such dreams were not to be taken lightly. "Do you know the place where this happened?" Stiff Leg asked.

Tohave shook his head. "But it was very real, and it worries me. The white man is not through with us yet, and it is dangerous to live so close to all these new white settlers who come to take over our land like ants on honey."

Two Moons, who was approaching, overheard the last statement. "If you are so much against the white man, Tohave, how is it you have an eye for a white woman?" he said teasingly.

Tohave whirled. Catching the younger man with the back of his hand and whacking him across the side of his face, he sent him flying against the tipi. Inside Rosebud let out a little scream as the tipi sagged but did not fall, and in the next moment she was outside.

"What has happened?"

Two Moons rubbed the side of his face, and getting back to his feet, he shook his head in startled surprise. The three newcomers were astonished by Two Moons' mention of a white woman and by Tohave's reaction. He had hit Two Moons, who was his good friend. Tohave looked first at Rosebud.

"It is nothing. The tipi is all right. Finish cooking me something, Rosebud, and I will help you pack a travois. You may use one of my horses to pull it. Stiff Leg will take you back to Pine Ridge."

She frowned and looked over at Two Moons, who glared at Tohave but made no move to retaliate, knowing full well that Tohave could pound him into the ground if he wanted. Rosebud asked no questions but went back inside; then Tohave faced Stiff Leg and the others.

"Two Moons is young. He talks too much sometimes, about things he doesn't really understand."

Stiff Leg and Old Smoke both studied Tohave intently. "Many white women have stirred my loins, Tohave," Stiff Leg said. "But I am a wise man, and I never look more than once. White women understand nothing about the Indian. I will ask no questions. A man does what he wants, what he feels is right. But be very careful, Tohave. You have no father or uncle to help you decide what is wise. If you wish to talk further of this thing that bothers you enough to cause you to hit your close friend, I will listen."

He put a hand on Tohave's shoulder, and as he held his gaze, he saw a trace of tears in Tohave's eyes. "The sun is bright this morning. It hurts the eyes." Stiff Leg grinned a little and then turned to leave with the others.

Tohave breathed deeply as he turned to face Two Moons, who was still rubbing his cheek. "When I want to talk about the white woman, I will mention her myself, in front of whoever I choose. I do not need you to do it for me." Tohave scowled. "If you want to ride with me and the others again, you will not speak of personal things unless they concern only you."

Two Moons looked at the ground. "I am sorry, Tohave. I did not know it was that close to your heart. I was teasing. I thought it meant nothing."

Tohave threw his head back and sighed; then he put a hand on Two Moons' arm. "It is I who am sorry. I know it is wrong, and it makes me angry. I took it out on you. Forgive me, Two Moons." He stepped away. "Tell Rosebud I am going to ride for a little while. I will be back soon to help her pack."

He walked away then, and Two Moons entered the tipi, the dark skin of his face white and puffy at one side. Rosebud looked up at him. "Tohave hit you?"

Two Moons nodded. "I was only teasing . . . about the

white woman."

Rosebud scowled. "That is bad. Very bad. It means his feelings for her are very deep, Two Moons. Do not mention her to him again. This is a bad thing for Tohave, but he must settle it in his own heart. If she did not belong to another, it would not be so bad. But she is white. Bad. Very bad."

"All things are bad for us right now. Why has Tohave made them even worse for himself? We have enough things to worry us."

Rosebud put a piece of meat on a tin plate for him. "Some things cannot be stopped or changed, Two Moons. You look at someone, and you want that person, and the longing is so bad that it hurts. You are young. You have not felt that way yet. But you will, and then you will understand. A person can wish certain feelings would go away, he can fight them; but there they are just the same, like weeds that grow back no matter how much they are trampled."

"Tohave is a fool."

Rosebud bit into a piece of meat. "We are all fools sometimes."

As the wagon rattled over hot, open prairie, Katie's heart was heavy as stone. The fort was far behind her, loneliness and brutality lay ahead. It was midafternoon when they saw the small herd of horses approaching, driven by four men. Spotting the wagon, one of the four left the others and headed for it, waving his hat. When he came closer, Katie cringed at the sight of him. He looked as though he had never bathed and his food-stained shirt was dark with perspiration stains. The man eyed Katie hungrily as he approached, giving her the chills; but Ezra seemed unmindful of his lascivious look and he greeted the man with a nod.

"Something I can do for you, mister?"

The man rubbed at a three-day beard and then sniffed. "Got some horses to sell. Figured you might be a new settler, lookin' for some good stock. We're on our way to Fort Robinson, but anything we can sell on the way is fine with us."

"Well!" Ezra braked the wagon and looped the reins around a wheel rim. "I'll be damned! I couldn't put my hands on a damned thing at the fort—thought I'd be going home without any plow horses. This is a stroke of luck. How much you asking?"

The man turned and signaled for the others to bring up the animals. "Depends," he replied, turning and eying Katie again. "I don't suppose you'd trade this here fine-looking young woman for a couple of my best steeds?"

Katie reddened. This man frightened her much more than Tohave had, and she expected Ezra to pull out his rifle and tell these four to leave. To her astonishment, however, Ezra just laughed the ugly, throaty laugh she had learned to hate.

"Now that's a thought," he replied. "If she keeps giving me trouble, I just might have to consider that."

Katie's skin crawled. Never had she hated Ezra Russell so! It was all right for this filthy white man to look so boldly at her and to suggest trading her for a horse, yet he'd been ready to shoot Tohave for much less. Surely Ezra could see that they were in more danger from these men than from Tohave . . . but he did not.

The trader rubbed at his lips as the others approached. "Well, sir, you change your mind, we'd be glad to oblige." He turned his mount and cut from the small herd, several pintos and Appaloosas. To Katie they looked very much like Indian horses, but she was not about to speak up. This was Ezra's deal, and she didn't care to make him angry or he just might take the man up on his offer to trade horses for his wife.

90

The other three men were staring at her now. Dirty and perspiring and unshaven, they eyed her as if she were a cool pond in the middle of a desert. The first man came forward with a roan mare and a very large, gray Appaloosa.

"These are the best for plow horses, mister. Not true draft animals, mind you, but with a little work, you could put the harness to them. Twenty dollars each. Or for one night with the woman, you can have one for twenty and the other free."

Katie felt faint when Ezra actually seemed to be considering the offer. Her eyes teared and her throat constricted. "I've got money from the sale of my farm back in Illinois. I need the horses, and I don't need my woman here hating me when I'm stuck alone on the prairie with her. And she's still new to me—got me a virgin. You know how it is. I don't think I'm ready to let somebody else have at her."

Katie sat staring at her lap, shivering and sweating at the same time. The four men laughed and their leader nodded. Then he leaned over and pinched his nose, snorting air through it to blow it out hard onto the ground instead of using a handkerchief.

"Can't argue that," he told Ezra. He handed Katie the ropes that were tied to the neck of the two horses being offered, but she would not even look at him.

"Take the damned reins!" Ezra growled.

Katie jumped, just then noticing the ropes held out to her. She took them, and the man made a point of putting a rough, dirty hand around her own as she did, making her feel ill. His fingernails and knuckles were filthy from being unwashed for many days.

Ezra stood up and pulled some money from his pockets. "I hope they do a good job and I have a good harvest," he told the men. "This is just about the end of my money."

"They'll do you good. They're strong," the first man answered, his eyes still on Katie. "They've not plowed before so they'll take a little working with, but they're young and strong. The male here has been castrated, so he'll give you no trouble."

He smiled at the way Katie reddened again and refused to look at him when he made the remark. There were a few chuckles from the others as Ezra handed the money to their leader. "Get down and tie them horses to the back," he ordered Katie.

She obeyed, hardly able to walk on her shaking legs, and more and more angry because Ezra did nothing when the men made no move to leave while she tied the horses. The four men watched her intently, as though they'd never seen a woman before. The deal was done. Surely Ezra knew they ought to leave and they were only staying to watch his wife.

She returned to the front of the wagon and climbed up, unable to do so without lifting her skirts slightly. Why was it all right for these scurvy white men to look at her and not all right for Tohave to do so? Why hadn't Ezra ordered her to hide in the wagon as he had when Tohave's men had come upon them? She hated Ezra Russell! She had been determined to be kinder to him, to try to love him and be a good, submissive wife, but any bit of respect she might have had for him as her husband had left her.

"I'm obliged," Ezra told them. He hadn't asked where the horses had come from, hadn't gotten a written receipt, hadn't inspected them. He kicked off the brake and slapped the reins, getting the mules underway and heading southeast, commenting that he hoped the cow and bull he'd left beside the stream at "home" were still all right. "Hope the damned Indians didn't steal them," he grumbled.

"If they're dead and partially eaten, it could have been those filthy men back there stealing a free meal," Katie

92

answered coldly. "Not everything out here is the fault of the Indians. Why didn't you get a receipt or ask where those horses came from?"

"Out here a man doesn't ask questions. They're good mounts. I know horses. Even if I can't put them to the plow, it's a good deal, and don't you be sassing me, woman."

She glared at him. "Why did you act like you were considering their offer to trade me for the horses?" she asked angrily.

He just chuckled. "I just figured if I got all hopped up, they might, and then they'd be more likely to take you whether I wanted them to or not. You don't rile men like that."

She blinked back tears. "I don't believe you. I think you really considered it," she said brokenly.

"You keep sassing me like that and I will. Believe what you want."

"I don't like them, and I don't trust them. Did they leave yet? I don't want to look."

He turned his head. "They're riding on." He glanced at her then. "Now ain't it something, you not caring if that stinking Indian Tohave looks at you, but worried about white men."

"Those white men are no better than the Indians— probably worse. Why did you let them look at me, talk about me, in that filthy way?"

"I told you why. Now shut up or I'll call them back. They'd do something to you that would shut your trap right good, I expect. If you weren't still so new to me I'd have thought more on it."

Her throat constricted. "Why?" she gasped. "I've been good to you, Ezra." She swallowed back an urge to scream. "Why do you treat me this way?"

"Because a man has to treat a woman with an iron hand or she ends up ordering him about. You're young

93

and learning, and I intend to teach you right. I'll admit you're improving. Give me a son and I might have a little more feeling for you, beyond being damned pleased with that body of yours. So far that's all you're good for, and even that isn't always very good. When are you going to learn to enjoy your man?"

She sniffled. "When he's kind to me."

"There you go, acting like a damned kid again, blubbering like a baby. I don't want any blubbering or arguing when we make camp tonight, understand? Try enjoying it for once and I won't have to hurt you. You're the one making it hard on yourself, not me."

She closed her eyes and forced back her tears. There was no talking to him, no reasoning with him. That night she tried her best to pretend she was enjoying him. She made no fuss, didn't resist. But her only reward was a harsh slap when he was through with her.

"You're a poor actress," he growled, turning over and going to sleep. She curled up and turned away from him. Then her loneliness overwhelmed her, and she wept quietly. She no longer cared how wrong it was. She would think about Tohave, and about the Browns. She must occupy her mind with something. Maybe by some miracle she would get pregnant soon. At least then he might not hit her. Maybe he wouldn't even mate with her for fear of harming the child. His first wife had never been able to have children. Perhaps that was part of what was wrong with Ezra. He had always wanted sons. She tried hard to understand him, to figure him out. How was she to go on this way if she could not somehow understand this man who she belonged to?

But she didn't really want to understand him tonight. She couldn't keep her thoughts on him. It hurt too much. She fell asleep thinking of Tohave.

*　　　*　　　*

Katie awoke in the early morning to a strong wind, frowning at the realization that there were no other sounds, no bird calls, no insects singing. She sat up with a start, her thoughts turning to the scummy traders. She turned her head then and saw Tohave and five others sitting their mounts nearby, watching them. Her eyes widened, and she pulled her blanket over her partially naked body. Surely they had been staring at her bare shoulders and arms! What else had been revealed while she slept! She turned crimson.

"What do you want!" she managed to ask.

Ezra stirred at the words. Tohave did not answer, but watched Ezra carefully, and Katie saw then that he held the ropes of the two horses Ezra had bought. In his left hand he held a rifle, pointed at Ezra.

Chapter Six

Tohave stared at Katie, hard. He could take her. He could just pick her up and ride off with her. He'd seen her smooth white shoulders and arms, wondered if she was that white from head to toe, wondered about her nipples, the hairs that covered the special place he wanted to own. But if he took her by force, she might hate him, and the soldiers would come and he might hang. On the other hand, if he killed her loathsome husband, she might hate him all the more, and he would certainly hang.

As their eyes held, she clung to the blanket, sure the wild boys with Tohave would do something terrible to her, for it was obvious she wore nothing under the blanket. Normally she dressed when Ezra was through with her, in case of emergencies like this one. But she'd been so upset she'd simply cried herself to sleep, a sleep that turned out to be deep because of her weariness from not having slept the night before. Now she was staring at the reason she hadn't slept and he was staring back, a hard look on his face.

"Wake your man," he said sternly.

Ezra was already stirring, but the whiskey he'd drunk the night before made him groggy.

"Ezra, wake up!" Katie's voice was shaking.

Russell was finally fully aroused. He sat bolt upright at the sight of the Indians, then scrambled for the rifle that should be beside him, but it was not there, nor was his revolver.

"Rest easy, my friend," Tohave told him, clicking back the hammer of his rifle. "We have your guns. When we leave we will drop them behind us after we are far enough away so that you cannot shoot us before we are out of sight."

"What the hell do you want! What are you doing with those horses?"

"They belong to my friend, Stiff Leg. We were out riding when I saw them by your wagon. I am taking them back to Fort Robinson."

"Those are my horses! I just bought them yesterday, for plowing!"

Tohave scowled. "Plowing!" He spat. "Our best Indian ponies are not made for pulling a white man's plow! It is bad enough that the white man plows and plants like a woman, but to use a well-bred Indian mount for such a thing—" He sucked in his breath. "If these were the old days, you would be dead, and I would have your horses and your scalp!" He shifted his eyes to Katie again, and she knew what he was thinking, but he did not say it. He could take more than the horses.

"Hand over those horses, Tohave, or I'll ride back and report you as a horse thief. You know what that means to the white man!"

"It means the same thing to the Indian! I am only taking back what belongs to us. You are the thief!"

"I bought those animals fair and square!"

"From thieves! Stiff Leg came to the fort just yesterday from Pine Ridge to report many horses stolen from the reservation. White men come and take our animals because the Indian raises the finest horses. They steal them and sell them for a profit, and fools like you do not ask where the horses came from. I am taking these to the white leader McBain so he can record that these two have been recovered."

"They're mine! I paid twenty dollars apiece for those animals."

"Then go back to the fort and claim your money, *heyoka!* You are not getting these animals. The mare belongs to my friend Stiff Leg, and the gray one to Deer Tail."

"How do you know for sure?"

Tohave just smiled. "No one knows his horses as the Indian does. There is no doubt they belong to us. Who sold them to you? Where did they go? My friend Stiff Leg also has a fine black gelding missing."

To Katie's humiliation, Ezra threw aside his blanket. He was totally naked as he reached for his pants. As she turned away, Tohave saw her embarrassment and revulsion. He pictured the cruel, hairy Ezra Russell forcing her to submit and his desire to kill the man became almost uncontrollable. But these were new times. He must be careful.

"Four men," Ezra was saying. "I don't know their names. They rode through this area yesterday, said they were headed for Fort Robinson. If you go in that direction you can probably trap them right there at the fort."

Tohave watched the man with disgust. He could smell the odor of an unwashed white man from where he sat. "We will go to the fort then and quickly," he announced.

Ezra buttoned his pants and grasped the bridle of Tohave's horse. "Leave those two here. They're mine now, bought and paid for!"

Tohave glared at him with flashing dark eyes. Then he yanked on the reins so that his mount jerked its head away from Ezra's hold. "A man cannot buy what another man cannot rightfully sell! I am taking them back. You

99

can settle with McBain."

"You redskinned bastard! If I don't get some money back or some horses, I'll have a piece of your hide for myself!"

Tohave looked down at him with a sneer. "Take it now or later, if you can, *vehoe!* Tohave is ready anytime!" He forced the hammer back down with his thumb, tossed his rifle to a companion, and then handed the ropes of the horses to another. As Ezra moved toward him, he put up his hands.

"Ezra, don't!" Katie screamed. "You'll start something that can't be stopped!"

Russell hesitated. Tohave glared down at him. "If you fight me, I will kill you, Ezra Russell." He sneered. "And then your woman will be sitting there all alone. Think of that, hairy one, or perhaps you do not care."

Ezra clenched his teeth. "The day will come—"

"I think not, my friend. Not because you fear for your lovely wife, but because you fear for your own life. We already know you would not give up your own precious hide for her, don't we?" He shook his head. "You white men are so ready to believe we Indian men will do the worst. I think perhaps you have abused your woman worse than I or my friends would. What is it they say about Indian men, that they rape their white women captives to death?" He laughed then and said something in the Sioux tongue to his friends, making them all laugh. "We have our own women," he added. "And if it were not so sad, the things you whites say we do would be a good joke." He sobered then. "It is you who are the bad ones! You come here and rape—our land and our women! You cheat us at the reservation, steal our horses, kill off all the buffalo, ruin the fresh waters!" He spat again. "The horses belong to us! I am taking them to the fort." He glanced at Katie once more. "Why do you cling to that blanket so? Do you not realize that if we meant you harm, we would have ripped it from you long before this?"

She was unable to answer, and the hard look he gave her suddenly changed to one of soft regret. He turned his horse then and rode off, the others following. Some yards away they dropped Ezra's guns onto the ground, then rode hard for the nearest ridge.

"Bastards!" Ezra screamed after them. He walked toward his guns as Katie hurriedly scrambled into the wagon to dress. They had slept outside because there'd been a cool breeze the night before. She wished now that they had slept inside. At least then the Indian men would not have seen her. She yanked a dress over herself, and minutes later Ezra came storming back to the wagon.

"Help me hitch up!" he barked. "We're close to home. I'm taking you there and getting you started on some planting. Then I'm going back to the fort. Somebody is going to make restitution!"

Her heart froze, but she climbed down out of the wagon and hurried around to help hitch the mules. "Ezra, don't leave me out here all alone," she said quietly. "Please."

"Shut up! I'm not too happy about you yelling at me to stop a while ago when I was going after Tohave! You shouldn't have done that!"

"But Commander McBain said—"

"I don't care what anybody said! If I have to start a goddamned war over those horses, I'll do it!"

She blinked back tears. "Ezra, don't leave me alone. What about those awful traders, and the Indians?"

"They're all headed for the fort. Those traders are long gone, and now Tohave and his bunch are on the way. You've nothing to worry about but getting some planting done, and you'd better do it right."

Her chest pained her; she was so terrified. It was bad enough to be out here in this wild land with Ezra, but

101

even he was company and some protection. She walked around the mules to face him.

"Ezra, just take me with you, please. It's only a couple of extra days—"

He grabbed her around the neck, quick and hard, choking off her air as he'd done many times before when he was angry. "A couple of days can make a big difference!" he growled. "There's no sense in both of us going. I said you were staying and planting, woman, and that's what you'll do. I'll leave you a rifle." He yanked her forward and shoved her then toward the wagon seat. "Now climb up there and shut your trap!"

Katie stirred the fire outside the entrance to her earthen home. She had known terror before, but nothing like this. Night . . . alone on the wide prairie. Something howled in the distance. Was it coyotes, or Indians? She could not be certain. The creatures of darkness were out there, hidden in the shadows, stalking; the crickets singing.

It was a muggy, still night, one of the rare times when she was not plagued by the constant wind, but she knew when the sun rose, it would pick up. Now she could only concentrate on keeping the fire going. Fires kept away wild animals, but they didn't keep away men, the kind of animal that frightened her most. She could not forget the ugly, dirty traders and the way they had looked at her. What if they had seen Ezra? They'd have known she was out here alone and helpless, and perhaps they'd have decided not to go to the fort.

She checked the rifle again. She was not even familiar with how to use one for she'd only had one quick, confusing lesson before Ezra had left. As she set the rifle aside, she wondered why Ezra Russell had married her. He might as well have bought a slave woman, for she was more that than a wife. She tried to determine what terrible thing she had done in her life to have been allotted this fate, but she couldn't come up with anything that made sense.

A coyote howled again. Was it Tohave? No. He'd gone on to the fort, hadn't he? What if it was? Should she be afraid? Alone! She was so alone! Was she wrong to believe that the one called Tohave would not harm her if he caught her out here without help? He knew he could have done as he pleased with her more than once, but he had not.

Tohave. What did the name mean? Whatever its meaning, it was a name that seemed to fit the wild land. She wished he had not come riding into her life, making things more complicated than they already were. She was miserable enough without a wild Indian man disturbing her thoughts. If only she could go back to Illinois and start over . . . But it was done now. She could only try to be a good wife, if such a thing was possible with Ezra, and to forget about Tohave and hope that he never showed up again.

She added more wood to the fire, hoping Ezra had left enough to last the night and wondering how she would stay awake all night to keep the blaze going. Never had she dreamed a land could be this big, this desolate, this wild. And never had she felt more alone and small than she did this quiet night on the wide, Nebraska plains. After midnight it became impossible to stay awake. Much as she fought it, her eyelids simply became too heavy, and against her will she let them close and drifted off to sleep. She wasn't certain how long she slept before suddenly jolting awake to realize the fire was nearly out. The wind was blowing again, but it was still dark and there seemed to be singing voices in the wind. A chill went through her.

Tohave? Her heart pounded so hard she could hardly breathe. She hurriedly put more wood on the fire, then

103

reached for her rifle, breathing deeply to try to slow her heart.

Then she saw it, a little beaded hair ornament, lying near her bedroll. Her eyes widened, and she picked it up with a shaking hand. He'd been there, right beside her while she slept! Perhaps only moments ago. It might be that that was what had awakened her!

She closed her hand around the ornament and set the rifle aside. Yes. If he'd wanted to harm her, he'd certainly passed up his best chance. Her eyes teared. She was not alone after all. Someone watched over her, and she knew that all her efforts at forgetting Tohave would fail. How could she not have a special feeling for him, when he showed more concern for her than her own husband?

She curled back into her bedroll, clinging to the little piece of beaded leather. She should be afraid, but she was not. She could sleep now. Tohave watched.

Any lingering fear was gone at sunrise. It wasn't so frightening to be alone when one could look out at the horizons and see what was coming. Katie washed and dressed and brushed her hair; then she walked to the dugout where the cow and bull were tethered. She untied them and led them to the stream, where she hobbled them. Afterward, as she carried a few things into her humble home, she longed for the time when Ezra would set up their bed so she could stop sleeping on the hard ground.

An iron cookstove sat inside the dugout, but Ezra had not gotten around to putting in the pipe, so she continued to cook over a campfire. But she wasn't very hungry this morning. Her thoughts were too full of Tohave, and his visit the night before. Surely it was he who had left the ornament. She'd shoved it under beads and necklaces in her little wooden jewelry box, afraid Ezra might see it but not wanting to throw it away or burn it.

Already it was growing hot, and she did not look forward to the day's work, but she'd best be doing it or Ezra Russell would make her sorry. Perhaps if she showed him what a good worker she was, he would be proud of her and show her a little more consideration. Always she hoped that in some way Ezra Russell would change, would love her more, if he was capable of love. Some people did not seem capable of it, and she felt sick at the thought that Ezra Russell must be one of them.

She tied back her hair and put on a bonnet, then took a hoe from a corner of the dugout and went outside. She'd been told to dig some deep trenches by hand and get some seed potatoes planted. It would not be an easy task, for the earth had not even been turned yet; but Ezra Russell had spoken. Plant them deep, he'd told her. Later he would help her loosen the soil between the rows, also by hand. Then he would use the plow horses he'd have bought and the plow he'd brought along to turn up more soil. They would plant even more potatoes, as well as a lot of corn. They would sell their produce at Fort Robinson, where Ezra had made arrangements with a man who came to the fort in the fall to buy the supplies and take them on into the Dakotas, to cities and to mining towns. But first the produce had to be grown. They could only hope that nature would be on their side this first year.

Katie looked around before beginning. No one was about. Had Tohave really come, or had she dreamed it? No. It was not a dream. She had the ornament. Perhaps he was watching her now from some hidden place. But where did one hide in this open land? Only an Indian would know. That thought made her shiver. She would rather he came out in the open and got it over with. What did he want? Why did he keep appearing out of nowhere?

She pounded the hoe into the hard earth, realizing at the first swing that this would be a miserable task. In minutes she was drenched with sweat, with only a few feet of trench dug. But her fear of Ezra kept her going, dig, dig, scrape. The hot wind blew against her skin but did not cool her. The sun blazed down relentlessly and the grasshoppers and crickets sang so loudly she wondered if they were laughing at her. How was it that wild things, insects and birds and Indians, got along so well without any of the possessions the white man thought he needed to survive? They did no work, did not worry about what they wore or who they impressed. Free! So free they were!

But she was not free. She was married to Ezra Russell, and if he came home and decided she had not done enough, he would be angry. She didn't like it when he was angry so she dug harder. Ezra would probably be gone one more night. That frightened her, yet in spite of the hot day, the hard work, and the thought of another lonely night, it was a relief to have him gone. At least she would have some peace while he was away. She could pretend she was her own person, her own master. No one would bother her at night or order her about during the day.

Dig. Dig. Scrape. Wipe off the sweat. Her hands quickly blistered, and by the time she had two long trenches dug she felt faint. She dropped the hoe and walked to the stream, where she removed her bonnet, slips, and shoes and literally fell into the water. She groaned at the cool relief the stream offered, splashing, drinking, putting her head back and wetting her hair. She let her dress soak. Perhaps a wet dress would keep her cooler. She unbuttoned the neck and pulled it off her shoulders, revealing the straps and front of her cotton undergarment. But what did it matter?

She sighed and lay back, closing her eyes and nearly falling asleep. The noon prairie was quiet but for the ever-present wind. The wind . . . Then a shadow loomed across her face. Katie opened her eyes and gasped, then sat bolt upright. Quickly jerking the shoulders of her dress back up, she slid over to the side of the stream opposite the man who stood staring at her. Tohave!

Their eyes held for a long, silent moment during which it seemed that time had stopped. She looked past him then, to see that no one else was about. When she looked back at Tohave, he scowled.

"That animal makes you work too hard. I watched. You almost passed out under the sun. A woman like you is not made for this land."

She put a hand to her stomach. She had no defense. Her rifle was not even nearby. "What are you doing here?"

His dark eyes roved over her soaked body. "I wondered if you were all right so I circled back, let my friends take the horses in. Then I saw your husband riding for the fort, but you were not along. I told myself you must be out here alone. So I came."

"Why? To hurt me?"

Pain showed in his eyes. "I left something for you last night. Do you not realize if I intended to hurt you, I'd have done so then? Why wait until the heat of the day?"

She reddened then and tore her eyes from him, feeling guilty at the thought his remark had stirred in her mind and not wanting to look at the virile man who stood before her.

"Why, Tohave? Why do you watch me? And why are you here now when I am alone?"

"Because this is the first time Tohave has had to speak with the white woman who is much on his mind. Do not ask why I watch you, because even I do not know. Perhaps Tohave pities you, because of that first time he saw you and asked if you were married by choice. You never answered Tohave."

She looked at the water. "It isn't your business."

She saw his feet splash through the water then. He was

107

nearly naked because of the heat, and she wondered if he was as oblivious to the temperature as he seemed. She wished she could expose her skin as he did, be cool and free. But his skin was dark bronze; it could take the sun. Hers would be bright red within minutes if she exposed it.

He sat down on the bank beside her, and she scooted away. There was a moment of silence before he spoke softly.

"Hemene." He said it so gently that she looked at him in surprise, meeting kind, dark eyes. "Why are you afraid of me?"

She looked away again. "I'm afraid of everything out here." She swallowed back tears. "I hate this land! I hate my husband! And I hate you for confusing me! I've known nothing but brutality all my life. Why should you, an uncivilized Indian, be any different! I'm all alone out here, and you've been watching me for days! Isn't that enough reason to be afraid?"

She sniffed and swallowed, angry with herself for beginning to cry just when she should be showing bravery.

"I suppose you think me just another foolish, weak white woman for crying," she choked out, wiping at her eyes. "I suppose Indian women never cry."

He studied her sadly. "And why should they not cry? When a woman is attacked in the night while she sleeps, the people of her village slaughtered, her tiny baby's skull crushed under a soldier's boot, her man bayoneted, her own body taken by five, six white men—why should she not cry? Oh, yes, Hemene, Indian women have wept many tears."

She met his eyes then, and became calmer. For the first time she was struck by the fact that he was a human being, that they all were human beings. His face showed compassion and sorrow now, but he had laughed the

108

other times she'd seen him. Didn't Tohave like a good joke?

"I'm . . . sorry," she told him. "I shouldn't have said that." She looked at the ground, unable to meet his eyes for long without being too aware of the moving urgency deep inside her. She did not like to feel that when looking at an Indian man. He was all power and beauty, a bronze man in a bronze land, wild and free and strong—and, amazingly, a man of compassion. He'd actually been worried about her. "I still don't understand why you are here, Tohave. There is no reason for you to care one way or the other about me. Your presence can only bring me more trouble, and it will bring trouble for you."

"I have been careful. Your husband will not come back until another moon has gone. We are alone here."

She moved farther away at the remark. "What do you want?"

"Only to talk. When my friends and I attacked your wagon, I did not know I would find such a treasure inside. When I saw you, it was as though something hit me hard in the chest. I lost my breath for a moment. I know it is supposed to be wrong for an Indian man to look upon a white woman with desire, but I could not stop the thoughts that passed through my mind and heart when I saw you. You are married to that hairy old man who is cruel to you, and I have wondered why. But never was there a chance to ask you. I could not ask in front of your husband, or in front of my own friends. Neither would understand."

She finally met his eyes again. "Why does it matter to you? I am white, you are Indian. We can't even be friends, Tohave. So what is the difference?"

He rose, sweeping his arm to signify the land. "Out here you will need any friend you can find, Hemene. If you are unhappy with your man, your loneliness will be

109

great. You cannot get away, but Tohave can come whenever he chooses. Tohave wants to be your friend. Is that so bad?"

She looked up at him, feeling dwarfed. Even standing she barely came to his shoulder. His dark eyes met hers again, making her feel weak. "I don't know, Tohave. I . . . I've never even known an Indian before, man or woman. And it . . . it just doesn't seem right . . . our ages and all." She reddened. "You know what I mean."

She looked away again, and in the next moment he was kneeling beside her. "Tohave knows what you mean. But if you did not have feelings for Tohave, as he has for you, you would not say it. Deny it, and Tohave will leave."

She sat there a long time, staring at the water. Then a tear slipped down her cheek. "I . . . can't deny it," she said in a near whisper. She rose and walked a little bit away from him. "But it isn't right, and it's only because I'm so unhappy," she added. "I'm . . . I'm simply . . . fascinated by you, that's all. I've never known an Indian before." She wiped away tears and faced him boldly. "I'm full of questions, just like you. I've wanted to talk but couldn't." She shrugged and folded her arms. "As long as you're here, we might as well talk and get it over with, and that will be the end of this foolishness."

He flashed the handsome grin that made her legs feel like pudding. "You first," he told her. "I am still waiting for an answer to my question."

She turned and looked at the water again. "My father forced me to marry Ezra," she admitted. "My mother died when I was young, and my father was not a kind man. I have a whole passel of brothers, most of them worthless. My father only kept me around to do the cooking and washing. I never had time to see young men, and after living with my father and brothers, I didn't want anything to do with them anyway." She raised her

110

eyes to stare out at the horizon. "Ezra was a neighbor to us, back in Illinois. My father liked him a lot, perhaps because they were so much alike when it came to their opinion of women. Then one day Pa just came home and told me I was to marry Ezra, who was a childless widower. Ezra was going west and wanted to take a wife along. My father wanted to get rid of me, said it was about time I got 'hitched,' as he put it." She met Tohave's searching eyes then. "When I protested, I got a good whipping with the belt until I agreed. That's all there is to it. I married Ezra Russell, hoping that somehow I'd be happier than I anticipated. Instead it's been worse than I thought, and now here I am, stuck in this desolate, hot, barren land with a man I hate."

He turned slowly, looking out at all horizons. "It is not a desolate, barren land. It is good land. You simply have to learn to listen to the land, Hemene. The wind, the singing insects, they are like music. The wind is like instruments, the insects are voices, and the grass dances to the music. Look at the land. Let it be beautiful for you. It is your own life that is ugly, not the land. The land, man—all creatures—are put here to live together, to share. That is what the white man does not understand— sharing. He wants everything for himself. Always he wants to say 'this is mine, that is mine.' Land, animals, the air, all belong to everyone. They cannot be owned."

Their eyes met and held. "I can already see how very different we are, Tohave," she said softly. "And what of Indian women? Are they owned?"

His dark eyes moved over her appreciatively. "Only for as long as they choose. Indian men are seldom cruel to their wives. If a man is, his wife can set his moccasins and belongings outside her tipi. This means she is through with him. But this does not often happen, for most of the time an Indian girl chooses her man and he chooses her

111

so their love is very great and lasting."

She looked away then. "What is that word you call me? Hemene?"

"It means mourning dove, mourning as in weeping. You remind me of a soft, white dove, full of sorrow. The first moment I saw you I saw sorrow. Tohave reads many things in the eyes. And although yours were the most beautiful I have ever seen, they were not happy."

"That shouldn't matter to you."

"You think I do not know that? But it mattered, whether Tohave wanted it to or not. I could not stop myself from coming back, looking at you again. And when I saw your husband being cruel to you, I was tempted to kill him, but that would only bring about my death and then Tohave would never see you again."

"Stop it!" she whispered, walking farther away, her cheeks crimson. "I've suffered enough shame."

He came closer, reaching out and touching her wet hair. "I saw nothing, Hemene."

"Don't touch me!" she said, darting away. "You shouldn't do that!"

He folded his arms. "Then I will not touch you again. You have my word. Do you wish Tohave to leave?"

She faced him again. "No. Not yet."

He smiled, staying back, his folded arms revealing bulging muscles. "What do you wish to know about Tohave?"

She put a hand nervously to her hair, pushing a piece behind one ear. "What does your name mean?"

"It is Cheyenne for wilderness. It is a good name, for sometimes I feel I am in a wilderness. I dreamed once, during the Sun Dance ritual, that I was lost, doomed to always wonder where I belong."

"Cheyenne? Aren't you Sioux?"

He sat down on the bank of the stream. "I am both.

112

Many years ago the Northern Cheyenne began living among the Sioux. Many intermarried. My Cheyenne mother was one of them. I speak both languages. And when I was young the missionaries came and tried to teach some of us white man's ways, so I learned the white man's language, but only to know better how to outsmart him. I did not like the way these men treated us, did not like their teachings. I could see even at my young age what they were after. Now they have it."

Katie frowned in concern. "What is it like . . . on the reservation?"

He smiled sadly. "Think of what your life is like, but many times worse," he answered. "That is why Tohave wanders. I do not like the reservation. There is too much sickness and sadness there. The young ones are bored, the old ones cry a lot. The things your government promises never come on time, and many die—from loneliness, white men's diseases, or too much whiskey drunk to forget their misery. The people are hungry, but there are no longer any buffalo to hunt, and when the white man's beef comes it is bad meat. The good meat is resold by agents and suppliers who get rich with white man's money while the Indian starves."

She came closer. "You should tell someone, Tohave."

He threw back his head and laughed. "Oh, yes! I should tell someone!" He laughed again. "And how many of your kind do you think will listen? We cannot get the messages to the right people. Those who get them are just as crooked as those involved. They all work together." He scowled then. "And you whites in the outside world know nothing of what goes on. Did you not think when you came here that all Indians are bad, all Indian men pant after white women, all Indians steal and kill, all Indian women are loose? Did you not think us uncivilized savages?"

113

He met her eyes then. Slowly, she sat down. "Yes," she answered honestly.

"And what made you think this?"

She looked at her lap. "The things I read. The things people say."

"There. You see? The agents and soldiers give out false reports so that they look good. Your Eastern newspapers print it that way. And you form your opinions. None of you can even begin to understand anything about the Indian, how he thinks, loves, plays, feels. To you we are not even human beings. We are shot down like dogs. If just one of us kills a white man, the whole tribe is punished, and back in the East the papers say we are again on the warpath." He sneered then, and turned to look at the water. "The whites even scoff at our religion, saying theirs is the only right way. We must change our God. We must change our way of living, our clothing, our hair, our houses, our speech, our games, all of our customs." He looked at her again. "Why? Who has made these rules? Who says they are the only way?"

She sighed and picked at a weed. "I never thought about it, Tohave. You have stirred my mind as well as new feelings." She met his dark eyes. "We are very different, but alike in wondering about the world. I see things now I never saw before. I don't know how to answer you, because I can't truly say that you are wrong. I've seen you laugh, seen compassion in your eyes. I guess I never thought an Indian was a real person, just like myself."

His eyes roved over her, noticing how the wet dress clung to her lovely form, and he longed to see her lying beneath him, naked and white; wanted to taste her pink nipples, invade the small body, and hear her cry out his name. But Rosebud was right. Two Moons was right. He was a fool to think on such things. He was treading in dangerous waters. She blushed under his gaze and rose again to walk a few feet away.

"Is it true you were at the Little Big Horn?" she asked.

"It is true. It was my first battle."

"You've . . . killed men?"

"Of course I have killed men. It is the way."

She swallowed. "And your mother? She was really raped and killed?"

He rose, studying her. Was she trying to find something out so she could tell the soldiers? No. Not this girl. There was an honesty about her. "She was. The men who did it regretted it." There. He had not said he killed them.

Katie shivered. Lieutenant-Colonel McBain had said the bodies of the hunters they had found were not a pretty sight. Could this gentle man of compassion have done that? She turned to face him. Of course. He was an Indian. He had his own kind of justice, and to him it was not wrong. That was one of the things she had to think about, to understand. He had killed men, yet she was not afraid of him. And she was impressed by how amazingly bright and well-spoken he was.

She faced him, and she could see by his searching eyes that he was actually afraid she might say something. "I won't mention it," she told him.

"And why did you not mention to your husband the times you saw me and he did not?"

She looked down. "I don't know. I was curious about you. I wasn't positive you meant any harm, and I didn't want my husband to shoot at you."

"Was it not because you care for Tohave, deep inside, just a little?"

She shook her head. "You'd better go. You said you'd leave if I asked, and I have my work to finish. Please go, Tohave. And don't come back."

He breathed out a long sigh. "I will go—only because you ask. I do not want to do so. But I will not promise that

I will not return. It will take time, because a white man owns you, and because we are so different, but more and more as you stay in this land you will think about Tohave, as Tohave thinks about you, Hemene."

"Please go!" she told him, her voice shaking.

He nodded. "When your heart is most heavy, when you are in danger, you will find that Tohave is near. And when Tohave is not near, he will pray to Maheo that you will have strength and courage, and will be well. You are a fine woman, Katie Russell, to try so hard to be good to a man who is so bad. You are strong and good. It takes much courage to come to this land you do not know, with a man you do not love. I will go now. But not forever."

He walked through the stream, and she watched him, wanting to call out to him. But her mouth would not open. It is wrong; let him go, she told herself as he walked far into the distance, where he suddenly disappeared. In this land that seemed so flat, there were dips and holes unseen at a distance. Suddenly, he reappeared, now on his horse. He turned for a moment and waved, then rode off.

Don't leave! Don't leave me here alone! her heart screamed. But it was a silent scream, and not until he was gone did she realize what a pleasure his presence had been. She had a friend, and there was so much more to talk about. But a friend like Tohave was not allowed. It was best this way, best that he go. But how empty and lonely she felt now.

She sucked in a sob. "Come back," she whimpered. But he was gone. She shook with tears as she turned back to her hoeing. But she had no strength or spirit now, so she chopped away, making little progress, then fell to her knees and wept. It was best that he didn't come back, for if he returned at that moment she would run to him and hug him just because it was good to have someone near, to have someone to talk to, to have someone to hold her

116

and tell her he cared.

Little did she know that Tohave's heart was just as heavy, just as lonely, just as confused. The hot Nebraska sun shone down on his bronze skin as he rode to nowhere, just as it shone on the weeping Hemene. And at that moment it seemed to both of them that there were no other people on the whole earth.

Chapter Seven

The night brought thoughts that could not be denied as Katie lay on her bedroll, physically exhausted from hoeing and emotionally exhausted by her feeling for Tohave. He was so much more human than she'd imagined, and he'd been easy to talk to. It would be nice to be able to talk to him whenever she wanted, like a friend. But such a friendship could not be, and the feelings he stirred in her were dangerous.

But they were there. Yes, they were. If Ezra were half the husband he should be, they would probably not be, but she was starved for kindness and friendship. She told herself that was the only reason it was pleasant being with Tohave. She tried to deny the fact that there was more to it than that. He was bright, compassionate, easy to talk to—things that surprised her in an Indian man. And he was undeniably handsome. For the first time in her life she'd thought about a man as a man, wrong as that was. A more perfect specimen than Tohave could not be found, and she began to realize in the deep recesses of her heart that it was possible to want a man. It was a new and frightening feeling, let alone wrong. But her young heart had never known real love, never known real desire, never known passion. They were natural things for a pretty, nineteen-year-old girl to feel, but they had never been allowed her and perhaps never would be. Such thoughts would have to be just that, thoughts. For her, there was no hope of true happiness. A woman did not just up and leave Ezra Russell, not out in the middle of a land that led nowhere. And a white girl certainly did not run off with an Indian man. She shouldn't even entertain such a possibility.

The crickets sang. Suddenly, after talking to Tohave, someone who was truly a part of this land, their sounds did not seem quite so terrible. *"The wind is like instruments, the insects are voices, and the grass dances to the music,"* Tohave had told her. What a beautiful way to put it. Beautiful thoughts from a beautiful man. Yes, she missed him. How could she deny it? She'd talked with him only a few minutes, and now she missed him. Perhaps, as she had asked, he would never return. It was best. But it left a sadness in her heart unlike any other unhappiness she'd felt. It was a special, precious sadness, her secret, something that changed everything, made other things more bearable. Much as it hurt, she had a secret all her own. She'd shared a moment that was just hers, done something daring. She'd talked with an Indian man and not been afraid. These days of being alone had been good, though frightening. Tohave had helped her feel braver, stronger—and beautiful. She'd never thought much about her looks. Neither her father nor her brothers had ever complimented her on her beauty, nor had Ezra. When he talked about her body he might have been referring to a prize animal, one that might win a blue ribbon. But now, for the first time, she was truly conscious of her body. She realized a man could appreciate a beautiful woman without pawing over her like an animal. It seemed that some men actually had respect for women. She'd had no opportunity to learn this on the farm, but she'd seen it in the soldiers at the fort, sensed it from Tohave's beautiful words.

Now she knew. There were men who honored women, and men who did not. There were men like Tohave, and men like Ezra and the traders. There was so much to think about. She wished she could talk to Dora, but it would be a long time before she saw her again, if ever. There were few chances for socializing in this land.

Something wild cried out in the night, far in the distance. Was it an animal . . . or was it Tohave? She fell asleep. She was too tired to lie awake and afraid, and she suspected, although she'd not seen Tohave since his visit, that she did not sleep unwatched. She held the hair ornament tightly in her hand, then pressed it against her cheek. It smelled of leather and the out of doors, a fresh, wild scent, like Tohave's. She kissed it and held it close, as her eyes closed to the music of the wind and the insects.

It was late the next night when Ezra returned, two new horses tied to the back of the wagon. Katie's heart fell, for she'd hoped she'd have one more night alone. She quickly put the hair ornament back into her jewelry box and went to greet him as he untied the horses. They were huge, broad-chested animals, both mares, one red and the other a golden color.

"Where did you get them?"

"McBain gave them to me," he answered, then led them to the stream. The night was lit up brightly by a full moon. "Tohave's friends had already got back with the two I bought and they'd told McBain what happened, so he knew I'd probably be along. He said rather than start an uprising over a couple of horses he'd give me two of his strongest animals, even though he really couldn't spare them. I'll have to work with them a bit to get them to work together in harness. I never knew good draft horses would be so hard to come by out here."

"Did the traders show up?"

Ezra shook his head as the animals drank. "They never did. They must have smelled trouble and avoided the fort. McBain says a lot of whites around here steal Indian horses because they're such good animals."

"That's terrible. They have no right."

Ezra shrugged. "The Indians have more horses than they need anyway. They aren't going anyplace anymore. But I agree that stealing them sure won't help keep the peace."

"I'm just glad it worked out, Ezra." She was surprised that he was carrying on a normal conversation with her and didn't seem so angry as he had when he left. "Now we have horses for plowing, or to ride to the fort if we have an emergency."

He turned with the horses then, standing in front of her. "Was that Tohave here?"

The question startled her, but she kept her composure, hoping her eyes would not betray her. "Tohave? No. Why?"

He studied her closely. "He never showed up at the fort. McBain says he's not seen him since the day we left." He looked her over. "But I expect if that bastard had been here, he'd either be dead by your rifle, or you'd be raped and scalped."

She breathed a sigh of relief and turned to walk to the animal shelter with him. "I was more worried about those traders, but I've been alone the whole time, Ezra. I got three long trenches dug and planted, like you told me."

He got the horses to the shelter and tied a hind leg of each to a stake so they couldn't run off. Then he turned to face her. "Well, now, since you're so good at doing what I say, how about helping me set up the bed. I haven't had you in a real bed in a long time."

Her heart fell. She was hoping he'd be too tired.

"Come on, woman, let's get busy." He led her to the wagon, where she hauled out the feather mattress while he unhitched the mules. She silently vowed to be as obliging as possible. So far he seemed to be in a good mood, so maybe they could get through this time without a beating. But she wanted to cry. How she hated this! She set the mattress down and pulled the iron headboard of the bed into the dugout, then walked back out into the cool night air. She looked at the full moon, and a wolf howled. She scanned the horizon, but saw nothing. Tohave. She realized that if it was Tohave who wanted her this night, she might actually look forward to being with him. What was it like to want a man, to take pleasure in a man? She might never know.

Ezra came up to her then. His odor offended her, for he hadn't washed in days and had perspired heavily during the long, hot days of travel. He jerked her close and kissed her, his stubbly beard scraping her chin, his breath smelling of whiskey again. All she could think about was Tohave's smooth face, his bright smile. Surely his lips were warm.

Ezra let go of her suddenly and picked up an iron slat for the bed frame. "Get the foot of the bed there and we'll put this thing together," he told her. "And get that gown off while you do it. I want to look at you."

"Ezra, please—"

"Get the goddamned gown off! Things are going good here. Don't go spoiling them by getting uppity."

She swallowed back tears and obeyed. Ezra was home. It was time to get back to reality.

They did the work of those who open new land. Plowing and planting. Day after day it was the same, back-breaking. Now Ezra truly was too tired to bother her at night, but Katie's work did not stop with helping him in the fields. There were clothes to be scrubbed in the stream, meals to be cooked. She finally convinced Ezra to get a hole dug through the earthen roof of their home so he could put in the chimney of the cook stove and that made preparing meals a little easier. Soon he would have to go for more wood. He'd found a place on the White River, several miles northwest of them, where there was some good standing timber, a spot not far off the route to Fort Robinson. Two days a week he would go and cut small loads, and in the fall when the crops were in, he'd go more often to store up wood for the winter.

The lumber for their house lay untouched, and when Ezra set her to work cutting sod squares to close in the front of their earthen home, she knew that this first winter would be spent underground. The only advantage to that was it would be warmer and out of the wind, so there'd be little danger of running out of wood. But she felt like an earthworm, and the thought of being buried underground with Ezra for weeks, maybe months, was not encouraging.

At least in these first weeks of hard work, he had not had the time or the energy to beat her or rape her, or even to get angry with her. Katie's own weariness helped her heavy heart. If hard work brought this kind of peace, she would willingly work herself to death, and sometimes she did not doubt that that was exactly what she was doing. She grew thinner, sweating off pounds in the daily heat, but there was little time for thinking during the day. There was only work, from sunrise to sunset, then supper and washing clothes, then sleep that allowed for no dreaming and wondering.

Dora and Jacob Brown were just a distant memory now, and Tohave had not returned. She had taken a few precious moments occasionally, when she knew Ezra was too busy plowing or hoeing to catch her, to remove the hair ornament from the jewelry box. She'd studied it fondly, touched it gently, pressed it to her face, then put it back. He was just a memory now, something to tell her grandchildren about, an Indian man she had known, a man who had visited her once. It would be an exciting story, her there all alone, visited by a wild Indian. She would smile at the thought of it, fully realizing there had been no danger at all, but it would be fun to tell others that there was. Tohave. Was he gone for good? He had said that when she needed him most he would be there, but perhaps he had decided it was best to forget about her and never come back. She had not felt his presence since that day. The wind was constant, but it did not blow in the eerie way it did when Tohave was around.

She had resigned herself to this life now. She would grow old before her time and die young, of that she was certain. She felt crazy sometimes with no one around but Ezra, who did not make conversation, and it was not even winter yet. Her attempts to love this land were failing. The beautiful things Tohave had said about it no longer were apt. Perhaps it was being with Tohave that had made it beautiful. With Ezra it just seemed hot and cruel and ugly. Maybe it was not the land at all. Maybe she could bear anything if she were with someone she loved, someone who loved her in return, like Jacob loved Dora.

Love! Why had she used that word? Was this what it felt like? Was it love when your thoughts were on someone in every spare moment; when a person's very presence made everything more beautiful; when a tiny part of that person, like the hair ornament, could be comforting just to hold? No! She must not think that way! It could not be love. It must not be love! Besides, he was gone and would probably never return.

She worked even harder. She would forget Tohave. She would forget Dora and Jacob. She would resign herself to this life, to a man who used her like his plow horses, without one word of gentleness or gratitude. She would do what was "expected of a woman," as Ezra put it.

There was a lull then. The crops were planted. Now they hoped for rain, but every day the sky was blue and the sun was hot. No rain came, and during the wait Ezra Russell drank. The brief relief Katie had had from his attacks was over. The drinking made him mean, and he seemed to get pleasure from hurting her before bedding her. She felt like a prisoner who was being tortured. For a short while she had had some hope for a relatively normal married life, but it had vanished when she'd realized it was only the hard work that had kept Ezra quiet, exhaustion that had made him leave her alone in the night. Now he had time to rest, to drink, to bed his woman amid tears and struggle. After all, he wanted a son, and there was only one way to get one. But there was never a kind or gentle touch, never whispered words of love, seldom a bath first. If she protested the least bit, she received stinging slaps, a twist of the arm, or a painful grip that left bruises on her flesh. Her tiny hope that he'd changed a little, that they could have a decent marriage, had been snuffed out, and more and more often she sneaked out the hair ornament and held it against her cheek. But Tohave was gone. There was only Ezra . . . and the heat . . . and the wind . . . and the constant singing of the insects. She no longer heard the music.

Tohave looked at the sky through the opening at the top of the sacred lodge. Someone turned his body, and he swirled, the sky and the paintings at the top of the lodge swirling also. He no longer felt pain. He was in a trance, a self-induced trance from days of fasting, days without even a drop of water. He had chosen to suffer the Sun Dance ritual for the second time. It had been years since that first experience, and most men did not suffer it more

126

than once, but Tohave needed to cleanse his thoughts and heart of a woman he could not have. Perhaps fasting and praying and suffering, offering his blood to Maheo, would help him forget, bring him a vision that would give him his answer, help him know what to do.

He hung by the flesh of his breasts and arms and shoulders, a buffalo head tied to his feet for additional weight. He would hang there with the other participants until the skewers under his skin tore through and he fell to the floor. It was necessary. It was an important part of the Sioux-Cheyenne religion. The whites on the reservation had tried to stop the rite. The government had considered outlawing it and had already tried, but it was as essential to the Indians as breathing. So they sneaked off to secret places to hold their summer ritual, their week-long celebration and worship, topped off by this most sacred sacrifice, this test of manhood for the young warriors. Everything was being taken from them, their land, their customs, their clothing, even their religion. They would let the whites believe they were changing, accepting new ways, but it was not so. How did a man give up that which had been bred into his people for generations, since the beginning of time? The whites could not just come in and say it all must change in a day.

Why did they not understand? Why must everything be their way? He was Indian! He had his own religion. The whites had taken the land of his people, their wealth, their buffalo, and their pride. Why did they insist on taking more, on taking everything that was precious to their hearts?

But that was not all that was bothering him. That was bearable. His thoughts of Katie Russell were not. Katie. Hemene. He swirled again. He wanted to suffer. It was right that he suffer. He wanted another man's woman. He loved another man's woman. That would be bad enough if she were an Indian woman already taken; but Katie was

127

white. To love her was not only a betrayal of her ownership, it was a betrayal of his own people, his own beliefs. Never in his wildest dreams had he expected to have such feelings for a white woman. It was as though that first time he'd set eyes on Katie Russell he'd been struck by the Gods, destined to love hopelessly.

Around him in the sacred lodge sat many young maidens who would marry him in a moment, if he but spoke to their fathers. They were beautiful. They were Indian. They would make good and devoted wives, give him full-blooded sons. He should be thinking of them, looking at them. But there was something unsettled in his soul, a restlessness, a need. He knew what that need was, but facing it was difficult. He wanted nothing more right now than to be one with Katie Russell, to touch her, taste her, show her how good it could be to know a man, teach her all the things Ezra Russell had never taught her. To Tohave she was like a virgin, for she truly knew nothing yet of sharing bodies joyfully, with passion and desire. The fact that it was wrong to have such thoughts about her did not stop them from coming, and his heart was heavy.

He had been hanging for hours, and he moaned as he felt the flesh tearing away, then grunted as he hit the ground minutes later as the last piece of skin gave way to his weight. Everything swirled around him and then turned to blackness. He was lifted later, unconscious, and the next thing he remembered was the sweet smell of herbs as Rosebud pressed an Indian concoction against his wounds to help heal them. He groaned with pain.

"Get me . . . water," he told her, his tongue swollen.

She soaked a rag and held it to his mouth, squeezing it so that he got fresh water very slowly. "Only a little at first," she told him.

He licked at it, sighing because of the refreshing wetness.

"I am making a broth for you," Rosebud told him. "Soon you must try to eat some."

He looked around the tipi as she stirred something over the fire. Yes. This was where he belonged, here in a tipi, among his own kind.

"Elk Man's young daughter has been asking about you," Rosebud said. "She is the prettiest on the reservation, you know. She is waiting patiently to see if you will awaken and be all right. She is worried about infection, but I will make sure there is none." She wet another rag and turned to him then, pressing its coolness to his forehead. "You should think about that one, Tohave. She is good, and strong. She has had her time and can bear children, and she is young and untouched. She would please you greatly in the night."

He closed his eyes. "I am not . . . ready. And I . . . have no passion for her . . . no longing. Do not speak to me . . . of those things. I am happy right here."

"No, you are not," she said, daring to argue with him. "You picture me with hair that is red in the sun, with eyes as blue as the sky, skin like snow, and nipples like pink wildflowers. Deny it, Tohave, and I will not speak of it again."

He opened his eyes then and met hers, and to Rosebud's astonishment his had tears in them. "I have . . . been with you too long, Rosebud. You know me . . . too well."

She smiled sadly. "This is true. Do you think I did not understand why you went through the ritual again? You want to suffer because of your guilt. You want to pray, to forget." She held his eyes. "Did it work?"

He swallowed. "What do you think?"

She rubbed the cool cloth over his neck and chest, carefully avoiding the wounds at his breasts. "I think not, my handsome warrior."

He sighed deeply. "I had . . . a vision." He could not

tell it to her. It was sacred. A man seldom told others his Sun Dance visions, those wild dreams that came to him when his mind and body was tortured. But all visions were important to Indians—all had meaning. In this vision he rode through the sky, from one cloud to another, Katie Russell in front of him, her reddish hair flying in the wind to brush his face, her blue eyes happy and dancing, her smile bright. She belonged to him, and there was no one to object, no one to stop them. But in the dream he also saw his people below, crying and weeping as bluecoats stomped on them until they disappeared beneath the earth. He would not tell Rosebud that, but he would tell Stiff Leg. Stiff Leg was wise.

"She was in the dream?" Rosebud was asking.

As Tohave started to shift he grunted with pain. Perspiration broke out on his whole body. "Yes," he answered in a strained voice. "I wish . . . to see Stiff Leg. Bring him . . . and leave me."

She obeyed, as she always did. Tohave provided her with food and protection. She owed him obedience. When she had left the tipi, Tohave stared up at the smoke hole. He wondered what was happening to Katie. He had not gone back, for he was deliberately trying to forget, allowing her time to forget also. It had been many weeks. Was she still alive? How was her husband treating her? Poor Hemene. Hers was such a cruel and unhappy life. He shouldn't care, for she was white, but the notion that she should belong to him would not leave him. And now he'd had the vision. He'd wanted one, but he was not sure what it meant. Minutes later Stiff Leg appeared at the tipi entrance, then slipped inside and sat down, cross-legged, beside Tohave.

"You sent for me," he stated. "Are you ready now, Tohave, to speak of this thing that has burdened your

130

heart since the day at the fort when I saw you hit Two Moons?"

They conversed in the Sioux tongue.

"What should I do, Stiff Leg?" Tohave swallowed back the pain. "It is not . . . like the old days . . . when I could raid her farm . . . kill her husband, and carry her away, and force her to submit to Tohave. And I would not want . . . to do it that way. She has known nothing . . . but force and cruelty. I do not want her . . . to know Tohave that way."

"You speak of dangerous things, Tohave, but I understand that a heart cannot always be controlled. Rosebud said you had a vision. Tell me of it. Then perhaps I will know better what to tell you."

"Give me . . . more water first."

Stiff Leg turned and dipped the rag again, squeezing it gently into the young man's mouth. Tohave swallowed and met the man's eyes as Stiff Leg straightened and waited for him to speak.

"I rode . . . through the sky . . . on a grand horse . . . the black Appaloosa. She rode in front of me, laughing and happy. We were . . . together . . . happy. Below me . . . the people wept and cried out as soldiers stomped on them . . . until they disappeared under the earth and cried out no more." He searched Stiff Leg's eyes. "What does it mean?"

Stiff Leg sat for a long time, staring at a painting on the wall of the tipi, thinking, rubbing his chin. "I think it has many meanings," he replied. "I think it means that somehow you will be with the white woman. But be careful not to think that means you can just ride out there and take her, Tohave. That would bring you imprisonment and perhaps even death. It must not be that way. It must be some other way. I cannot tell you what it is. The Spirits will guide you." He sighed and

131

rubbed his chin again. "The vision of the people being stomped into the earth worries me. There will be another slaughter, I fear. Already you had one dream about this, and many of the old ones are restless. It is not over yet for us. There is too much unrest over this latest treaty, over more whites coming into this land. Sitting Bull feels it also, danger. The people are too unhappy. It is not good, Tohave."

"You say . . . someday I will be with her. How can this be? We are of two different worlds. She is owned . . . by a white man, and my own people would turn me away, as would hers."

Stiff Leg thought again for a moment. "I do not know about her people. It is true they would probably be unkind to her, though some would not—the good ones like the Browns who live a little way from here and offer us food and friendship. They would understand. Our own people would be the same—some accepting, some not accepting—but if she were good to them, they would not long be against you, Tohave. This is not the thing with which to be concerned. It is the difference in your way of life that should be considered. She must allow you to be Indian, respect your ways, your religion. How can you be a husband to a white woman? You cannot push the plow and plant the seed. You do not own things or have any white man's money. You have never lived in a white man's house."

"I would find a way. My love would help me find a way. I could do . . . anything . . . to be able to hold her in the night. But I will not push a plow. I would find another way to make the white man's money . . . so she could have a proper house."

"Then remember that your children would not be full bloods."

Tohave closed his eyes. "I have thought of that. I believe that was part of the meaning of my vision, Stiff

Leg. While my people were dying beneath the earth . . . I was riding away with my white woman. Do you not think that could mean it is time for a new way . . . time for sharing both ways? Is it not possible that mixing our lives will help us learn the new ways? Is it not possible . . . to live beside the whites, keep our own ways . . . yet be able to love their women? Already many of their men marry our women. Why is it so wrong for our men to marry theirs?"

Stiff Leg grunted. "The white men have strange ways of thinking. They want our women, but they want their own women, too. They look at Indian men as unworthy to touch their own, yet they say it is all right for them to touch our women, willingly or unwillingly. I do not know how it is that the white man has come to believe that he is superior to others, that his ways must be for all. We do not tell him how to live, whom to worship, whom to marry. Why must he tell us?" He shook his head. "I am through trying to understand the white man, his need to own things, to collect things. Some of our people have gone to the East where there are many whites, and they say there are many poor ones with little to eat or wear. I do not understand how a people who can make so many wonderful things, own so many things, will let some of their own kind starve. If these people refuse even to take care of their own, if they are so selfish as to hide food in closets while their own people go hungry, how will they find it in their hearts to help people they think inferior and worth less than dogs? I do not know if you are right about being able to live side by side peacefully, Tohave. I do not even know if it is right for you to love one of those people."

"But she isn't like them. I know it in my heart. She feared me at first . . . only because she did not understand and because she had been told things that are not true. If I could talk to her more . . . she would

133

understand. She has much love in her heart but no one to give it to, Stiff Leg. If you saw her, saw the sadness in her blue eyes, you would know. She is young and has never known kindness and love. Her man is cruel to her. When he takes her, it is no different than when a soldier rapes one of our maidens. He hurts her. She did not choose him. She told me so."

Stiff Leg frowned and stiffened. "When?"

Tohave swallowed. "I went to her one day . . . when her husband was gone."

Stiff Leg scowled. "That was bad, Tohave!"

"I did not touch her. We only talked. I just wanted to know her a little better . . . wanted her to know I meant her no harm. I could see that if she did not belong to another, she would let me court her. She would not be afraid of what others would say." He met Stiff Leg's eyes. "She is brave, Stiff Leg. She is strong and good. And she is beautiful . . . like a flower. But a flower that has not yet fully bloomed."

Stiff Leg sighed. "And you think you could make it bloom?"

Their eyes held. "Someday she will open her petals and take me inside as if I were a bee going after the pollen," Tohave replied. "I am as sure of it as I am sure the sun rises every morning."

Stiff Leg looked very serious. "Then there is no use telling you it is wrong. There was not even a reason for me to come here, because your heart and mind are already decided. Did you think the pain and suffering of the sacred Sun Dance would change that?"

Tohave frowned now. "I hoped it would, but it has only made me more sure."

"Then I will pray for you, Tohave. You will need prayers. It is wrong, and it is dangerous. You know this."

"*Ai*. I know it. I will be careful. I will wait for signs. Tohave will be patient, for he wants his woman when it is right. It must be her decision, but somehow, some way, she will be mine forever. It might take a winter, two winters, three. But Maheo will not desert me. The Spirits will not make me suffer forever. This I know, because of the vision."

Stiff Leg put a hand on his shoulder. "My heart is heavy for you, Tohave. You are alone. It would be easy if you chose one of the Sioux girls who looks at you with hope, but you have chosen the hard way, the long road. It is not an easy choice."

Tohave closed his eyes, listening to the wind and the singing insects. Did Katie hear the prairie sing now?

"It is much harder for her, Stiff Leg," he declared. "She is sad and lonely. She doesn't even have someone to talk to as I do. She has no one to turn to in the night while I can turn to Rosebud. And there is no song in her heart. She does not hear the birds or listen to the wind. I will teach her those things . . . someday."

Chapter Eight

The days were hot and long, and at night Ezra Russell invariably invaded her tired body. It mattered little to him that once the daily farm work was done, he could rest, while Katie still had other chores to do. "Give me some sons and you won't have to work in the fields," he'd tell her. She wondered if he wanted them as a father wants sons or as plow horses, slave labor like she was. She wasn't sure that she wanted children if the poor things were going to be raised by Ezra Russell. And what if she had a daughter? Would he treat the child as she had been treated, as if she were worthless because she was a girl? Katie hadn't the courage to run away from the man, but she vowed that if he ever mistreated their children, she would find a way to get them away from him. And she continued to pray that somehow, someday, he would change.

Rain would not come, and as the drought grew worse, so did Ezra Russell's mood. The corn that had sprouted was withering, and only water would save the crops. There was only one way to get it to the plants—carry it by hand. It was nearly August. How many days or weeks they had gone without rain, Katie was not certain. She had no choice but to join in the effort to save what remained of their crops. It would not have been so bad if the temperature had remained normal. But it soared two days into their hand-watering project.

Katie felt as though she were in a kind of trance. She was so miserable that she was almost numb. Every day was the same: rise with weary bones, dress, get the bucket, and start watering. Walk to the creek, which was itself getting dangerously low, fill the bucket, carry the water to the fields, and pour it on the crops. Back to the creek, fill the bucket, carry it to the fields, and water the crops. The mornings were not quite so bad, but when the sun rose in the sky it became unbearably hot.

Trenches could not be dug from the creek for irrigation, for if they tried that, the bone-dry earth would quickly lap up whatever water was left before it ever reached the crops. The water must be left in the creek bottom, where the ground was still damp, muddy in some places. There it would last a little longer. Irrigating by hand must continue if anything was to be saved.

Katie knew that if she were doing this for a grateful, loving man, she would not mind the work half so much. But Ezra ordered her about and cursed at her. "Hurry it up . . . don't put too much on one plant . . . you'll take a rest when I tell you to." Her arms ached fiercely, and she wondered how she still worked. The animals moved slowly, hanging their heads from the heat. Even they could hardly bear it, and they had no work to do. Katie had suggested that they rig up something so the mules could carry water, but they were needed for "other things" and must be "spared," according to Ezra. He would "spare" the animals from the heat, but he gave no such consideration to his young wife. The animals were more important to him.

The work continued until Katie wondered if she was still human. Up in the morning. Feed the animals. Get the bucket. Water the crops for the rest of the day. Tend to the animals again. Wash a few clothes. Cook a meal. Mend, Bake. Had she slept the night before? She could not remember. Surely she had. Ezra took the wagon to Fort Robinson in the midst of all the work to trade two mules for some chickens and feed. The chickens would provide meat and eggs. But they, too, had to be fed— another chore assigned to Katie. The feed would be stored for the winter for the animals. But the livestock would need more than that. Their only hope was that the crop would survive and provide money for feed. The buffalo grass of the plains was dry. A rain would green it up again; then the animals could be hobbled farther out on the prairie to feed and they would have plenty to eat until the snows became too deep to find the grass.

Yes. This was a hard land. How had the Indians survived? Katie pondered that as she worked. She had to think about other things besides the heat and the work. As she did so, she began to understand why the Indians hated the reservation, hated being kept in one place. They had survived by moving around. Surely weather like this would find them in the mountains, where it was cooler. They had followed the buffalo and the seasons, like migrating birds and animals. It was their nature to migrate. To keep them in one place was like caging a wild animal. Didn't caged animals often die? The Indians were dying, Tohave had told her so. It made her heart sad. Tohave. Where was he? He had never returned. She knew that was best, but she missed him and the thought of never seeing him again brought a sick ache to her heart. Was this love? What else could make her miss him so? What else could evoke such pleasant urges at the thought of his handsomely chiseled face, his warm, bright smile, his wild, powerful body?

But that love would have to remain a dream, and that was really all it had been from the beginning, wasn't it? She must learn to accept her fate and deal with it as best she could. Other women did, and so would she. But she envied the woman lucky enough to choose her husband, the one who loved her man and enjoyed pleasing him because she had a man who was grateful and pleasant and loving. Dora Brown had no idea how lucky she was. She often wondered about Dora. Had she had her baby yet? How nice it would be to talk to her again, to be able to visit with anyone once in a while. She longed to talk with Tohave, to find out more about his people, his ways. But she had sent him away and told him not to come back. In her heart she secretly hoped that he would, but she had no idea what she would do or say if he did. She only knew she missed the sweet knowledge that he was out there, watching over her. He'd said if she needed him badly, he would be there. But was that a joke? Was he still playing games, teasing the foolish white woman and laughing about it with his friends?

She could not believe that. There was too much sincerity in his warm, brown eyes. Tohave might tease, but he was not a liar. Still, it was probably stupid of her to think about him at all now. It had been many weeks since he had left. Perhaps he had married some pretty Indian girl and was riding with his woman on some cool mountainside. Why did such a thought bring such pain to her heart? She knew, but she could not admit it to herself. She must forget him.

Although it seemed impossible, the heat grew worse. The stream they had been using to water the crops was down to a trickle, but Ezra insisted they salvage what they could. Katie was worried. Her husband had not stored much water in the spring, as Jacob Brown had advised him to do. He had taken it for granted the stream would provide all they needed. But this was not Illinois, where, in some places, water lay just beneath the earth,

140

where there were lakes and streams and where rain fell frequently. This was Nebraska—the highest, dryest section of Nebraska. Here the wind blew constantly, drying up what water there was. Would they die on this vast prairie? First the crops, then the animals, then Katie and Ezra Russell?

Carry the buckets. Carry the buckets. The heat was overwhelming, and against her better judgment, Katie ripped the sleeves from her dress and opened the neck, tucking the bodice around the straps of her undergarment and pushing some of it inside around her breasts. She then took off her hat, for the straps tied under her chin were more than she could bear in the heat. Finally, she cut away the lower part of her dress, around her ankles, so more air could get to her legs. She felt crazed by the heat and the work.

Ezra had picked one of the hottest days to ride upstream and see if there was more water elsewhere. As he'd loaded barrels into the wagon he'd ordered her to water the crops as best she could. She'd watched him rattle away, wanting to go with him, for if he found good water, she wanted to jump into it. She looked at the crops. What good would it do to water them? They were beyond salvaging. She turned to stare at the pile of lumber still waiting to be made into a house. There would be no real house, she was sure. This was what her life would be. She picked up a bucket and headed for the pitifully diminished stream.

No house. No happiness. No love. Nothing to look forward to. As she filled the bucket with the slowly trickling water, she pictured a fine home with polished wood floors and cool halls, nice furniture and curtained windows—a house with light, a house full of laughter and love, with a large kitchen where she would bake for a loving husband and their children. Did some women really live that way?

She carried the bucket to the fields, and in a moment the water was on the ground, disappearing so quickly that it seemed she hadn't brought water at all. She stared at the dry earth and laughed, harder and harder, feeling like a madwoman. She walked back to the stream and refilled the bucket, back to the fields to watch the water disappear and to laugh. And so the morning went. She had ripped away her clothing late in the afternoon the day before, and her skin had quickly reddened. But the sun had gone down before it could do its worst damage. Now she was spending the better part of the day in that sun, oblivious to the danger its rays presented to her fair skin. Back and forth she walked, her silly, mad laughter beginning to change to tears. She struggled against them, afraid that if she started crying she would never stop.

The heat! How much longer could she bear it? Back to the stream. Back to the fields. Feel the sun. Try to see through tears. Carry the bucket. Water the crops. Stop and feed the animals. She should eat, but when was there time, and where did one get an appetite in such weather? Morning wore on into noon, and noon into early afternoon. As Katie bent over to empty another bucket, her mind swirled, everything swirled. She wanted to rest. Yes. She must rest. She lay down, right in the middle of a cornfield, her mind confused because of the heat. She would lie here and sleep. Yes. That would be good. Take a little nap. Was that the sun, so hot on her skin? No matter. She would lie here just a little while.

How long was it before she sensed someone lifting her? Why was her mouth so dry and swollen?

"Hemene." Someone was speaking softly close to her ear. She smelled leather and sage and wild things. Then, suddenly, it was dark and cool, and she was lying on something soft. Surely she was in her earthen home, lying on her own bed. Something cool touched her skin

142

and she stirred.

"Lie still, Hemene." It was a man's gentle voice. This certainly was not Ezra. Something cool dripped over her burning eyelids, then touched her cheeks. She blinked, then saw a blurred dark face bending over her. "Why did you let the sun shine down on your fair skin?" he asked. "One such as you is not made for that much sun. The sun does not harm Tohave. Tohave was born to it." Something cool touched her neck then, her chest. "Tohave should have come sooner."

She breathed deeply. Tohave! He had come back! Her heart beat with joy, but her skin burned like fire. "Water," she whispered.

He held her head gently and put a canteen to her lips, letting her drink only a little. Then he dribbled some over her forehead and into her hair to cool her.

"Tohave has a special salve, made by the Indian for too much sun. Tohave will put some on you, and your skin will not burn so much," he told her.

She could not answer right away. She just lay there, while he removed her shoes. "Tohave should undress you so you can truly rest well," she heard him say. "But if Tohave did that and your husband came, Tohave would have a hole in his back like a canyon, before he could even explain. Still, I could not let you lie out there to burn up and die, not my fair, sweet Hemene. Let your husband think what he will. Tohave will not let you die."

He smeared something on her forehead, and instantly the burning pain diminished there. Gentle fingers then rubbed the salve over her cheeks, her lips, her chin, her neck. She opened her eyes and watched him as he rubbed the ointment over her chest, gently massaging the salve into the skin on that part of her breasts that had been revealed to the sun, and she felt a fire deep in her blood hotter than the fire in her burned skin. He met her eyes, feeling the same fire, but he said nothing, as he moved his fingers back over her chest, over her shoulders.

"It's been . . . so long, Tohave," she said in a near whisper.

He dipped his fingers into the pouch of salve again and began to apply it to her arms. "You told Tohave not to return."

"We don't always . . . say what we really feel."

"That is one bad habit of the white man. The Indian always speaks the truth."

She watched him lovingly, able to study him closely for the first time. How remarkably handsome he was, hard and strong and perfectly formed. How could such a big man touch her so gently, and how could a wild man who had killed be so soft-spoken and concerned? She studied his clean, long, dark hair; his large, dark eyes. Everything about him was dark and mysterious and beautiful. Tenderly, he smeared the salve on her other arm, and it was then she noticed the fresh scars on his chest and upper arms.

"Tohave!" she muttered through swollen lips. "You've been . . . in some kind of . . . terrible fight!"

He saw the direction of her eyes and looked down at his scars, smiling sadly. "No fight. I took part in an Indian ritual, a test of manhood, a time for visions and prayer."

She frowned, struck again by their differences, by the wild, uncivilized side of him. "Why?" she asked. "Why would you submit yourself to torture?"

He met her eyes, and their gazes held a long time. "I was trying to forget something . . . someone." He returned to applying the salve. "But it did not work."

She watched him, her eyes filling with tears. He meant her, and she knew it. All her attempts to forget him, all her vows never to think of the Indian called Tohave had been in vain. A tear slipped down the side of her face and

144

he quickly wiped it away.

"Do not cry, Hemene. We must not speak of it. There is nothing to say. Not now. You are badly burned. Why did you lie down in the sun?"

"I don't know. I was . . . so tired. I didn't even feel it burning me." She licked her lips. "I must . . . look terrible."

He grinned a little. "You can never look terrible. Here, sit up. I will put some salve on your back. You did not expose much there. It is not so bad." He helped her rise, and she breathed in his comforting scent as she rested her head on his shoulder while he rubbed on the salve. How nice it must be to be held by such a man. How comforting it was just to have him near. He had come when she needed him most, just as he'd said he would.

He helped her lie down and then wiped his hands. "I will get you more water," he said, and reaching for his canteen, he held it to her lips. "Drink just a little."

She drank the cool liquid and then closed her eyes. "Have you ever . . . seen the Rocky Mountains, Tohave? Are they cool . . . on days like this?"

He set the canteen aside, wetting a rag first, folding it, and laying it on her forehead. "*Ai*. Tohave has seen the great mountains. And it is true they are cool when the valleys and plains are like an oven." If you were mine, I would take you there, he wanted to tell her.

"And the place . . . called Yellowstone. Have you been there?"

"In the days when the Indian was free to roam, we went there often. Once we rode there and beyond, hunting buffalo, going to the cool mountains to get away from the heat."

"Is it true that the waters there bubble and are warm, that one can bathe in them in the dead of winter?"

"It is true."

She opened her eyes and met his own. "It's strange,

145

Tohave. I'm supposed to be . . . more educated and civilized than you. Yet you know so much about life . . . about survival. You've been to wonderful places. We whites . . . are so easily defeated. But the Indian seems . . . so strong."

"In some ways," he answered. "In other ways we are weak, Hemene. Being penned into one place makes us weak. Our strength comes from the land, from freedom to worship in our own way, to roam and hunt and live where it is best, according to the seasons. The white man tries to take all this from us." He rubbed a little more salve onto her cheeks. "And in other ways we are weak. Sometimes our hearts tell us to do one thing, and our good sense tells us to do another." Their eyes held again. "When our heart wins, we do foolish things. It is that way for all people, white and Indian."

"I suppose," she whispered.

He took his hand away. "Where is your husband?"

"He rode up the creek to find water, to fill the barrels. Even the animals . . . don't have enough water now." She closed her eyes and sighed. "Oh, I still haven't fed them! The chickens! And they need water, too. I have to get up . . . take the cows and horses to the stream—"

"No, Hemene. Do not move. Tohave will do it."

"No. I have to. Ezra will be angry."

"Let him be! I am not afraid of your man or of what he thinks. It is he who should have been here to help you. He should not have had you out there working."

"But if the crops fail—"

"You white people make life so hard when it is so simple. The land holds everything you need. Why do you toil away at work that brings you white man's money so you can buy more 'things,' gather up a whole big houseful of them, useless things that sit around on tables and shelves? If a man has a good woman, sons, a few good horses, he has everything."

She breathed deeply against the burning pain. "You see the kind of house I have, Tohave. A dirt house. I would like a nice house . . . but I could not be happy in the most beautiful home if I could not live in it with the man I loved. I would be happy with the simple things you speak of . . . if I had a good husband. I understand that possessions don't bring happiness. If I could love and be loved, I could—" She blinked back tears. "I understand you better than you think, Tohave. I only work this hard because I must, so my husband won't be angry."

His eyes held hers a moment; then he turned away. "I will feed your animals."

Alone, she fell into a light, fitful sleep, awakening later to a gentle hand on her hair. "I am back, Hemene. How are you feeling?"

"Tired . . . so tired," she whispered. "And I'm on fire."

"The salve I put on you will help greatly. I will leave some."

"But how will I explain—"

"Do not worry. I will talk to your man myself. He will listen, or he will wish he had."

She met his eyes. "Don't kill him, Tohave."

"It is something I have thought about doing many times."

She frowned. "No. He is my husband, and according to my religion, that would be a bad thing. It would be hard for me to live with that. And then the soldiers would come for you. I don't want anything bad to happen to you."

He smiled sadly. "I will not kill him."

Their eyes held. "Why, Tohave? Why did you come back? You confuse me. I had almost forgotten about you."

He frowned. "Truly?"

She swallowed back tears. "No," she whispered. "No.

147

I just . . . wanted to forget. It would all be so much easier."

"It was the same for me. I suffered deliberately. I wanted to feel pain, to fast and pray, to forget. But it did not work for me, and I could not stay away any longer, for I wondered what was happening to my Hemene, if she was well."

"Don't call me that, Tohave. Don't call me yours. It isn't true. It can never be true. It's wrong."

"Why? Because you belong to another, or because Tohave is an Indian?"

She held his dark eyes. "I . . . don't know. A little of both, I guess."

His eyes hardened a little. "And is Tohave not just a man, like any other? Do you not see that?"

She sniffed. "You know I do," she whispered. "I'm not thinking of my own feelings. I only mean . . . others . . . how they are . . . the way they think."

"Worrying over what others think is senseless. They will think what they will no matter what you do. But you still do not look at Tohave without seeing an Indian. You must look beyond that, Hemene. One day you will, but now it is true that you belong to another. Tohave prays every day that there will come an answer, and until it comes, Tohave will only watch . . . and wait. You will be comforted just knowing someone watches."

"Tohave, it can't be. We can't—" Her eyes widened then at the sound of the rattling wagon. "He's here!" she gasped. "Ezra is here!"

Tohave rose and went to the entrance as the wagon rattled closer, then stopped. For a moment there was only silence.

"What the hell are you doing here!" she heard Ezra growl. "Where is my Katie! What have you done to her!"

Both men were now outside, but Katie could hear their words. "I have helped her. Your woman fainted in the fields. She lay in the hot sun, burning to death."

"You're lying! If she's been touched by your stinking red hands, I'll skin you alive!"

The next moment, Ezra was inside the dugout, standing next to Katie and looking down at her red skin and swollen face, shiny now with Tohave's salve. "What the hell happened? What's that Indian doing here!" he roared.

Katie's heart pounded. "He helped me. Can't you see, Ezra? For God's sake, look at me!" she answered in as strong a voice as she could muster. "I passed out in the fields. If he hadn't come by, I might be dead."

He clenched his fists. "A fine thing! Now you won't be able to do any work!"

"What's the use!" she choked out. "We can't save the crops now. We should just try to keep the animals alive."

Tohave came inside then. "I put a special salve on her, to take away the pain," he told Ezra. "It is an Indian salve, made from herbs that soothe burns. I will leave it for her."

Ezra's face darkened. "You put it on her?"

It was Tohave's turn to become angry. "Would you prefer that I left her in the field, so you could come home to a burned, dead woman?" He spat the words through clenched teeth, finding it difficult to keep from hitting Ezra. "What kind of a man are you?" he growled. "She is not a plow horse! She is a woman, still young and learning, and she is not made for this land! How can you be angry with someone who has saved your woman's life!"

Enraged, Ezra breathed heavily. "I'll let this go, redskin, only because she was in need of help. But that's the last time you'll put your dirty hands on her."

"Ezra!" Katie sobbed, humiliated.

"You shut up! I'll settle with you later!" He turned back to Tohave. "The fact remains you were out there,

149

skulking around like the sneaking redskin you are!" he continued. "I leave my woman for one day, and you come! How can I ever leave her alone now?"

Tohave boldly stepped closer and looked down at Ezra Russell with hot eyes. "If I meant her harm, I could have hurt her many times, you white fool!" he hissed. "And I have had more than one chance to put my knife to you and show your guts to the sun! But I did not do it! Since this is the way you show your gratitude, I tell you this, white eyes, hurt her, and Tohave will kill you—slowly!"

Their eyes held, and Ezra backed up a little, studying the big Indian. "What do you want for helping her? Whiskey? Tobacco?"

Tohave laughed sneeringly. "What a fool you are! Cannot a man help another without expecting something for it? That is the way you whites think. Is nothing done out of the goodness of the heart?" He picked up his canteen. "I want nothing from you, *heyoka!* Just your promise that you will let her keep the salve and use it as she needs it. And do not let her back out in the sun for six or seven suns, unless you want to bury her!"

Ezra looked him over. This was not the time to anger the big Indian further. He didn't want the other whites and the soldiers on his back for doing something that might lead to trouble.

"Get out!" he ordered, trying to seem brave, but inside he feared that Tohave would take his knife from its sheath and sink it into his belly. "She can keep the damned salve!"

Tohave nodded. "Such a generous man you are." He sneered. He glanced at Katie as though to tell her not to be afraid, then turned and left. Ezra stood looking at the doorway until he heard the sound of a horse riding off.

When the sound drifted away, he glared at Katie and then walked over to the bed. "You can stay inside till you're better."

"Thank you, Ezra," she replied weakly.

Then, without warning, his hand struck the side of her face, the slap bringing almost unbearable pain to her already badly burned skin. She cried out the moment he hit her.

"That's for letting that dirty redskin touch you!" he growled. "No white woman lets an Indian man touch her, no matter if she's dying!" He walked out then.

His words sounded distant to her ringing ears as she shook from pain and the shock of her sunburn. She rolled onto her side, grabbed a pan, and vomited into it. Tohave was gone. Ezra was back.

The next few days were agonizing for Katie. To her relief, Ezra did not bother her in the night, and finally in the second week of August they heard thunder in the distance. Even Ezra got excited.

"You hear that?" he called out. "Get out here, Katie. Look at the clouds in the west! I think it's really coming this time."

She walked slowly outside, wincing at the bright sun that had not met her eyes since Tohave had rescued her. She looked out at ominous black clouds. They seemed to be moving toward them at an amazing speed. Perhaps that was because there were no trees to break the oncoming thunderheads, perhaps it was because the prairie was so broad and endless; but Katie did not like the looks of them, even though they meant rain.

The air turned suddenly cold, and the grazing animals began to whinny and bray uneasily.

"I think we should put the animals in the shelter!" she told Ezra. "That looks like a bad storm coming."

They had both been warned about prairie storms. Was this one of the big ones people had told them about, the kind of storm that left behind destruction and flash

151

floods? Ezra headed for the animals. "Come and help!" he shouted.

Katie hurried over.

"Something tells me there's no time to lose," he told her.

They loosened the cow and the bull, and Katie led both of them toward the shelter while Ezra brought the mules, cursing at the animals because they didn't move faster. Katie tied the creatures in their earthen stall while Ezra went back for the two horses. The chickens would have to fend for themselves. After tying the horses, they ran for their earthen home just as the wind whipped up.

"Ezra, what is it?"

"Might be a tornado," he told her, shoving her inside.

Her heart pounded furiously. She hated storms, and one of this magnitude terrified her. Within moments they heard a blood-chilling roar. It sounded like a hundred locomotives coming toward them at full speed. The very earth seemed to shake, and although the storm lasted only minutes, it seemed they crouched in their sod hut for hours. Sleet and hail, several inches deep, now covered the ground. They could see it piling up because Ezra had not built a doorway yet. Then came the rain, a sheet of water that quickly turned the prairie into a lake, flooding the dugout.

"Oh, no!" Katie whimpered.

They stood upon chairs as water filled the room, and when the rain finally ceased, an odd silence fell over the land as the sun broke through. Never had Katie experienced such a sudden, severe storm that moved on so quickly.

The two of them stepped down into the water, Katie lifting her dress as they walked outside. The once-parched crops were now completely submerged.

"From not enough water to too much," Ezra muttered. "Now they'll rot." He ran a hand through his hair. "We might have to go back to Illinois."

Her chest tightened. How long had she prayed for that? Now, suddenly, she didn't want to go. "Go back?"

"Depends on what we can salvage from this, how fast the water goes down. We might be able to stick out the winter and try once more next year. We'll see."

He walked toward the wagon, from which the canvas top had been torn by the wind. It lay far out in the field. A few chickens staggered about in the water, clucking, and a few lay drowned; they had been too soaked to climb or fly to safety. Some had been killed by wind and hail. Katie began to pick up the ones that were still alive, and she carried them to higher ground that was not waterlogged. She looked at the sod house. It would be a mess now, the floor just mud. Yes. Illinois did sound good. She hated this land. But as she scanned the horizon she knew deep inside that something was making her love it, knew how hard it would be to leave. What about Tohave? Had he been out in the storm? What did Indians do when such storms came?

She turned and watched Ezra checking over the wagon. When she called out his name, he turned.

"What do you want?"

"I . . . I think I'm pregnant." Why she had chosen this moment to tell him, she wasn't sure. He was her husband. She felt sorry for him because of the crops and the chickens. Maybe telling him she suspected she was pregnant would brighten his day. She should not be thinking about Tohave now.

"Well, it's about time!" he shouted back. He almost barked the words, and her heart fell. She'd thought he would be happy, excited. What could she do to please this man? She picked up another chicken and petted it, tears filling her eyes.

153

Chapter Nine

They lost about half the chickens, but salvaged the wagon top. About half the corn and potatoes were rotted. There would be enough to get them through the winter, for they had planted other vegetables for their own use, but some of those were also gone. It would be a lean time since they had barely enough left to break even after selling their crop to the supplier at Fort Robinson. Ezra had planned to buy a second wagon. She would drive it, and they'd have two wagons loaded with food for the Dakota miners. But now there would not be enough to fill two wagons, let alone money to buy a second one.

The prospect of a poor harvest only made Ezra's temper worse. Katie's pregnancy was something he took for granted—another "woman's duty" that she had "put off" for too long—and he promptly informed her that she was not going to use pregnancy as an excuse to get out of work. Her chores would not change. "We'll see what kind of woman you are, Katie Russell," he told her. "A real woman can bring in crops and do her chores and have a baby, all in the same day."

Katie wondered at his reasoning. If he wanted a child so badly, it seemed he would do everything to ensure that her first pregnancy went well. She was terrified by the thought of delivering a baby in this land, with no one but Ezra to help—a man without compassion. And if the baby came on a day when Ezra was gone, she would be completely alone. She knew little about having babies, except that she'd seen her cat and a couple of cows deliver back in Illinois. When women she knew had had babies, the infants were born behind closed doors, with much screaming and carrying on. Was it that painful?

It did no good to dwell on it. There was work to be done. The land had dried and was reasonably hard now, but the dugout smelled of wet dirt, and it nauseated Katie. Rain had run down the stovepipe the day of the storm, dripped right through their earthen roof, and the floor would not dry. The dugout was too enclosed. There was no sun, circulating air, to help dry up the mud. It upset Katie to live in such a mess so she dug a little trench through the middle of the floor and out the doorway, hoping it would help drain the floor. But when that didn't work, they resorted to knocking down the sod walls at the front of the dugout to allow more air to get in.

That meant more work for Katie. She would be expected to rebuild the sod walls; Ezra had other things to do. It mattered little to him that his wife was not completely over her deadly sunburn; or that she was having fits of nausea and vomiting from the combined effects of the sunburn and her pregnancy. But those things and the extra work the storm had caused at least kept the man silent and away from her in the night most of the time, which was just fine with Katie. She was down to her last hope, that once she had the baby, her husband would change. It was all she had left.

She wondered occasionally why she had not told Tohave she might be pregnant. Perhaps she'd been too embarrassed. There was only one way for a woman to get pregnant, and in telling Tohave she would be admitting she had lain beneath Ezra Russell, which shamed her in spite of the fact that he was her husband. Ezra had made it all so ugly for her that she felt she was doing something wrong, even though it was legal. Not once had their coming together been enjoyable, nor had it ever been without pain deliberately inflicted by him. How a beautiful, innocent baby could come of such a union seemed incredible. But the thought of one made the union a little more bearable. After all, Ezra was her husband and the father of the life in her womb. But to tell Tohave about the baby would embarrass her.

Tohave. This only made friendship with him even more impossible. Not only was she white and a married woman, she now carried a child, Ezra's child. All doors to happiness were closing. There had been fleeting moments when she'd thought it just might be possible to be free, to love a man, to choose a man. Why she had ever entertained such hopes, she couldn't be sure. They were foolish and useless; the baby had settled that. The hair ornament and the sweet memories of their brief moments together would have to be secrets she treasured forever, and one day told her grandchildren about.

The fourth day after the storm the soldiers came. The front walls of the dugout were mostly knocked out, and Katie was digging a second trench. The floor was finally beginning to drain and harden again, and Ezra had stuffed a mud and grass mixture around the chimney to seal it tighter against another storm. But their sod house would never be truly waterproof, and Katie longed for the day when they would have a real, wooden house.

She looked up from her digging to see a small company of soldiers led by the young lieutenant who had first greeted them at Fort Robinson, and she was suddenly self-conscious about her appearance. There had been nothing but work since the storm, and mud. She had not

157

even had a chance to really clean herself up. Her hair was pulled back into an untidy bun, and her hands and the hem of her dress had mud of them from her morning's work. Her sunburn had left her skin a mixture of pink and brown, for she was peeling badly. She wore the dress with the ripped-out sleeves and folded-down neck, and Ezra quickly ordered her to button the neck.

"It's bad enough that your arms show," he grumbled, setting aside a hoe and going out to greet the soldiers.

"Mr. Russell, I believe it is," the lieutenant called out. "I'm Lieutenant Rogers. I met you several weeks ago at the fort, when you first arrived in Nebraska."

"I remember," Ezra answered with a frown. Katie stepped bashfully out of the dugout, pushing a piece of hair behind her ear. The lieutenant glanced at her, pity quickly filling his eyes. Her lovely, fair skin had been badly burned, and she looked tired and beaten. This poor young girl would age quickly out in this land, especially with a husband like Ezra Russell. He looked back at Ezra.

"We're out on patrol checking on the settlers, Mr. Russell. That was a pretty bad storm we had. There was a lot of flooding. We're just out checking to see if anyone needs any help."

"We're fine," Ezra answered, folding his arms and assuming a proud look. "I do things myself. Don't need any help. We lost a few chickens and part of our crop. That's about it."

The lieutenant again glanced at Katie. "What happened to your wife, Mr. Russell? She seems to need medical attention."

Katie looked down, embarrassed by her peeling skin.

"She took a bad sunburn, but she'll be all right now," Ezra answered. "And it's a good thing you came along. I've got another complaint about that Indian, Tohave. That bastard came here one day while I was gone, like to scared the death out of my woman."

158

Katie glanced at Ezra in surprise, which quickly turned to anger. If it were not for Tohave, she might be dead.

The lieutenant looked at Katie again. "That true, ma'am? Did Tohave give you trouble, harm you?"

Katie frowned, angry now. "No. I don't know why my husband told you that. I was passed out in the sun. Tohave came and carried me inside and put a special Indian salve on me." She looked angrily at Ezra. "He probably saved my life. He did nothing wrong and meant me no harm."

Ezra's look told her she had said too much, but she didn't care. It wasn't fair of him to give the soldiers a distorted picture.

"You shut your mouth, woman!" he growled. He looked up at the lieutenant. "It's true he helped her. My point is, what was he doing out here in the first place? How did he know she was here alone and needed help? He's been skulking around, and I don't trust him not to harm her one of these times."

The lieutenant glanced at Katie, suspecting that Tohave might appeal to her because of her cruel husband, even though Tohave was an Indian. He sensed trouble, and it worried him. "Are you afraid of him, Mrs. Russell?"

Katie swallowed, realizing Ezra's angry eyes were on her. "No," she answered.

The lieutenant removed his hat and wiped sweat from his brow. "Well, fact is, we've been looking for Tohave. That bunch he rides with is back at Pine Ridge for the moment, but Tohave isn't with them. Of course, they aren't about to tell soldiers where he might be."

"He in some kind of trouble?" Ezra asked.

"No. No trouble. It's just unusual for him to ride alone. He's usually with his wild friends. They say he's been acting differently lately, even went through the Sun Dance ritual for the second time. A man doesn't usually suffer that more than once, and he's lucky to live through it then. We've tried to outlaw the ritual, but it's probably the Indians' most important religious ceremony. They go off and hold it secretly."

"Well, when you find him, you tell him to quit hanging around my farm," Ezra told the lieutenant. "You tell him that if I see him around here again I'll shoot him."

"Ezra!" Katie was furious. "He saved my life!"

"And what did he have in mind for you if you hadn't been passed out from the sun?" her husband shot back. "You know damned well the real reason he was spying."

"He wasn't spying. The Browns said he visits them often. They talk with him. They're his friends. Dora Brown has been alone many times when the Indians came."

"Dora Brown isn't nineteen years old and beautiful and looking at young men for reasons she shouldn't be! Especially not at Indian men!"

Katie's face turned crimson. She was so angry she was about to cry. She whirled and walked into the dugout, while the soldiers looked away uncomfortably. Lieutenant Rogers would have liked nothing better at that moment than to hit Ezra Russell, but he was a soldier. Soldiers did not go around hitting settlers.

"I'd be careful who you shoot, Mr. Russell," he warned. "The peace around here is very tentative, and Tohave has never hurt any settlers. It's true he strays from the reservation too often and he likes to play games with new settlers, but we only get onto him because we don't want his games and tricks to lead to something serious. How long ago was it he was here?"

Ezra scratched his chin. "Ten days or so, I guess. I've been watching out for him, but he never came back. When a man has a young, pretty wife, he has to be careful of those things, you know."

Katie felt like shooting him as she sat listening inside

the dugout. Why did he have to talk like that? He'd made her look like a loose woman, yet here she sat, his own baby in her belly, and most of the time she worked like a slave for him, doing everything she could to be a good wife. She hated him more than ever. What must the soldiers think of her after the way Ezra had described Tohave's visit. She bent over on the bed and wept quietly, then quickly stifled her tears in order to hear all that the soldiers had to say.

"If you see him, Mr. Russell, please don't get trigger happy. Kind words and hospitality can go a long way. And we'd appreciate your telling him we're looking for him at the fort. There's a man there who'll only be around a few more days, and he wants to see more of Tohave's carvings."

"Carvings?"

Katie sat up to listen.

"Yes. Tohave is quite good at carving things from wood—animals and such. He does beautiful work, when you can corner him long enough to make him sit down and do it. He leaves his carvings at the fort, and travelers buy them. This man is an art dealer. He'd like more of Tohave's carvings, wants to deal with him. He says they'd sell well back East—original Indian work, that kind of thing."

Katie wiped at her eyes and blew her nose. Carvings! She didn't know Tohave could carve, and she didn't doubt that what he did was beautiful. There was a gentle, beautiful spirit about him that surely came out in his work, and she longed to see something he'd done. Could hands such as his carve anything but beauty? Yet those hands had also killed men. What a mysterious, complicated man he was.

"Well, I'd tell that art dealer not to count on the likes of Tohave," Ezra grumbled. "Indians aren't reliable."

"I'd say that's for the dealer to decide. At any rate,

161

we'll keep looking and asking. You'd best store up good. The cold months can get pretty bad out here. You folks going to make it through the winter?"

"We'll make it," Ezra boasted. "It takes a lot to stop Ezra Russell."

The lieutenant glanced at the dugout. How did a pretty young girl stop such a man from using her whenever he chose? he wondered. But that was not his business. He'd seen a lot of cruelty since he'd been in this land, and there was little he could do about it. "Be sure to come to the annual autumn dance, Mr. Russell," he said. "Every year, in late September, we hold a get-together at the fort for the surrounding settlers. It goes on for days, since it takes some people that long to get there. and traders and suppliers come to buy up whatever you have to sell."

Ezra nodded. "We'll be there."

Katie was surprised he had said "we." She looked forward to it already. People again! Maybe she'd see Dora! The coming weeks would go very slowly.

"Be sure to come, any time in the last couple of weeks of September. You can store up then on supplies for the winter." He looked around again, glancing at the lumber that still lay in a pile. "You sure you don't need any help? I could spare a couple of men to help you get a house started."

Katie's heart lifted, until Ezra dashed it to the ground again. "Not now. We'll just concentrate on saving what we can of the crops this year. Maybe next year we'll build a house. My wife's carrying. By next year there will be three of us, and we'll need the house."

"Well, congratulations!" the lieutenant replied, putting his hat back on. "Don't make her work too hard now. It isn't easy carrying a baby out here in the middle of nowhere. Have her see the camp doctor when you come in September."

"She don't need a doctor. She's young and healthy."

Again the lieutenant quelled his anger. "Well, it never hurts to be sure, now, does it? A woman has to be careful with that first one."

Ezra folded his arms. "I'll tend to my business and you tend to yours, lieutenant. Yours is to find Tohave and make him high-tail it back to the reservation. Mine is here, and we don't need any help so you might as well go on and see who might."

The lieutenant eyed him darkly. "I'll do that, Mr. Russell. But you remember what I said—about not shooting Tohave. If that happens, and war breaks out, the citizens in these parts will hang you by your heels. You remember that."

He turned his mount before Ezra could reply, then waved for his men to follow. A few of them glanced at the dugout, feeling sorry for Katie Russell, but it was not their affair. Minutes later they were gone.

Ezra stormed to the dugout, jerking Katie up by the arm. "What's wrong with you, talking out of turn like that!"

She glared defiantly at him. "I only spoke the truth! Tohave saved my life. You could have spoken a good word about him just this one time! You had no right making him look bad—and certainly no right making me look bad, not after all I've done for you! I've been a good wife, Ezra. How dare you make me look bad in front of those soldiers!"

A hand slammed hard across her face. She was jerked up and hit again, over and over until she tasted blood.

"Pregnant or not, you'll not get away with that kind of talk around me, woman! Tonight I'll be showing you who your husband is. I'll take your mind off that Indian, and that young lieutenant you were making eyes at!"

"I wasn't making eyes . . . at anyone!" she screamed, swallowing blood.

"Well, now you'll be sure not to, won't you? Don't you

163

dare speak out of turn like that again and defend an Indian! And now that that baby has took good hold of your belly, don't be expecting me to stay out from between your legs at night. But since you're supposed to be so delicate, I'll let you out of your chores today. You rest up, Katie girl. Be ready for your man tonight."

As he walked out, she curled up on the bed, licking at bruised lips. She grasped at her stomach then, praying she would keep the baby, her only hope of having something to love and to love her back, her only hope of a change in Ezra Russell.

It was not a night Katie wanted to remember. For the first time in her marriage she had dared to speak out against her husband, and in front of others, defending an Indian no less. Ezra Russell was not about to let her do so without suffering for it. A woman had her place, and that was not in front of her husband, contradicting him; it was behind him, quiet and submissive.

He beat her and her muted screams carried across the dark prairie, unheard except by one man—Tohave. His self-control that night amazed him. The soldiers had been there, looking for him, no doubt. Ezra Russell would have spoken against him. To kill the man would draw blame to himself, and he would lose all chance of helping and having Katie Russell. He must wait. The Spirits had told him there would be a right time, that some day he would have Katie Russell and their love could be right and free.

He had to smile at the thought of how close he'd been when the soldiers were there talking. Tohave was not found unless he wanted to be. Now that he knew about the white man from the East who liked his carvings, perhaps he would go back to Fort Robinson, but not before he saw Katie again. She had spoken in his favor, and she was paying for it at the hands of her angry husband. But Ezra Russell had said she was with child; surely he would go easy on her. Nonetheless, the thought of him hurting Katie sent flames of rage through Tohave, and he cursed these new days when a man could not take his own justice. He'd exacted retribution for his mother's fate and he'd gotten away with that. Yet he knew that killing Ezra Russell would only seal his fate and leave poor Katie all alone.

His hand gripped his knife, and he was on the verge of going against his common sense and charging in to sink his blade into Ezra Russell's belly when Katie's screams finally quieted. He knew then what was happening, and the thought of it made him sick inside. Ezra Russell should not touch a girl like Katie that way. Only a man who truly loved her should touch her. He stood up and paced, his fists clenched. Someday. Someday it would be Tohave who made love to her, and she would know kindness and gentleness. He waited, his rage making him feel as though he would explode at any moment.

He would watch and wait, and pray. Perhaps when her husband slept she would come outside to get away from him; then he could go to her and comfort her. His hand gripped his knife again. He would rather go now, sink his knife into Ezra Russell's back while the man raped his wife, throw his body off her and carry Katie Russell away.

No sound was more welcome to Katie's ears than that of Ezra Russell snoring. She eased her way out of the bed. He would sleep hard, for he had drunk too much whiskey. She stood up and turned up a lamp but did not look at him. If she looked at him she might be tempted to pick up the rifle and shoot him.

She held up a mirror and studied her bruised face. This

165

was not the face of the Katie Russell who had first come here. It was bruised and peeling, the eyes sadder, the lips chapped. She would look normal again in a few more days, but how soon would it all start showing—the wind, the work, the hard life, the abuse? How long would it be before she looked like an old woman?

She set the mirror down and heated some water. She wanted to wash—wash away Ezra Russell's filth. She soaped up a rag minutes later and sponged herself, then pulled on clean underthings, praying every moment that her baby was still all right. Ezra had been careful not to hit her in the stomach. Mostly he'd struck her face, and he'd grabbed her arms cruelly so that they, too, were discolored. This was the worst beating he'd given her since their marriage. But then after the first one she had submitted. His anger over her words in defense of Tohave had made him impossible to reason with; and her own anger at his lies and insinuations had made her unable to submit. She didn't really care how much he hit her. She wanted to fight him. If he liked hurting her before he invaded her, then give him reason. What good had it done to be submissive and obedient, to do everything he told her, work herself almost to death, even get pregnant, something he'd been wanting since marrying? Even that had not changed him.

She felt cold now. She would be a good wife, but one with no desire to make her marriage work. She would simply accept her fate and wait for the baby. The baby. He or she would change everything. She would love it with her whole being. And if Ezra Russell was cruel to their child, she would find a way to run away, no matter what the danger. But she must wait. It was bad to go off alone and pregnant. She wouldn't know where to go. She must first try to make this work. She would wait and have the baby, and then perhaps a change would come over Ezra. In spite of all her suffering, she clung to the hope

166

that she could accept and stay with Ezra Russell. If he would show her just a little kindness, a little appreciation, a little gentleness, she knew that in time, she would try again to be kind to him, but right now, this night, there was no room in her heart for any good feelings or intentions. She felt only hate and revulsion.

She pulled on a clean dress and brushed her hair, leaving it long and loose. She could not bring herself to get back into the bed. She needed to get away from his smell, needed some fresh air, needed to look at the stars and pray. She walked outside into the quiet, dark night. The moon was half-full. She breathed deeply of the air. At this time of night even the mosquitoes were at rest. They did not bother her.

She listened to the crickets and tried to remember Tohave's lovely words about their singing, but she couldn't hold a tender thought. Her throat was tight with tears that wanted to come but which she refused to release.

As the wind picked up a little, she shivered. In the distance a coyote yipped, and her heart pounded harder when she sensed his presence.

"Tohave," she whispered. She realized then how she'd longed to see him again.

"I am here, Hemene."

She whirled. He was standing behind her. "Tohave!" she said, a little louder. She wasn't sure what possessed her, but she needed someone to hold her. She literally ran to him, hugging him about the middle and bursting into the tears she'd been trying to hold back. Strong arms came around her then. Such wonderful warmth and comfort! She could feel their power, their tenderness.

He held her tightly, swaying slightly as he rocked her in his arms, though both of them were standing. Her tears wet the skin of his chest, but that did not bother him. He patted her long, loose hair, relishing this first chance to

167

truly hold her, touch her lovingly. Feeling the thick, reddish hair beneath his fingers, he smelled her clean, soapy scent.

Katie, in turn, breathed deeply of his aromas of wild sage and leather, glorying in being held and supported and comforted. At the moment she didn't care that he was an Indian or that it was wrong. She needed a friend. Tohave had said he would be there when she needed him, and he was, just as he'd promised! She understood why he could not stop Ezra Russell. They would not speak of it, for she was sure he'd been on the verge of coming to her defense and, in doing so, risking his own life as well as the lives of many of his people, who would suffer for what he had done. That was the way it was out here. If one Indian committed a crime, they all suffered.

"Do not cry, Hemene. You have suffered enough this night. You will lose the child in your belly."

She clung to him. "How . . . did you know?" she whispered.

"Tohave heard. He was close enough to hear the soldiers and your husband—what they said."

She pulled back slightly, looking up at him in surprise. "You were here?"

He grinned a little. "You never know when I am near. Why do you think the soldiers have so much trouble finding us Indians when we do not want to be found?"

Their eyes held, and in the moonlight he could detect the bruises. He sobered. In the next moment he leaned down, rubbing his cheek gently against her own, and she did not resist. It was comforting. His long, loose hair brushed her face, and it smelled sweet and clean. "My poor, Hemene," he groaned. In the next moment his lips gently caressed her ear, her cheek, her neck, until she pulled away.

"Please don't, Tohave," she said quietly. She took a handkerchief from the pocket of her dress and blew her

168

nose and wiped at her eyes.

"I only want to hold and comfort you," he said gently.

"I know, but it's all hopeless. I'm just being foolish tonight. I am with child now, Tohave, Ezra Russell's child. My fate is sealed."

He reached out and touched her bruised cheek with the back of his hand. "Is it? Tohave does not think so. Tohave thinks some day your life will be different."

"I've given up ever thinking it can be. And someone like yourself is in no position to change it." She met his eyes then. "We might go back to Illinois, Tohave."

He studied her in the moonlight, his heart pounding wildly. "No!" he whispered. "He cannot take you back."

"There may be no choice. If the crops are this bad next summer, we'll go, at least for the winter. Ezra can work there, build up some money again if we live with my father. And it . . . it might be best all the way around. Perhaps that would put Ezra in a better mood, and I could see my friends again."

He frowned. "Do you want to go back?"

She looked down. "I don't know anymore. There was a time when I would have given anything to go back. Now . . . I'm not sure I want to leave."

"Because you are learning to love the land?"

She turned and met his eyes. "You know that's not the reason. It isn't the land I'm learning to love."

He came closer again, and she could not take her eyes from the dark shadowy man who hovered over her. "It is Tohave you love."

It was a simple statement and she could not deny it. As he bent closer, she did not resist, for she thought he would do no more than touch her cheek. Instead warm, beautiful lips gently caressed her mouth, carefully, so as not to hurt her bruised, chapped lips. As he plied her with loving little kisses, she went limp, and he pulled her close then, crushing her breasts against his powerful chest and

169

searching her mouth more forcefully. Never had she dreamed she could feel this way in a man's arms, so alive and afire, with urges she had never known.

But the horror of Ezra was still with her. When Tohave moved a hand to her hips and pressed her against himself, she felt the hardness that came to all men who wanted a woman, and sucking in her breath, she pushed him away. She was afraid. This was wrong.

"Tohave—"

"No. Do not say we cannot be," he answered, his voice husky. "I know now that one day we will be as one, and it will be right."

She shook her head and turned away. "It's all foolish, Tohave."

"You want Tohave, even though it frightens you. I will return soon, when you are alone. And you will know joy such as you have never known before, Katie Russell. You will know love and gentleness."

She whimpered and shook her head, but then his arms came around her from behind. In her agony and sorrow she could not help but rest her weary head against his muscular arm. Grasping it with her hand, she rubbed his flesh as his lips caressed her hair.

"Someday you will belong to Tohave," he told her softly. "And the music in my heart when I think of you will live in your heart also. You do not sing now. You do not smile. Someday you will do both, and you will whisper Tohave's name in the night, against Tohave's ear, softly in desire, not screaming in pain and hatred. This Tohave promises."

"You can't make a promise like that," she whimpered.

"I can, and I have."

A sob shook her, and she pulled away. "You must leave, Tohave! This is wrong! I'm grateful that you came . . . grateful for your concern, the risks you've taken to help me. But I don't want you to get into trouble.

170

Please, please, go now and don't come back."

When she turned to face him, he looked like a lost little boy. She wanted to embrace him again, to be embraced by his strong, warm arms, to taste his lips. But these were only stolen moments. Reality lay in the dugout, snoring; and in her belly.

"Go, Tohave. You'll just be killed or bring harm to your whole tribe. We must think of others, of the terrible things that could happen if we were ever seen or found out. Having fond thoughts of each other is bad enough, but we can never have more than that without destroying our own lives and those of others."

He stepped closer, putting a hand to the side of her face. "So you are never to know man in the way you should know him, never truly to enjoy your man?"

"Don't!" she whimpered, moving back. "You must go now—away from here. Go to the fort and see that man from the East. Then go back to the reservation so that the soldiers are satisfied. You're going to be blamed for any little thing that goes wrong. It's dangerous for you."

"I do not care."

She swallowed and sniffed. "Then do it for me."

Their eyes held. How handsome he was in the moonlight, how utterly provocative and beautiful! He turned and leaped up onto his mount, pulling out a lance and riding the horse up next to her. He cast down the lance, sticking it through the hem of her dress into the ground.

"It is as I told you, Katie Russell. Someday you will belong to Tohave."

She choked back a sob and reached out to touch his leg. Then he put his large hand over her small one, and squeezed it gently. "*Nemehotatse, Hemene,*" he told her in a strained voice.

She knew no Indian words, yet she knew he had said, I love you. She kissed the back of his hand. "Go now,

171

Tohave," she whispered.

"I will go. But soon Tohave will return, when your bruises are more healed. Then you will be a woman for the first time." He spoke as though he had no doubt that it would happen.

Then he turned his horse and quietly disappeared into the darkness. She stared after him, her heart pounding wildly. He came and went like the wind. It seemed as though he hadn't been there at all, but the lance was still stuck fast in her dress.

She grasped it with shaking hands and yanked it out, wondering what to do with it. Ezra must not see it, but she wanted to keep it. She ran her hands over its smooth surface, and from what she could see in the moonlight, it was beautifully painted. Feathers were tied to the spear end. She knew she would never see it in full daylight, for she must hide it quickly.

She carried it to the dugout where food was stored—Ezra seldom went there—and getting down on her knees, she began to dig with her hands until she had made a trench long enough to hold the spear. She laid it into the trench and covered it, then walked back and forth over the spot so it would not look freshly dug.

Finally she left the dugout, her heart heavy as a rock. This was how she must deal with her feelings for Tohave, bury them, like the lance. If he came back again, she would not let him touch her, for if he touched her . . .

Chapter Ten

If Ezra had any remorse about beating her, it was only slightly detectable. He seemed withdrawn and more quiet than usual, and Katie wondered if that was because she had actually fought him that horrible night. She had not made excuses, said she was tired, but had actually fought him. He had been quiet ever since. She wondered what he planned next, nonetheless she was grateful that he was not touching her at night. But she knew that when he decided to go on another binge, it would·happen all over again.

Nothing else had changed. When he spoke it was to give her an order. The days turned into weeks, and some of the corn and potatoes that had survived was ready to harvest. There was still no sign that Ezra was grateful for the meals Katie cooked, the work she did, or the fact that she was pregnant. He made no apology for the beating, no inquiry about her health. She found herself grateful for the work the harvest created. It kept them busy, and Ezra Russell was too tired to force himself on her in the night.

Any bit of warmth she might have had for him was gone now. He had beaten it out of her. Her only consolation was the memory of Tohave holding her in strong, dependable arms. In spite of his wild ways, she knew instinctively that he would never beat his woman, never force her in bed. He would be proud of her, proud that she carried his child in her belly, and he would protect her with his life. Tohave would tease her, talk for hours with her, make her laugh and sing. Tohave saw the beauty in life and in the land . . . the beauty in love. How she missed him! How she treasured the memory of his comforting arms, his sweet mouth.

But to think of him was hopeless. She never should have let him hold her that night, kiss her. But she'd been frightened and broken and hurting. She'd needed to be held, and who else had there been to turn to on that lonely night? She had no friends, no family, to help—no one who cared except Tohave, wrong as that was. How strange their meetings were—brief, beautiful moments that brought life and joy to her tired body, followed by days or weeks of dreary loneliness. How long would this go on? She could not live like this forever. She could not spend the rest of her life with Ezra Russell, unless the man changed, but with or without Tohave, how did a woman get away from a man like Ezra? A woman couldn't just leave her husband. It simply wasn't done.

Tohave? Yes, he would help her if she asked it of him, but that would only bring him much trouble, trouble for his whole tribe. A white woman running off with an Indian . . . In her heart she now looked at Tohave simply as a man, a beautiful, wonderful, gentle man. But others . . .

It was impossible. Tohave was her only refuge, but she could not go to him. She was Ezra Russell's wife. Maybe he wouldn't beat her anymore. Maybe he would change. She needed to be held, longed to be loved. If only he would bathe once in a while, shave, clean his teeth. In their months alone on the prairie he'd turned into more and more of an animal.

At night she lay thinking of Tohave, wrong as it was.

How else was she to keep her sanity? She must occupy her thoughts with something beautiful, keep reminding herself that someone out there really did care. Tohave had said that somehow they would be together, but how could that be? And what about his statement that he would return when she was healed and alone. Would she be able to turn him away? Thoughts of being his woman brought warm surges inside her. The thought that he might come made her tremble with both fear and excitement. She must, of course, send him away if he did. It was the only right thing to do.

But how wonderful it must be for a woman to love freely. It seemed she had nothing to live for now but the nights, the still, quiet nights, when, in the distance, a coyote yipped or a wolf howled. Were they just animals?

Her days were filled with hellishly hard work and with threats of another beating. Finally Ezra announced that he was going to the fort on one of the horses. He was out of whiskey. Katie's reaction was mixed. She was glad that he was going, sorry that he would come back with a new supply of whiskey.

"Can't you wait until we go to the harvest festival?" she asked him carefully. "It's only two or three weeks away."

"I might as well die as go that long without whiskey," he grumbled. "And don't be preaching to me, woman."

She put a hand to her stomach and turned away. "I hate being alone, Ezra. So many things can happen out here."

"Quit whining. I won't be gone long, one night probably. On horseback I can go a lot faster than by wagon. If I start early and ride till past dark, I can be there tomorrow night and back here the next." He burst into the throaty laugh she hated then, and came up behind her, running his hands over her breasts. "Don't worry, Katie girl, you won't be long without your man. And there's something about that whiskey that makes you even prettier to look at."

He yanked open the front of her dress, startling her and pulling off a few buttons. As he reached inside her undergarment, she closed her eyes, steeling herself against his touch, wanting to scream and run. "I'll be expecting a decent farewell tonight," he told her, "so no smart talk or arguments." He squeezed one of her breasts painfully. "Understand, woman?"

"I understand," she answered coldly. Her brief relief from his advances was over. Ezra Russell wanted his woman. She felt like an object, something being used up and banged up. Her sunburn was healed. The bruises from her last beating were gone, except for a faint one on her left cheek.

"Fix me some supper and something to take along," he told her. "And make sure you tend to the animals while I'm gone. We'll get back to harvesting whatever we can when I get back."

He sat down to their makeshift table, then noticed she was just standing and staring at him. "Well, get busy!" he yelled.

She jumped, blinking. Then, closing her dress, she turned and set a pan on the stove.

Her mind was made up before he even came. The night before she had known cold abuse and terror. She now had no hope that Ezra Russell would change. She needed to be held. She wanted Tohave to come to her. She watched the horizon for him. Tohave. He had said he would come when she was alone. Ezra had left for the fort. She would steal this moment, if Tohave came. She wanted to know—she had to know—and she was in love with him.

176

Yes, she was in love! How good it felt to admit it to herself. Being with Tohave would be as natural as breathing. And if she went to hell for that, so be it. Something permanent might never be possible, but at least she would know if it was really true that a woman could enjoy a man. She was starved and beaten and lonely. She wanted to love and be loved.

She bathed and then brushed out her long, thick hair before putting a clean sheet on the bed and going out to search for wildflowers to put in a little vase on the crate table. She realized then that she was humming. When had she ever done that? Certainly not since she'd married Ezra Russell. Her heart pounded with hot anticipation, and she worried that perhaps Tohave would not come after all.

What was she doing? What kind of fool was she? How wrong was she to hope that Tohave would come riding in and catch her alone? She didn't want to answer those questions. It didn't matter anymore. She had never forgotten that night he'd held her, his tender kiss. He'd said he would come, and she did not doubt him. Tohave kept his promises.

She fidgeted with a bow at the front of the yellow dress she had put on, and then she heard it—a horse. She hurried outside, and even in the distance she knew it was he. Tohave!

Now she was not so sure of her decision. He came closer, looking grand on the large pinto, his hard, bronze body naked, except for a bone hairpipe necklace and a brief loincloth. What was she doing! She watched him, not moving. She should get her gun, shouldn't she? She should tell him to go away. But she did not.

He rode ever closer, a part of the land, a wild thing that belonged there. Their eyes held from a long way off, and as he came alongside her, a gentle breeze blew the coup feathers braided into one side of his long, black hair.

"I saw him go," he said quietly, looking down at her with commanding dark eyes. "Tohave told you he would come when you were alone."

"He's gone to the fort," she managed to say, and he saw in her eyes that she was asking him to stay.

He swung a leg over and dismounted, standing close to her. Then he reached out and grasped part of her hair, bringing it around to the front of her shoulder and fingering it, running his hand down it so that the back of his hand just lightly touched her breast. The small touch made her take a quick, deep breath. Her legs would not move, her mouth would not speak. Then she was suddenly lifted in strong arms. She said nothing. She only wrapped her arms around his neck and rested her head on his shoulder.

He carried her into her earthen home and laid her on the bed, then knelt beside her, stroking the hair back from her face. "You have made yourself beautiful this day. You knew I would come."

Her eyes teared and she finally spoke. "I knew," she whispered.

His smile sent fire through her veins. "Tohave has watched and waited. When I saw your man go, I knew the Spirits were with Tohave." He leaned closer. "The Sioux woman Tohave sometimes lies with once shared her bed with a white trader. She learned the white man's way of touching mouths. I want to touch your mouth again, Hemene, as I did that night I held you. Did Tohave do it right?"

A tear slipped down the side of her face. "Yes," she answered. "He did it just right."

She was too lonely, too hurt, too miserable to pass up this moment of beauty and compassion, things she had not yet known. It was all wrong, yet it did not matter now. They hardly spoke. They were alone—totally alone. There was no visiting first. It was simply something that must be done before they died from the need of it.

His lips were touching hers, and never had she known anything like this kiss. It was hungrier, more determined and demanding than the gentle kiss he'd given her out of pity the night of her beating. Could a man truly have lips like these, use them this way? So warm and sweet they were! A surging urgency filled her from head to foot, her breasts suddenly aching to be touched, a throb teasing her deep in her belly. She was returning his kiss then, against her will, as hot passion suddenly swept through her, glorious and sensuous. She reached up and put her arms around Tohave, and he gently moved onto her bed, their kiss unbroken. His tongue flicked at her lips teasingly, making her whimper, until finally his lips left her mouth and gently caressed her cheek, while with one hand he began to unbutton her dress.

She stiffened and grasped his wrist. "What are you doing?"

His warm lips on her neck, he said, "You know what I am doing. And you will not fight Tohave, because you do not want to fight him. Have you ever been touched this way, Hemene, gently, slowly, by a man who truly loves you?" His big hand moved carefully over one of her breasts, still covered by the dress, and she gasped with desire. "I think not," he continued. "It is time you knew man, little one, in the right way."

He raised up, seeing the protest in her eyes, mixed with curiosity and terrible need. "You are like a virgin, in spite of what you have been through with the animal who calls you his wife," he told her, unbuttoning the rest of her bodice and pulling it away from her. She allowed him to raise her so he could remove the dress and the undergarment beneath it, and when his dark eyes fell on her full breasts she was afire. She wanted him to look. She wanted him to touch her, to show her what it was like to be a woman—a real woman. He was right; she did feel like a virgin. Even though she carried another man's life in her belly, it was as though no man had yet touched her, for never once in her marriage had she felt what she was feeling now.

She sucked in her breath when Tohave came close again, caressing her neck and shoulder with sweet lips, moving a big hand under one full breast and pushing up on it, as his lips moved down to kiss its white fullness and then gently taste of the pink nipple as he put his other hand to the back of her neck and gently laid her back down, his lips lingering on her breast, making her breathing quicken.

He breathed deeply himself, his body tense and warm, his dark eyes glazed with desire as he moved to taste her other breast.

"You are more beautiful than I thought," he told her in a husky voice. "And this is not wrong, Hemene. What you have with that man Ezra Russell—that is wrong. You did not choose such unhappiness. To love a man, to give yourself to a man in joyous passion is not wrong, not when you love him, when he is the only one truly in your heart. There is nothing wrong in lying with the man of your heart, the man the gods intended for you. Tonight you will give yourself in a way you never have, and you will find pleasure you have never known."

There was no stopping him then, nor did she consider doing so. She wanted to forget Ezra Russell, forget this land that she hated, forget work and hardship. She was in love for the first time in her life, in love with an Indian called Tohave. And that was not wrong. She would not lose this moment.

He removed her last undergarment, and she lay naked beneath him, on fire and hardly able to breathe. She gasped when his fingers probed a place where she had only known pain at Ezra's touch. What was it Tohave was doing to her? Her husband had never done that. Ezra had

180

never made her want to cry out in utter joy and pleasure, had never done this wonderful, mysterious thing with his fingers that made her want to open herself to him the way she wanted to open herself to Tohave.

As his fingers slipped into the moist depths of her lovenest, then swirled around in a teasing way that made her groan, something built inside her that made her grasp his long hair and tangle it in her fingers, pressing his lips to her breasts while his fingers worked their magic. Then his warm mouth moved down over her belly, which was no longer flat though it did not show the baby that was inside, and he kissed her groin, her thighs, while his fingers continued their teasing movements. Tohave. Tohave was touching her, looking at her nakedness and taking pleasure in it, and she could not stop him.

Something exploded inside of her then. That had never happened to her before, and she cried out Tohave's name, whimpering and arching toward him. His hand moved around to her hips, rubbing at them as he drew himself up to meet her lips again, kissing her savagely and groaning with desire. He again caressed her breasts, still kissing her while he quickly untied his loincloth, then rose to his knees for a moment, to remove it. He was naked and Katie drank in the beauty of him, her blue eyes glazed with heated desire. This was the first time she had wanted to look at a man, to touch that part of him that before now had only frightened and repulsed her. She looked down at his manliness, and she gently grasped him. He breathed deeply, his nostrils flaring with desire, and she wondered if he was trembling as much as she was. She met his dark eyes then, and a tear slipped down the side of her face.

"May the Gods forgive us," she whispered, reaching up to him.

He came down closer then, moving between her legs. "There is nothing to forgive," he told her. "Tohave

181

wants you. You want Tohave. You are with the man of your own choosing, the man of your heart."

He reached down and guided himself into her, and she cried out, arching up to him as he buried his face in her long, auburn hair, reaching under her and grasping her hips to help her come up to him, filling her tightly with his glorious manhood. To her utter amazement it was not painful, even though she knew Tohave was more man than Ezra had been. Was it because she wanted this man, desired him, or had the magic thing he had done made her want him this way? It had created the moistness that made his movements soft and smooth, and the rhythm to his lovemaking made her groan for more. She whispered his name in his ear, just as he had predicted she would do one day. All his predictions had come true, except that she could not see how they could ever be together this way forever. But she would not think about that now. She would only enjoy this ecstasy, this man whose caresses and sweet words and perfect movements brought her such tremendous joy and womanly satisfaction. She was taking and receiving pleasure. Yes, a woman could lie with a man and enjoy it. It was a surprise to her, this wonderful, new feeling. She never wanted it to end. It must last forever. Tohave! Her beautiful Tohave!

They moved in heated rhythm, groaning, whispering. His tender Indian words only added to the magic of the moment. She did not understand them, but she knew they were words of love and desire—compliments. She didn't have to know their meaning. They were beautiful, musical words.

How could a man be this beautiful? She thought of his description of the prairie music, the dancing grasses. How mysterious he was, capable of killing men, yet gentle and loving.

She cried out then when he suddenly swelled inside of

her and his life poured into her, and he groaned at the release, shuddering and saying something in the Cheyenne tongue. Then he breathed deeply, rolled a little to the side and pulled her close.

"My Hemene," he said softly. "Never have I felt so wonderful with a woman. You are Tohave's now."

She frowned, her heart tightening at the impossibility of the statement, but she didn't want to talk about it yet. She kissed his chest and curled up against him. She was a woman for the first time. She could not stop the tears.

He kissed her hair. "This time you do not weep from pain and ugliness. This time you weep from beauty, from joy, and because you know you love Tohave."

"Oh, God! Oh, God, Tohave!"

"*Hoshuh, Hemene.* Do not cry. Somehow we will make it all right."

She huddled against him. "I love you so, Tohave. I do. I love you so. You're the most beautiful man I've ever known."

He smiled softly and wiped at her tears. "And you are the most beautiful woman Tohave has ever touched. *Nemehotatse, Hemene.* Tohave loves you more than his own life."

He began to caress her gently, running his hand over her, wanting to touch every part of her, from her lustrous hair to the tips of her toes.

"We will make love again, little one. That was just the beginning. Tohave will not be able to get enough of you in one night."

She smiled and met his eyes. "I never thought I would want a man, let alone more than once in one night."

He smiled back, the brilliant, provocative smile that made her feel weak. "This is because you were never with Tohave before. I told you that one day you would belong to me. Now your body and soul are mine, and your heart. You have never really belonged to another. Now you will

183

know the music of the land, and your heart will sing. Now you see that Tohave is not Indian. Tohave is just a man, is he not?"

She ran her hand over the hard muscles of his shoulder and arm, then reached up and touched his handsome face, fingering his tempting lips.

"Oh, yes, Tohave, you are that. You are a man, more man than any I can think of. You make my heart sing."

His lips met hers again. She was tired, but she did not want to sleep.

The singing of birds and bright sunshine announced morning. Katie stirred and stretched, opening her eyes and remembering that it was not Ezra Russell who slept beside her. A strong arm came around her from behind and pulled her close.

"*Pave-voonao, Hemene,*" he said softly. "How do you feel this fine morning?"

She smiled and turned to him, snuggling into his shoulder. "Do I dare feel happy, Tohave?"

"Of course you dare. We have only to wait a little while, Hemene."

"What do you mean?"

"I mean we will go away together, far to the north to the Grandmother's country—Canada. But we cannot go until it begins to be cold. When the snows come, tracks cannot be followed. Tohave will take you to the mountains of Canada. In this land there is no longer any place for the Indian to hide, but up there, we could be together forever."

She frowned and pulled back, meeting his eyes. "Tohave, we can't—"

"We can. Tohave has decided. Tohave will let you know—later—after the harvest festival at the fort. Do not worry if you do not see Tohave much before then. It is wise if he stays away. No one must suspect our feelings for one another."

"Oh, Tohave!" She burst into tears. "It would never work. It's wrong! I carry another man's child—"

"He is an animal, and not of your choosing!" Tohave hissed. "You did not ask for this hell, Hemene. It was forced upon you. No God, yours or mine, would wish this for you. When you lie with the man who owns your heart, you are not being bad, and Tohave owns your heart, not Ezra Russell!"

She cried harder, huddling against him as he held her close, stroking her back and kissing her tousled hair. "Do not weep, little one. You have time to think before Tohave sees you again at the festival. There you will give your answer, and when the moment is right, Tohave will come."

She could not control the tears that were long overdue. She wept hard and long, her shame mixed with jôy, her hatred and despair mixed with love and hope. If only she were truly free.

"It isn't . . . that simple, Tohave." She could feel her heart shattering. "I carry . . . his child. And I'm white . . . and married. It's all wrong, no matter how bad my marriage is."

"It is not a marriage at all. You whites live by too many rules. A piece of paper says a man and woman belong to each other. How foolish can you be? It is not the paper that makes you one. It is love, sacrifice, desire. It comes from the heart. There is nothing of the heart between you and Ezra Russell. You are worth no more to him than a prize cow. You have never belonged to him at all. But you do belong to Tohave, in a way you have never belonged to that man. He does not deserve you."

She hugged him tightly. "Oh, Tohave, how I wish I could really go with you."

"Then you will. Tohave will protect you. Tohave can

185

keep you from the soldiers long enough to get you to Canada. We are already married the Indian way. I have claimed you, and you took me willingly. That is all there is to it. I would be a good father to your son, and we will have more sons."

"I'm afraid to really believe we could do it," she said hesitantly. "I love you so, Tohave, and I want so to be free, but I'm afraid of Ezra. When he drinks . . ." She cried harder. "God forgive me, but I would go away with you if you came for me."

"Then we will do it."

He ran a hand over her bare skin, and the magic he had shown her more than once the night before began to work again. How wonderful it was to lie with a man she really loved and wanted. She didn't care if he was Indian. She didn't see him that way anymore. She saw only a man of strength and beauty, a man who would die for her, a man with feelings and tenderness yet one with skills and bravery and fierce pride.

Their lovemaking was sweet, as it is with parting lovers. The thought of his leaving brought savage desires to life in them, passions that needed to be fulfilled, quickly. Never had she known such intense feelings, such utter ecstasy.

He moved over her as though she were a soft, small kitten, his bronze skin in a sharp contrast to her fairness. His gentleness was amazing, considering his size and strength, and again his whispered Indian love words only heightened her passions. She took him gladly, moving rhythmically with him, still shocked that being with a man could be so enjoyable. This time the wonderful explosion deep in her groin came while he was inside of her. She felt as though she were floating then, into a whole new realm, one removed from the real world, a place where passion knew no bounds. She could not get enough of him then, and he obliged, holding his own

186

release until he feared that to take her any longer would hurt her. He had never known such ecstasy himself, for he had never done this with a woman he wanted with his whole being, a woman he wanted to be with forever. He shuddered with the excitement of it. Mourning Dove! He was one with her, mating with the sweet white girl with the sad blue eyes who had never taken a man by choice. She was beautiful, wonderful, loving. She could be a good wife, even to an Indian man with whom she had nothing in common.

As his life force poured into her again, a moan left his lips. They lay together then, still joined, for several seconds, before he finally pulled away from her, he kissed her lightly and stood up, covering her.

"We must be careful. We will wash and dress now, and Tohave will go."

She felt sick inside. Ezra had gone to the fort to buy whiskey. How would she bear the next few weeks?

"Do not fear," he told her, seeming to read her thoughts. "It is only a little longer. The snows not only cover tracks, they also discourage others from following. It will not be easy, Hemene, but we can do it. You must be brave and strong until Tohave can come for you. If it were the old days, Tohave would kill that man and take you away. But your white blood could not live with it. I know how you think. You would feel guilty, and you could never look at Tohave without remembering and feeling bad. I do not want it to be that way, much as Tohave longs to make Ezra Russell suffer for what he has done to you. It will be hard enough for you to go, for you are married to him, but you must forget about that piece of paper, little one. It means nothing, just as our treaties have meant nothing, for it was signed against your will."

He put some water on to heat, standing naked before her. It all seemed so natural and right. She had always thought a man ugly, until now. She raised herself up on one elbow.

"What about your people, Tohave, this land? You would miss both. Perhaps you won't want to stay away forever. I don't want to take you from the place where your heart lies buried."

He met her eyes. "My heart lies with you now, wherever we go. We will survive. We will find a way. Tohave is a good hunter, and he can build us a good, warm, sturdy tipi until, in the spring, he can build a log house. I have watched the white man build cabins, helped build one or two."

"You didn't answer me, though, Tohave—about your people. You belong here."

He turned away, pouring some lukewarm water into a pan. "Not anymore. It is not the same. Tohave can live in a new land."

She lay down, staring at the dirt ceiling while he washed. So many things were wrong about the plan, yet it was worth the risk to be away from Ezra Russell forever and to share Tohave's arms. How good he was, so good and brave to be thinking up such a scheme. She would not think about what would happen if they failed. They would not fail.

Time moved too fast after that. She washed and dressed and straightened the bed. Ezra would not notice. He cared little for neatness and cleanliness. He would probably be so drunk when he got home that he would see two beds before him anyway. But that would mean . . .

She shuddered at the thought of having to share the same bed with Ezra Russell after what she had known with Tohave. It would be like being raped by a stranger, which was all their joinings had ever been, and now that she knew the beauty of such intimacy, that would be even more unbearable. She breathed deeply. She must be strong and brave, just as Tohave had told her.

He was behind her then, and she turned and hugged

him. "I must go now," he said gently. "Do not be afraid. Think of Tohave, and of this time we have had together, Hemene. We will do this again. It will not be long."

"Oh, Tohave, I love you so," she whispered.

"And Tohave loves you as his own life. Be strong, Hemene."

He let go of her then, bending down and kissing her tenderly as he did so, her lips, her cheeks, and her throat. "Farewell, my Mourning Dove," he told her in a husky voice. He straightened, and she was surprised to see tears in his own eyes. "It is not easy to leave you. But I must."

He turned then, walked out, and quickly mounted his horse. "*Wagh*. Soon we will be together forever."

She nodded. How grand he looked on the horse! It was difficult to realize she had actually been bedded by such a man, that she was loved by him. Why? Why had he chosen her? If only they had more time to talk. She had so much to think about, but right or wrong, she would never regret these last beautiful hours with Tohave.

"Good-bye, Tohave," she said softly.

He rode close and took her hand, squeezing it. "Dreaming of you will make Tohave's nights restless."

She wanted to ask about the Sioux woman. Did she dare? There was no time. The thought of Tohave lying with anyone else tore at her insides with jealous claws. He belonged to her, and she belonged to him, though each might lie with another until they could be together forever.

"God be with you, Tohave." Tears ran down her cheeks, now unchecked.

"And with you, Hemene."

As he whirled his horse and rode off at a hard gallop, she shook with sobs. Had she only dreamed all of it? She half-stumbled back into the dugout. A feather lay on the floor near the bed. She picked it up and held it to her breast, crying harder then. No. She had not dreamed it.

Right or wrong, it was done. Now they must wait for winter. At least she would not spend it buried under the ground with a man she hated. She would spend it with Tohave, this winter and all winters to come. She must believe it. She must hang on to that hope. And perhaps before winter came they would find a chance to lie together again. How could she bear to wait so long before feeling his arms around her, before tasting his sweet lips. Surely he would find a way to come to her again.

Chapter Eleven

Ezra returned, with a new supply of whiskey. The moment he arrived, any guilt Katie bore for having lain with another man left her. Ezra half stumbled from the wagon, and the look in his eyes told her all she needed to know. Things would be as bad or worse than ever.

She dreaded living through the next few weeks as though nothing was changed. In her heart everything was changed, but outwardly she must not show it.

In spite of her pregnancy, she was expected to help with the harvest—hot, hard work that sometimes made her vomit. But to Ezra she was only being "weak." With September came cooler nights, but the days were still in the nineties. The heat was draining, and Ezra seemed even worse since returning. He constantly gave her orders and complained about everything.

Despite her strenuous days, Katie was almost grateful for the work. It made the time go faster. Somehow she would see Tohave again, and then it would be winter! Winter and Tohave! Yes! She would go away with him! She heard the music of the prairie now, and she was filled with joy and love in spite of Ezra Russell. Her thoughts dwelt on what it was like to lie with a man out of desire and love. How different it had been! Joyous and beautiful! She missed Tohave's arms, his voice, his teasing smile. She ached for him night and day, and she prayed that they could be together forever.

She saw beyond Ezra Russell now. She had hope, and that helped her to bear her husband's cruelties. She clung to the memory of Tohave's love so she could bear to be alone with Ezra Russell.

Now that she had known Tohave it was even harder to suffer her husband's mauling in the night. Ezra had plenty of whiskey now, and when he drank he took his woman. She had objected strongly the first time. After being with Tohave, how could she lie with such a man? Even though he was her husband, it seemed wrong. She wondered if this was how a prostitute felt, that she was simply performing an act without feelings or emotion. But she had no choice. Her objections had brought another beating. She knew she must hang on, for in a few weeks she would be with Tohave forever.

So she closed her eyes and allowed her husband his "privileges." But he was her husband on paper only. She had never truly given herself to this man. In her heart she was married to another, and it was thoughts of Tohave that kept her going during those long hot days of work, and the hideous nights.

She didn't care anymore if it was right or wrong that she was going to run away with Tohave. She was tired of trying to please Ezra Russell, tired of his brutality, tired of everything, almost tired of living. If it were not for Tohave . . . and the baby . . .

She wondered what her wedding night might have been like if she had been with Tohave. He'd have been sweet, slow, understanding, of that she was certain. Perhaps it would not even have hurt quite so much that first time if she had been with a man she loved, a man who loved her and was patient and careful. Her wedding night was something she tried not to dwell on too much, for to think of it brought the panicky horror that made her chest tighten and her heart pound.

Tohave. She must struggle through these lonely weeks until she could be with him again. For now there was the harvest. She must work hard to keep Ezra happy.

She tried to ignore the pain in her palms from the constant potato digging, day after day. Potato fork in hand, she did her best not to poke it through any of the potatoes, for piercing them made them rot faster; but it was almost impossible not to pierce several, for digging potatoes was entirely new to her. Every time Ezra found a ruined potato he became furious, cursed her, and told her how stupid and useless women were. A few times he even waved the wicked-looking potato fork under her chin threateningly, making her back away.

The creases in the skin of her hands and fingers seemed permanently dirty. No matter how much she scrubbed them, she could not get her hands and nails completely free of the dirt ground into them from pulling potatoes from the dirt and shaking the soil from them. Her back ached from the constant bending, and the joy and beauty of lying with Tohave was fading more and more every day, becoming more unreal. She began to fear that she would never see her love again, that perhaps he would not come back, that he would not be at the fort for the fall festival, that he wouldn't come for her when winter was upon them.

Would there be only this then . . . backbreaking work even when pregnant, hands that were never clean, an earthen house, a cruel husband? Was she destined to waste away on this prairie and die young, but with the face of an old woman?

She stuffed potatoes into sacks, the rough burlap making her hands raw after hours of handling. Day after day it was the same. Sacks of potatoes were piled near the house, and some were stored for their own use over the winter. What they had to sell would bring barely enough to get them supplies to last until the next spring planting.

After several days of digging, the potatoes were harvested. Katie sat down wearily inside her one-room dirt home, her hands raw. Every bone in her body ached. Ezra came inside with a handful of potatoes she had unintentionally pierced with the potato digger.

"Here's some more of your carelessness," he snarled. "Might as well make them for supper. They're no good to save." He dropped them on the floor. "Tomorrow we start picking corn."

Katie sighed, staring at the potatoes. "I'm too tired, Ezra," she mumbled. "And now you've got them all dirty again."

He reached for a bottle of whiskey. "Don't be sassing me, woman. Pick them up and cook them. I'm hungry."

She looked at him blankly, thinking of Tohave. Tohave would tell her to lie down and rest. "I said I was tired, Ezra, and I'm not hungry. Why don't you fix them yourself for once?"

Ezra took a swallow of whiskey, then slowly lowered the bottle. As he eyed her closely, a chill crept over her. But it was too late. She already knew he'd taken her remark the wrong way. She felt an urge to be stronger, to tell Ezra Russell exactly what she thought, to just walk off and leave him. Being with Tohave had opened a whole new world to her, but she could not yet free herself of the terror and submissiveness in which she had been reared. Her fighting spirit quickly vanished when Ezra set the bottle aside and came closer, grasping her arms painfully.

"Where'd you get that sass, girl?" he snarled. He shook her slightly. "My woman doesn't talk to me that way! Now I said fix those potatoes!" He shoved her hard then, and she fell against the iron stove.

She got up slowly, rubbing at her arm and struggling against tears. She must hang on. It wouldn't be long now,

194

would it? Soon the harvest festival would be held, and she would see Tohave again and be reassured that he was going to take her away. She picked up the potatoes and set them on the stove, then wet a rag to clean each one off, while Ezra slugged down more whiskey. Her hands shook as she cleaned the potatoes, and her mind and heart screamed for Tohave. If only she could run to him this very moment . . . if only he could hold and protect her now, take her away from here! . . .

She sliced the potatoes into a pan, sniffing quietly, feeling more lonely than she had since coming to this land.

"I want some meat, too. Go kill and clean a chicken for me," Ezra ordered. He lay on the bed with his whiskey. She knew he was just trying to be mean now. Killing and cleaning a chicken was the last thing she wanted to do, even though it might delay what he had in mind for her after supper.

"We'd be eating late, Ezra," she replied. "It takes a long time to pluck a chicken and you know it. But if you want to wait that long, I'll do it."

"Then do it."

He was testing her. Refusing to sass him again and give him an excuse to beat her, she finished slicing the potatoes, then picked up a small hand hatchet and walked outside. She detested killing chickens, even when she wasn't so tired that every move was an effort. She moved among the chickens, which seemed to sense her errand. They scattered away from her, clucking and flapping their wings and tails, feathers coming loose with their every movement.

"Come on now," she said softly. "This is why God made chickens and eggs." She moved slowly among the balking hens, grasping at a few and missing. "Don't give me any trouble tonight," she told them. "I'm too tired."

She chased one particularly fat one toward the

storehouse. When it ran inside, she smiled victoriously. She had it trapped now. As she started to enter, an arrow whizzed past her and landed in the earth above the entrance to the storehouse. She gasped and jumped back, staring at the arrow, her heart pounding hard with fear until she realized that Tohave was telling her he was nearby!

Her breath came in short gasps as she whirled to look. She saw no one. Yes. It must be Tohave. No one else could hide so well or shoot so straight as to put an arrow so near her without harming her. Her eyes searched the horizon, but he was not to be seen. She looked at the arrow, then grasped it. Turning it in her hands, she closed her eyes, breathing a deep sigh of relief. Suddenly Ezra's anger and drinking didn't seem quite so bad.

Tears trickled down her face. He was out there. He loved her. He still wanted her. He would come for her. It was not a trick. He had not used her or lied to her. It wasn't that she had doubted him, but her life had been so full of cruel disappointments that it was difficult to believe anything wonderful could happen to her. Her night with Tohave had been wonderful, but she was afraid to believe it had been real, or that she could ever know such beauty again.

Now she held his arrow. She smiled and pressed her cheek to it, not caring that the chicken scurried out of the storehouse right past her feet.

"I'm hungry!" Ezra shouted from the house.

Katie jumped and quickly wiped at her eyes. She stuck the arrow into the dirt, pushing it down until it was buried and could not be seen. Then she turned and ran after the chicken again, her heart suddenly lighter. When the chicken stopped and pecked at something, she lunged at it, falling to the ground as she grabbed it around the neck. She carried the bird to the chopping block and quickly ended its life. She hated that task, but told herself

196

it was to better to kill a chicken than to get a beating for refusing to feed her husband. Then she began the chore she had never gotten used to, cleaning the bird, which continued to move and twitch even after it had lost its head. She blinked back tears and tried to concentrate on Tohave.

He was out there! He had found a way to come back. He had to be so careful now, so the soldiers, and even his friends, did not always know where he was, careful not to arouse suspicions that would ruin their plan to run away together. But he had not been able to resist coming back before the harvest festival. Surely he wanted to see her as much as she wanted to see him. But with Ezra at home, they could not be together. The most he could do was send her a message that he was close by.

Cleaning and plucking the chicken took her longer than it normally did, for she was too weary to hurry. By the time she got the naked bird inside, Ezra was red-eyed from the bottle. he looked at her with a hungry grin, and she felt sick inside. This would not be a pleasant night, but she would try not to scream and cry, for her cries might bring Tohave, who might try to help her. She must be careful for Tohave's sake, and to keep Ezra from suspecting that her heart and body belonged to someone else.

She heated up the pans and began to fry the chicken and potatoes, wondering if she would ever get to sleep that night, longing for rest, needing it badly. Ezra's eyes drooped and she began to take hope that he was drinking so fast he would pass out before he touched her. Her heart pounded with hope that he would, and she took her time cooking the food. By the time it was ready Ezra could barely sit up straight to eat it. He dropped pieces of meat on the floor and only half chewed what went into his mouth before swallowing it. He ate fast and heavily, then flopped back onto the bed and ordered her to

197

undress and lie down beside him.

She shuddered and turned down the lamp, then undressed slowly. She'd been so certain that he would pass out from the whiskey and food, she was shocked when, as she lay down carefully on the bed, he suddenly grasped her hair and threw a leg over her.

"It's a damned good thing you did what I told you, woman, killing that chicken and all," he growled. "I've been testing you out all night, Katie Russell. Something is different about you. You, by God, better behave if you know what's good for you!"

He pinched her breasts painfully, and she struggled not to cry out. Then, with his knee, he shoved her legs apart and moved between them, giving her a hard slap before dropping his full weight on her in a sudden drunken slump. She could barely breathe with his weight against her chest, and he reeked of whiskey and perspiration. He moved rhythmically but nothing was happening. He was too drunk to perform, and didn't even realize he was not accomplishing anything. She was afraid to protest or try to move him off her. She could only lie there and hope he would fall asleep after all.

The minutes seemed like hours, and she longed to take a deep breath, to get away from him, to wash and hold a cool cloth to her breasts. Finally she felt him relax. She pushed at him slightly, and he mumbled something, then rolled over onto his back, his arm flung out. His breathing was slow and rhythmic, and he snored deeply. The whiskey and meal had finally taken over. He would sleep hard.

She was too upset and sore now to sleep herself. She shuddered from fear and revulsion, as she picked up her gown, soap, and a towel, wrapped herself in a blanket and headed outside. The cool, clean air smelled wonderful. If only Tohave were with her . . . But surely he had gone again. She broke into wretched sobbing. She needed him!

198

How much longer could she bear this? Could she really last until winter?

She stumbled to the stream, removing the blanket and walking into the water. There was not much of it, but the water in the barrel was stagnant. The stream was cooler and cleaner. She bent over and cupped some water in her hands, splashing it on her face and through her hair, then holding some against each sore breast. Picking up the soap, she rubbed it over her skin, bending down and scrubbing her hands. Suddenly it seemed important to get her hands clean, and it annoyed her that she could not. She could hardly see them, but she knew the wretched dirt would not come out and for some reason that depressed her. She scrubbed and scrubbed at them, her sobs becoming deeper and louder, until suddenly she heard her name called softly in the dark night. She whirled to see Tohave standing nearby on the bank.

"Oh, thank God!" she whimpered. She dropped the soap and quickly rinsed herself, running to him without even drying off or putting on her gown. "Hold me! Hold me, Tohave!" she whispered.

Strong, reassuring arms enfolded her naked body, and he pressed her close, kissing her wet hair.

"Do not cry, Hemene," he said soothingly. "I should not be here, but I could not stay away any longer." He held her close, rocking her gently. "It will be all right. Tohave will make everything all right."

She did not wonder or care how he got there so quietly. He apparently had left his horse someplace farther away and had come in on foot. She was so depressed and hurting that she wanted nothing more than the feel of his arms around her, no matter how or why he had come. She turned her face up to his. How handsome he was in the soft night! His lips found hers, hungrily, and she could not imagine a more beautiful moment than this one, when she needed him so badly, the stream nearby babbling quietly, the night warmer than usual for this time of year, the scent of this wild and free man permeating her senses. She was more sure than ever at this moment of how much she loved him, Indian or not; more sure than ever that it was right that they should go away together.

He moved his lips to her neck. "Come with me, Hemene, a little farther from here. Just for a little while. Does he sleep?"

He released her and bent down to pick up the blanket as she looked toward the sod house. "Yes," she answered, feeling cold hatred. "He drank a lot of whiskey, too fast. He sleeps hard when that happens. He . . . tried to . . ." She swallowed as he put the robe around her shoulders.

"Did he hurt you?"

She hung her head, pulling her wet hair behind her neck. "It's all right."

She felt his hands tighten on her shoulders. "It is not all right!"

She reached up and squeezed one of his hands. "You must not do anything to him, Tohave. You know that. It would bring so much trouble we'd never be able to go away together." Turning to look up at him, she asked, "You did mean it, didn't you? About going away together when winter comes?"

He touched her face gently. "You know that I meant it. Tohave will come for you." He looked toward the house. "Come. Be with Tohave for a little while." He looked back at her. "He will not know."

She glanced toward the house again, then picked up her gown, the towel and soap. It was wrong, but she didn't even care. Any moments she could have with the man she loved were precious, and worth taking. She looked up at Tohave, who stood tall and dark in the moonlight. She smiled to herself. If she did not know

200

him, he would seem frightening indeed, towering over her as he did now. How odd that she did not fear this huge, half-wild Indian man, yet she was afraid of her own husband. "Show me where to go," she said quietly.

She could see the white of his teeth when he smiled. He bent down and kissed her cheek, then whisked her up in his arms and carried her over the stream and several yards beyond it to a spot where the land sloped down until she could no longer see the house. There he laid her down on a soft blanket already spread out, and sat down beside her. She set her things aside and smiled inwardly. Apparently he had been sleeping here himself, wanting to be close to her. He must have heard her crying at the stream.

She met his eyes in the moonlight, and for a long moment they just looked at each other, passion burning in their souls. The dark night, the soft moon, the warm breeze, all added to the sharp desire heating their blood, for their love was new. That first time had only whetted their appetites for the glorious pleasures they found in each other.

He reached out and pushed the robe away from her milky shoulders, then bent closer, lightly kissing them. She breathed deeply at the thrill of his touch. When he pushed the robe down farther and gently grasped at her breast, she gave out a little gasp, and he frowned and took his hand away.

"What is it?"

"I . . . he pinched by breasts, Tohave. They hurt."

He sighed deeply, turning away for a moment. She knew he was struggling with his anger, and she could almost hear the thunder of it.

"I'll be all right."

He got up to pace, and his hand gripped his knife. "If this were the old days—"

"It wouldn't matter, Tohave. It still would be wrong.

201

We'll simply go away together and that will be that. Come and sit beside me. We don't have very much time. Don't spend it being angry."

He turned and stared at her. Their eyes were accustomed to the dark now so it was easier to see each other. He sat down beside her again, and she could feel his tenseness. She leaned forward and kissed his cheek, then his lips. "Make love to me, Tohave. Don't let him spoil that for us."

He relaxed a little, put a hand to her face. "Are you sure? You must be very tired, and after what he did—"

"I am tired. But not too tired to lie with my Tohave. I'd die to have moments like this with you." She kissed him lightly again. "A while ago the last thing I wanted was this, because I hated the man who was touching me. But when I'm with you, it's all different. And he didn't . . . I mean, I'm just yours tonight. He was . . . too drunk."

The thought of any other man touching the woman he loved overwhelmed Tohave, and he kissed her hard, possessively. Then, laying her back on the blanket, he ran a hand over her naked body, carefully avoiding her sore breasts.

She shuddered with awakened passion as his gentle fingers moved over her, finally seeking that place she never dreamed she could enjoy letting a man touch. The way he used his hands relaxed her so that she forgot the horror of the earlier hours, forgot how tired she was, how sore she was. She didn't want to think about anything but being here with her lover in the soft night, being a woman, giving herself, enjoying it, and most surprising of all, taking pleasure in a man, wanting him, hungering for him.

His lips moved to her breasts, ever so lightly kissing them in a desire to make them better. Her whole body trembled with sweet love as he almost magically took

202

away the pain by gently massaging her breasts with his soft tongue, while his fingers brought forth the moistness of heated desire. Nothing existed for her but this moment, this man. Tohave! She had not dreamed that first day she'd met him that it would lead to this, had not imagined that an Indian man could be this sweet and gentle, this beautiful and desirable.

He kissed her breasts over and over then, moving his mouth down over her belly, her thighs; working such lovely magic with his hands and lips that it was hard not to cry out with the glory of it. How did he know how to touch her so perfectly, in all the right places, in just the right ways to bring such utter ecstasy? This was like a delicious appetizer before a royal feast. She could not stop the urgent explosion that she would have preferred to save until they were one, but that mattered little. It would not take away from the final act, only enhance it.

He got to his knees, kissing her thighs, and he lifted one of her legs as he sat up to kiss her calf and foot. He rose then, removing his vest and weapons belt, leggings and loincloth, before kneeling between her legs again and running his hands over her weary muscles, massaging, watching her, deliberately letting her desire build to almost painful proportions.

"Stop teasing me, Tohave," she said with a smile, her voice husky with the want of him. "Is this some new Indian torture?"

He laughed lightly. "Is it painful?"

"Very painful. Now put me out of my misery."

He came down on her then, resting on his elbows and nibbling at her lips as he pressed himself against her. "You are Tohave's prisoner. I think I will torture you a little longer."

She ran a hand over his muscled arm, then over his chest,wriggling it down along his side until she grasped him and gently caressed his manhood. She found it

203

amazing that she wanted to touch this part that Ezra Russell had made her hate.

"Then I shall torture you also," she teased back.

His breathing quickened and he grinned. "There are many things Tohave can suffer, but this is too much."

He raised up slightly, and as she guided him into depths of passion and ecstasy, he groaned with pleasure. She arched up to him, unable to stifle at least a small cry of utter pleasure. Instantly, they moved in perfect rhythm, pushing hard, knowing this might be the last time they shared bodies for a long time, for they were taking a great risk. But it was worth it to be together.

She hated having to steal such moments. She wanted to spend every minute of every day with him, longed to sleep in the warmth of his arms every night, to cook his meals and have his babies. If only the life inside her belly were Tohave's and not Ezra Russell's . . . But she would love it just the same, and she would give Tohave sons of his own someday. She must believe that would happen, that they would escape to Canada and live happily ever after. It must come true! It must!

She reached around his neck and pulled him closer, feeling the need to reassure herself that he really was with her, and he took her hard and fast then, unable to control his own heated desire. He moaned something in the Cheyenne tongue as his life poured into her.

As they lay relaxed, he pulled her close, lying on top of her but careful not to rest his full weight on her or hurt her breasts. He longed to torture Ezra Russell slowly and then kill him, but she was right. He must not do such a thing. She could not live with it, and it would only bring trouble that would keep them from being together.

He carefully pulled away from her then and lay down beside her, pulling her robe over her so she wouldn't get a chill.

He kissed her eyes. "I wish we could stay here all night

and make love again," he told her. "But you had better go back soon."

She nuzzled into his neck, unable to stop her tears. "I wish I never had to go back, Tohave. I love you so!"

He stroked her hair. "And Tohave loves you. We will be together some day, Hemene. It is a promise."

"Let me lie here awhile, Tohave. Just a little while. I feel so safe and loved when I'm beside you . . . and I'm so tired."

He held her tighter then, putting one leg around her own and pulling her between his legs while he pressed the rest of her close against his chest and made sure the robe covered her back. He gently rubbed her back, and within minutes, when she was asleep, he sighed deeply as his own quiet tears flowed.

Was it wrong to love a white woman? Would his people turn him away for it? Perhaps some would, but not all of them. It didn't matter. Much as he loved this land and his people, he would take her to a new land, if that was the only way they could be together. Everything was different now anyway, with so many new settlers, more land sold away from the reservation. The old days of riding free, hunting, making war on enemy tribes, they were gone. Nothing he could do would ever bring them back. Some of his people still believed that the Great Spirit would do something miraculous to make everything the way it once was, that the buffalo would return, the white man would go away, dead ancestors would rise up, and the Indian would be strong again. But those were just foolish dreams, and he knew it. He wanted to believe them but could not. Now this white woman had come along, beautiful and sweet. She had stolen his heart the first moment he'd gazed into her wide blue eyes when he'd looked into her wagon. Why a white girl had won his affection he would never understand. He only knew that he loved her and wanted to be with her forever, and he would do whatever he must to make that happen.

She stirred slightly and he gave her a squeeze. He hated to let her go back to the white man he hated so. He wanted to hold her forever, protect her, never again let anything bad happen to her. She was his woman. It wasn't right that she should go back to that man, yet for now it must be done. It was torture for him. He would kill for her, die for her. Sending her back went against everything that made him Tohave. Since the white man had come to this land it seemed the Indian man was forever going against everything that was his nature. The unhappiness that brought had made many of his friends turn to the firewater, and some had even taken their lives rather than go on living this new way.

He kissed Katie's hair and rubbed at her back again. He would take her away where he could be a real man again, where he could hunt and provide for his woman instead of standing in line for a handout from the government. They would be free. He would protect her and make a shelter for her, and she would give him sons. A small distant voice told him that was impossible, but he would not listen to it.

He let her sleep nearly an hour, then moved away from her and retrieved her gown. Gently, he pulled it over her head, then lifted her up. She stirred awake as he helped her put her arms into the gown before drawing it down over her. She rubbed at her eyes and put her arms around his neck, resting her head on his shoulder.

"I'm so tired, Tohave."

"I know. But you must go back." He laid her back down and reached for his canteen, bringing it around and wetting her towel with the contents. Then he pushed her gown to her waist and washed her as she stretched while trying to wake up completely. But his gentle touches only made her want him again.

"Can't we make love once more, Tohave?"

He grinned. "I would like nothing better. But we have already taken a great risk. It matters little to me what your husband would do to me if he found us. It is you I worry about. I want no harm to come to you. Come now. I will walk you back."

He helped her to her feet, and she pulled on the blanket and rolled the soap into her towel. Tohave dressed and rolled up his blanket. "The soldiers and agents have been watching me more closely," he told her. "I will go back tonight, and I probably will not see you again until the festival. You will be there?"

"Yes. I'll make sure Ezra doesn't leave me behind, but it will be hard to see you and not be able to hold you, Tohave."

He turned to her and pulled her close. "It will be the same for me, but after this, we must not be seen together. You are sure, about going away with Tohave when winter comes?"

She rested her head against his chest. "I've never been more sure about anything in my life. I know we will make it. You know the land, the mountains. I'll not be afraid with you, Tohave."

He held her close and kissed her hair. "We will go. Until then Tohave will pray for you and dream of you. I did not think we could be together this way again before winter, but I could not help coming out once more. I had hoped in some way you could come to me, but I was prepared just to watch you and be near you. Still, I should not be here at all, and I must leave quickly now, Katie."

He turned her and walked back with her over the rise. Then he stopped and studied the shadows, seeing nothing. Turning, he bent down and his lips met hers. She dropped her towel and flung her arms around his neck, and he lifted her off her feet, kissing her almost violently in his agony over leaving her. He pressed her

207

close and it hurt her breasts, but she didn't care. She hated to let him go! Their kiss lasted until they were both almost breathless, as they tasted one another, saying a desperate goodbye. For Katie, it was cruel not to be able to be with him, now that she had discovered the pleasure and joy of wanting a man, now that she knew love.

His lips finally left hers and moved over her face and neck. "I hate letting you go, but I must. I will watch, Hemene. If anything goes wrong, I will come and help you. If he still sleeps and all is well, come to the door with a lantern; wave it and I will know all is well. After that, I will wait a while longer to be sure he has not tricked you."

He gently pushed her away then, and she bent down to pick up her towel and soap. When she rose, her eyes were brimming with tears. "I love you, Tohave," she whimpered.

"Nemehotatse, Hemene."

She turned then and ran back toward the house. If it must be done, then she would do it quickly. She reached the door and looked back, but could not see him. Inside, Ezra lay sprawled in a sweaty sleep, snoring loudly. She could tell he had barely moved since he'd first rolled off her. He had never wakened.

She put the towel and soap away, then picked up the lantern from the table. It was still dimly lit, so she carried it outside and held it up, waving it back and forth a few times. She heard something that sounded like an owl hooting, and she knew it was Tohave signaling that he'd seen her light.

She smiled and went back inside, setting the lantern back down. Ezra still snored. She felt secretly victorious over his cruelty. He had hurt her this night, but while he slept she had lain with another man, a kind and gentle man who loved her. All of Ezra Russell's ugliness could not take away the beauty Tohave had brought to her. Her

208

sore breasts banished any guilt she might have felt for loving another man. She had not chosen Ezra Russell. How could she be expected to love him?

She lay down carefully on her side of the bed, not wanting to disturb Ezra, safe in the knowledge that Tohave still waited outside to be sure she was all right. She had merely to scream and he would come running. But Ezra snored on, oblivious to the fact that his wife had not been in his bed for several hours after he'd fallen into a drunken sleep.

Katie turned and hugged her pillow, wishing it could be Tohave. But she must wait now. She would see him at the harvest festival. How would she control herself when she saw him? It would be difficult not to run to him and hug him in front of everyone. It would not be possible to be alone with him. They would have to just look, make love with their eyes, smiling inside, sharing their beautiful secret.

Soon! Very soon! And while she waited, she knew he was out there somewhere, also waiting, also aching for her. But he dared not be seen, dared not come again in the night. He could no longer watch her from afar. He would be careful now. They both would be careful.

Chapter Twelve

For once there was something joyous to look forward to. It was late September, time for the harvest festival at Fort Robinson. They would sell their meager supply of corn and potatoes; but according to Ezra, if they were to make it through the winter, they would also have to sell at least one of the horses in order to buy enough supplies. Katie agreed, though she did not plan to spend the winter with Ezra Russell.

The wagon was loaded, the mules were hitched. Ezra announced that on the way back they would stop at the place several miles from their dugout where he had found good timber for wood. They would load the then-empty wagon with wood, after which he would keep going back for more until they were well stocked for the winter. Katie suddenly loved the sound of it. She had dreaded winter, until now. The thought of spending months alone with Tohave made her smile. Yes. She could stand that. Tohave . . . a sweet, warm friend; someone who cared, who could be kind.

She was so full of him she felt like an excited little girl. She was in love! For the first time in her whole life she was in love!

It had seemed incredible that a woman could truly want a man. She had never once felt that way, until tiny urges had started poking at her whenever she'd seen Tohave. And then that night, when he had come to her after her beating . . . the trembling desire he had created in her—a desire consummated that one beautiful night she had shared her bed with him, and in their secret night on the prairie while Ezra slept.

Katie climbed into the wagon eagerly. She wore her best blue calico, with a matching slat bonnet. For the first time in many days, Ezra had shaved; and for the first time in weeks, he had bathed. He wore a clean cotton shirt and pants, and Katie supposed that if he had been a good man, he would not seem so ugly. It was his attitude that made him ugly. That day, although there was little more than cold silence between them, he seemed to be in slightly better spirits, and he was clean. Perhaps they could get to the fort without a drunken rape.

She breathed deeply of the clean, September air as Ezra kicked off the brake, and they were off, one horse tied to the back to sell, their two mules pulling the wagon. Their other animals were staked near the creek, with plenty of hay and feed left nearby. The chickens would run loose as they usually did; food had been scattered for them. It was impossible to take everything along, and out here there were no neighbors to watch a man's belongings. They could only hope no one would come along to steal the stock.

Katie knew that Ezra had actually considered leaving her behind. She had trembled with dread. But he'd finally consented, because he wanted to show off his young wife to the other settlers and to brag that she was "carrying." His reasons for taking her didn't matter. She was going. As they headed northwest, she wondered if Tohave would be there when they arrived. The thought brought a warm flutter to her heart, but also a tiny dread. She hoped there would be no trouble.

Several wagons and tents stood just outside the fort when they arrived, and traders and suppliers milled about among the farmers' camp, buying up supplies to sell to the mining camps. Everywhere there was movement, and the activity seemed wonderful to a young girl long buried on the wide prairie, with no one to talk to but a cruel husband who did not care to answer her, except with a slap.

In the distance a few tipis were placed in a circle. Indians, too, had come to trade. "Probably looking for whiskey," Ezra muttered, as though he never touched the stuff himself.

Katie searched the camp for Dora and Jacob Brown, but her eyes also sought someone else. Near the fort entrance a group of men played fiddles and banjos, and just inside the fort there was the rich smell of the roasting pig being turned slowly over a pit of coals by soldiers. They were cooking it as a free meal for the settlers.

It was a picture of peace and togetherness. There was much visiting, and Katie could hear laughter. It was a wonderful sound to a lonely young girl. She wished Ezra would let her see the Army doctor about her pregnancy, but he insisted that in her young, healthy state she didn't need such attention. Nonetheless, she didn't feel healthy. How could she after his beatings and rapes, and after being made to work until she nearly passed out? But there was no arguing with Ezra Russell. She didn't feel like being hit again so she said nothing more about it.

"Ezra, there are the Browns!" She cried as she saw them camped in the distance. "Let's go camp beside them."

"I don't like them. They're too friendly, and you'll be carrying on with that woman."

"Ezra, please. We owe it to them to visit. And we have a long winter ahead of us. Let me visit a little. Please, Ezra."

He scowled at her and turned the wagon. "Thank you, Ezra." She knew that while they were at the fort she could talk him into allowing her to do a few things she wanted, only because other people were around and Ezra Russell didn't want others to know just how badly he treated his wife. As he had back in Illinois, here he'd put on a show for others.

They headed for the Browns' camp, Katie's eyes carefully searching as the wagon rolled. Tohave! Was he here? How would it feel to see him again after . . . Her face flushed and fiery trembling overtook her. It would be so hard only to look at each other. Now she began to fear he had changed his mind. She could not spot him anywhere, yet he'd promised to see her here. She needed to be reassured that he intended to take her away.

Perhaps something had happened to Tohave, or perhaps he had only told her of his plan to get into her bed. No. Not Tohave. The memory of his eyes, his loving words . . . no. Tohave would keep his promise. He was too honest and sincere. He would not betray her.

Her heart ached at the thought of him! How could one person be this much in love? If only she'd been given the right to choose her husband . . . Now she must run away like a wanton woman, but surely God understood. She put a hand to her belly. So what if Ezra's child rested there? Tohave would be a much better father than Ezra Russell could ever hope to be. She would have her baby deep in the mountains of Canada, and Tohave would help her. Then they would all live together, peacefully and happily. She would have her baby to love . . . and Tohave. She would be in paradise.

Dora Brown looked up with tired, circled eyes when they approached, but she broke into a warm smile at the sight of Katie. Katie noticed that her stomach was flat again. However, Dora looked thin and tired.

"Katie!" she called out, reaching up.

Katie climbed down and the two women hugged while Ezra maneuvered the wagon into position to camp. Dora seemed to cling to Katie longer than necessary, and when they finally parted there were tears in her eyes.

"How are you, Katie?"

Katie smiled sadly. "It's been a hard summer, Dora. There are so many things I'd like to tell you." Did she dare tell the woman she was in love with Tohave? No. She must be careful. But she needed desperately to talk to someone, and Dora could be trusted. She looked down at the woman's flat stomach. "You had your baby!"

Dora squeezed her hands. "He died. He was only a week old."

Katie's eyes teared. "I'm so sorry! Oh, Dora, what happened?"

"I don't know. Out here . . . how can one get a child to the doctor in time? He just . . . stopped breathing." She swallowed and turned away. "We're going back, Katie. There is still time before the snow comes, if we take a train. We only came here to sell what we could, and then we're going back to Ohio."

Katie felt as though someone was wrenching out her heart. The one and only woman friend she had was leaving. She liked Dora. She'd had little chance to talk with her, but she hated to think this woman was going. Soon she would leave, too, and she would never see Dora Brown again.

"I'll miss you, Dora, even though we've hardly had a chance to get to know each other very well."

Dora nodded and turned. "I guess it looks like we're giving up, but we have each other." She swallowed back more tears. "Poor Jacob is heart broken. It was a boy. He blames himself, for coming out here. He thinks if we had stayed in Ohio it wouldn't have happened. Who's to know? Perhaps it was something a doctor could have done nothing about."

Katie put a hand to her stomach. "I'm pregnant myself, Dora."

The woman looked at Katie's still-flat stomach, then back at her eyes. "When are you due, Katie?" Ordinarily this would have been wonderful news, and she would have congratulated the girl. But Dora knew how hard a pregnancy could be in this land, and it would be even harder for a woman married to a man like Ezra.

"I'm not sure. I don't know much about these things. Sometime in the spring, I guess." She blinked back tears. "Oh, Dora, I'm so scared."

Dora grasped her arms. "Keep your courage, child. Maybe Jacob can talk Ezra into going back now, for your health and safety."

Katie wiped at her eyes. "Ezra doesn't care about my health and safety," she whispered. "You don't know . . . what he's like when we're alone. I'm living in hell, Dora. And the worst part is . . . I don't know if I want to go back to Illinois . . . in spite of Ezra . . . and in spite of what this land has been like."

Dora frowned. "I would think it best if you went back."

Katie sniffed and blew her nose, then walked several yards from the camp while Ezra and Jacob maneuvered Ezra's wagon and began unhitching the team. She turned and faced Dora once they were out of hearing range.

"Dora, the strangest thing has happened."

Dora frowned. "What is it, child?"

Katie swallowed, reddening slightly. "I . . . I don't want to go back, because . . . because I don't like the thought of never seeing Tohave again. I . . . I'm in love

216

with him, Dora." There! She'd finally told someone!

There was a moment of silence. "Tohave?" Dora whispered.

Katie met her eyes proudly. "I'm not ashamed of it. He's come to . . . to see me . . . a couple of times when Ezra wasn't around. It was nothing bad. We just . . . talked . . . like friends. He's wonderful, Dora!" How could she tell the woman the whole truth, that she had let Tohave make love to her? "The last time . . . was after Ezra had beat me badly. I was so lonely, Dora. I let Tohave . . . hold me." Her eyes filled with new tears. "He loves me, Dora. He told me so. And I have . . . feelings about him that no woman should have for someone who is not her husband . . . and an Indian besides. But I can't rid myself of them, and I don't see him as an Indian. He's just a man . . . a man I love and who loves me."

Dora put a hand on her shoulder. "Katie, there is nothing terrible about loving an Indian, but the attitude of others could create serious problems for you. And you are a married woman, carrying another man's child."

Their eyes held. "What am I to do!" Katie choked up. "I've never loved Ezra, Dora. My father . . . forced me to marry him. He's been cruel to me in the worst ways. I keep hoping . . . that he'll change. I thought knowing I was pregnant would help, but it didn't. When he last beat me he knew I was pregnant, but it didn't stop him."

Dora's eyes widened, and she put an arm around Katie's shoulders. "This is very dangerous, Katie. There is nothing wrong or sinful about loving an Indian. It's the consequences it could bring that are bad, and the fact remains that you are married, no matter how cruel your husband is. I don't know what to tell you." She faced the girl then. "Katie, you should understand that you may feel for Tohave only because of the way Ezra treats you. Don't you understand how very different you two are?

217

Even if you were free, it would be very difficult to live with someone like Tohave."

The love in Katie's eyes was shockingly obvious. "I know. But we could make it work. I know we could! I would never stop him from being Indian, and I don't think he'd stop me from being white."

She dropped her eyes then. Had she said too much? Did she dare tell Dora Brown she planned to run away with Tohave? Maybe the woman already suspected, but she would say no more. Tohave had told her not to say anything to anyone.

Dora frowned. This was serious. "I know Tohave," she said. "I know how easy it would be for a young, unhappy girl to love such a man. But you couldn't have picked a more impossible love, Katie. I'm so sorry for you, because you've never had the chance to love the way I've loved Jacob, to have a love of your own choosing. You're in a difficult situation, and I don't know what to tell you."

Katie turned and raised her eyes to stare out at the horizon, her back to Dora. "The worst part, Dora, is that if . . . if Tohave ever tried to . . . make love to me . . . if I ever allowed his lips to touch mine . . . I don't think I could stop him." She swallowed. "Does that make me a bad woman, Dora?" She needed to know, though she would not tell her Tohave had already made love to her.

Dora put a hand to her waist. "It only makes you human, Katie. You're a young girl who's never known her first true love. You've never known anything but cruelty. You want to love and be loved, but you're trapped in a situation you can't control. I can't honestly say your feelings and desires are bad. I just wish I knew what to tell you. All you can do is pray and follow your heart. I wish—"

"Katie, get over here and help set up camp!" Ezra hollered.

The two women looked at each other, and Dora gave Katie a smile. "Somehow it will work out. It has to."

Katie forced a smile in return. "What a ridiculous conversation, after not having seen each other for so long. We should be talking about . . . quilting . . . and the crops . . . and—" Her eyes teared. "Oh, Dora!"

"Hang on, Katie. We've all known sorrow. It seems there's more of that than joy in life. I'll pray for you— and I'll miss you. I'll send you an address so you can write to me and tell me what comes of all of this."

"I would love to write, Dora, but we only get to the fort a couple of times a year. I couldn't write often." *I won't be here!* she wanted to shout. *I'm running away with Tohave!* "Thank you for understanding Dora," she said aloud. "It feels so good to be able to talk to someone about it, but please don't tell anyone, not even Jacob."

"I won't tell," Dora responded, patting Katie's hand. But inside she was sick with concern, and she hated the idea of leaving and not knowing what happened to poor Katie. The girl was toying with disaster, yet it was so sad that she could not love freely.

"Quit your gabbing and start some supper," Ezra ordered. He scowled at Dora. "Your husband says you're going back to Ohio."

Dora sobered. "Yes. After three bad years and losing a baby, we're going back to get control of our lives. Perhaps we'll come out again, but I doubt it."

"Well, we're sticking it out, aren't we, Katie girl?" He slapped Katie on the rear. "Katie here is strong. She'll have no trouble with the child."

Dora glanced at Jacob, who just looked away. Then she looked back at Ezra Russell. "I was strong, too, Mr. Russell. I had no trouble with the birth. Our son died a week later. If I were you, I would not take so many things for granted, and I wouldn't make Katie work too hard. She looks tired and she's too thin."

219

Ezra grasped the harness of a mule. "I think I'm the best judge of my own wife, Mrs. Brown," he grumbled, leading the mule to the back of the wagon to tie it up.

Katie glanced at Dora, then looked away. There was work to be done.

That evening they visited with other farmers. There was feasting on roast pig, and dancing. Katie longed to dance, to whirl her skirts and be young, to enjoy the festivities. But Ezra would not dance, and he refused to let her dance with someone else. She searched the crowd for Tohave, but he did not appear. Her heart tightened anxiously, and the voices and activities around her seemed far away and unimportant. Suddenly, she didn't care about any of them. She could not even eat. Tohave. Would he come?

Later she slept restlessly, hearing drums and chanting in the distant Indian camp. Was he there? The sounds made her realize how different they were. Yet the vision of the free and wild Tohave hovered over her.

She curled into her pillow and struggled to sleep.

Morning brought more activity. Suppliers milled about making deals with farmers; Indians traded handmade jewelry and moccasins and blankets for food. Katie was allowed to wander about as Ezra talked with suppliers, and near the entrance to the fort she noticed a very young Indian seated beside a table full of carved wooden objects. She walked closer, studying them, and picked up a carved eagle.

"This is beautiful," she told the young Indian. "Are these for sale?"

He looked at her strangely and she thought him familiar. "You are the one," he told her.

She frowned. "What do you mean?"

"The white woman Tohave talks about."

She reddened slightly. Tohave! "Is he here . . . at the fort?"

Joyous anxiety was evident in her eyes. The Indian scowled. "You should not see him!" was his only reply.

Katie's heart pounded. "But I must! Are you his friend? Can you get word to him?"

"I am Two Moons. I rode with Tohave that first time we surrounded your wagon. I saw you the last time at the fort—at the races. Yes, I am Tohave's friend, and I am warning you that you will bring Tohave much trouble. You should stay away from him."

She carefully set down the eagle. "I don't want him to get into trouble any more than you do, Two Moons." His face was dark and stern, and she decided it was useless to try to explain. She picked up a horse, sleek and beautiful in its carved state. "Is this Tohave's work?"

"It is." Two Moons scowled. "They are for sale, for food and tobacco, or money. But only silver or gold, not paper money. Tohave does not trust the worth of the white man's paper money."

She sighed and set down the horse. "They're beautiful," she said, her eyes tearing. "Tohave is a bright and talented man." She touched the other objects lovingly, owls, wolves, bears, all carved in exquisite detail. "My husband would never let me buy one though."

"Then take one for free." The voice came from behind her.

She turned, and her heart nearly stopped beating. Tohave stood there, wearing bleached buckskins beautifully painted and beaded, his dark skin looking even darker against the white of the clothing. It was the first time she had ever seen him in full Indian regalia. He looked magnificent, and she felt herself turn crimson under his brilliant smile and searching dark eyes.

"You look much better, Hemene. I see no bruises. Has

that animal, your husband, been treating you better?"

She trembled at the sight of him. Oh, if only they could embrace! If only she could shout her love! She could see by his eyes that nothing had changed. Thank God! If only they could go away together right now, this very moment!

She put a hand to the bow at the high neckline of her dress. "The bruises are hidden," she replied. "But I'll survive, as long as I know you're coming for me."

His face darkened with hatred. "I would like to kill him!" he hissed.

"Please don't say that, Tohave! It would be the worst thing you could do. If we keep calm, we can get away."

He stepped closer, his jaw flexing as he restrained himself from kissing her sweet lips and her bruises, promising her that no one would ever hurt her again. She could see tension make his whole body tremble. He breathed deeply for self-control. He wanted to take her away then and there. "I will talk to you again in a better time and place. Take one of the carvings if you like . . . my gift to you."

"I can't. Ezra would ask where it came from."

"Tell him Dora Brown gave it to you, that she got it from a settler's son and gave it to you as a parting gift. I know they are leaving."

How wonderful he looked! "The eagle," she told him. "I like the eagle."

He turned and picked it up, handing it out to her. "I have missed you, Hemene."

"And I have missed you," she said quietly. His fingers touched hers as she took the eagle, and her legs felt weak. "I love you," she whispered.

"Soon," he replied. "I will let you know when to be ready."

Six men rode out of the fort then, passing close by. "Well! Well!" one of them yelled, turning his horse and trotting it up to where Katie and Tohave stood. Katie quickly put the eagle into the pocket of her dress. "Look what we have here. The little lady we saw out on the prairie."

Katie stepped back, her blood chilling. The traders. And they had a couple of extra men along now. They smelled bad, even at a distance. Tohave stiffened as the leader of the men spit tobacco juices at his feet and then turned chilling dark eyes on Katie.

"And here we thought we had to treat you like a lady. Ladies don't go around talking to Indian bucks." He turned threatening eyes on Tohave. "And Indian bucks don't go around laying eyes on white women."

Tohave's hand rested on the handle of his knife. "I do not know this woman," he lied, wanting to protect Katie. "She was looking at my carvings."

The trader snickered. "That so?" He looked at Katie again. "I've had trouble getting you off my mind, little girl. You'd best not let yourself be caught alone, now that we're back in these parts."

Tohave's jaw flexed in anger, and he stepped in front of Katie. "Do not give the white girl trouble! She has done nothing to you."

Katie considered telling Tohave that these were the men who had stolen the horses Ezra had bought, but she decided that might create too much trouble. The trader moved his horse closer to Tohave's carvings.

"I don't like redskins telling me what to do. You're the one called Tohave, ain't you? Don't tell me what to do." He suddenly kicked out at the table, sending the carvings flying.

Katie screamed and stepped back, and in an instant Tohave had charged into the man, yanking him down from his horse.

"No, Tohave! They'll kill you!" Katie screamed.

As the two men tumbled on the ground, Katie backed,

her mind and heart torn. Deciding she should not be seen in the middle of this meleé, she quickly stepped back into the milling crowd that had already gathered. Suddenly there was a gun in the trader's hand. Tohave grabbed the man's gun arm and bent it up behind his back. The men with the trader moved closer, drawing pistols, but Lieutenant-Colonel McBain hurried to the scene with several other men. Tohave bent hard on the trader's arm until there was an odd crack as the elbow was displaced. The trader cried out and the gun fell.

McBain's men had surrounded the traders, and now McBain moved in on Tohave and the trader, slamming a rifle barrel into Tohave's side. "Let him go, Tohave!"

"He kicked over all of my carvings!" Tohave raged.

Katie's heart ached for him. The beautiful carvings lay scattered on the dusty ground, Two Moons stood nearby, his eyes hot with anger, and the beautiful white buckskins Tohave was wearing were covered with dirt.

The trader sank to his knees, groaning with pain and holding a limp arm. "One of you get him to the medic!" McBain ordered.

"Tohave tried to tell Orin his business," one of the other traders spoke up. "We caught him talking to a white woman."

Katie had already moved to the back of the crowd, behind a wagon. Ezra must not find out!

"What white woman?" McBain asked.

The man looked around. "I don't see her now."

"You scared her away!" Tohave roared. "I do not even know who she was." He looked at McBain. "She was only buying one of my carvings. Many whites buy my carvings. You know that. Men and women alike! There was nothing wrong going on." He tossed his long hair behind him. "Ask them how many Indian women they have talked to—or worse!"

Mutterings went up from the crowd, and a few gasps.

"I have seen these men before," Tohave growled. "Around the reservation. I have seen them selling firewater and trying to trade for Indian women!"

"Don't try to get out of it, Tohave. Everybody knows what a troublemaker you are," one of the traders retorted.

McBain looked up at them. "You men get your friend after he's been treated and you ride out of here! Things are nice and peaceful at this fort, and they're going to stay that way. The way I see it, you had no cause to knock over Tohave's carvings. You men know better than to deliberately start something with an Indian. Tohave's been selling his carvings to whites for a long time."

There was not much the traders could say. If they told McBain they knew the woman, they would have to explain about the horses. Perhaps the man they had sold them to had already discovered they were stolen and had reported it. If so, McBain would put it all together and they would be arrested. They were already risking arrest for Tohave had accused them of hanging around the reservation and trying to trade whiskey for women.

"Come on, boys," one of them said. "Let's go see to Orin."

Grudgingly the three men rode back into the fort, and McBain turned to Tohave. "I want no more trouble over this, Tohave. You hear me?"

Tohave gritted his teeth. "I hear! It is all right for the white man to start trouble, but not all right for the Indian to finish it! How badly is a man supposed to allow his pride to be trampled?"

McBain sighed. "I'm sorry, Tohave. But you remember what I said. One wrong move out of you, and the government will have that reservation surrounded so tight your people won't be able to pee without permission. The settlers in these parts are just waiting for one wrong move. You came close today. What if I hadn't come along? Would you have killed that trader?"

"Why not!" Tohave sneered. "He was going to kill me. Was I to stand there with open arms and welcome his bullet?"

McBain rubbed at tired eyes. "If you would stay where you belong, Tohave, there would be fewer problems. Everyone knows you roam around at will. Don't you realize that if something bad happens, you'll be blamed? Stay away from the Russell place."

Tohave frowned, and Katie put a hand to her chest. She had moved with the crowd and stood just on the other side of a high log fence, where she could hear them talking.

"Who has told you I go there?" Tohave asked.

"Lieutenant Rogers. He rode a patrol a few weeks back—said Ezra Russell complained about you hanging around there. You went to see his wife when she was alone."

"Did he explain why?"

McBain nodded. "Rogers said the woman stuck up for you, said you saved her life. She'd passed out in the sun and you took her inside and gave her some kind of Indian salve to help the burn. I understand all that, Tohave. But the fact remains you were close by. Ezra Russell thinks you have an eye for his wife. That true?"

Tohave blinked, then turned away and brushed himself off. "No. Ezra Russell is an evil, jealous man. Have you met him?"

"I've met him."

"Then you know what I mean."

"I only know what I just saw in your eyes, Tohave, and I'm telling you it's the most dangerous thing I've ever seen. Stay on the reservation, for your own good."

"The reservation makes Tohave sick! Give your warnings to those who need it, Mr. McBain. Tell those traders to stay off our land!" He faced the officer again.

226

"And tell them to stay away from the settlers. Those men threatened the white woman who was buying my carving. They are dangerous. That is Tohave's warning to you."

"And if their threats made you so angry, the white woman must have been Mrs. Russell."

Their eyes held. "It is best her husband does not know she was around here. He is cruel to her. He beats her."

McBain sighed again, shaking his head. "I figured that. But that's not your affair, Tohave. Do you understand? It is not your affair. From here on, you stay out of it. I won't say anything to Mr. Russell."

"Tohave makes no promises. But I thank you for your understanding."

McBain held his eyes. "The thing I understand most of all is that an Indian man looking twice at a married white woman can mean only trouble. Don't expect me to back you too many times, Tohave."

The man turned and walked away, and Tohave brushed himself off a bit more. Two Moons straightened the table and began to pick up the carvings and blowing dust from them. A few were ruined, the foot or heads broken off.

"Bastards!" he muttered. He looked at Tohave. "I told you the white woman was trouble."

"She didn't do anything. You shut up about her or I'll send you flying like the carvings!" Tohave answered.

He turned then, catching Katie's eyes as she peered around the fence at him. He saw the anguish there, the doubt that they could truly be together, and he ached to be inside her again, to lie with her tonight and every night . . . forever.

He glanced around at the dispersing crowd, then walked in her direction, not looking at her. He stopped near her. "We must not be seen together again here," he told her. "But do not despair. It will be as Tohave promised. I will come. I am glad I could see you, Hemene. Know that I love you, little one. Tohave did not lie to

227

you. You will not have to put up with Ezra Russell much longer."

"Those traders . . . they'll make trouble, Tohave," she said quietly.

"I think not. Not here. And do not fear when you leave the fort. Tohave will keep watch."

"I love you, Tohave," she whispered.

He looked at her quickly, passion and love in his dark eyes—and tears. He left then, and her heart felt heavy as a stone. She wished she could help pick up the carvings. How many had been broken? How many hours of work had gone into each one? It wasn't right that the Indians should be treated as they were. Their land had been taken, and now people wanted to take their women, their horses, their very pride. She wished she could go to him, hold him.

Suddenly she trembled. Tohave! How grand he'd looked, and how weak her legs had felt when his fingers had touched hers. She hurried to the wagon. She could only pray that Ezra would not find out. The traders had been ordered to leave, McBain had promised not to mention it, and soon they would be leaving. But once she and Ezra had left, when would she see Tohave again? Waiting even a little while seemed unbearable. She slipped a hand into the pocket of her dress and fingered the lovely eagle. The beauty of the carving bespoke the beauty of the man. Only a man with compassion and love could capture the movement and beauty of wild things in wood. She would keep the eagle forever, no matter what happened to her.

Orin Slavens walked out of the medic's office, followed by his men. His right arm was wrapped and tied to his side, so he grasped his saddle horn with his left hand while one of his men boosted him onto his horse.

228

"We leavin', Orin?" another asked.

Orin glared at him with eyes that were slits of hatred. "We'll leave, like the commander said, but we'll find a way to get even with Tohave. And by God, we'll look up that woman when her husband ain't around. I saw how she looked at that Indian buck. You can damned well bet he knew her, all right. Any white woman looks at an Indian that way must like men, and soon as my arm is a little better, she'll have about six of them to take pleasure with."

"She's a fair one, that's for sure. I've had my fill of Indian bitches," the man responded.

Orin licked at his lips. "You aren't the only one. That pretty little thing with the big blue eyes looks mighty tasty to me. The way I figure it, we'll all have a turn at her, then kill her and leave a few Indian things about. When we come here and report we found her that way, who do you think will be the first to be blamed?"

The other man grinned, then laughed. "Tohave!" he shouted.

Orin nodded. "Tohave." He turned his horse. "Let's go."

for her, and she worried about him. Yet her heart beat with excitement and with ... fluttering away. She prayed that

Chapter Thirteen

The ride home would have been dreadful if it were not for Tohave's promise. She would see him again. He loved her and he would take her away. The fort, the people, dear Dora Brown . . . all were left behind. Katie would probably never see Dora again, and if she had had no more than a winter with Ezra Russell before her, she would not have been able to bear leaving the fort.

But how difficult would it be for Tohave to come for her? The commander of the fort had warned him to stay away from her farm, and Tohave had made trouble for himself by fighting the traders. If he were wise, he would go back to the reservation, but Katie knew he would not do it. The risk he was taking was for her, and she worried about him. Yet her heart beat with excitement and with fear at the thought of running away. She prayed the soldiers would not catch Tohave near her farm and arrest him.

She had considered telling Ezra about the traders. They should have been reported as horse thieves, but they would have told Ezra about seeing her with Tohave and what could be proven against them now? Tohave probably already suspected them, but if his suspicions were verified, perhaps he'd do something even more foolish, and she did not want that to happen. She was haunted by the look in the eyes of the man called Orin, by his threat to come for her when Ezra was gone. His threat chilled her blood. But surely Tohave would be out there somewhere, watching over her. She should not be afraid.

Gathering wood was hot, hard work. Ezra chopped and split it. Katie could only throw it into the wagon once it was cut.

Ezra cut mostly small trees that he could chop through once they were down. Using a saw was even harder work; for one man to saw through a big tree took hours. He left some of the logs whole for longer burning. They were heavy, but Katie loaded them silently. For four days they cut and split and loaded until the wagon could hold no more wood without breaking down.

Then they headed home, hot and dirty and covered with mosquito bites inflicted by the swarms that surrounded them at night. The trees were near a river and the dampness encouraged the breeding of the devilish pests. Katie wondered, even if she was happy with her husband and next year's crops were better, whether life would ever be easy in this land. Would it ever be civilized? Someday would there be a town near the place where they had lived?

She watched the horizon all the way home, but saw no sign of Tohave—or of the traders. She still could not get out of her mind the way the trader Orin had looked at her.

They arrived home to find the animals still there, though their feed was gone and they tugged at their ropes restlessly to get to more grass. It was dusk and Katie was so tired she felt faint, but the animals had to be fed. Hurriedly, they moved the livestock and their only horse from the spot where they were staked to a fresh, clean place along the stream. Katie fed the chickens while Ezra fed the stock, muttering that he hoped the bull had enough sense to breed and there would be a baby calf in the spring.

"Sometimes I wonder if this bull knows what females are made for," he muttered. Yes. That was the way Ezra Russell considered sex—an animal act for the male's pleasure and for breeding.

Katie was chilled by the thought, but she helped unhitch the mules and stake them out for the night.

"We'll unload the wood in the morning and you can stack it while I go for more," he told her. He looked around. "I can hardly believe Indians didn't come and take everything we own while we were gone," he commented. "You can't trust those red devils. At least you'll be here next time to watch over things."

He walked into the dugout then, after pulling out sod they had stacked up at the doorway to keep animals out. The inside smelled of earth and dampness, and Katie curled her nose.

"I'll be glad when we have a real house," she commented, as though she planned to stay. She raised an iron plate from the stove and stirred some old, unburned wood. Then she put in some kindling.

"No house till we get the farm going better," Ezra grumbled.

"It smells bad in here."

"It's shelter. It don't bother me any."

She turned to see him take down a bottle of whiskey. No! He was bad enough in his normal state, but the whiskey made him truly mean. She opened her mouth to protest, but he cast her a warning look.

"Mind your business, woman. Cook us up some supper. We've got something to tend to that has been neglected since we left for the fort. I'll be leaving in the morning soon as we clear out the wagon."

233

She swallowed, hardly able to breathe because of her aching chest. She was so tired! How could he even think of it? Surely he was tired, too.

"I've let you be long enough," he growled, slugging down some whiskey. "You're getting spoiled. You'll never learn to like it that way. Practice makes perfect, don't they say?" As he broke into the guttural laugh she'd learned to hate, she wondered if his mind wasn't right. Perhaps there was something wrong with Ezra Russell that all the kindness and obedience in the world would never heal. Hadn't her father told her once the man had been wounded in the Civil War? Yes. A bullet in the skull, he'd told her. Ezra had been a young boy then, barely old enough to be fighting.

As she got a fire going in the stove, it all began to make sense. Sometimes it took years to realize the aftereffects of a bad wound. *"His folks didn't think he'd live,"* her father had said. *"I remember he was in a coma for a long time, was kind of violent, too, for quite a while after he came out of it. But he calmed down, worked hard on the farm, and married Jennie. Too bad Jennie never gave him any sons before she died."*

Jennie Russell. Katie remembered very little about her. She'd been much younger when the woman had died. How had she died? A fall, they said. A bad fall.

She froze for a moment, her blood suddenly cold. A bad fall. Perhaps it had not been a fall at all. Perhaps Ezra Russell had beaten her to death! Yes. It all made sense now, too much sense. A head wound followed by a coma and then violence. A wife dead of wounds from a fall. It was not a fall at all!

She swallowed and put the plate back over the burner, setting a black frying pan over it and throwing in some grease. She would fry the rabbit Ezra had shot that day. She actually broke into a sweat. Why was it suddenly so clear? What kind of a man had she married? She blinked back tears. Tohave! Suddenly she wanted to run to him, to scream for him to take her away—right now! She turned to look at Ezra again. He was drinking more whiskey. Perhaps the whiskey acted on his injured brain and made him violent. She would have to be careful tonight.

She was torn. If what she was thinking was true, in a way she had to feel sorry for Ezra Russell. But that had happened long ago. What kind of man had her father forced her to marry? What kind of man was she doomed to spend her life with, and just how long would she live if she stayed with Ezra? When would he decide she, too, must die; and who would know out here? He could say she'd been trampled, or had fallen down a bank and hit a rock.

She opened the gunny sack that held the rabbit and washed the meat, then laid it in the hot grease. This would be a pleasurable task, if done for a man who loved her. Suddenly her appetite was gone. She put all the meat in the pan, then turned to face Ezra. When she spoke his name, he turned and looked her over.

"What?"

"What . . . what was Jennie like? I don't remember her very well. I was much younger when she . . . died."

He looked at her for a long time, as though he wondered if she suspected something.

"What does it matter?" he finally said. "She's dead. And she never gave me any children. You'd better give me a healthy offspring."

She put a shaking hand to her stomach. "I'll try, Ezra. I . . . I want to be a good wife."

"Then get the damned supper cooked and then get them clothes off. I haven't felt you naked against me in a long time. I'm as restless as a horny bull chained close to a cow in heat. Only difference is, you're never in heat. But that makes no difference to me. I still get my

235

pleasure." He drank more. "Now get busy like I said."

She forced a faint smile, hoping to keep him in a decent mood. She would not fight him tonight. She would never fight him again. She suddenly realized the kind of man she was dealing with.

"You don't need to order me, Ezra. It's been a long time for me, too," she lied. "I won't fight you."

He grunted a reply and swallowed more whiskey. She turned around and began turning the rabbit, her quiet tears making the grease sizzle as they fell into the pan. Tohave! When would she be in his arms again? Reminding herself that she would be with him soon was the only way she could bear this present hell.

In the morning he was gone. She didn't care anymore that she would be alone and defenseless. It was good to be alone. Ezra Russell was dangerous. Nothing would convince her otherwise. She must be careful what she said, how she looked at him. She no longer felt guilty about not loving him. She had not chosen Ezra Russell, and a man like Ezra did not understand love or even want it. He only wanted his "pleasure."

There was nothing left now but to hope he got no worse before she and Tohave could run away. Her thoughts were full of Tohave, especially after the ugly intercourse she had experienced the night before. Ezra had not been satisfied with taking her once. He had wanted to "make up for lost time," as he'd put it. And make up for it he had, while she'd been silently screaming for Tohave. How many more times would she have to bear Ezra Russell's touch? With Tohave, she had wanted to make love more than once. How could it be so different with someone else?

Tohave! Maybe he would come now while Ezra was gone. But no. It was still too soon. They must be very

236

cautious. Winter was not upon them yet and it was too soon to run away. Yet she could not help but feel he was somewhere close by. If he came to her they could be alone again, together. But even if he did not, she would not be afraid. Tohave watched. She would never be afraid again.

They still had their own vegetables to harvest for the winter so she dug a few late potatoes and, placing them in gunny sacks, carried them to the cool dugout where food was being stored for the winter. She stashed the last sack toward evening, and as she prepared to leave the dugout, she remembered the lance—Tohave's lance—the one he'd pinned right through her dress when he'd announced that one day she would belong to him.

Her throat ached. Ezra was gone. She would dig up the lance and look at it again. She'd never seen it in full daylight. She scratched with her fingers, suddenly desperate to see it again, to have something of Tohave. The hair ornament and the carved eagle remained hidden in her belongings, but they were not as important as the lance. Surely an Indian man's lance meant a great deal to him. When she felt it, she dug harder, then pulled it up and carried it outside to a water barrel. She dipped her apron into the barrel and carefully wiped the dirt from the beautifully grained and polished wood. She was sorry now that it had been kept buried. It was exquisite, just as his carvings were exquisite. It was painted with tiny horses, each depicted in surprising detail. A beaded piece of soft leather was wrapped around the middle, at the spot where a man would grasp it to hurl it. The spear end was metal, and two feathers were tied at its base.

She held it up like a warrior and mimicked throwing it. Then she could not resist the temptation. She threw it, but not quite hard enough. It stuck in the ground for a moment, then fell over. She laughed. How good it felt to laugh! Even in his absence Tohave had brought a smile to her lips, something Ezra had never done. She picked up the lance again and studied it lovingly, running a hand over the smooth surface. Then she kissed the leather at the center. Surely Tohave's hand had touched that spot many times. Her eyes teared.

She carried the spear into the sod house—somehow having it nearby made her feel safer—and she plunged it into the ground right at the doorway, then stood back and looked at it, smiling and crying at the same time. Who would enter a house in which an Indian's lance graced the doorway? She laughed again, feeling like a little girl. Then she flopped down on the bed and stretched out. She was not going to worry about anything tonight. She was going to be happy and free, and she would sleep well. Tohave's lance guarded the doorway.

Katie slept deeply, and she was surprised to find the sun had been long up when she awoke. She jumped up. The lance was still in the doorway. She smiled and began to wash. Having dressed, she prepared herself a breakfast of fresh eggs and some bacon they had brought from the fort. She ate leisurely, then fed the animals and picked corn. She would spend the afternoon husking it.

It was a lovely, crisp, early October day; the humid heat of the summer was over. Soon she would probably wish for that heat again, but for the moment she looked forward to cold temperatures—and nestling with Tohave somewhere in the Canadian Rockies. That thought made everything else less ugly. She decided she would stack the wood the following day. It would take the rest of the afternoon just to husk the corn she had picked that morning. Tomorrow, after stacking the wood, she would cut the corn from the cobs, some to be dried, some to be pickled. Even though she was running away with Tohave, she must do the work Ezra expected. She must not arouse his suspicions.

She piled the corn at the front of the dugout. It was too nice outside to sit in her hole in the ground. She had had enough of dwelling under the earth. Now she would enjoy the afternoon sun. She brought out a small barrel to sit on, as well as a large washtub, into which she poured some water. Then she began husking the corn, throwing the ears into the tub of water.

An hour passed, two. She lost track of time and of her work. It became automatic, so automatic that her mind could wander and she could think of Tohave again. She had reburied the lance, just in case Ezra came back early. She'd hated to put a thing of such beauty under the ground, but she'd had no choice.

Tohave. She began to hum, then stopped husking and looked out at the prairie grass blowing in the distance. Yes. It truly did dance when one looked at it with happy eyes. She listened to the wind. Was that violin music? She smiled and hummed some more, then set down the corn and rose to walk out in front of the sod house and put out her arms. Humming, she whirled and dreamed, pretending she was a grand lady dancing with her prince. Her prince was dark and utterly handsome, dressed all in white. His face was Tohave's, as were his scent and his smile.

She watched nothing. She listened for nothing. She was lost in her dream. She had not pretended or laughed or danced in so long! How good it felt! She sang a little song she had learned as a girl, whirling meanwhile and sometimes closing her eyes so that she was dizzy. So lost was she in her fantasy that she did not hear the horses until it was too late. They thundered toward her at amazing speed, and when she finally heard them she just stopped and stared. Was it Tohave and his "wild boys?"

Her heart began to pound furiously then. It was not Indians! It was white men! She did not need to see them close to know who they were. They certainly were not soldiers. Instinct told her they were the traders!

The rifle! Where was the rifle? In her panicked state she could not remember. She had carried it with her to the animal dugout that morning, hadn't she? Yes. She'd left it there while taking the animals to the stream, had forgotten about it for the rest of the day.

She ran to get it. But a shot rang out and a bullet hit the dirt not far ahead of her. She stopped and screamed, then ran again. Another shot was fired, digging up dirt in front of her. She whirled. No! To lie with Ezra was bad enough, but these men had the same thing in mind, only she knew they would do even worse things to her—ugly things she could not even imagine. And it would not be only one of them. Her breath would not come. Ezra she could bear out of necessity, but not this! Not this!

"Tohave!" she screamed. Why had she screamed his name? He was not there. "Tohave!" she screamed again. But there were only thundering horses, ridden by ugly, dirty men wearing shaggy buffalo coats that made them look like giant monsters to her.

She began to run then. She'd never get to the horse in time to get away, and they were not allowing her to get to her rifle; but what else could she do? How had they known she was alone? Was Ezra dead? She ran until her chest ached, but the pounding hooves came ever closer until something caught her up and brought her to a jolting halt. She was jerked back and she fell to the ground, a rope tightly circling her arms and breasts.

Someone who smelled of old blood from a poorly tanned buffalo robe grabbed her up then, laughing. When she kicked and screamed, a hand slammed across her face. Her protests would only excite them, she knew that, yet she could not help resisting. The horror these men would wreak was more than she could bear.

"Now we'll see what's under all them skirts," Orin

240

MORE PASSION AND ADVENTURE AWAIT... YOUR TRIP TO A BIG ADVENTUROUS WORLD BEGINS WHEN YOU ACCEPT YOUR FIRST 4 NOVELS ABSOLUTELY *FREE* (AN $18.00 VALUE)

Accept your Free gift and start to experience more of the passion and adventure you like in a historical romance novel. Each Zebra novel is filled with proud men, spirited women and tempestuous love that you'll remember long after you turn the last page.

Zebra Historical Romances are the finest novels of their kind. They are written by authors who really know how to weave tales of romance and adventure in the historical settings you love. You'll feel like you've actually gone back in time with the thrilling stories that each Zebra novel offers.

GET YOUR FREE GIFT WITH THE START OF YOUR HOME SUBSCRIPTION

Our readers tell us that these books sell out very fast in book stores and often they miss the newest titles. So Zebra has made arrangements for you to receive the four newest novels published each month.

You'll be guaranteed that you'll never miss a title, and home delivery is so convenient. And to show you just how easy it is to get Zebra Historical Romances, we'll send you your first 4 books absolutely FREE! Our gift to you just for trying our home subscription service.

BIG SAVINGS AND FREE HOME DELIVERY

Each month, you'll receive the four newest titles as soon as they are published. You'll probably receive them even before the bookstores do. What's more, you may preview these exciting novels free for 10 days. If you like them as much as we think you will, just pay the low preferred subscriber's price of just $3.75 each. *You'll save $3.00 each month off the publisher's price.* AND, your savings are even greater because there are never any shipping, handling or other hidden charges—FREE Home Delivery. Of course you can return any shipment within 10 days for full credit, no questions asked. There is no minimum number of books you must buy.

Slavens growled.

Screams welled up from deep within Katie as one man removed the rope and pulled her arms up, while Orin ripped away her skirts.

"Hell, Orin, there's a bed inside. Why don't we tie her to it?" This was another man's voice. "It's a hell of a lot softer than the damned ground, and once she's tied we can have us a right good meal of woman, two at once if we want."

As Orin stood up, throwing down the material he'd ripped away, Katie kicked out at him, catching him in the knee and making him cry out.

"You bitch!" he bellowed. He placed his heavily booted feet on each of her ankles, making her scream with pain, while he reached down and ripped at her lacy, knee-length underpants, tearing off one side and exposing a bare leg and hip. He grinned then. "You might be a bitch, but by God you're a pretty one, missy." He stepped off her ankles then. "Get her to the house. When we're through with her we'll leave a couple of feathers and a moccasin and a few other things. Once she's dead, she can't say who did it. Tohave will have trouble getting out of this one!"

They all laughed, while one man dragged her toward the house despite her screaming and kicking. Tohave! They were going to kill her and blame it on Tohave! She wanted to die before they touched her, but what about poor Tohave? No one would believe his innocence!

Her abductor continued to drag her on, while Orin ordered the others to dismount and water their animals. "Me and Clay will be awhile, boys. Then you can have your turns."

She heard their ugly laughter. But then there was an odd silence, followed by a whirring sound and a strange thud. The man dragging her suddenly dropped her and fell to his knees. Katie quickly scooted away from him, staring wide-eyed at the arrow protruding from his back. Suddenly there were shrill war whoops.

"Tohave!" she whispered. She crawled farther away, as Tohave himself charged into Orin Slavens, jumping from his horse and knocking Slavens to the ground before the trader could get off a shot. Tohave's "wild boys" surrounded three more of Slavens' men, but the fourth had already taken off at a gallop, having been the first to see the Indians coming. He had not even warned the rest of Slavens' men. He'd been too frightened to speak.

Tohave and Slavens tumbled on the ground in a bitter, ugly fight, two big men, each filled with hatred of the other. Tohave's huge knife was out, and Katie watched in terror. Even if Tohave won this fight and killed Orin Slavens, what kind of trouble would he be in? She crawled farther away, glancing meanwhile at the rest of the Indians, who had knocked Slavens' men down with rifle butts and war clubs. As one trader's throat was quickly slashed, Katie cried out and looked away. She did not want to see what happened to the other two.

Tohave and Slavens struggled, and Slavens kicked up, catching Tohave in the groin with his knee. Then he threw Tohave over his head, but Tohave quickly came up, knife still in his hand. Slavens had his own knife out by now, and he was waving it menacingly at Tohave.

"No!" Katie groaned. Out of the corner of her eye she saw one of the Indians stabbing a man repeatedly. She put her hands to the sides of her face, trembling and weeping but unable to take her eyes from Tohave's struggle. The men slashed out at each other, but Tohave was quick and skilled. He sliced into the trader's arm, making Slavens cry out and drop his knife. Then he moved in for the kill, plunging his knife deep into Slavens' chest.

Katie cried out and covered her face. Then all was

quiet. In the next moment strong hands were pulling her up and wrapping her in their warmth.

"*Hoshuh, Hemene,*" came the gentle voice. "I will take you away from here."

"Don't let go of me!" she screamed, her face buried against his powerful chest.

"I do not wish to let go of you," came the gentle reply. She was lifted in strong arms then and she did not even ask where they were going.

"My . . . husband," she groaned.

"Do not worry. My men will watch for his return. They will signal if he starts back. They know where he is. He still cuts the wood."

"But . . . how . . ."

"Tohave saw your man cutting the wood so I came here quickly, remembering the trader's words to you, remembering the trader rode south." He kissed her hair. "My friends will load up these bodies and when I return we will take them to the fort and explain."

"One got away, Tohave," one of Tohave's friends spoke up. "He will get there before us. He will tell lies."

"I will come back in the morning," came Tohave's voice. "We will go to the fort then and explain to McBain."

"This is not good, Tohave."

"I do not care," he answered. He set Katie on her feet and wrapped her in a warm, soft blanket. Then he lifted her onto his horse. This time he rode the grand Appaloosa that was nearly all black. He mounted up behind her. She didn't care where they were going. She was safe. She was with Tohave. He wrapped an arm around her and picked up the reins in his other hand.

"You know where I will go," he told his men.

"You should not do it, Tohave," someone declared.

Katie's head lolled back against his chest. "Don't leave me here alone," she whimpered.

"Not to fear, little one," he answered. "I go!" he said louder. "And none of you will speak of this to anyone."

His horse began to move at a gentle trot.

"The . . . corn," she said in a whisper.

"It will keep. My friends will stay and feed your animals. You will stay with Tohave this night. We will go to a special place, away from where your memories are bad."

She did not argue. She was with Tohave. She was safe.

Chapter Fourteen

A gentle and unusually warm wind graced the prairie
twilight. Katie breathed in its sweet scent, or was that
Tohave's sweet scent? He was lifting her down from the
black Appaloosa, and moments later she was inside some
kind of dwelling, being laid on something soft. A gentle
hand stroked the hair back from her face.

"I must go tend to my horse, Hemene. Tohave will
only be a moment."

"Don't leave me," she heard herself saying. "They'll
. . . come back."

"Not anymore. They will not bother you again, little
one. Lie still and rest."

She sensed his leaving, and she rolled onto her back,
breathing deeply and trying to get her thoughts together.
Tohave. The traders. The fighting. All the blood. Blood!
She whimpered and sat up. Tohave. He had come! He had
stopped those men from doing vile things to her—from
murdering her—but he had killed Orin Slavens! What
would the soldiers do to him? Perhaps Orin was not the
only one he'd killed. The man who was dragging her had
been shot with an arrow. Tohave's? And what about
Tohave's friends? Would she be the cause of their
deaths?

Tohave. He had swept her up in his warm, strong arms and brought her here, wrapped in his own blanket. She looked around then, realizing he must have brought her to a tipi. In awe, she stared about. She was actually sitting inside an Indian tipi. It was roomier than she had imagined, and cleaner. She looked down at a bed made of clean buffalo robes, and her heart began to beat harder. She was sitting in Tohave's tipi on Tohave's bed. How many Indian women had shared this bed?

She shook away the thought, suddenly feeling too warm. Tohave. She was alone here . . . with Tohave. *"You will stay with Tohave this night,"* he had told her. She remembered now. She had not thought they would be together again this soon, but he had been watching over her just like he'd promised. The thought of it was wonderful, exciting.

She looked around the tipi, at a myriad of paintings: running horses, men with lances, the sun, circular designs. A circle of various scenes of Indian life decorated the dwelling, and everything inside was neat and tidy. She thought how much nicer this would be than her home under the earth. How simply the Indian lived! These roomy, pleasant dwellings could be collapsed and raised again in moments.

She looked up at the smoke hole, where several poles were tied together. A rawhide rope came down from the center of them and was tied, taut, to an anchor peg. The smoke flaps at the top were open, and she could see stars beginning to twinkle. It was getting dark. But there was just enough light left, combined with the illumination from the dying fire inside the dwelling, for her to see the tipi's sturdy structure and its paintings.

There was little inside it besides the bed and the small fire. The fire was situated toward the now-open door flap, as was the smoke hole, and she realized the tipi was not truly circular, as she had supposed one would be. It was

246

wider and higher at the back, where the bed was placed. She supposed there was a reason for the way it was structured, and she could not get over how big it was inside.

If this was how she and Tohave would live in Canada, she would not mind at all. But there would be so much to learn. She knew nothing about how to build a tipi. She remembered hearing that the Indian women did that, sewed the skins and put up and took down the dwellings. Could she really live this way?

Of course! She would be with Tohave. And this tipi was so much cleaner- and fresher-smelling than her earthen home. It wasn't where or how she lived that mattered. It was the man she lived with that mattered. With Tohave she could bear any burden and bear it joyfully.

Tohave's horse whinnied, and her heart nearly skipped a beat. She forgot about the wonder of the tipi. This was Tohave's tipi, and night was coming. And the traders . . . She put a hand to her face, still hot and sore from Orin's hard slap that had knocked her to the ground. As she did so, the blanket fell away from her slightly, and she realized she still wore the top half of her dress, but it was ripped, one sleeve nearly torn off and her arm bleeding. Her eyes filled with renewed tears prompted by re-membered terror. She opened the blanket, to see that her underwear was nearly gone, just the elastic waist left and one side completely torn away so that her hip was bare. There were ugly scratches at her waist, where Orin had grabbed the material.

Tohave came inside then, and she gasped and threw the blanket back over herself. As their eyes met, she found it difficult to draw breath.

"Do not cover yourself," he told her, coming closer with a canteen. "You have wounds. Tohave will clean them."

She clung to the blanket staring at him. "Tohave, what

will happen to you?"

"It does not matter. Whatever happens, it is better than what you would have suffered at the hands of those men. No other man will touch you besides your husband, except Tohave. And one day soon even your husband will never touch you again."

The statement was made matter-of-factly, and his dark, hypnotic eyes held her blue ones. "Tonight we will be together, Hemene."

She shook her head. "We . . . can't."

He only smiled a little, setting down the canteen and taking the blanket away from her shoulders and opening it.

"We do not know what tomorrow will bring. We have only tonight, and if we are forced apart for the rest of our lives, we will have this memory, and the memory of that first time Tohave claimed you."

Her eyes filled with tears. "What are you saying?"

He studied her blue eyes lovingly. "I am an Indian, and I have killed white men. There are some who will not care why I killed them."

"Tohave!" she cried, and she threw her arms around his neck.

"Do not fear." He kissed her hair and held her close. "If Tohave can get to Mr. McBain, he will protect Tohave. And when your husband returns, you must make him bring you to the fort to explain. When they all hear the truth from your lips, no harm will come to Tohave and his friends."

She pulled back. "You should go now then, Tohave! Right now! And you should take me with you."

He frowned, kissing her bruised cheek. "No," he said softly. "Tonight Tohave will make love to his woman. Tomorrow is soon enough. It is already getting too dark. We will go to the fort and take the bodies with us. We will tell them we waited the night, until your husband's return, because one of the traders got away and we feared he would come back. My friends will not tell anyone that you and I went off alone. They understand. But you cannot go to the fort with us. If you are seen riding with us, a white man might think that we took you against your will. It is best that you come to the fort with your husband. We will go before he returns. You explain to him. Make him come to the fort. We cannot wait for him. The one who got away is probably now on his way to the fort to tell his own story. We must go in the morning, and take the bodies with us as proof we tell the truth. The soldiers will probably hold us at the fort until you come."

"But Ezra might not be back for two more days! I'll worry about you, Tohave!"

"It is best we go soon, right away, and you should not be seen with us. We will be all right, Hemene."

She rested her head on his shoulder. "But McBain knows we have feelings for each other. He told you to stay away from here."

He kissed her hair. "That does not change what the traders did. It was right that we helped you."

She ran a finger along a vein in his muscled arm. "It worries me, Tohave. You killed a lot of white men. I fear there will be trouble over it, in spite of what they tried to do. Someone might twist the story and make people turn against you."

"It was right what we did. As long as no one knows about you and me, there is no problem."

"My own husband might not believe what happened. He'll ask why you were around here, and he won't care what might have happened to me. He'll be more angry about the fact that you were here."

"Then he is a fool," he told her. He pulled back and gently stroked her face. "Make him come. Tell him the truth. Then when it is all settled and Tohave is free, I will come for you as I promised, when the snow begins to blow."

Their eyes held, and she felt lost in him as he unbuttoned the few remaining buttons of the bodice of her dress and removed it. "Tohave will bathe you and put a salve on your wounds; then we will sleep together. I have missed you so. The nights are painful, Hemene. I have never known such beauty as the nights we spent together. When I saw you at the fort . . ."

His lips covered hers then, hungrily searching, and his bare chest pressed against her breasts as he groaned from his need for her. He trembled as he moved his mouth over her cheek then, and her throat. She whimpered when his lips found a full, pink nipple and tasted of its fruit.

"Tohave!" she whispered, closing her eyes and kissing his hair, holding his head gently in her hands and pushing toward him, wanting to feed him, satisfy him, give him pleasure. How wonderful it was to feel this way about a man, to know it could be so good, so gratifying, so beautiful.

His lips shifted to kiss the cleavage of her breasts; then he gently laid her back on the bed of robes. "First we must clean your wounds," he told her, his voice husky with desire.

As he removed the rest of her clothing, she lay there naked, blushing but unafraid. He wet a rag with water from his canteen and sponged the scratches on her arm and at her hip. Already they were beginning to scab over. "Bastards!" he muttered. "They all deserved to die!" He set the canteen aside and gently ran a big hand over her belly. "Do you still carry his life?"

She closed her eyes. "Yes," she whispered. "But I'm worried, Tohave. It seems I should be getting bigger by now."

He frowned and bent down to kiss her belly, and hot desire rushed through her at the realization that this was Tohave touching her, kissing her, drinking in her nakedness.

"The way he treats you, I am surprised you still carry the child at all," he said, anger in his voice. "Lie still and rest now. Tohave will build up the fire and then massage you with a sweet oil."

She pulled a blanket over her, and watched him as he added wood to dying coals, studying his hard, beautiful form, his dark handsomeness.

"Why, Tohave?" she asked suddenly. "Why me? I thought you didn't even like white people."

"Ones like your husband and those traders I do not like. Ones like Dora and Jacob Brown I do like. They are fair. They look at me as a man and not some kind of wild animal that should be shot."

She frowned. "But I should think a man like you would consider only an Indian wife. Your sons would not be full bloods."

He sat down, stirring the coals, his dark eyes sad. "What does that matter anymore? We are a dying race. If we are to survive at all, we must learn a new way. Tohave hates the thought of it, but he is also wise enough to know that it is true. We are just two people, but in our own way we can learn together and perhaps help others. Someday perhaps we can return and be with my people, and somehow help them. I do not know for certain yet why the Spirits led me to you. I only know how I feel when I am near you, and there is a certainty in my heart that you should belong to Tohave. I will be true to you, Hemene, and Tohave will never hurt you."

"I know that," she answered softly. She pulled the blanket closer as the new wood began to burn. "How did this tipi get here, Tohave?"

"It is—was—my mother's. A woman kept it for me. The last time I was at the fort, when you and your husband were there, I decided I would watch over you because of what the traders did. I brought the tipi on a travois and set it up myself, planning to stay out here as long as necessary and wanting good shelter."

She fought back her jealousy. "The woman who kept it. Is she the one who . . . who taught you how to kiss?"

He grinned. "She is the one. She is called Rosebud, and is a childless widow. I provide meat for her sometimes. She provides for my needs."

Katie sobered into a scowl. "I see," she answered quietly, fingering the fur of the buffalo robe she lay on.

Tohave laughed then. "You see all right! You are jealous, Hemene!"

"I am not!" she pouted. "I just wondered, that's all. If you think I'm jealous, you think an awful lot of yourself."

He laughed more and then came closer to her, his gaze holding her blue eyes. "And Tohave is jealous of any man touching you. So we are even." He pulled the blanket away from her breasts and kissed each one lightly. "Tohave has not slept with Rosebud for many suns, not since being with his Mourning Dove."

She touched his hair. "Truth?"

He raised his head and met her lips. "Tohave always speaks the truth," he said softly, kissing her eyes then. "How could anything match this? And soon we will be together forever, so it will not matter. We can be one as often as we choose."

She touched his face lovingly. "I've been so lonely, Tohave."

He sobered. "Tohave has also been lonely. I am a homeless man who has lost whatever was dear to him. I will not lose you, Hemene, now that I have found and claimed you. Even I do not understand fully why I have chosen to love a white woman. Perhaps it is some kind of sign, a sign that we are not so different after all." He

252

smiled sadly. "Perhaps if the white man had been more honest with us from the beginning," he continued, "perhaps then it would be easier for my people to want to learn new ways. But there is so much fear and hatred. There have been too many lies, Hemene—too many broken treaties, too many massacres of peaceful Indian villages, butchered women and children, too much rape and plunder. Yet when one or two Indians do something bad, the whole tribe is made to pay. If that is white man's justice, then I want none of it. The white man lives by strange rules. To murder is against his religion, yet to murder an Indian baby or an Indian woman, or an old man begging for his life, is not bad. I do not understand this. If a man's skin is dark, he is worthless as a buzzard. Why? Perhaps you can tell me. The Indian has always had enemy tribes, but we fought one another for good reason, sometimes over ancient wrongs. It never was to do with the color of a man's skin. In the beginning the Indian did not have a quarrel with the white man. I try to understand this strange thinking that the white man is superior, but I cannot understand it for sometimes he is very much a fool and I wonder why he is supposed to be smarter than Tohave. Some white men do not even know how to survive out here in this land where the Spirits have provided all they need."

"If I understood myself, Tohave, I would explain it to you, but I don't."

He sighed and met her eyes. "Someday we will sit and talk of these things. We will teach one another what goes on in our minds and hearts, why the Indian is the way he is, why your white race is so different. We will talk and we will learn, and in some little way we will help."

She smiled, tears in her eyes. "It will be so wonderful, Tohave, to sit alone by a fire, deep in the mountains, and talk and learn . . . and make love all we want."

The fire crackled and the night darkened. The attack of

the traders seemed far in the past. Katie could forget it for now, for she was surrounded by beauty and love.

Tohave stood up to remove his weapons belt and leggings, and his loincloth. When he stood before her naked, Katie wondered if she was on fire, she was so warm. Striding to his parfleche, he took out a small leather pouch that resembled a canteen. He unscrewed the cap and came to her side, kneeling beside her.

"Remove the blanket, Hemene."

It was a gentle command, and she obeyed. He poured something into his palm from the leather pouch, then rubbed his hands together and bent over her.

"Turn onto your stomach," he said.

Her eyes widened and he saw fear in them. He frowned. "What are you afraid of?"

"What are you going to do?"

He frowned, curiously. "What do you think I will do? I am going to rub this oil onto your back, over all of you. It will relax you. An Indian man often does this to his new wife, to relax her before he takes her for the first time. After what happened to you—"

He stopped, seeing tears in her eyes, and when she sat up and hugged him, he frowned in surprise, then placed his oily hands on her back and gently rubbed. "What is it, Hemene?"

"I thought . . . you were going to do something ugly . . . like Ezra," she whimpered.

She felt him tense then, and he held her closer. "Oh, how I long to kill him!" he hissed. "Tohave would not make you do ugly things, or anything you would not want to do, Hemene," he told her softly. He kissed her hair. "Do not ever be afraid of Tohave. Come now. Lie down and pull your hair away so I do not get this oil on it."

She complied, her face red with humiliation for she'd revealed some of the ugliness of her marriage. On his part, Tohave was filled with rage. Perhaps he would come

254

for her sooner, he thought. To leave her in the hands of Ezra Russell was like tossing her to the wolves. Was her husband much different from the traders? He thought not.

"Do not cry, little one," he told her. "The Spirits are with us. We will be together."

She sniffed and pulled her hair back as she lay down on her stomach and closed her eyes. What she experienced then was the most beautiful, most provocative act of love she had ever been shown. His hands moved over her in gentle circular movements, covering every inch of her, finding every muscle, soothing, relaxing, gently loving her. He worked from her arms, over her neck and shoulders, down her back and spine, over her hips and the backs of her legs, never touching a private place rudely, moving over her calves and the bottoms of her feet in the most glorious way. Then he moved back up, urging her onto her back and beginning the process all over again, gently massaging her breasts, her stomach and thighs, yet not touching her in that special place reserved for other things.

By the time he was through, she wanted him to touch other places, wanted him to taste and enjoy her body, to make love to her. Never had she felt so relaxed and beautiful and loved. She looked at him, her eyes glazed with love and desire as she opened herself to him. How wonderful it was to want to take a man.

"Make love to me, Tohave," she whispered.

He grinned and came down to her, rubbing his chest against her. "You are slippery tonight, little white flower," he told her.

She laughed lightly. "We will move easier then."

His smile faded, and as his mouth covered hers they both suddenly felt they could never get enough of each other. This one night could not be long enough. She gasped when he entered her quickly, pushing hard, needing, wanting, filling her with his manhood and glorying in his love for her.

They moved in desperate rhythm, making up for all the time they'd had to be apart, wanting to remember their coming together in the days to come when they must be apart.

She ran her hands over the hard muscles of his arms and shoulders, breathing deeply of his sweet scent. His long, black hair brushed her shoulders and his lips devoured her, moving over her eyes, her lips, her throat, gently pulling at her breasts so that she arched up to him. The wonderful explosion inside of her came again then, the beautiful thing that only Tohave had made happen; the ecstasy that made her cry out his name, made her want to laugh and cry at the same time, made her whimper and push up toward him to take every bit of him that she could. Moments later it was his turn to experience the lovely explosion, and he groaned with pleasure as his seed poured into her.

He kissed her over and over then, tears in his own eyes. "Do not move, Hemene," he groaned. "I must have you again. Please do not tell Tohave no."

"I would never tell you no," she whispered, leaning up and kissing his chest. "Never."

His lips found hers, and she felt him growing inside her. Nothing mattered now—not the traders, not Ezra, not what the soldiers might do, nothing. There was only this night . . . and Tohave.

Morning found Katie and Tohave lying wrapped together. When they awoke, they lay motionless at first, simply enjoying the feel of their flesh touching, listening to the birds singing outside. If only this moment could last forever! His lips tasted her neck, then her ear. "Once more," he whispered, "before I must leave you."

"No, Tohave," she objected, pushing at him. "We should never have stayed here this long. You must leave quickly!"

"Not before making love to my woman once more," he argued, his lips against her neck.

"Tohave, we're taking a great risk. That man probably already made it to the fort. Soldiers might be searching for you. My husband might—"

Her words were stifled by his gentle mouth. He kissed her hard, pushing her hands out of the way and lying on top of her, deliberately lengthening the kiss until he felt her relax, felt her own desire building again. Finally his lips left hers and sought her breasts. He nuzzled the soft white mounds, kissing the sweet pink fruits that made him tremble with the want of her.

"Do not argue with your man," he told her softly. "We do not know what lies ahead for us. We will have this moment."

Her eyes teared. How could she argue now, when he touched her this way, when he reminded her that if something went wrong, this might be their last moment together? She grasped his hair and whispered his name as his lips moved over her entire body, kissing, searching, teasing, caressing. They made love quietly, and it seemed sweeter than ever before. Too soon it was over.

"We will wash and eat," he told her, moving away from her then. "I am glad I thought to bring a white woman's sweet-smelling soap for you." He poured water from his canteen into a porcelain pan and set it beside her, handing her the bar of soap she had used the night before; then he turned away and began to stir the old coals, oblivious of his nakedness. Katie wished she could be that free, but she washed quickly and bashfully. And just like the night before, he did not turn and watch her.

She was struggling against tears, wishing they never had to part again! But it was as he had said. He must go with his friends to the fort and explain—quickly. She would make Ezra go, too, and she swore that if he would not take her, she would go alone.

Tohave shoved a skewer through a thick piece of deer meat and hung it on a spit over the fire he had built up. He turned then and carried the pan of water she had used outside, saying nothing. When he returned the pan was empty and he wore a clean loincloth. Again she was amazed at how important cleanliness seemed to be to him. He smelled of some kind of sweet herb, which she suspected he had rubbed onto his skin for her, an Indian man's way of perfuming himself for his woman.

"I should be doing that," she said, as he turned the venison.

He smiled at her. "You will be, soon enough. Do not expect me always to do this after we are settled in Canada."

She smiled back, but then their smiles faded. "We will be able to go, won't we?" she asked.

His dark eyes studied her lovingly. "We will go. You will see. And Tohave will not let anyone find us." He picked up the buckskin shirt that lay near him, and handed it to her. "You can wear this, since your clothes were so torn. Take the torn ones with you. Show your husband. Tell him what happened and do not be afraid of him. Make him take you to the fort. I will tell McBain we did not bring you with us because we feared being found with a white woman. He will understand."

She took the shirt, and he drank in her nakedness once more when she stood up to put it on. When she had slipped it over her head, they both laughed. The sleeves were much too long, and it came to her knees.

"At least you are covered," he told her. "When you get home you can put on a dress."

Katie's heart tightened. She didn't want to go back. She didn't want to let Tohave out of her sight. She wondered if the escaped trader had reached the fort, wondered what he was telling the soldiers. Tohave seemed to read her thoughts. He reached out and took her hand.

"Do not be afraid, Hemene. We will be together. We belong together."

She sat down beside him and he put an arm around her. Then they both watched the meat cook then, saying nothing. What was there left to say?

Finally the meat was done, and he took it from the fire, breaking off a piece and handing it to her. "Eat. We must go soon."

She blinked back tears. "We could go right now, Tohave. We could run away right now and never come back."

He smiled sadly and kissed her eyes. "No. After this thing with the traders, the soldiers would hunt us with much hatred. It must be settled first. Tohave must not have a bad name. I will come for you, I think sooner than winter, for Tohave is tired of waiting. Your husband will make many more trips for wood, and one of those times I will come, for he is gone three, four days. That will allow us to get away before he knows you are gone. We will be almost to Canada before he and the soldiers figure out what has happened. Even then, they will not know where to look for us. My people will tell them nothing."

They kissed lightly, and he pushed the meat into her hand. "Obey your man and eat," he told her.

She tore her eyes from his and forced herself to bite off a piece, but she had no appetite. She chewed slowly, then met his eyes again. "Am I your wife, Tohave?"

He nodded. "I told you once that you were Tohave's woman now. In our gods' eyes, you are not married to that Ezra Russell. You are married to Tohave. No matter what happens now, you are my wife. That is how Tohave thinks of you."

"Tell me again that you love me."

He smiled and leaned forward, kissing her cheek. *"Nemehotatse, Hemene."*

"Nemehotatse," she replied. She smiled bashfully then. "Did I say it right?"

His eyes teared. *"Ai, Hemene.* You said it right."

"Rider coming!" a soldier called out as the lone horse thundered into the fort, the horse lathered and its rider practically falling off when he dismounted. A sergeant grabbed the man's arm and wrinkled his nose at the man's smell.

"Got to see . . . your commander," the man panted. "Quick!"

"Sure, mister. Calm down." The sergeant aided the man as he walked to McBain's office. The lieutenant colonel was immediately alarmed by the sight of the man. He remembered him from the day of the fight between Orin Slavens and Tohave.

"What's happened?" he asked quickly.

"Indians! I think Tohave and his bunch. They attacked the Russell place. They were trying to rape Mrs. Russell. Me and Orin and the others tried to stop them. But they all got killed, sir. All of them!" The man took a deep breath. "I just got the hell out of there! I don't know what happened to that poor woman, but there was nothing I could do to help her. They're gone by now, probably trying to get back to the reservation. It was awful, sir."

McBain eyed him warily. "Tohave and his men attacked the place?"

"Yes, sir. Yesterday! I rode all night to get here!"

"And where was Mr. Russell?"

"I . . . I don't know. I never saw him. I just saw Tohave rope that poor woman and drag her to the ground!"

260

McBain scowled and looked at the sergeant. "Work up two patrols. Take one to the Russell place, and have the other scour the area between there and the reservation. Try to find Tohave and that bunch he rides with. But I don't want anyone hurt, understand? I want them brought directly here until we talk to Mrs. Russell, if she's still alive."

"Yes, sir." The sergeant quickly left and McBain turned his eyes to the trader.

"You'd better be telling the truth, mister. A war could start over something like this. Tohave has been a troublemaker, but only with pranks. He's never brought harm to a settler before."

"You know how a young Indian like that looks at a pretty woman like that Mrs. Russell," the man answered. "I tell you we came upon that place and found that bunch attacking her."

"Well, we'll see, won't we? You stay around the fort until we know for certain what went on out there. You say the others in your party are dead?"

"I think so. Those redskins fought like the savages they are, cut them up something awful. I got away because I took off before I saw the last man go down."

"I see." McBain frowned disgustedly. He wondered about the woman. This man was a coward to have ridden off without trying to help her, but that was beside the point. "You can leave," he told the trader. "But only after you go over your story once more and give me your name. And by leaving, I mean you can leave this office, not the fort, understand?"

"Yes, sir. I've got no call to leave. I want to see justice done. My name is George Hammer."

"Mmm-hmm." McBain began filling out a form. "Now, let's have the details."

Hammer sat down, already plotting how he would steal a fresh army horse and sneak out after dark. He did not intend to stay around. Things might not work out the way

261

he was hoping they would. He would head south for Mexico, and let his lies wreak havoc in his absence. He had made plenty of trouble for Tohave, no matter how things turned out. The Indian would not be trusted again, and perhaps if he saw soldiers, he would put up a fight and be killed. Either way, Tohave was a doomed man. If he lived, he would be watched like a hawk by the agents and the army. Even if he was proven innocent, Tohave, an Indian, had killed white men, something settlers did not like, no matter what the cause. Tohave was a branded man.

Hammer felt like laughing. Tohave had kicked him in the groin once when he was just about to get his way with a squirming little Indian maiden. Hammer had not forgotten, and now Tohave would pay. It was just too bad Orin and the others couldn't be around to see the trouble this incident would bring upon the Indian they hated. Fact was, once Tohave and his friends had finished off Orin and the others, there would be a white woman there, alone and half-naked. Tohave and his friends would not pass up such a temptation. Surely they had raped and killed her by now, and would try to get out of it by saying the traders had done it. Let Tohave try to get out of this one!

He smiled inwardly as he enlarged on the tale he was telling McBain. Tonight he would get as far away from the fort as he could, and if the uppity Katie Russell still lived, she would have a lot of explaining to do.

Chapter Fifteen

Tohave's friends waited anxiously, the bodies of the traders wrapped in blankets bound tightly with rawhide cord slung over their own horses. Katie avoided their dark, unapproving looks as she and Tohave rode up to them. She knew Tohave's people disapproved of his involvement with her, just as her own people would disapprove of her loving an Indian. Tohave gave her a reassuring hug as he halted his mount. He got down then and lifted her down.

Katie pushed aside all thoughts of how impossible their relationship was, telling herself that, with love, anything was possible. How could she go on living if she had no hope of being with Tohave?

"I will be ready soon," Tohave told the others.

"We must go! We have already waited too long, Tohave!" Two Moons said angrily.

Tohave tensed. "I need only a moment." He urged Katie toward the house then. "Take off the shirt and put on your own dress," he told her quietly. "If your husband finds the shirt he will wonder why you needed it if you were right here all the time."

Katie hurried to her trunk and took out fresh underwear and another dress. She blushed as she removed the shirt, and Tohave's blood rushed with renewed desire. How he hated to leave her! Katie quickly pulled on her underthings, then slipped the dress over her head.

"I'm afraid for you, Tohave."

"It will be all right. We must tell the soldiers the truth. Come to the fort as soon as your husband comes. I will leave one man behind to watch from afar until soldiers come or your husband returns, just in case that trader who got away tries to come back."

She frowned. "Why would he do that?"

"He probably thinks we would stay behind and violate you, then kill you, just because we are Indians. Then he can blame us for the whole thing. With you dead it would be his word against ours—an Indian's word. Who do you think would win?"

She grasped his vest. "Tohave, be careful!"

He smiled for her. "Do not worry about Tohave. I will leave Running Deer, but you will not see him. As soon as your husband comes, he will leave. I would stay myself, but it is best I go to the fort. It would look bad if Tohave was the one to stay behind, since McBain knows I have feelings for you."

Their eyes held. Feelings. Yes, such feelings! He kissed her gently. "Soon, Hemene. Be brave and strong for Tohave. Come to the fort, and when you do, do not look at Tohave with eyes so full of love."

A tear slipped down her cheek. "That won't be easy."

He kissed the tear. "Nor will it be easy for Tohave. I go now. My love will be with you always."

"And mine with you."

They kissed once more, a sweet kiss of farewell, before he pulled away. It was hard to leave her, hard for her to let him go! He turned then and without another word hurried out and mounted up. When she ran to the doorway, their eyes met once more. Then, like the wind, he was gone.

"This is bad, Tohave," Two Moons told his good friend. "That trader will not speak the truth."

"Katie Russell will tell them the truth," Tohave replied.

"Then we should have brought her along. You know how quick the soldiers are to accuse."

"If white people saw us riding with her and leading white men's horses with dead riders, they would not ask questions before shooting at us, and she could not ride into the fort with Indians. A white woman alone with a bunch of young Indians, that would look bad to those white men. You know how such men think. They think bad things."

"Then what will they think of her when she runs away with you?"

Tohave looked over at his friend as their horses trotted side by side. "Keep your voice low!" he hissed. "What makes you think that?"

"I see it in your eyes. I know you better than you think, Tohave."

Tohave looked ahead again. "Should that happen, I trust you as my friend to keep still."

"You know I would. But I would miss you greatly, Tohave, so would many others. And I think you would miss our homeland more than you know."

"It is the only way I can be with her."

"She is white! She cannot long live your way, Tohave!"

"One can do many things for love. We will both be making sacrifices. I lead my own life, Two Moons."

The younger man sighed and blinked. "We all look to you, Tohave."

Tohave glanced at him, then looked forward again. "I

would miss you, too, Two Moons. Someday I will find a way to return. It will all work. You will see. The Spirits have willed it."

"And what if you are wrong about the meaning of your visions?"

"I am not wrong. Speak no more about it."

"You should stay, Tohave. Maybe something else will happen that will give us back our power; then you can just take her freely."

Tohave frowned. "What are you talking about?"

"That new faith, the one everyone whispers about. Even now the prophet Wovoka, the Paiute, tells his people of this religion. It is called the Ghost Dance religion, and they say that if one believes, someday all white men will be buried and the land will be covered with sweet grass and trees. The buffalo will return in great herds, the wild horses will come back, and our dead ancestors will return."

Tohave shook his head. "The Fish Eaters beyond the Shining Mountains are telling tall tales."

"I do not think so. It is rumored that when the snows of winter have melted Sitting Bull might send someone into Paiute country to learn about this new religion. You should stay, Tohave. Perhaps better days are coming."

Tohave scowled. "I have given up wishing for better days. They will not come. I have already seen days of glory, Two Moons, and I have seen our people cut down. I saw them flee to Canada, and I fled with them. Many died there, and those who were left struggled back, their pride and power gone. Red Cloud, our great chief who led us to so many victories, now sits at Pine Ridge, his pride and power broken also. The buffalo are gone. The whites watch our every movement. I do not see how a new religion will change anything."

"Think what you wish. I want to know more about it."

"I will not be here to do so. I am going to find my own

peace and happiness. I am going to a place where I can live as I wish."

"It might not be that easy, Tohave. You will be hunted."

"Perhaps. But I will never be found."

"It will be hard for the white woman."

"I will protect her and provide for her. I will not let anything happen to her. We will find a way."

Two Moons sighed. "You must love her very much then."

Tohave smiled. "Finally you understand, my friend. I wondered if you ever would."

Two Moons smiled sadly. "Then I will pray for you, Tohave, even though I think it is wrong."

"Tohave thanks you." He drew up his horse then, squinting his eyes and staring out at the horizon. "Look out there, Two Moons. I think it is soldiers."

Two Moons shaded his eyes, and the others drew up to a halt.

"Do you think they come for us, Tohave?" one of them asked.

There was a long moment of silence before Tohave spoke. "I think that trader went to the fort just as we feared. He has told them something that is making them seek us out. I do not trust any of the whites except McBain."

"I knew we should have left last night. Now they are already out searching for us."

"McBain would tell them not to shoot at us until he knows what happened," Tohave reassured him. "We should ride out to them."

"I am afraid, Tohave. You know the soldiers, how they are," Short Arrow put in.

"If we were guilty, why would we ride to the fort and bring the bodies with us?" Tohave replied. "It is our best proof."

"Were the Cheyenne guilty at Sand Creek or at the Washita?" Two Moons shot back. "Were the Nez Perce guilty at the Bear Paw Mountains? And what about our Cheyenne brothers at Fort Robinson, the very fort to which we are going! What about the winter they were imprisoned there when they were only trying to get to their homeland? They meant no one harm. Many times the soldiers have slaughtered us when we were peacefully camped. If they can crush our babies' heads and murder our women, what will they do to young men who they think tried to rape a white woman? I am certain that is what the trader has told them."

Tohave hesitated. If only he could be sure McBain was with the soldiers ahead of them. He saw the uniformed men turn and ride toward him and his men.

"They come," he said quietly. "We will wait here for them. Make no sudden moves. We will let them take us to the fort if we must. The white woman and her husband will come and tell the truth."

"Perhaps her husband will not let her come. He is a stupid and cruel man."

Tohave's eyes softened. "If he does not let her come, she will come alone," he replied. "I know her heart. She will not betray us."

"Perhaps not, but I trust no whites. And the soldiers have not talked to her yet, only to the trader. They will want blood," Short Arrow declared.

"Do not panic. We must get to McBain," Tohave assured him.

They quieted then and sat their mounts, watching, waiting, but as the soldiers came closer, Short Arrow grew restless. "They are riding harder now that they have seen us," he said. "We are nearly a full day away from the white woman's house. If we ride hard, we can get to the fort and to McBain."

"No!" Tohave ordered. "If we bolt now, they will

think we are running away, that we are guilty. It is the worst thing we could do."

"No Indian tells another what to do in battle," Short Arrow retorted. "It is each man for himself. I say we ride hard for the fort and outrun the soldiers. Our swift horses can do it. They are burdened down with their gear and heavy clothing. An Indian can always outrun a soldier."

"And the soldiers have rifles," Tohave warned. "They do not need to be close to shoot you off your horse."

"We can use our riding tricks. Leave the dead traders here for them to find and bring in. When they get to the fort, we will be safe with McBain."

"I think it is a good idea," another stated. "I choose to ride for the fort with Short Arrow."

"I tell you we should wait and go in peacefully!" Tohave's dark eyes were fiery and threatening. "Do not run, Short Arrow!"

The soldiers were riding harder now, leaving a cloud of dust behind them. The clinking of their gear and sabers evoked ugly memories in some of the Indians.

"There will be no more Little Big Horns, Tohave," Short Arrow told him. "The soldiers look for any excuse to slaughter us. I am not waiting here to find out what it will be this time."

He turned his horse. "No!" Tohave shouted. But the man galloped off, heading away from the soldiers, intending to circle back around them. A second man followed. Two Moons' horse reared and he turned it. "I go, too, Tohave."

"Wait with me, Two Moons. Do not do this."

They both watched some of the soldiers break away to chase the two fleeing Indians.

"*Katum!*" Tohave swore. "They think we are running!"

A shot rang out then, and that was all Two Moons and

the one other man remaining with Tohave needed. They sped away, leaving behind the traders' horses and bodies. The four fleeing Indians scattered and soldiers followed hard behind them.

"Get the red bastards!" Tohave could hear someone shout.

Another shot rang out and Tohave saw Two Moons fall. His eyes widened in anger and despair. "No!" he growled. He rode hard toward his good friend. Somehow he must help him. If not, he would count coup on the soldier who had shot him. All reason left him. His pride and spirit were hot. They had come in peace, and this was what they received. They had already been judged. Why had he thought this time would be any different?

As he rode hard, toward Two Moons' body, not caring that bullets whizzed around him, his heart cried out for Katie. What would happen now? Could he keep his promise and take her away? Two Moons lay on the ground, blood pouring from his side. As Tohave reached down for his friend, it hit him, the searing pain in his upper back.

Everything spun around him, and he felt himself hit the ground. His last thought was of Katie. He could see her face, feel her body in his arms. Then even that vision faded.

Moments later he heard voices, far, far in the distance, seemingly coming through a tunnel.

"They were bringing in the traders' bodies. We shouldn't have shot at them."

"How were we to know? They ran!"

"McBain will be pissed about this. What a mess! We might have started a goddamned war."

"You heard what they did! They attacked that Russell woman."

"Then why were they coming toward us with the bodies of those traders?"

270

"Who knows? Did the others get away?"

"All but these two. That one is Tohave, I think. The dumb bastard rode right toward us. I don't understand it."

"He was riding to help the other one. Are they dead?"

There was a moment of silence. "This one is. I think Tohave is still alive, but he won't last long. Look where that bullet hit."

"Jesus Christ, why did it have to be Tohave?"

"Just our luck. Let's wrap them up and get them to the fort. We'll lose our stripes for this one. McBain said no shooting."

"Well they shouldn't have run! Guilty men don't run!"

"Maybe not, but scared Indians do. Some of them have pretty bad memories of bluecoats. You gotta admit they aren't usually treated very fair."

"As fair as they deserve. Come on. Let's get these two to the fort. The other patrol should be on its way to the Russell place. They'll bring the woman back to the fort, if she's still alive. I hope we can straighten this out without any Indian trouble."

Katie could not sleep. She knew something was wrong. Just what, she was not certain, except that it involved Tohave. Never had her instincts been stronger.

The night was long and lonely, and too quiet. She thought about her night with Tohave, their tender parting. Now he was in danger. Perhaps he'd been arrested, or had something terrible happened to him? For the first time since her marriage she actually wanted Ezra to come home. She had to get to the fort, and quickly. She didn't care what Ezra thought about it. She would not let him stop her.

Tohave. Her only comfort had been the memory of

lying in his arms, being one with him. Her only hope had lain in his promise to take her away. If only the traders hadn't come! Those ugly men had spoiled things for two people who only wanted to be together. Why were there men like Ezra? Bad people always seemed to triumph, good people always lost. Tohave was good. Would he lose? If he did, then so would she, and there would be nothing left to live for.

She sat up most of the night cutting corn from cobs. She had to keep herself occupied somehow. Tohave had been gone a day and a night. Surely it was settled now. The soldiers would probably come soon to check on her, and everything would be fine once she told them what had happened.

Somehow night finally stretched into dawn. As a fiery pink sunrise met Katie's tired eyes she walked outside to feed the animals. She surveyed the horizon but saw no one, yet she knew Tohave's friend watched somewhere as Tohave had promised. But why did she feel this anxiety about Tohave? What was wrong?

It was midmorning when Ezra finally arrived with the load of wood, three days and two nights since the traders' attack. Katie ran out to him and he frowned at her when she grabbed his arm.

"Ezra, we have to go to the fort! Those traders who sold us the Indian horses came, and attacked me! They would have raped and killed me if Tohave and his men hadn't come! They killed the traders and—"

"Slow down, woman!" He took off his hat and ran a hand through his hair. "What the hell are you talking about?"

She took a deep breath. "The day after you left. Those horrible traders came through here. I told you I didn't trust them." Her eyes filled with tears. "I ran for my rifle but they shot at me and kept me from getting to it. Then one of them threw a rope around me and pulled me to the

272

ground. He hit me and tore at my clothes. They talked about the ugly things they were going to do with me, but then Tohave and his men came and attacked them and killed them—all but one. One got away and God only knows what he told the soldiers. Tohave and the others took the bodies and went to the fort to explain to McBain, but they'll need me there to back them up. We must go right away, Ezra. They might be in trouble. I'm sure the one who got away lied about it."

Ezra sighed and looked her over. He grasped her chin and turned her head, studying the bruise on her face. He let go and looked her over again. "You got other wounds?"

"My right arm is covered with scratches, and my . . . my left hip. I have my torn clothes, too. Ezra, it was horrible. They rode in so fast, shooting at me, shouting filthy things. They roped me so I couldn't move my arms. The one left should be punished. And Tohave's doing a brave thing, riding into the fort with those bodies. He saved my life. We have to make sure the soldiers know the truth."

Ezra scratched at his beard and looked around. "You get that corn picked and shucked?"

Katie stared at him in disbelief. Didn't he even care? "Yes."

He nodded. "We have wood to unload before we can do anything."

"We could take the horse. It would carry both of us."

"I'm not going to save some damned Indian's neck before my own work is done!" He looked her over scathingly. "You sure it wasn't just Tohave who was here? Did that redskin rape you and did you decide you liked it?"

Her eyes widened in indignation, and suddenly she was not afraid of him anymore. Tohave had given her courage. "If you are as concerned about me as a husband

273

should be, you will report those men and you won't leave me alone again, Ezra Russell! And if you don't care about me, then why should it matter to you if I live or die, or if another man touches me! I'm living in hell, trying to be a good wife, carrying your child in my belly. I'm too tired and beaten to care anymore what you think about me or what you believe. Go ahead and beat me if you want. Beat me until I'm dead! I'd be better off! But I'm going to that fort, with or without you! I didn't want to have to go alone, but I will. And if you care one jot for your wife, you'll come with me!"

As she started past him, he grabbed her arm. "If Tohave went to the fort with those traders' bodies, the soldiers will come out here. They'll want to check on you, see if you're alive or dead, find out what the hell happened. You don't need to go to the fort."

She jerked her arm away. "If they don't come by tonight, promise me we can go first thing in the morning. Promise me, Ezra!"

There was a new strength to her, a new determination that surprised him. "All right. We'll go in the morning." He walked to the mules to unhitch them. "It's a damned good thing you weren't stupid enough to go to the fort with Tohave."

She just turned away. "I'll start stacking the other wood. I'm sorry the traders interrupted my work." She looked back at him. "I suppose if I'd got all the chores done, you wouldn't have cared what else happened to me."

He just scowled. "The traders are dead now, according to what you say. So there's nothing left to worry about but Tohave. After this, we won't have to worry about him either. Maybe he saved you from those men, but he was skulking around here again and he wasn't supposed to be. This time I'll make sure the soldiers make him stay on the reservation. For all you know he had the same thing in mind for you as the traders, only he caught them at it first and decided to make himself look good. You'd better quit thinking you can trust that redskinned bastard, Katie Russell. He's been a problem from the start, and I'm going to put a stop to it."

Katie checked an urge to defend Tohave. She realized she had to be careful or her love for him would show, but she was sick inside with worry over him.

The afternoon seemed to last forever. As Katie stacked wood her heart was torn with worry over Tohave. In the early evening, when soldiers finally appeared on the horizon, Katie's heart quickened. She brushed off her dress and smoothed back her hair though she was tired and half-sick from stacking wood all afternoon, worry over Tohave, and the after effects of her encounter with the trappers.

"Ezra, soldiers are coming," she called out to him. He turned from chopping wood and walked up beside her.

"Don't be defending that Tohave too strong. You already did once, you know. You'll look bad to those men if you do it again."

"He saved my life twice. Apparently that doesn't matter to you."

He scowled and looked down at her. "You're looking to add another bruise to that face, woman?"

"I don't care."

He stared at her, surprised again by her boldness. The soldiers rode in then, led by Lieutenant Rogers, who motioned for the others to halt. Dismounting, he removed his hat and walked up to Katie and Ezra, looking at her as though he'd expected to find her half-dead.

"Mrs. Russell." His eyes swung to Ezra. "Mr. Russell."

"We know why you're here," Ezra told him. "It's about Tohave."

Rogers sighed. "A trader came to the fort a couple of

days ago carrying on about Tohave attacking this place, and his men tried to stop Tohave and his friends and they got killed, except the one who rode to the fort." His eyes sought Katie's. "That true?"

"No," she replied boldly. "It was the other way around. The traders came here. They shot at me so that I couldn't even get to my rifle. They threw a rope around me and intended to—" She reddened then and looked down. "One hit me so hard I was senseless for a moment. They . . . tore at my clothes and . . . said things . . . what they would do. One of them intended to kill me and let Tohave take the blame. The next thing I knew the man who was dragging me toward the house fell, an arrow in his back; and in an instant Tohave and his men were attacking the others. One got away."

"Did you witness Tohave killing any of them?"

She hesitated. "The biggest one. Someone called him Orin, I think." She did not want anyone to know she'd already seen the man at the fort and had heard his name there on the day Tohave had fought with him. She met the lieutenant's eyes. "He shouldn't be blamed for it, Lieutenant. The Indians were only helping me. They did me no harm whatsoever, and they even camped here that night in case the one who got away decided to come back."

The lieutenant noted the plea in her eyes, and he glanced at Ezra. "Where were you, sir?"

"I was up at the river cutting wood. I just found out about all this this morning."

"You can see where they hit me," Katie told Rogers, turning her face. "And I have . . . scratches and bruises elsewhere . . . and my torn clothes. Tohave left with his men to take the bodies of the traders to the fort and to report what happened so that his name will be cleared. I was going to go to the fort if you didn't show up by tomorrow morning."

276

"Well, I have no idea whether Tohave showed up yet. McBain sent out two patrols. Mine was to come here. The other was to roam around and see if they run across Tohave."

"They won't hurt him, will they?" she asked anxiously. "They'll wait to hear his side of the story."

"McBain's orders were to bring him in alive and to get your story. But Tohave and his men were out here when they weren't supposed to be, and they killed white men."

"But they did it in my defense!" Katie answered, alarm in her voice.

"I know that, ma'am, but people can twist that all kinds of ways. I'm only saying that Tohave has our protection, nonetheless it won't be easy to keep people from getting riled. If we're real lucky, this will just blow over for winter's almost upon us, and nothing will come of it. We'll warn Tohave to stay where he belongs."

"If he had been where he belongs, I might be dead," Katie answered, tears in her eyes. "He has saved my life twice. It isn't right that he should be blamed for anything." She struggled to maintain control. She must not let her feelings show too much.

"I understand that, ma'am. But Tohave and his men didn't have to kill all those men. They could have brought them in alive, or at least a couple of them."

"In that kind of situation a man can't always stop at just wounding. Surely you know that, Lieutenant. You've probably been in battles."

"In a case like yours, we would have surrounded the traders and brought them in. This is an example of how hot-blooded an Indian can be, quick to kill, Mrs. Russell. There are some things about the Indians you don't understand. You haven't worked with them like we have."

She dropped her eyes. "I suppose so," she replied, feeling sick. What would happen to Tohave? Everything that had occurred in the last few days suddenly overwhelmed her, and she covered her face and wept. No one knew she was weeping for Tohave, for fear that their plans were ruined.

"Look, she told you how it happened," Ezra put in. "There's nothing else to tell. How you men handle Tohave is your business. Just make sure he stays away from here after this. For all we know he had plans for my wife himself and the traders just beat him to it. Maybe he just used them to make himself look good."

"That isn't true!" Katie spoke up despite her tears. She wiped at her eyes and looked at the lieutenant. "It isn't true. Tell Lieutenant–Colonel McBain that he was only helping. That trader who got away was lying."

Rogers sighed and looked at Ezra. "You want to file any kind of a report?"

Ezra glanced at Katie and then turned back to Rogers. "I suppose not. It's up to McBain what's done now. The traders are dead, so there's nothing left to report, except the one that got away ought to be punished. Fact is, the reason those traders came here is because they'd already seen my wife once. I bought those Indian horses from them, only I didn't know at the time they were Indian horses, or that they were stolen."

"Tohave has complained about them before, making trouble on the reservation. If they're the ones who sold the stolen horses, we can press charges against the remaining man for that, too. Maybe that will satisfy the Indians." He put his hat back on and looked over at Katie. "I'm very sorry, ma'am, for having to upset you this way. I know it's hard for you to talk about, and I understand why you sympathize with Tohave and his men. We'll let you know what happens."

Katie just nodded. The lieutenant glanced at Ezra once again. "Good-bye, Mr. Russell. We'll be in touch. We'll make a wide sweep through the area on the way back, see if we can find Tohave. If he's being honest about all this, he's probably at the fort right now. But Indians do have a way of turning tail because they think they won't get the proper justice."

He turned to mount his horse, thinking how foolish Ezra Russell was to leave his wife alone in the first place. Theirs was obviously an unhappy marriage, and he felt sorry for Katie Russell. But there was nothing he could do for her. He glanced at the weeping Katie once more, then nodded to Ezra and turned his men. As the soldiers rode off, Katie wondered that would happen to Tohave.

Chapter Sixteen

The days crawled by. Katie dried corn and canned some. Then she and Ezra buried vegetables in the good dugout, and she was glad she had buried the lance toward the back where it would not be discovered. The waiting was hell. She continually wondered why someone didn't come, what had happened to Tohave. She deliberately stayed up late at night working on canning and washing and mending, desperately trying to avoid having to go to bed with Ezra, but he had made no advances and he looked at her strangely. Did he know? Or did he think she'd been raped by the traders? She didn't care what he thought if it kept him away from her. She could no longer figure out Ezra Russell, when he would behave in a relatively normal way and when he would turn into a beast. But he had stayed away from the whiskey, as she had prayed he would.

That prayer was being answered, but what about her prayers for Tohave? She could not get over her feeling that something was wrong, that all had not gone as they'd planned, and it was even more of a reality to her that the Indian did not get justice. If white men had saved her, they would not be punished for killing her attackers. Instead, they would be praised, like heroes. But Indians had done the killing.

Ezra stayed six days and then was gone again. In spite of what had happened to her, he made no effort to urge her to go with him. There were chores to be done. But she didn't really care now. She wanted to stay, in case someone came with word of Tohave. Perhaps Tohave himself would come!

Alone, she didn't go anyplace this time without her rifle at her side—she would not be caught off guard again—and this time she was fearful at night. She couldn't be sure that Tohave watched over her, and she felt truly alone. If nothing was wrong, he would have come by now, but he hadn't and his absence made her terror greater.

Tohave! She ached for him. She loved him. What was wrong? Why didn't he come? Most of the crops were in now, and soon winter would be upon them. Where was he?

On the third day of Ezra's absence she saw the soldiers, only five or six, approaching. She hurried inside the house and removed her apron, pushing back a piece of hair that had fallen out of the tight bun she'd pinned it into. Soldiers! Why soldiers instead of Tohave? What did this mean?

She walked back outside, shading her eyes and holding her rifle, just in case it was some kind of trick, but moments later she recognized McBain. He looked even grayer, and his face was lined by the sun and worry.

"Mr. McBain," she called out, waving.

He motioned for his men to halt and rode forward alone, nodding to Katie and dismounting.

"I wondered if anyone would ever come!" Katie gave him a relieved smile. "How is Tohave? Did he get to the fort?"

McBain sighed and nodded toward her door. "Can we go inside, ma'am?"

Her heartbeat quickened. Something was wrong! No! She paled slightly and turned away, leading him into the humble hut made of dirt. Her legs moved, but she could barely feel them so she sat down on the edge of the bed while McBain removed his hat and came closer.

"Have a seat, Mr. McBain," she told him in a weak voice. "We have nothing but humble crates for now, but they do. Would you like some coffee?"

"No thank you, ma'am." He sighed and held her eyes.

"What is it?" she asked quietly. "What has happened to Tohave?"

He swallowed. "I'm afraid he was shot, Mrs. Russell. It was all a misunderstanding."

"Shot!" Her eyes widened and she paled alarmingly. "How? When? Is he badly hurt?"

McBain sighed deeply. "I'm afraid he is, ma'am. Very badly. It's doubtful he'll live. His people came and took him from the fort. They wanted to take him 'home' as they put it, and they felt they could take as good care of him as anyone. Actually, there wasn't much our own doctor could do anyway."

She could not stop the groan that came from her throat. "No, it can't be!" she said, her voice only a whimper. "How? How did it happen?"

McBain watched her closely. He was now more convinced than ever that there had been something between Tohave and Katie Russell. "Tohave and the others were bringing the traders' bodies to us. One of our patrols spotted them and rode toward them. Apparently a couple of Tohave's men panicked then, probably figured they'd get no justice from the soldiers, or maybe that they'd be shot down. It's happened before. At any rate, they bolted, and to my men that meant they were guilty and were running. My men started shooting. Then more Indians bolted. One was shot down, and Tohave rode toward him, apparently to pick him up and ride away with him. But Tohave was shot, too. The man he was intending to rescue died. It was his friend, Two Moons. Did you know him?"

"My God!" she whispered. "Yes." She met his eyes with her own tear-filled ones. "Tohave?"

"He was shot in the back, near the spine. He never spoke again, never moved. He's paralyzed, as far as we could tell, since he couldn't talk. Our doctor says it's only a matter of time before he dies. He could be dead by now. The trader who started it all disappeared from the fort during the night and hasn't been found. He's probably hundreds of miles from here by now, having a good laugh over all of this."

She broke into bitter sobbing. Tohave! Her beautiful Tohave! It couldn't be! How could life be this cruel? Her sweet, loving wonderful Tohave! This was all her fault! She should have insisted he go back that very same night. Perhaps then he wouldn't have run into the soldiers. But he'd been so determined to have one night with her, and now their hours together might be her last memory of the only man she had ever loved.

McBain sat and watched awkwardly as she wept tears no one would shed for a mere friend. What had happened between them, and who could blame her for it when she had to live with Ezra Russell.

"Where is your husband?" he asked gently.

"Cutting . . . wood . . . up the river," she sobbed. "Oh, God! Oh, God! Tohave! My poor Tohave!" She suddenly met his eyes, her face wet with tears. "I have to go to him! Take me to him, Mr. McBain! I should be with him."

McBain frowned and shook his head. "I'm sorry, ma'am, but I can't do that. It would be very dangerous for you and for the soldiers who took you. The Sioux are in an ornery mood over this. They're calling it another unnecessary attack, which it was. My men panicked just

284

like Tohave's men did, and the result was disaster, as it always is. Tohave's other men got away, and Tohave could have, too, if he hadn't ridden after his friend. So far there has been no retaliation on the part of the Indians and I intend to keep it that way. To bring a white woman into their camp, especially the one they think made all this trouble, would create havoc, and you'd be right in the middle of it."

"They . . . blame me?"

"Some do. I've done some scouting around. They think you were bad luck for Tohave." He leaned forward, resting his elbows on his knees. "And think of your husband, ma'am. What would he think of your going there to see Tohave? He'd suspect something that might anger him into hurting you."

She held McBain's gaze with her tear-filled eyes. "You know?"

He smiled sadly. "Anyone can see it in your eyes, ma'am." He looked at her steadily. "Give it up, Mrs. Russell. It's impossible, and Tohave is most likely dead now. It wouldn't do any good for you to go there. It would only make things worse, between the Indians and the settlers and between you and your own husband. Surely you know that."

She wept harder. "I can't let him die alone!"

The man reached out and put a hand on her shoulder. "He won't die alone. He'll know why you couldn't come. I simply can't take you there, ma'am, and I don't think Tohave would want you to come anyway. He wouldn't want you to risk your life or to start a war over this. And most of all, knowing Tohave, I don't think he'd want you to see him the way he is now, limp and helpless. He'd want you to remember him as he was, proud and strong. Surely you understand that."

She put her head in her lap and wept harder. What would she do now? What hope was there for the future, for any kind of happiness? Tohave! It couldn't be true!

"You don't . . . know all of it," she sobbed. "Tohave . . . was my only . . . hope!" She couldn't help letting it out, even though she was talking to a stranger. What he thought of her didn't matter. Nothing mattered now.

McBain patted her head. To him she was a mere child, and he didn't doubt Tohave had been the first man she'd really loved. "It could never have been, Mrs. Russell. Surely you know that. It simply could not have been. I don't know what went on between you, or what you had planned, but it couldn't have worked, whatever it was."

He couldn't help feeling sorry for her. Apparently Katie Russell really cared for Tohave, and McBain knew the kind of husband she had.

"When will your husband be back, ma'am?"

"Tomorrow . . . I think," she sobbed. "Please stay. Please camp here . . . for the night. I don't think I could . . . bear staying here alone. I . . . I have to keep busy. Let me cook a meal for your men."

He set his hat on the table. "Well, I suppose I could manage that. Is there anything we can do for you?"

She wiped at her eyes. She couldn't think of anything that mattered now. The baby. There was the baby. "The . . . wood," she said brokenly. "There's more wood to be stacked."

He nodded. "All right." He stood up then. "You stay in here and rest awhile, and we'll stack the wood. I'll tell the men you don't feel well and I have decided to stay here for the night to make sure you'll be all right, seeing as how you're carrying and all. Your husband mentioned it the last time you were at the fort."

She blew her nose and wiped her eyes. She must be strong. Tohave would want her to be strong. "What will happen to Tohave, if he lives?"

McBain shook his head. "Nothing will happen to him. There was wrong done on both sides. A few citizens might say Tohave should be hung, but I know that's not true. And some of the Indians are worked up, especially Tohave's friends, but they know it's useless to start something now.

"Will you tell me if . . . if he dies?"

McBain nodded. "I'll tell you."

"Can you go to him? Would it be safe to tell him you've seen me, and that I . . . that I love him and I'll wait for him?"

McBain shook his head. "It's hopeless, ma'am."

"I don't care!" she answered, wanting to scream it. "Please promise me you'll try to talk to him, that you'll tell him—explain why I can't be there. Please, Mr. McBain!"

The man rubbed at his eyes. "All right. If it will comfort you, I'll go and tell him."

She nodded. "Thank you. Thank you for understanding . . . and for not telling anyone else. You knew that day at the fort, when Tohave got in the fight with the traders. You knew then, didn't you?"

He sighed deeply. "I only had to look at Tohave's eyes, just as I am looking in your eyes now. What about your husband? Does he know?"

She looked at her lap. "I don't think so. My husband has no conception of love, Mr. McBain. I am a mate, someone to bear him children and do his work and look pretty on his arm. That's all. And after a few years out here, I won't have any looks left. At any rate, I don't care anymore what he thinks. I'll not tell him, but he can assume whatever he likes." She ran a hand through her hair. "Nothing matters." She met his eyes proudly. "I've known love, the most beautiful kind of love. Nothing and no one can take that away from me, and damn anyone who looks down on me for loving an Indian! If Tohave and I were free to be together, I would go to him in a moment and not be the least bit ashamed."

McBain rose and patted her head. "You rest. I'll get the men to work on the wood. There are only five of us, but if a meal is too much work, we have our own grub."

"No. I'd like to cook. It would help me. And I feel I owe you for coming out here and telling me what is happening, and for understanding about me and Tohave."

McBain headed for the doorway. "I've seen a lot of things in this land, ma'am—a lot of heartache, a lot of death. Too many people come out here with no idea of what to expect, and they learn some hard lessons. I'm sorry it had to happen to you."

Her eyes hardened. "I've been learning hard lessons all my life, Mr. McBain. I don't know why I thought that could change. Tohave gave me hope."

McBain left, and she curled up on the bed. Tohave! Her beautiful sweet, gentle Tohave! Never in her whole life would she know that kind of love again. She could not bear the thought of never seeing him, never feeling his touch, never looking into his teasing, dark eyes, never being held by him. But she must be strong, stronger than she had ever had to be in her young life.

When the soldiers left, Katie walked out onto the prairie and watched them until they were out of sight. She was alone, more alone than she had ever been. It seemed strange that before she'd met Tohave, her loneliness had not been so intense, so terribly painful. Then she really hadn't known what she'd missed in life. Now she did, and it hurt.

She stood there, a small dot on a vast land, the land Tohave loved. She turned slowly under the brassy autumn sky, drinking in the entire horizon. The crickets sang and the grass waved in the gentle wind, but it was hard now to hear the music or see the grass dancing. Yet

Tohave had taught her to do so. She must remember how. She'd hated this land when she'd first come here! She wanted to hate it now, but oddly enough she could not. This was Tohave's land. He loved this vast, endless prairie that had once signified the freedom of his people. All of it had once been their domain. Perhaps it was better for a man like Tohave to die, rather than live only to see more and more of his freedom die away. He'd lost so much.

She breathed deeply for courage. Tohave had given her something she would never forget—courage, beauty, love, joy. He had made her laugh; he had made her heart sing with the music of the prairie.

No. She would not let this land defeat her. She would stay here because here she was near Tohave. And if Tohave lived, he would come for her—someday. She might have to wait all winter, live buried under the earth with Ezra Russell, but she would do whatever she had to, wait forever if necessary. Now she could only pray he would live. She must cling to the hope that someday he would come riding out of the horizon on his grand black Appaloosa and sweep her up in his arms and carry her away. If she did not harbor that thought, she would not stay sane.

And if he died . . . part of her would die with him. But she would remember his smile, his touch, the joy he had brought to her dreary life. He would live forever in her heart. Men like Tohave never really died. They lived in the wind, in the singing crickets, the flying birds, the swaying grass, and the rippling waters. They lived in the land. They were the land. She would cling to her memories of Tohave, draw strength from them, and hope that one day she would be in his arms again.

Ezra returned with the wood. To his surprise, all the

other wood was neatly stacked next to the dugout. He walked inside to find Katie sitting on the bed, knitting a blanket for the baby.

"You're in the right spot," he told her. "This is my last load of wood, and I feel like celebrating. You over that mess with the traders?"

She just looked at him as he reached for a bottle of whiskey.

"I'll never really be over it," she said quietly, realizing he had no understanding of the horror of their attack, or of the kind of beauty she'd shared later with Tohave. If only Tohave would come riding to her rescue at this moment . . . But she must be strong, for Tohave.

"You sure those bastards didn't touch you? Maybe you decided to find out what it was like to be with somebody besides Ezra Russell."

She set down her knitting. "If I'd wanted to know that, I'd have chosen someone who wouldn't beat me first," she told him coldly. "How can you think I enjoy giving myself to any man who leaves bruises and cuts on me and forces me?"

He stared at her, slowly setting down the whiskey bottle. "You saying you don't enjoy being with me?"

She smiled bitterly. "What do you think?"

He watched her carefully. She was different. Something had changed.

"I think you're getting a little uppity, little girl."

"Maybe I am." She sat up straighter. "Those men didn't touch me, Ezra, and neither will you, not for a long time."

His eyes darkened. "What are you talking about? You're my wife."

As she pulled out a handgun from under the blanket, pointed it at him, his eyes widened and his hand tightened around the bottle.

"Yes. I am your wife, and you will treat me like a wife,

not like an animal or a whore. If you beat me again, I'll kill you, Ezra. And when you drink, I'll leave. I don't care if I have to spend all night alone on the prairie. I am carrying your child, the one you wanted so badly, so leave me alone until it is born. I've taken all I can. I'm surprised I still carry this child, but now he or she is all I have to live for and I'm going to have my baby. You're not going to do something to make me lose it. I have nothing else to lose, Ezra. If you choose to beat me when you catch me off guard, then you will either have to beat me to death, or I'll kill you the next chance I get. I have only this baby, and I intend to protect it."

He just stared at her and then blinked. This was not the submissive, frightened, whimpering child he had married. This was a woman, and she meant every word she said.

"You wouldn't shoot me," he said cautiously.

"Wouldn't I? Try me, Ezra. Mr. McBain was here earlier. I told him that you beat me, that I'm afraid of you. He's going to come out here every once in a while to see how we're doing. If I'm ever found dead, you could be in a lot of trouble." It was a lie, but she could see it was working. "But if I shoot you, I probably won't even be blamed. I would just be defending myself against a brutal husband. I'll be a proper wife to you, Ezra, but you're going to treat me the way a proper wife deserves to be treated."

She had to be strong until she knew about Tohave. She had to stay here and wait. But she could not bear to put up with Ezra Russell's abuse while she waited. If Tohave died, she would be alone again. Nonetheless she must survive until spring, until the baby.

Ezra moved back. "What was McBain doing here?"

"He came to tell us about Tohave." She struggled not to break down. "He was shot. A couple of Tohave's men ran and the soldiers started chasing them. They must

291

have panicked. Tohave and one of his friends were shot. The friend is dead, and McBain says Tohave will probably die, too. He was shot in the back. He's paralyzed. His people took him back to the reservation."

Ezra looked relieved. "Well, at least we're rid of him."

She cocked the gun. How she wanted to fire it! "Tohave was a good man. He saved my life twice, but that's all you have to say about him? Go to hell, Ezra Russell!"

He frowned in disbelief, staring at the gun. Then he picked up the whiskey bottle and walked out without saying another word.

Chapter Seventeen

Stiff Leg and Old Smoke sat in the council of Oglala Sioux at Pine Ridge. All the best warriors were there, all looking to Red Cloud for answers.

"I say we kill every Bluecoat we see!" Short Arrow said angrily. "I was there. I saw them shoot down Two Moons and Tohave. And now Tohave, once a strong and free man, lies weak and dying, imprisoned in a body that will not move or even speak!"

"You should have waited for the soldiers," Stiff Leg declared. "You should not have run."

"And how many times have our people approached soldiers carrying white flags, only to be shot down!" Short Arrow retorted. "Too many to count. That trader had already told them lies about us. They were looking for blood; we could tell. They were not going to let us explain. I wanted to get to the reservation, to let them come here for me. That would have been safer than going to them out where there was no one to see what they did to us. McBain would have come for us. Tohave himself said McBain was the only one to trust."

"You should not have been out there," Old Smoke put in. "You have been warned many times to stay within the reservation."

293

"What Indian can stay in such a small area?" Short Arrow grumbled.

"We know it is hard for the young ones," Old Smoke replied. "But you must try harder."

"If it were not for the white woman, none of it would have happened." Stiff Leg scowled. "This is the result of Tohave's weakness for the white woman."

There was a moment of silence before Old Smoke spoke up again. "Think back, my old friends, to the days when you were young, and your blood was hot for the first young girl you truly wanted for a wife. You wanted to claim her. You would give many horses for her. Which one of us did not take risks for that girl, foolish though they might have been. When a man is young and in love, he does not think clearly. If matters not that the girl is white or Indian. I think she must be good, and must love Tohave, or he would not have been so reckless. Let us not be swift to blame her. Tohave went there of his own choosing."

"The woman is married to a white man," Short Arrow retorted.

"Tohave said her husband is cruel to her," Stiff Leg stated. "She did not choose him. She was forced to marry him, and white women cannot just put a man out of their tipi as an Indian woman does. It is different for the white people. They sometimes marry for strange reasons, but not often for love and the kind of hot desire our young ones feel. And once they marry, there is no changing it. A piece of paper says they must stay together forever, even if they are unhappy. I do not understand it, nor did Tohave. I think the white woman wanted to put her husband out and take in Tohave, but she was afraid, because of white man's rules. For this I do not blame her. It is Tohave who should have been wiser. He should have known that to go to her could only lead to something like this. Now he lies crippled, and it is unlikely he will live much longer. All this because he was weak for blue eyes and fair skin."

"I do not think it was just that," the one called White Horse replied. "I also rode with Tohave. I saw the girl. I remember when they came back from being together, after the traders attacked her. I saw her face, the way she looked at Tohave and the way he looked at her. It was not just that she was white. I believe they truly loved each other. She did not see him as an Indian, and he did not see her as white. They were only a man and a woman who wanted to be together."

"It does not matter now," Old Smoke said. "It is done. I say that it should be finished, here and now. No more killing. No retaliation." He looked at Red Cloud. "What does our chief say about this?"

Red Cloud sat staring at a fire, listening carefully, weighing the facts. All the Oglalas looked to their still-great leader for answers. Even the Minneconjous of the Cheyenne River Reservation, the Hunkpapas of Standing Rock, and the Santee and Teton Sioux on the Rosebud Reservation, all waited to know what Red Cloud would do. If there should be war again, they were ready to fight. They only needed Sitting Bull, now of the Standing Rock Reservation, to agree with Red Cloud.

Red Cloud, in his early sixties but still handsome, took a deep breath and scanned the circle of warriors. "Red Cloud, more than some of you, understands the recklessness that desire for a woman can cause."

Some of them grinned, knowing full well that Red Cloud, especially in his early years, had had many women. He was a handsome man and had had more than one run-in with Indian men whose wives were attracted to him. He smiled mischievously at his own remark before continuing.

"Many of you remember the good days, when I led our people against the soldiers in the place called Montana, when we fought so well that the soldiers fled and burned their forts. We did well, my friends. We won that fight. The Bighorn River country, the Powder River country, the Black Hills then belonged to the Sioux. For many years we have fought, watching our numbers decrease, while the white men came in an endless line from the East, where the whites swarm like ants. We must face the fact that to start another war would be useless. It hurts my heart to say it, but it is true. We are at peace. There is little enough land left that is still our own. Let us not risk losing even that over one little white woman. The traders are dead. That is good. None of us was punished for it. That is good also. It is over now. I do not think it is something worth bringing upon us the slaughter of more of our women and little ones. And that is what would happen."

Red Cloud rose and left, as others nodded their heads in agreement, but Short Arrow scowled. Was there no hope of ever riding into war again? He had seen his best friends shot down, had seen Tohave become only a shell of the man he once was. His blood was hot. He wanted to kill a soldier, to go to war. But there would be no more war, and it seemed there was no purpose in life for a young warrior.

He stalked to Rosebud's tipi, his eyes hot with tears. Rosebud stood beside it, waiting.

"Red Cloud says no war," Short Arrow muttered. "There will be no revenge for what has happened to Tohave. I go now. I think I am going to be sick."

Rosebud hung her head and ducked inside the tipi. In the dim light of her fire Tohave lay motionless, already losing weight. It was all she could do to force hot broth down his throat. If he did not get better soon, at least eat enough to recover, he would die.

She knelt down beside him. It was torture to watch him die so slowly, this strong virile man who had once smiled so often, teased her, hunted for her and made love to her in the night. But then the white woman had come, and Tohave had stopped sharing her bed. Rosebud did not blame Tohave. He was in love. But why couldn't he have chosen an Indian girl?

She wet a rag and bathed his face again. "My poor Tohave," she said softly. "How I wish you would speak to Rosebud. What are you thinking, my warrior? What goes on behind those closed eyes and those silent lips? Do you dream of her?" Her eyes teared.

Someone jiggled the little bell at the entrance to her tipi then, and she looked up. "You may come inside," she declared.

Stiff Leg entered and came to kneel beside Tohave. "He is the same?"

Rosebud nodded, her lips pressed tight.

Stiff Leg sighed deeply. "He cannot last much longer. I don't know what has kept him alive this long."

She wiped at tears. "Perhaps he thinks of her."

Stiff Leg nodded. "He may be seeing his vision again, be riding with her through the clouds. Perhaps the only way he will be with her is in death."

Rosebud leaned down and kissed his cheek.

Moments later there was much shouting, mixed with women's eerie wailing of death songs. People were running past the tipi. Rosebud looked at Stiff Leg with frightened eyes. "What is it?"

"I will go and see. Stay here with Tohave."

When she was alone, the wailing outside pierced Rosebud's heart. Another tragedy had come to them. But what? Several minutes later Stiff Leg returned, his face ashen.

"I remember in Tohave's vision, he saw our people being stomped into the earth," he told her, his voice strained. "And others have had visions of more bad things happening to us. In spite of Red Cloud's words, I

297

do not think it is over, Rosebud. There is death in the wind."

"What happened?"

He looked long at her, his eyes filling with tears. "It is hardest on the young men. Short Arrow has hung himself."

Rosebud turned away, resting her head on Tohave's shoulder and weeping. Yes. It was hardest on the young men.

The winter wind swept down from the Rockies and across the prairies with a lonely howl. And along with its complaint, Katie Russell's heart groaned. Tohave had not come. She knew it was possible he was dead, that because of the weather no one had been able to come and tell her. She wondered how one person could bear so much hurt.

Tohave! They should be together now, huddled in a warm tipi sheltered in some mountain cave that would block the wind. There would have been little for them to do but lie together and talk . . . and make love. What a beautiful winter it would have been. What a beautiful "forever" it could have been. She would have learned to sew skins and make things for Tohave, while he hunted their meat. She would have taught him the white man's ways, and he would have educated her in the Indian ways. They would have explored in body, mind, and spirit. How beautiful it would have been.

Katie was no longer sure how many times she had considered taking her own life. If it weren't for the child in her belly, she would have. But she could not condone taking the life of an innocent child who had not yet had the chance to live. Indeed, the child was the only thing that helped her bear her present heartache. It was all she had to live for.

Since her threat, Ezra had been surprisingly quiet, and he had not touched her. She realized she should have been stronger from the beginning, but she had known only brutality, had been taught from childhood that women were to be seen and not heard, that they had been put upon the earth to serve man, and if they did not they would feel the consequences. Tohave had taught her something new and wonderful, that she was a human being with certain rights that no man should violate. She had known love, real love, and the sensual fulfillment that came from it. She would not let Ezra Russell spoil that for her, even if that meant she would never again lie in a man's arms.

She tried not to think about the future. She could not turn her husband away forever. Perhaps, after the baby was born, if Ezra had learned she meant business, he would change just enough so that she could bear to continue being his wife. If Tohave had died, she would try to make her marriage work, as long as Ezra Russell stopped beating her. Apparently, she had surprised him by announcing that if he beat her again she would kill him. Now she was not sure she really would have, but the day she had told him that, she'd been so full of hurt that she most certainly had meant it, and he had seen that she did. His only alternative had been to beat her to death, and he had known that would only bring him trouble. If there was anything in their marriage to salvage, she would try to do that, but only if Ezra tried to do the same. If he did not, and if he abused their child, she would leave him, no matter how hard she had to scratch to support her son or daughter, no matter how frightening it would be to go off alone. She now knew she could be strong. She would survive.

Twice Ezra had drunk, and twice she had left their earthen home as soon as he'd opened the bottle, taking the handgun with her and huddling in the food dugout, determined to shoot if he came for her. The first time he had come after her, full of threatening words. But he'd backed off and gone back to the house. The second time he had not come. Both times she had waited until she'd been certain he'd be deep in drunken sleep before she'd returned to the house.

Sober he was bearable. He treated her with a new but obviously grudging respect. She was polite to him, did not snap at him or neglect to make his food or keep his clothes clean, but there was no warmth between them. Still, they were on speaking terms, and the weather provided a topic of conversation, for the winter winds hit them hard and fast, bringing heavy snows with them. Their days were busy. They kept the animals fed, brought in wood, trudged to the food dugout, and brought back just enough for daily meals so that nothing spoiled.

At least their house under the earth was warm and naturally sheltered from the winds. On some days Ezra would leave to hunt for fresh meat. Those were the best times for Katie. She spent them knitting and dreaming about Tohave, praying aloud for him. Before winter set in hard, some soldiers had come to visit, bringing old newspapers and a few books, for they realized how lonely and maddening a long winter on the prairie could be. Katie treasured the reading material, savoring it on her days alone, reading slowly, every article, every word. From the papers she learned that Benjamin Harrison was president, having gotten more electoral votes than Grover Cleveland, though Cleveland had gotten more popular votes. She smiled at that news, for she knew that Tohave would wonder how a few men could change the vote of the whole nation.

She also read that North and South Dakota and Montana might soon become states. The thought of it brought a little pain to her heart. Another door was closing on the Indians. All Indian country would soon be under the rule of the white government. What did Tohave think of this . . . if he was alive?

She had to shake off the question. She must not think of him as dead; she could not bear it. He would come. He would take her away.

There were days when she felt she was losing her mind. She lost all track of time and dates. It was easy to do when the days were so short and cold, and there was nothing to do but huddle inside the dugout around a warm stove. What did Indians do in winter? How did the little children play? What did the adults— Her blood rushed warm. Surely husbands and wives found things to do, lovely things. There were many joyous ways to pass the time when two people were happy and in love.

January came in furiously. Ezra had framed and set in a wooden door at the entrance of their home, and snow actually blew in through little cracks, the wind was so strong.

"This will be a bad one," Ezra muttered, putting his hands to the cracks. "It's a heavy snow and it's sticking."

Katie sat next to the stove for warmth, listening to the wind, the constant wind. Did it cry for Tohave? Or was that Tohave's voice she heard when it howled? Was it a death song? Still he had not come, and she feared now that he never would.

In the morning when Ezra opened the door to go out, snow was packed against it, higher than his head, with only a crack at the top.

"Oh, my God!" Katie gasped.

"We'd better try to get to the animals," Ezra muttered, picking up a shovel.

"It's still blizzarding, Ezra. They say men can get lost twenty feet from their own houses in this weather."

"I'll shovel as much snow as I can to the outside, but I'll have to dump some inside until I can break through better," he replied. "We'll tie a rope to my waist and you

301

can hang onto one end so I won't get lost. It will take me the whole goddamned day just to get to the animals, maybe even part of tomorrow."

As he started jamming at the snow, knocking some into the house, Katie's heart froze with fear. This was like being buried alive. She wanted to scratch her way out, but she forced herself to stay calm, for the sake of the baby.

Ezra worked, steadily, diligently. She watched him, and again she experienced a small hope that he would change. In these moments when he worked extra hard, she could not help feeling a little sorry for him. What did he want out of life? He worked so hard to make this desolate land into something profitable. How could a man have such a dream, yet be so cruel to his own wife and not even let her share his dream? She might have learned to love him, if he had been kind to her. That was all she had wanted. Indeed, she had done everything in her power to bring out whatever kindness he possessed, yet it was only when she had been firm with him that he'd showed her an ounce of respect. This was as close to kindness as he had come.

He dug all day, stopping only for coffee once or twice and to eat a little something. The snow was banked so high on both sides that it wasn't even very cold when, at times, Katie left the door open, for the winds blew over the tops of the banks, which were higher than the doorway. It took three days of digging to reach the animals. When it was done, Ezra returned to the house and sat down wearily at the makeshift table.

"The horse is dead," he said dejectedly. "I don't know what the hell I'll do for plowing next year. Maybe I can rent some horses from the fort cheaper than I can buy them. Or I could trade the two mules, but I'd rather use mules to pull the wagon. I guess I'll have to use horses for both. I can't afford to keep the mules and have two horses besides. The cow doesn't look too good either. I think I can get a little milk out of her though. I'll see what I can do."

She sighed deeply, blinking back tears. "I'm sorry about the horse, Ezra."

He looked at her strangely then, as though he wanted to weep. He turned away then. "I know I'm ugly, Katie, and there isn't much about me you like. But I need a woman, and you're my wife. You told me not to force you, so I'm just plain asking."

She stared at him in disbelief. Ezra Russell asking his wife for permission to bed her? For the first time she had mixed emotions about her husband. She was still afraid of him, did not want him or love him. Yet he might be all she had now, and this might be the beginning of a livable life for them. If she said no now, perhaps he would revert to his old ways.

"I never called you ugly, Ezra. All I've ever wanted was a little kindness."

He sighed deeply, removing his coat. "My mother never failed to tell me how ugly I was. Neither did my first wife. Maybe my mother hated me because my father always beat on her. I was his offspring, I came from his seed, and she hated him." He swallowed. "I don't want you to hate the baby, Katie."

"I never thought that I would hate it. I want this baby very much." She put a hand to her stomach, now obviously swollen. "You don't have to be violent to get what you want, Ezra. Is that what you think, that you're so ugly a woman could never really want you, that to make her submit you have to inflict pain?"

He turned and looked at her with a scowl. "A woman has her place. That's what my pa always taught me. My first wife was as ugly as I was, and a bitch. I expect we made a good pair. She tried to boss me, and I wouldn't stand for it, no more than my pa would. But I never killed her. I know people thought I did, and I know you thought it. It isn't true. And I knew when you married me that you didn't want me. I knew your pa beat you into it. I figured, you being so young and pretty, there was no way you'd ever want me for me, ever have any real feelings for me, and I resented you because I knew you hated my guts and thought I was ugly. I knew you felt like throwing up every time I laid my hands on you. And then that . . . that Tohave came along. I saw how he looked to you, even though he was an Indian. Fact is, a lot of younger, more handsome men probably looked good to you."

"Ezra—"

"No, let me finish. You're carrying my child now. I'm getting old. If there's anything we can do to have a halfway civil marriage, you tell me what it is. If you hate me all that much, then next spring, after the baby is born, you decide. You can stay with me or have your freedom, just as long as you don't hate the child like my ma hated me."

She covered her eyes. "My God, Ezra, why didn't you talk to me like this a long time ago?"

"Because women aren't for talking to. They're for a man's pleasure, and for chores. That's the way I was brought up. Sometimes when you acted like you wanted to make it work and tried to be nice to me, it only made me madder. I figured you were laughing at me on the inside, that you were just a bitch like all the others. And when you turned weak and were sniffling and I could see the disgust in your eyes, it only made me angrier. It made me want to hurt you. But when you held that gun on me and said you wanted to keep the baby, I was surprised. I'd figured you'd hate it and wish it wouldn't be born. That got me to thinking, and I figured, if you can love my child, I'll do what you say. But I won't crawl, Katie. I won't take orders from a woman. A man still has his pride."

She swallowed and looked up at him. "I don't love you, Ezra. You know that. I didn't marry you by choice, but I wanted it to work if that was possible. Still, there's been so much hurt since then, so much cruelty. I can't just forget it all in an instant. I can't say what I will choose to do in the spring, but I can say that I do want this baby, very much, and I most certainly will love it. And if . . ." Her heart beat with dread. Tohave! Where was Tohave? And how wrong would it be now to be with him? Her husband was trying in his clumsy way to do something about his cruelty, to offer her the possibility of a bearable marriage. Why now? Why had he chosen to do it now? "If you have . . . needs . . . I will oblige you. It's my duty as a wife. But that won't mean that I love you or intend to stay with you." She met his eyes. "I can't tell you that I will because I just don't know what I'll do yet. My only request is that you don't drink first, and that you don't hurt me. You don't need to hurt me, Ezra. Hurting a woman is no way to make her want you."

He nodded. "All right." He sat down wearily. "You make any supper?"

She rose and went to the stove. "Stew—from that rabbit you killed."

"I'll have some."

She blinked back tears. What a strange conversation it had been. She had thought he might come to her, hold her, something. But he'd only asked for stew. She did not want him. She wanted only Tohave, and she would be happier if Ezra had made this effort months ago. Now she was more torn than ever, between her terrible need and longing love for Tohave and her duty as a wife. At least Ezra had opened up a little, and now there was some hope of a marriage without horror and beatings. That might be

305

all she had to cling to. It was nearly the end of January, and there had been no word of Tohave.

She placed a bowl of stew in front of him, but she could not eat. She would have to oblige her husband this night, much as she did not want to do it. He had been fair about it, and he did have his rights. Wasn't that the way it was supposed to be? But Tohave had said no man had such rights, not even a husband, if the woman did not want him. Still, when she was making such miraculous progress with Ezra Russell, she was not about to argue the point. Tohave might be dead, and this might be all she had. She would do what she could to make it work, for the sake of the baby.

But what about Tohave? Her dreams were shattering, blowing away with the howling winter winds. If only she knew what had happened to Tohave . . . Had he suffered? Had he cried out for her? What strange twists life took. Fate had led her to this land, had ripped her heart to shreds. There was nothing to do now but wait . . . wait for spring . . . and the baby. Her hope that Tohave would live was fast fading. It was time to face reality.

Chapter Eighteen

Never had Katie Russell known more maddening loneliness than in that winter of 1888-89. If it were not for newspapers and books, she would have gone insane. Ezra kept his word about not harming her, but she could not help but feel she was balanced on a razor's edge. She had lived with him too long and suffered too much at his hands to be ready to believe he would never hurt her again. Nonetheless, as the weeks passed, she relaxed somewhat, and he even carried on conversations with her and let her read to him to help pass the time during the dreary winter days.

It was a loveless marriage and probably always would be, but Katie was grateful for the relative peace she had managed to glean from it. Perhaps there was a God after all, and he had helped her through a winter she had thought would be full of horror. But she was not certain she could go on living with a man she did not love. There was still no softness about Ezra Russell. He voiced no tender words, and in bed he was rough and quick. She obliged him only because he'd promised not to hurt her, and she was afraid to press the issue. After he had so surprisingly told her his feelings she had thought that an opening for a closer relationship had been made. But he was still Ezra, the only real change being that he didn't beat her anymore.

In late February soldiers came, bringing more newspapers, and it was wonderful to see other human beings. There were only four of them, so Katie invited them into her humble earthen home and served coffee and biscuits. She wanted to ask them about Tohave, to find out whether he was alive or dead, and she tried to think of a way to approach the subject while Ezra talked about the dead horse, about how he wasn't sure how he'd get his planting done in the spring. "Mules get too stubborn," he was saying. The soldiers suggested he come to the fort when the weather warmed a bit and trade them for a horse. "A lot of the area settlers come to the fort in the spring. They need new supplies and such. A lot of trading goes on," one soldier told him.

None of these men were familiar to Katie. Would they know anything about Tohave? She couldn't ask about him in front of Ezra anyway. The mention of his name might anger her husband, and it would show that she was still interested in the Indian. "If this year's crop fails, I'll have to go back to Illinois," Ezra was saying. "I've got some money set aside for a train, and there's a factory back there in a town near my old farm. I could work there during the winter, live with my wife's pa and save up, then maybe come back."

"You ought to try buying one of those new fangled steam tractors," a soldier told him. "You could have one shipped up from Denver to Cheyenne by train and then hauled here by wagon. It's been done before. We can order one by telegraph."

"Well, if I make a profit the next couple of years, I might do that," Ezra returned. "But I'll have to stick to horses for now."

Tohave! Katie was screaming inside to ask about Tohave.

"Considering feed and care of horses, a tractor would pay for itself in no time."

Ezra nodded, and the men conversed about farming and the hard winter while Katie poured more coffee. She was surprised that Ezra had allowed them inside. The fact that he was actually politely visiting with them and had allowed young men into his house, around his wife, only proved what a lonely, maddening winter it had been. Even Ezra was glad to see new faces. Perhaps, since his wife was great with child, in his mind she was not attractive to other men. Whatever his reasons, Katie didn't care. It was good to be around other people.

The visit was ending too soon for the soldiers had other settlers to check on. Had there been any Indian trouble? Ezra finally asked. "Things have been pretty quiet," one soldier answered. "Of course it was a hard winter so the Indians didn't move around much. That's why winter is a good time to attack when there's war. Their ponies are hungry and weak."

As Ezra followed the men outside, one lingered behind, buttoning his woolen cape. Katie took advantage of the moment.

"Mr. Lewis," she said quickly, "have you heard anything about Tohave?"

He frowned. "Tohave?"

"Yes. There was a little skirmish last year and he was shot. He was an Indian—Sioux and Cheyenne—a leader of sorts. Have you heard whether he lived or died?"

He shook his head. "Sorry, ma'am. I'm pretty new out here."

"But . . . didn't Mr. McBain give you any message for me about Tohave? He told me he'd let me know."

"McBain decided to retire early, ma'am. He's gone to Denver to be with his wife. Lieutenant Rogers has been in command since then. I never even met McBain."

She turned away, struggling not to cry. McBain was

gone! She felt she had lost a good friend. He was the only one who understood. "Thank you," she said quietly.

"Why do you care so much what happened to an Indian, ma'am?"

She shook her head. "Never mind. If . . . if it's possible, I wish you'd try to find out about Tohave for me, and perhaps send a message with the next men who come out." She turned and looked at him, reddening slightly. "I . . . I don't want my husband to know that I asked. You may think what you like about it. I don't have time to explain. Tohave was a . . . good friend. It is important for me to know what happened to him."

Lewis put on his hat. "I'll see what I can do, ma'am."

She managed a smile. "Thank you." Their eyes held a moment, then he glanced around the dugout, wondering how such a pretty young girl ended up living under the earth with a man so much older who didn't look very kind. And why had she asked about an Indian? How could she have become friendly with one? It wasn't really his business, but he felt sorry for her. Pain and loneliness were evident in her lovely blue eyes. He glanced at her swollen stomach.

"When are you due, ma'am?"

"In about two months."

"Maybe you should have your husband bring you into the fort before then. We have a doctor there, and he—"

"He won't bring me. But I'll be fine."

He could see the fear in her eyes. He sighed and nodded. "Yes, ma'am. Thanks for the coffee and biscuits."

"Any time, Mr. Lewis."

As the man turned and left, Katie suddenly felt very tired. If McBain were still at the fort he'd have sent her a message. Now she would have to wait to find out whether Tohave had lived, whether in the spring he would come for her. Ezra had said she could decide in the spring, after

310

the baby, whether or not she would stay with him. Would she wake up some lovely spring morning and see Tohave on the horizon, watching her as he used to do? Or would he be just a memory now, one bright and beautiful spot in a dreary life. Sometimes it seemed she had dreamed it all. She had gone to heaven and floated there in the arms of Tohave. Now she was back in hell.

The soldiers left, and when the farm was behind them Lewis turned to his sergeant. "You ever hear of an Indian called Tohave, sir?"

The sergeant eyed him. "She ask about him?"

"How did you know?"

"Rumor has it there was something between Mrs. Russell and Tohave. Nobody knows for sure. Tohave saved her from some white men who attacked her sometime last year. There was some trouble over it, and for a while we thought there might be all-out war. Tohave ended up being shot by panicked soldiers. We've not heard a thing about him since. We haven't had reason to go to the reservation. I don't know if Tohave lived or died."

"I think it's awful important to her to know, sir. I could see it in her eyes."

"It's something that's best left alone. Let her find out her own way. Soldiers should stay out of it, understand? There was a big enough mess over it last year. No sense opening up old wounds. Besides, the way I heard it, there was no way Tohave would live long. He was paralyzed— took a bullet in the back near the spine. Our doctor couldn't help him. 'Course I hear this new one that's coming here is topnotch, fresh out of doctoring school, you know? He's supposed to know all the new fangled ways to use a knife. I just hope he never has to use one on me."

The man laughed and rode forward. Lewis could not help but feel sorry for Katie Russell, but he'd been

311

warned to let things be. Besides, no one seemed to know about Tohave anyway. If the man was alive, he'd probably go and see Katie Russell himself.

Six weeks had passed, and the snow was gone, leaving behind a sea of mud as the earth thawed. Ezra hitched the mules to the wagon. He was going to the fort to see about plow horses and pick up supplies. Katie would not go this time. She was too swollen with child. She ached to go so she could learn something about Tohave, and be around people again! But she could barely walk around, let alone climb into a wagon and make the bumpy ride to the fort. Her big belly had kept Ezra away from her in the night for several weeks now, and he had even told her not to try to do any work. It was the first time Ezra Russell had ever voluntarily shown her such consideration since their marriage.

She wondered if he would ask about Tohave. He might wonder about the man, but he might not. If she didn't find out something soon she felt she'd go crazy. Should she be happy, or should she mourn? If Tohave had lived, surely he would have made an appearance by now. But then perhaps he couldn't, not in the dead of winter, not when Ezra was with her night and day. But Ezra was leaving now, so perhaps he would come! Yes, of course! He'd been waiting until Ezra was gone and they could be alone.

She watched Ezra ride away, then went inside and sat down on the edge of the bed, moving her hands over her swollen belly. Yes, he would come while Ezra was gone, and she would know if he still loved and wanted her. And he would. Tohave wouldn't care that she was big with child. She would still be beautiful to him. He would come, and he would hold her and comfort her. She would be free of Ezra and with Tohave her life would be a good

312

one. She got up and lumbered over to the dresser to look into the mirror. Her face was pudgy from her pregnancy. She pouted at how terrible she looked and then began to brush her hair. She had to make herself look good for Tohave would surely come.

In her anxiety, she looked for ways to keep busy. Despite her awkwardness, she lumbered out to the dugout where the animals were kept. It had to be cleaned out. She staked the cow and bull outside. The cow was now heavy with a calf. Katie patted the animal.

"Looks like we're in this together, girl," she told the animal with a sad smile. "Are you as scared as I am?" She sighed and shook her head. "Probably not. These things come naturally to animals. You'll know just what to do, but I don't know anything about giving birth."

She picked up a rake and went into the stall. She hadn't seen the horse since that first blizzard. When the snow had melted a little, Ezra had used the mules to drag its carcass away. She had no idea where he'd taken it, and wolves or coyotes had probably picked its bones by now. She shuddered. This was truly a wild land. How long would it take the white settlers to tame it? It was stubborn and hard, like Tohave. Her heart quickened. It seemed her every thought led to him. How much longer must she bear the burden of not knowing? She raked manure out of the dugout. She knew she should not be working so hard, but how else was she to spend the long, lonely hours? She wished she could have gone to the fort, seen people, visited. Perhaps she would have found out something about Tohave. Now she might not get to the fort all summer.

She raked for over an hour, cleaning out the dugout and leaving everything in a pile outside. Ezra could use the manure for fertilizer. Then she wiped her brow and set the rake aside. It was gloriously warm, a clean spring day on which a sweet smell came down from the

313

mountains. She wished every day could be like this. All too soon this welcome spring warmth would turn into sizzling heat, the kind of heat that had almost killed her last summer. How she dreaded it. She looked down at her hands and pushed up the sleeves of her dress. Her skin was smooth again, no sign of the awful sunburn. She was sure the salve Tohave had given her was responsible for that.

She blinked back sudden tears. How lovely his first touch had been. She'd known the moment his fingers had run over her skin that she wanted him, loved him. Oh yes, she loved him! She walked wearily toward the house. So much had happened to her in the past year. She'd been forced to marry a man she did not love, had found out, in the cruelest way, about sex, had trekked long, hard miles to a new and foreign land in a covered wagon, had met Tohave, had gotten pregnant, and had been subjected to Ezra's beatings. She was amazed that after the hard, hot work of the past summer and all the emotional pain she'd been through, that she had kept the baby. Not even the attack by the trappers had caused her to lose it. God was allowing her to keep one beautiful thing, even if she lost all else.

She picked up a pan of feed and began scattering it for the few chickens that had survived the winter. Then she saw it, the black Appaloosa. Her heart pounded so hard it hurt. She set the pan aside and walked toward the two mounted figures on the horizon, placing a hand to her chest. There was no mistaking the horse. Tohave's. How grand he always looked on it. But the person astride the Appaloosa did not look like Tohave. He was smaller.

She fought to suppress her mounting fear as the man on the Appaloosa rode forward. The other man stayed behind, and as the Indian approaching her came closer, Katie saw that the rider was a woman, a very beautiful, older Indian woman. She rode proudly toward Katie,

314

though she looked around cautiously as she did so. Her hair hung long and loose, and she wore a buckskin tunic and knee-high moccasins. Katie felt as though a clamp was being tightened around her heart. Why hadn't Tohave come? He had either changed his mind about her . . . or he was dead.

The woman came very close; then, halting the horse in front of Katie, she just stared at her for a moment.

"You are Katie Russell?"

Katie nodded. "You're Rosebud, aren't you?"

As the Indian woman nodded, Katie fought her jealousy. This was the woman who had taught Tohave how to kiss so beautifully, the woman who had shared his bed until he'd fallen in love with his white woman. But she could feel no real animosity toward her now. Something was wrong, or this woman would not be here.

Rosebud dismounted and stood in front of Katie, holding the horse's bridle. She studied Katie intently. "You are very beautiful, just as Tohave said."

Katie blinked back tears and put a hand to her hair. "Not so beautiful . . . right now," she answered self-consciously. "I'm fat with child."

Rosebud looked at her as though she wanted to hate her but could not. "Tohave told me once that you were carrying the white man's child. I was not sure whether you had had it. I think I have come at a bad time."

Katie turned away and walked up to the Appaloosa. Putting an arm around its neck from underneath, she laid her head against its mane. "He's . . . dead . . . isn't he?" she asked quietly.

"Yes," Rosebud answered. "He died in the first blizzard. We were surprised he lasted that long."

Rosebud had felt no pity for the white woman until she actually saw her. Now Katie broke into wretched sobbing that alarmed her. As she clung to the horse, Rosebud walked up behind Katie and put her hands on the girl's shoulders. "It could not have worked anyway. We all knew it. But we would not have wanted it to end the way it did. I also loved Tohave."

"It could have worked!" Katie sobbed. "Our love . . . would have made it work." She went to her knees in the mud. "Oh, my God! My God, Tohave!"

"Do not do this. It is bad for the baby," Rosebud told her. She grasped Katie under the shoulders. "Come. Get up and let me walk you into your dwelling."

Katie struggled to her feet and followed the Indian woman blindly. Men like Tohave did not die. They were too full of life, too virile, too strong. They loved life too much. She let herself be led inside, and the next thing she knew she was lying on the bed. She grasped a pillow and wept into it.

Rosebud looked around and found a can of tea. The kettle of water on the stove was already hot. She took down a cup and made some tea, adding a little sugar before bringing it to Katie. Then she sat down on a crate beside the bed.

"Try to stop crying," she told the girl. "Sit up now and drink this tea. Then we will talk."

Katie could not stop her wretched sobbing, so Rosebud set the cup down and touched her hair. "Tohave would not want you to do this, Katie. He would want you to be strong. He would want you to have your baby and be happy with your child. Come now. Try to stop, and drink some tea. I will fix myself a cup also."

As Rosebud rose to pour herself some tea, Katie took out a handkerchief and blew her nose and wiped her eyes. She thought she would never stop crying for Tohave. She had known he might die, but she had refused to face it. Not Tohave! He was supposed to come for her. Now the memory of their last night together was even more painfully sweet and beautiful. It was all she would have.

Rosebud came back and sat down, picking up Katie's

cup and handing it to her. "Drink some. It will help."

Katie took it with shaking hands and forced some down her throat. "Who is that . . . on the hill?" she asked, her voice husky and choked.

"It is Stiff Leg. He was a good friend to Tohave and often advised him about things. I needed someone to bring me here. We are not supposed to be off the reservation, but because of Tohave's feelings for you, I knew you would want to know."

Katie held back another sob. "Oh, God, it's my fault! I could have made him leave right away, or I could have sent him away in the first place and never let it get so serious. You and your people must despise me."

"Some do," Rosebud answered. "The few who do not understand. I despised you myself, until I saw how important you had become to Tohave. And even then I was angry with you for making him think there could be something between the two of you. It was a foolish dream, Katie. I tried to tell Tohave that, but he would not listen."

Katie wiped at her eyes again and took another sip of tea. Then she met Rosebud's dark eyes. "I wanted so much to come to him, but I couldn't. Mr. McBain—at the fort—he knew. He understood. But he couldn't take me to Tohave. He was afraid your people might bring me harm or get angry and start something. And then of course . . . there is my husband. I always wondered if Tohave called for me, needed me, wondered why I didn't come." When tears started to flow again, Katie covered her face with her hand, and Rosebud grasped her arm gently.

"Tohave would have understood more than anyone why you could not come, but I don't think he even knew, Katie. I think he was in a sweet dream, and you were with him in spirit. He never opened his eyes, never spoke or moved. I do not believe he was aware of your absence.

317

Physically he was only a shell of a man. I fed him as best I could, bathed him, cleaned up after him. He had good care."

Katie met the woman's eyes again. "Of course he did. He spoke of you. He said you were a good friend."

Rosebud smiled sadly. "We were lovers, but not in love. He was in love with you. He would have given his life for you, and I guess that is what he ended up doing in a way."

Katie dabbed at her eyes again. "Did he . . . suffer?"

Rosebud shook her head. "It is hard to say. He never spoke, but he never cried out or moaned. I do not think his mind was alert enough for him to be aware of how bad off he was. He seemed to be paralyzed, so there must not have been any pain. I like to think that there was not."

Katie sighed deeply, the shuddering sigh of one who has wept so hard her body trembles. Then she blew her nose again. "I know what my people would have thought of it and what his people thought of it . . . but I loved him, Rosebud. I didn't see him as an Indian. And I don't think he thought of me as white. We just . . . loved each other. It was all so . . . so natural and seemed so right. We were going to run away and spend the winter in the Canadian Rockies. We were going someplace . . . where no one would ever find us." She wiped at her eyes. "I suppose that sounds childish now, doesn't it?" She sipped more tea, the hand that held the cup shaking. "I suppose it was, but we both wanted so badly for it to work, we wouldn't let ourselves believe otherwise. That isn't reality, is it?" She swallowed back more tears and looked around at the dirt walls of her home. "This is reality . . . living under the ground, pregnant by a man I don't love and destined now to stay with him." Tears started to come again. "I should have known better than to think I could ever . . . find real happiness. I've never had it . . . and now I never will."

Rosebud took her hand. "You had it for a little while, Katie. At least you have known that kind of love, and you still carry your baby. The baby will bring you a new joy. And you have the memory of Tohave and the things he taught you. He was a man whose very presence brought a smile to one's lips, was he not? Did not your heart sing when he was near?"

Katie choked back a sob. "He taught me . . . to love this land. I hated it before I met Tohave. He taught me to hear the music of the wind and the insects. I never knew there could be such joy and beauty in life . . . such gentleness. I never had that when I was growing up."

"The Indian sees things that white men do not. We enjoy the simple things that the white man takes for granted and does not see or hear. It was not easy for me when he died. I lost a good friend. Many of us lost a good friend."

Katie wiped at her eyes again. They were now red and swollen. "What about his other friends, the ones who rode with him? What happened to them?"

Rosebud sighed. "Two Moons was killed. Tohave was riding to his rescue when he was shot. The others got away and the soldiers did not come for them."

"My God, what happened? They were going to the fort to explain. They even had the bodies with them. Why were they shot?"

Rosebud's eyes hardened a little. "For the same reason Indians are usually shot. White men are too quick to judge. They see Indians only as hostile, uncivilized, dangerous. In the beginning we were none of these things. It is the white man who taught us what it is to be hostile, uncivilized, and dangerous. We learned long ago that we could not trust him. Too many times we have done so and ridden in to surrender ourselves, only to be shot down. Those with Tohave were afraid this would happen again, so they ran. When they did, the soldiers

319

decided they must be guilty of something, and they started shooting. There was no stopping it then. It could all have ended peacefully if no one had been afraid, but if you knew what our people have been through, you would understand that kind of fear."

Katie thought of Ezra. "I think I understand it better than you think." She stood up then and walked to the doorway. "I'm surprised his friends who got away haven't come here to kill me."

"They would not do that. They respect you because Tohave loved you. Mostly, our people were angry at the soldiers. It is hard for the young ones not to make trouble over this. They wanted to very badly, but our chief, Red Cloud, warned them not to do it. Our young men feel very hopeless and they are depressed. That is why so many of them drink the firewater, to feel happy again. And that is why some of them just end their lives. One of Tohave's friends hanged himself."

Katie closed her eyes and hung her head. "Dear God," she whispered.

"You should understand all these things, so that you know Tohave was also searching for something when he found you. He was looking for hope, happiness, a reason for going on, just as you were searching for those things. If it makes you feel any better, you gave him much happiness for that short time. He did love you. He spoke highly of you and would not let anyone speak against you."

Katie put a hand to her chest. "If only I could have seen him before he died, told him once more that I love him . . . if only I could have held and comforted him."

"He knew how you felt, Katie. I am sure of it." The woman pulled something from a pouch that hung on her belt. "I brought this for you."

Katie turned. It was a carved horse, a rearing wild stallion, beautifully detailed, its mane flying back in the

320

wind, its muscled shoulders rippling so that one expected it to actually move at any moment. "It is one of Tohave's carvings. He spoke of how much you liked the eagle and wished you could have more. I thought you would like this one."

Katie took it, touching it carefully, running her fingers over the smooth wood. Tohave. What beautiful things he had made! She closed her eyes and cried, clutching the horse in her hands. Rosebud gently urged her to sit back down.

"I am worried about your baby. I am sorry to come at such a time."

"It . . . doesn't matter." Katie wept. "I'm due at any time. I want it to come soon. I need this baby . . . now more than ever."

Rosebud sat down across from her on a crate. "You are lucky, Katie Russell, that you can have a child. I cannot. That is why I cannot find a real husband. I am getting older, and I can bear no children. I have lost two husbands to death. And now no man will take me as a wife because I am barren. Children are very important to the Indian, for they represent life, and a continuation of our blood. They assure us that we will not die out. I wish I could have given some man a son. I will never know this joy."

Katie wiped at her eyes again and looked at the woman. "I'm sorry, Rosebud. We all have our burdens, don't we?" She thought about Dora Brown and her dead baby, and she quickly prayed that her own baby would not meet such a fate. It must live! It was all she had.

"I have something for you," she told Rosebud. "Help me outside . . . to the place where we store our food."

Rosebud took her arm and led her from the dugout, and Katie nodded toward the place where she wanted to go. As Rosebud helped her walk to it, Katie breathed deeply for she feared she would pass out from the horrible grief that consumed her. She pointed to the back of the dugout. "Over there. Tohave gave me a lance one night. He speared my dress with it . . . and told me that one day I would belong to him. I did . . . for a little while. I think you should take the lance. I've always been afraid that my husband would find it . . . and now I don't think I can bear to look at it. Perhaps one of his friends would like to have it."

Rosebud left her side and dug around until she found the lance. After several minutes she wedged it out of the earth and brushed it off. Closing her eyes for a moment, she held it tightly in her hands. Tohave would not use it again. She turned to Katie, her own eyes filled with tears.

"The lance must be very important to you. I will give it to Stiff Leg. He will treasure it, and he will know the good woman you are to give it to him. Thank you, Katie Russell."

Katie swallowed. "And thank you for coming and telling me. You didn't have to."

"I knew it was best."

Their eyes held. Both women had loved a man. Both had lost something. But it was Katie who had suffered the biggest loss. The knowledge that she would never see Tohave again overwhelmed her, and a black pain swept through her abdomen. She paled and went to her knees.

"What is it?" Rosebud rushed to her side.

"I think . . . it's the baby," Katie groaned. "Don't leave me, Rosebud! Please don't leave me here alone. My husband . . . went to the fort . . . won't be back until tomorrow or the next day."

Rosebud put an arm around her to help her walk back to the house. "Your husband will wonder why I am here."

"I . . . don't care. I'll tell him . . . myself. Just don't leave me here alone. I think the baby's coming! I don't want it to die, Rosebud. It's all . . . I have."

322

The Indian woman walked with her back to the house and got her onto the bed. "I will go and explain to Stiff Leg. He will stay out there and wait. He does not trust whites. He will not come in, but he will wait for me. I will take him the lance."

"Come back. Please come back!" Katie groaned.

Rosebud did not want to stay. She did not want to like Katie Russell. But now that she had met this woman that Tohave had loved, she knew that Katie was a good woman. She had not been toying with Tohave. For Tohave's sake she could not leave the girl here alone to have her first child with no help.

"I will come back," she told her. "Lie still, Katie."

Rosebud hurried out then, and lance in hand, she mounted the Appaloosa and rode out to Stiff Leg.

"She has gone into labor. I cannot leave her. She is alone. Tohave would want me to stay with her."

"You told her that he is dead?"

"Yes. This is a lance he gave her. She asked me to give it to you and thank you for bringing me here and for being Tohave's friend."

The man frowned and took the lance, studying it carefully.

"It has dirt on it because she buried it so her husband would not find it. She is a good woman, Stiff Leg. She is not bad. She had much love in her heart for Tohave. I think it was the news that Tohave was dead that brought the baby. It was very hard on her. Maybe I should not have told her."

"It was the best thing to do. We agreed. The soldiers do not ask anymore, and we do not tell them Tohave still lives. It is best she thinks he is dead. He can never be a man for her again, can never come for her. As long as she thinks he lives, she will wait for him, perhaps make more trouble for him. That would be bad for Tohave, but for her also, for she would want to see him, and her husband would be angry. She is about to give birth to her husband's child. She should think only of him now and forget Tohave. You know Tohave. He would not want this white woman he loved to see him as he is now—useless. He has only managed to open his eyes and learn to eat. That is all he will ever do. It would break his heart for him to see how she would look at him if she saw him now, to see the agony in her eyes. It might even kill him. Let her bury him and go on with life with her new child."

Rosebud nodded. "It is best, but it is all so sad. Tohave truly would be better off dead than the way he is now."

Stiff Leg studied the lance. "Sometimes I think his spirit has already left his body and rides on the wind." He held up the lance, and a rush of wind blew the feathers tied to it. A scream came from the dugout then, and he met Rosebud's eyes. "Go and help her. I will wait for you."

Chapter Nineteen

The earthen walls of the dugout muffled Katie's screams as Rosebud pounded a stake into the floor of the dwelling, then helped Katie undress and put on a flannel gown. She then spread a blanket on the floor and urged Katie to kneel on it and hang on to the stake.

"No. I must . . . lie down," Katie groaned.

"This will help you. This is the Indian way, and this is the way it should be. A woman should not lie on her back to give birth. There is more pain. This way is better; it is easier to bear down."

"Oh, Rosebud, I don't want it to come! I'm afraid!"

Rosebud stroked her hair. "Do not be afraid. I have helped with these things before. Let the child come, Katie. Do not fight it. That only makes it worse. Once it comes you will feel so much better, and you will have your little baby to hold. He or she will comfort you."

It began then, the long night of agony, as gnarled fingers of pain gripped Katie's insides and pulled at them against her will. This was not like anything she had ever experienced. Perhaps it would have been easier to bear if Ezra had not so cruelly planted this life in her womb. But at least he wanted the child. Now she could only hope it would make Ezra a happy man.

Over and over black pain swept through her, tearing at her inside and forcing screams from her.

"Try to breathe rapidly, Katie. Get lots of air and take quick, shallow breaths. Hang on to the stake and push. Push, Katie."

What would she have done if this had happened while she was alone? What a terrible experience it would have been. Perhaps she would have died. Maybe she would die anyway. How could she live through this pain?

The hours dragged on until dawn broke. Katie was now groaning deeply. There were no more screams. She was too tired. Rosebud massaged her back and stomach while speaking soothing Indian words that Katie did not understand, yet they were comforting. They reminded her of Tohave and of the way he'd sometimes talked softly when trying to comfort her.

Tohave. Poor Tohave! She would never love that way again. Never. How could she ever get over the grief of it? This baby truly was all she had. She prayed between pains that it would be born healthy and would not die like Dora's child.

The sun was peeking above the horizon when the baby finally started to come. Sixteen hours of labor were finally leading to birth. Katie bore down, her muscles taking over naturally so that she had no choice, and she gritted her teeth and groaned with each deep, rushing pain.

"It is coming!" Rosebud told her excitedly. "Keep pushing, Katie. You will have a fine baby soon."

Again and again deep spasms came spontaneously until suddenly there was a rush of life exiting her body. Katie felt limp then.

"Kneel down lower now. I have the baby, Katie. Put your head down a moment and rest."

Rosebud quickly cut the cord, and Katie turned to see a bloody, blue-looking piece of life lying on the blanket

326

beside her. Rosebud quickly cleaned mucus from its mouth and nose, then bent over and breathed into the baby's mouth in quick, short breaths. The infant made a little bubbling sound, and Rosebud raised it up then, by its heels, and lightly patted its bottom. In fear, Katie watched the little blue thing stiffen and open its mouth. Then its tiny fists clenched and it suddenly gulped in air and started crying.

Rosebud smiled and looked at Katie. "It is a boy, see?" She laid the baby down on its back. "I will get some warm water to bathe him. Then we must make sure all of the afterbirth is out of you."

As she hurried to get a pan of water, Katie studied the infant. She was too weak to pick it up. She reached out and touched one tiny cheek, so soft. So soft and tiny! The child continued to cry until Katie stroked its cheek again. Then he turned his head to try to suck her finger.

"He's hungry!" Katie exclaimed, surprised.

Rosebud laughed. "All newborn babies are hungry."

"But . . . he was just born."

"It does not matter. As soon as they are out of the womb, they are ready to eat."

Katie smiled. Life! Here was something to live for. Ezra would be pleased that it was a boy. And he was perfectly formed, every beautiful finger and toe there, a shock of dark hair on his tiny, perfectly shaped head. Rosebud quickly washed him, despite his angry protests, and Katie had to laugh. But it was a weak laugh. All the hard work she had done had never made her this tired. Her every muscle seemed achingly weak. Rosebud laid the infant on the bed and then began working to rid Katie's womb of any residue of afterbirth. Katie wanted no more of pushing and pain, but there was no choice.

That done, Rosebud bathed Katie and then helped her into the bed. When Katie opened her gown and drew her new and still-crying son to her breast, he quickly found what he was looking for, and Rosebud carefully laid a blanket over both of them.

"There now. It was worth it, no? Will the baby not help ease your grief for Tohave?"

Tears filled Katie's eyes as she stroked the baby's fuzzy head. "Yes," she replied quietly. She looked at Rosebud. "He seems healthy, doesn't he? I don't want him to die out here, Rosebud."

"He is a fine, strong son."

"How can I ever thank you? What would I have done if you weren't here?"

"Perhaps the Spirits guided me to you at just the right time."

"Perhaps it was Tohave's spirit."

Their eyes held. "Perhaps." Rosebud was tempted to tell the woman that Tohave lived, but Tohave would not want her to know, would not want her to see him as he was now. No. Katie Russell must start to forget Tohave. Whatever else she did with her life, it would not involve Tohave. He could not help her now.

"Rest now, Katie Russell," she said. "I will clean everything up and make you some food. Then I will ride out to Stiff Leg and tell him the good news. He was very happy to get the lance. He says you are a good woman."

Katie smiled through her tears. A good woman. It was the best compliment she could have received from one of Tohave's friends. But how long would her aching loneliness for Tohave persist? The baby would help, but her pain would be with her for some time. Tohave was gone. It was done.

Stiff Leg gave the signal. The white man was returning. Rosebud had stayed another day and night with Katie.

Now she must go. She was afraid of the white man. She leaned over Katie and gave her a hug.

"Your husband comes. I must leave."

Their eyes held. "I'll miss you, Rosebud. How can I ever thank you? You've been a good friend when you didn't have to be."

"Tohave loved you. I could not leave you alone that way. He would have wanted me to help you." She touched the baby's head and leaned down to kiss him. "Remember that Tohave's spirit is always with you, Katie Russell, but now you have your son to live for. Love him. Be thankful you have him. A child is something Rosebud will never have."

Katie reached up and they clasped hands. "God bless you, Rosebud."

"The blessings of *Wakan Tanka* be upon you, Katie Russell." She squeezed Katie's hand, then picked up her things and hurried out. As Katie heard her ride away, fresh tears came. It was as though the last bit of what was once Tohave was gone now, forever.

Several minutes later she heard the wagon roll in, and in a few minutes Ezra Russell came inside. He frowned when he saw her in bed, then hurried over. "The baby?"

She pulled back the blanket. "You have a son, Ezra. You tell me what to call him."

The man blinked and stared, then sat down slowly on the bed. He opened the blankets more to study the sleeping boy's anatomy, seeing that he was healthy and perfect, before he looked back at Katie. "You had him all alone?"

Katie swallowed. "No. An Indian woman was here when I went into labor. If it were not for her, God only knows what would have happened. She helped me deliver and get rid of the afterbirth, and she got our son to breathe. Then she watched over me until she knew you were coming."

He frowned, touching the baby's hand. "How did she happen to be here?"

Katie took a deep breath. "She was a friend of Tohave. She came to tell me that Tohave died. Since he had helped me against those traders and was shot for it, she thought I should know. It's a miracle of God she came when she did. I wouldn't be alive, and neither would our son, if she had not."

He studied the baby for a long time without speaking. Then he sighed deeply. "I don't suppose her telling you about Tohave had anything to do with your going into labor? Seems like quite a coincidence to me."

She held her baby closer. "It was no coincidence. It had everything to do with my going into labor."

He met her eyes then, anger passing through his own, then resignation. "I told you last winter that come spring, after the baby was born, you could have your freedom if you wanted it. I'll not argue about that woman being here because she helped deliver my son. I'd like to be with him. I never thought I'd have a son, and I respect you for that. Do you love him?"

She smiled a little. "Of course I love him. I love him more than my own life."

"And what about you? Will you stay, or do you want your freedom?"

She studied him closely, wishing she fully understood this unpredictable man. Tohave was dead now. She had a new son. She would try again to make her marriage work. "I'll stay, as long as you keep your promise not to hurt me."

He nodded. "Agreed."

She wished he would kiss her, smile, do something gentle. But he'd responded as if they'd made a business

330

agreement. He looked at the baby again. "Can I hold him?"

"Of course you can."

Ezra carefully picked up the boy. "He's so small. Seems like he'd break."

"He won't."

He looked at her again. "I expect I owe you a thank you. I wasn't sure you had it in you, Katie, or that you'd care about him."

"I can't help but care about him. He's my son, Ezra. What would you like to call him?"

He cradled the infant in his arm, the first sign of true gentleness Katie had ever perceived in the man. "I had a brother. He was killed in the war," he answered. "His name was Benjamin. I'd like to call him Benjamin."

She nodded. "Benjamin is fine. Why didn't you ever mention your brother? I didn't know."

He shrugged. "Actually he was a half brother. My ma's first husband was a good man, so she favored Benjamin. I was born by her second husband, the one who was cruel to her. She took it out on me. But I always liked Benjamin. He used to bring me food and toys after my ma beat me. I felt real bad when he got killed. That's when I decided to volunteer to fight."

She shook her head. "Ezra. Why do you hold all these things back from me? You keep telling me things I should have known a long time ago."

He laid the baby back down beside her. "Nobody ever cared to listen. I didn't figure you would either, considering your age and all, and the fact that you didn't exactly choose to marry me." He got up from the bed. "But don't go thinking I'm getting soft. I'm just explaining things, that's all. If Benjamin is all right with you, I'll write it down on a piece of paper, his name, when he was born, all that, so we'll remember. Benjamin Ezra

331

Russell. That okay?"

She kissed the baby. "It's just fine." It was done. She closed her eyes. She would continue to be Ezra Russell's wife because it was his son she held in her arms. Her childish dream of a beautiful life with her beautiful Tohave was over now. This would be her life. She could not bear it as long as Ezra Russell did not again become the brutal man he had been those first few months. In her marriage she would never know a deep, abiding love, for she had not been allowed to choose, but they had a son now and Tohave was gone. She must resign herself to making her marriage work.

"Do you think you could start building a house this year, Ezra?" she asked carefully. "It won't be long before little Ben will make this dugout seem awfully small."

He nodded. "We'll see. First comes the plowing and planting. I got two good plow horses for the mules, used them to pull the wagon back, and I got them supplies you needed. How long do you think it will be before you can help with the planting?"

She covered the baby. "I don't know. Two weeks perhaps."

He nodded, folding a piece of paper and putting it in the top bureau drawer. "I'll be starting without you then. I can't start on a house till you're better and can help with some of the chores again."

"I understand."

He walked to the door. "I'm grateful for the boy," he told her before going out.

She blinked back tears. "You're welcome, Ezra."

It began all over again, plowing and planting. After two weeks Katie joined her husband in the planting. Seed potatoes, saved from the year before and stored underground, were now covered with sprouts. With what little savings he'd had left, Ezra had bought corn seed from the suppliers who had come up from Denver and Cheyenne, and camped outside Fort Robinson to sell to farmers. He already had seed left over from the year before. This year he would turn up more ground and plant more corn, hoping to sell it to a trader for cattle feed. Wyoming was fast filling with ranchers, and he intended to buy a few more cattle himself if things went right. The big money was in beef.

This year the planting did not seem so bad. It was a cooler spring; Ezra, though still not a warm person, was not as cruel; and she had little Ben. To Katie's surprise Ezra built the boy a cradle, and every day Katie carried little Ben out to the fields with her, shading him with a makeshift awning she devised out of a towel and stakes. She planted until the boy needed to be fed, then stopped long enough to breast-feed him. The baby meant more work, more hand scrubbing at the stream, but she didn't mind. Little Ben could not have come at a better time. She needed him now. He eased the pain of her grief and helped calm Ezra Russell. He was like a little miracle for her.

Spring was good to them. There was plenty of rain, at just the right times, and within a month, plants started to appear. Ezra actually had time to make four wooden chairs and to start cementing a stone foundation for a house. He never again mentioned Tohave. Katie wondered what he thought about her declaration that the news of Tohave's death had caused her to go into labor. Had he guessed that she had loved the man, that she might have run away with him? She would have expected a beating if he had, but there had been none. Had he feared losing her? She wished he had told her more earlier in their marriage, but she still worried about the

333

whiskey. Right now he seemed determined to leave it alone. It seemed to bring on his violence, and Katie was still not convinced that his old head injury did not have something to do with his brutality. She wondered if he went through periods of violence and periods of bearable behavior. Would there be another wave of violence? She had known so much of it in those early months that it was difficult to forget or forgive, or to allow herself to believe it would never happen again. Perhaps it was something she would have to deal with again.

It was late May when James and Elizabeth Hembre came visiting. They had just settled on land to the south of them, and they were the first real company the Russells had had since the soldiers had visited in February, except for Rosebud's short stay when the baby was born.

"Just came to find out who our neighbors are!" James Hembre explained as he climbed down from his wagon. He put out his hand to Ezra, and Ezra shook it rather grudgingly. Russell was not a man who enjoyed visiting. "How much land have you got here?" Hembre asked Ezra, once the introductions were made.

"About a hundred and fifty acres. I plan to buy up more soon as the profits start turning."

"Good idea," Hembre replied. He was a slender but strong man in his mid thirties, with sandy hair and brown eyes. "I have two hundred and fifty myself. To work it I brought a steam tractor out by train. If you have need for it, let me know."

"I do fine on my own," Ezra replied. "I'll show you around."

"Come inside and I'll make you some tea," Katie said to Elizabeth Hembre. "It's been so long since I've seen other people, and I'm so glad you drove up."

Elizabeth Hembre was blond and young, but not as

334

young as Katie. She smiled and nodded. "I'd like that. I feel the same way. Don't you get awfully lonely out here, Katie?"

Pain nudged at Katie's heart. "It gets very lonely. You learn to cope with it, though. In the winter you should keep lots of newspapers and books around. I'm afraid my humble house is made of dirt, Elizabeth. My husband has started a real house, but there's so much work—"

"Oh, I understand. We built a sod house. It's such a different way to live, but I told James if this was what he wanted I'd come with him. I love him too much to do otherwise or to see him unhappy."

Katie smiled sadly. "I'll show you my baby."

"Baby!" They walked inside. "You had a baby out here?"

"Yes. A boy. His name is Benjamin and he's nearly two months old." She reached into the cradle and lifted the boy out.

Elizabeth took him, oohing and aahing over the handsome child. "I've not had a baby yet. Oh, Katie, however did you manage it? There's so much work, and surely you didn't have any help out here."

"Pregnancy doesn't have to stop a woman from working," Katie answered. She wasn't going to tell Elizabeth about Ezra's beatings or about the day she'd nearly died in the fields or the time she'd been attacked by traders. Why plant more fears in her? Besides, she apparently had a husband who was more kind than Ezra. Elizabeth Hembre probably wouldn't have to work in the fields as Katie had. James had a tractor.

"An Indian woman helped me deliver the child," she told Elizabeth.

The woman sat down, the baby on her lap. "An Indian woman! How did that happen? Do you have Indian friends? I can't imagine having an Indian for a friend!"

335

Katie swallowed back tears. "They're just people, Elizabeth, like you and me. They're no different. And the Indians around here are basically friendly. If they should happen to visit you, don't show fear, and don't treat them badly. Just be neighborly—offer them some food or something." She turned and looked at the woman. "I met this woman at the fort," she lied, not wanting to mention Tohave. "She had come to visit me, to bring me some things she had made." She thought about the carved eagle and horse, and the hair ornament she still kept buried in her jewelry box. The eagle and horse were buried under some clothes in a dresser drawer. She had not looked at any of those things since Rosebud had told her Tohave was dead. She could not bear to look at them yet. "At any rate, lo and behold I went into labor while she was here. It's a good thing, because my husband was gone to the fort, and I would have been alone if it weren't for Rosebud. She helped me through it, knew just what to do. She virtually saved my life, and my son's. I'm afraid I wouldn't have known what to do."

Elizabeth shook her head. "You're very brave, Katie."

Katie stared at the steaming pot of water. "Oh, I don't know. Sometimes we're brave for others, but not really brave. I guess it's love that makes a person brave, isn't it?"

Elizabeth toyed with the baby's fingers. "I guess so. You must love your husband very much."

Katie felt the pain in her heart again. "Yes," she answered. There was no use in confiding in this woman as she had confided in Dora Brown. She didn't feel Elizabeth would understand. This woman had not known Tohave as Dora had, and she was much younger. Katie decided she might as well give the girl some courage in whatever way she could.

"Oh, but Indians! I'd die if Indians came to my house,

336

Katie. I thought they were all on reservations now."

"They are, for the most part." She smiled for a moment, her back to the woman. It had been impossible to keep one called Tohave on a reservation. "The young ones are the most restless. Sometimes they break loose just to ride free and have a good time. They mean no harm."

She turned and poured hot water into two cups.

"I thought any Indians who left the reservations were shot," Elizabeth said.

Katie met her gaze, her own eyes showing her hurt. "Some are," she answered. "But there's no sense to it. Some of them are fine people, Elizabeth. Don't judge them wrongly. And it would certainly be unwise to shoot an Indian just because he is an Indian."

Elizabeth reddened. "I . . . I didn't mean any offense. I suppose if you were able to make friends with them, we can, too."

Katie sighed. "I am more tolerant of them than my husband. Please don't bring up the subject in front of him."

Elizabeth frowned then, picking up the baby and cradling him in her arm. It was obvious there was more to Katie's statement, but she was not about to pry. "I won't mention it."

Katie dipped a basket of tea leaves in each cup. "It's a long story, Elizabeth, and one I don't care to share with anyone now. But I do like to tell people to be friendly with the Indians. It can save a lot of heartache."

"I will remember," Elizabeth told her. "Do you know other Indians, besides the woman who helped you?"

Katie stirred her tea, staring at it for several seconds. "Yes," she answered quietly. "I knew some others. But they're dead now." her eyes teared, and Elizabeth quickly looked away, nuzzling the baby.

337

"You have a beautiful baby, Katie, and I still say you're braver than I'll ever be."

Katie swallowed. "I'm not so brave, Elizabeth. I've only done what had to be done." She breathed deeply and blinked back tears. "It's a rough land out here, but a person can survive. Remember that. Don't let yourself hate the land. Listen to it. Let it . . ."—she choked up a little—"let it . . . sing for you. Pretend the wind is music, and the grasshoppers and crickets are singing, and watch the grass dance to the music. It seems barren and empty . . . but it really isn't. It really is beautiful when you look at it with loving eyes. It has a way . . . of becoming a part of you. Sometimes I look out at the horizon, and I feel like I could just start walking . . . and walk and walk . . . and just disappear forever. The land will play tricks on you like that, make you wonder sometimes if you still have all your senses."

She looked at the woman and a tear slipped down her cheek. She quickly wiped it away. "I'm sorry. I've talked too much. I don't often get company. Let's talk about other things. Tell me where you're from."

"Indiana," the woman answered, seeing the pain in Katie's eyes and wondering what story lay behind her sorrow. How beautifully she had described the prairie.

The Indians knew before anyone that they were coming. They could hear them in the wind, they could see them on the horizon. They were the *hahkotaho*, the grasshoppers, coming to eat the *maoestse* and the *hekonoestse*, the prairie and buffalo grass, and anything else lush and green that lay in their path. To the inexperienced eye the cloud on the horizon looked like a distant raincloud. But the Indians knew what it was, and they began to gather around the wooden buildings of the

338

reservations, leaving their tipis. They would soon go inside them and wait.

Out on the prairie many new settlers were unaware of what was coming, including Katie and Ezra Russell. Ezra was working on the house, and Katie was scrubbing clothes at the stream. Little Ben lay just outside the dugout in his cradle.

It was several hours before they heard the strange, almost roaring hum. Katie frowned and looked up at the oncoming cloud, squinting, listening to the strange sound. Then she stood up, her chest tightening at the ominous hum.

"My God!" she finally whispered. She turned and started to run. "Ezra! Ezra some kind of bug is coming. Look at the sky!"

She no more got the words out than the green insects began landing on her, catching in her hair, sticking to her dress. She screamed, and Ezra threw down his tools, staring at the unbelievable horde of insects that had come down upon them like a giant storm.

Katie ran toward the cradle. The baby! She swatted at grasshoppers, then bent down to swish some off the baby's face before she picked up the cradle and ran into the dugout, quickly closing the door. Ezra soon came in behind her, to find her screaming and hitting at the grasshoppers she had brought in on her clothing. He helped her swat them, but her panic was building. What was happening? Would they be eaten alive? Thank God the dugout had no windows, but a few were crawling under the door.

"Ezra, the door!" she screamed.

He turned and quickly grabbed a blanket, stuffing it under the door. Katie picked up Ben and held him close, backing up to the bed and sitting down on it and staring wide-eyed at the ceiling of the dugout. They could literally hear the insects eating the grass above them. Suddenly she burst into terrified tears, hugging Ben and rocking him. "What is it?" she whimpered.

Ezra sighed and sat down. "I've heard of it happening before. Grasshoppers come in swarms and eat everything in sight. This will be the end of our crops."

She stared at him, wiping at her eyes. "What will we do?"

He shook his head. "I've got nothing to fall back on, Katie. If they ruin my crops, I'll have to go back to Illinois."

Her chest tightened. Illinois! A year ago she had wanted to go. Now, even with Tohave dead, she could not bear the thought of leaving this land that he had loved and that she had learned to love.

"There must be something—"

Ezra shook his head. "No sense talking about it until we see."

They both sat quietly then, and the scraping, munching sound above made Katie shiver.

The decision was made, and Katie could not argue against it. She had chosen to stay with her husband, and he had chosen to leave his Nebraska farm for a year. The Hembres, better set financially, could survive the grasshopper attack. They would watch over the things Ezra would leave behind, including the cow, the bull, the calf and the chickens. Furnishings, dishes, and such would be loaded into the wagon and taken to the Hembre place as well, to be stored there. Katie and Ezra would take the baby and their most personal belongings, and ride the horses to the fort, where they would sell their mounts for fare on the coach to Cheyenne. From there they would return to Illinois by train. Ezra wanted to get back as soon as possible, in spite of the cost of the train fare. The sooner he got a job, the sooner he could start saving to return. They would live with Katie's father and her brothers.

Now there was nothing Katie hated more than the thought of leaving Nebraska and going home to the father she hated and the brothers who teased her, but perhaps if she went back as a mother she would get more respect. It wasn't so much leaving Nebraska that hurt, it was that leaving meant truly letting go of Tohave.

It had all happened too fast. They were packed, and the animals were with the Hembres, who had already hired a man to build them a house and barn. Upon leaving her earthen home, Katie's emotions were mixed. She had known loneliness in it, and horror. But it was there that Tohave had taken her for the first time and had brought beauty into her life, there that she had delivered little Benjamin. How could one young girl go through so much in one year? She had learned many lessons on these Nebraska plains, most of them hard, and the pain in her heart would probably never go away.

Good-bye, little earthen house! Good-bye chickens and faithful old cow. Good-bye sun and wind and crickets, and all free things who were friends of Tohave. Good-bye Tohave! Perhaps Ezra would decide not to come back. Perhaps this was the end of her last thread of hope that by some miracle Tohave would ride over the horizon and she would see him one more time, even though she had decided to stay with her husband. If only she could have seen him just once more, told him that she loved him. But that was all a dream now. The garrison at the fort had changed, and most of the faces were new. Even Lieutenant Rogers was gone. Everyone from this strange year in her life was gone. Dora. But the hardest to forget would be Tohave. Katie had received one letter from

Dora. Ezra had brought it with him when he'd come back from the fort the first time. Katie had answered it, sealing the envelope before Ezra could see it. She'd told Dora of Tohave's death, for she knew Dora would understand her hurt. She also told Dora about Benjamin, and said that she would send her their address when they reached Illinois.

They rode to the fort, the baby in a home-made sling which Ezra and Katie took turns carrying on their backs. The horses would be sold at the fort, and they would spend the night there, waiting for the next stage to Cheyenne. As it turned out Ezra slept outside on a bedroll, but Katie was offered the use of an officer's quarters, because of the baby. The officer slept in a chair that night.

In the morning they were dressed and waiting for the stage. A few tipis were perched outside the fort, and as an Indian woman approached the gates, Katie recognized Rosebud. Her heart quickened, and she called out to her.

The woman stopped, looking startled. She seemed shaken, but she came closer. "Katie Russell?"

"Oh, Rosebud, I'm so glad to be able to see you and say good-bye." She embraced Rosebud before the Indian woman could respond, the baby squeezed between them for it was cradled in Katie's arm.

Rosebud blinked and frowned. "Good-bye? Where are you going?"

"The grasshoppers ate everything. We just can't afford to start over this year. We're going back to Illinois, where Ezra can find work and save up some money, but I have a feeling we won't come back, Rosebud."

Their eyes held. "So this is a final good-bye," Rosebud said softly. She put a hand on Katie's shoulder. "I wish you happiness, Katie Russell."

Katie's eyes quickly teared. "I don't want to leave this

342

land. It's like leaving Tohave's memory behind."

Rosebud squeezed her shoulder. "It is best. For you it is best not to come back. How are you? How does your husband treat you?"

Katie sighed deeply. "Better. I'm going to stay with him, for the baby's sake. I don't think he wants to be parted from his son. He's with an officer now, selling our horses." She pulled a blanket aside. "Look at little Benjamin."

Rosebud gazed down at a fine, strong, fat boy. She smiled. "Oh, Katie, he is beautiful!"

"I'm so proud of him, Rosebud." Katie looked around. "What are you doing here at the fort?"

Rosebud averted her eyes. "I only came to trade some robes I have sewn for some supplies that we cannot get on the reservation."

Katie nodded. "I see." Her eyes teared more. "Oh, Rosebud, I'm so glad I saw you, but it only makes it harder for me to go. I suddenly don't want to leave this land I once hated."

They embraced again.

"You will be fine now, Katie Russell." Rosebud pulled away. "I must go now. How else can one say good-bye but to say it and go? That is what I do now. May the Spirits bless you on your journey."

She hurried away, as though afraid to stay any longer. Katie watched her go, and moments later she saw an Indian man walk after her. He stopped for a moment and stared at Katie. He was handsome like Tohave, only older, and her heart ached. He brought back vivid, painful memories. Tohave! If only he were standing before her. The man turned quickly and caught up with Rosebud.

The stage was loading then, and Ezra joined her. As the Indian man and Rosebud disappeared inside the fort,

343

Katie boarded the coach while Ezra threw their baggage on top and then climbed in beside her.

Inside the fort Stiff Leg caught up to Rosebud. "That was she, was it not? It was Katie Russell."

Rosebud stopped and turned. "Yes. She and her husband are going back to Illinois. It is best. I hope they never return."

"You did not tell her?"

"Why should I? She stood there with her son in her arms, her husband coming for her, ready to get on a stage coach to return to her own land."

Stiff Leg sighed, his eyes sad. "I suppose you are right. It would have been useless. We do not even know if this new doctor can help Tohave."

"He eats and moves his eyes, even his head now. And he cries. He tries to speak. Think how much better that is than when he was first shot. Perhaps he can be helped, Stiff Leg. They say the new doctor here is very good at removing bullets from dangerous places. We must take the chance. We cannot let Tohave go on this way, but even if he gets better, it might be years before he recovers. I know he wants to die. I see it in his eyes. Only two things can happen if this doctor will agree to take out the bullet. He will get much better, or he will die. Either way he'll be better off than he is now. If he dies, Katie Russell will never know the difference. If he lives, it might be many more months before he is a whole man again. It is wrong for her to think any more about Tohave."

"But perhaps Tohave would have a better will to live if he could see her again."

"And what would that do to Katie Russell? She has a man and a child. She is where she belongs, where she always belonged. We both know that."

344

Stiff Leg nodded. "It is true, but my heart bleeds for Tohave."

"We all bleed for Tohave. Let us go find that doctor now and see if he will help our good friend."

As they walked toward the doctor's quarters, the stagecoach disappeared, and Katie Russell had no idea how close she had been to Tohave, who lay staring and helpless in a tipi just outside the fort.

Chapter Twenty

Katie watched the rolling prairie pass swiftly outside her window. She couldn't understand why she was missing her little earthen house, she had known much suffering there. Yet if she had not come to this land, she would never have met Tohave, would never have known beauty and love and gentleness, or what it was like to share bodies in passion and genuine love. She longed for that kind of passion, that joyful giving and receiving, but she would never experience it again. Perhaps it would have been better for her if Ezra had not brought her out here. One can't miss what one has never had. But at least meeting Tohave had given her the courage to stand up to her husband, and that had seemed to change Ezra a little. At least it had made him bearable. But that was all he would ever be. There would be no passion in her marriage, no real love. She would lie with her husband to perform her wifely duties and for no other reason, for her body truly belonged to someone else and it always would. As long as Ezra treated her fairly and with some respect, she would not be untrue to him or consider freeing herself of him. According to a piece of paper, Ezra was her husband, but in her mind, her husband had already died. He lay buried in Nebraska, hard as that was to believe, for men like Tohave should not die.

Now she was leaving it all behind—the land . . . the crickets . . . the Nebraska wind . . . Tohave. Gone, like the music in her heart. She must be strong now. And Ezra was trying in his own clumsy way to be a better husband. She wished he had tried sooner. Perhaps then she would not be so tormented by a combination of guilt and sorrow over her lost love. But what else was she to have done when she'd had a husband she did not choose? Tohave had been everything she needed then: a friend, a protector, a lover.

She put her head back and closed her eyes. She could not bear to look any longer. She held little Ben closer and struggled not to cry. What was the use of remembering? What could come of thinking about Tohave now? She knew the answer: even though he was dead, to think of him filled her with joy and warmth and remembered passion. Her memory of him was sweet but painful, a special secret known only to her own heart. It was her special treasure, something all her own, like the hair ornament and the carved eagle and the horse.

The train rumbled on, its whistle echoing eerily over the Nebraska plains like the call of the wolf, its wheels rumbling like the thundering of buffalo hooves. But the wolf and the buffalo were part of another era, something from the past, disappearing, just like the Indian was doing. She felt almost guilty for being part of the white settlement that had done so much damage to the Indian. Perhaps it was better that Tohave was dead. He would not see how much worse it would be for his people.

Little Ben squirmed, and she opened her eyes and looked down at him. He was a handsome boy, with big dark eyes. He smiled at the touch of a finger to the corner of his mouth, and Katie smiled back, bending down to kiss his chin. Thank God for him. Her life would be utterly lonely if anything happened to her baby, and she suspected the child was the only thing that kept Ezra civil toward her.

She wondered if someday she would tell Ben about Tohave. She could never tell her children of their intimacy. That they must never know. But she could tell them about the time Tohave rode down on their wagon and the time he came to take the horses. She could relate how he'd rescued her from the wicked sun and from the traders. It saddened her heart that in the future the whites would probably talk about Indians as something from the long ago, something that was only a memory. She did not doubt that in places like Nebraska there would be whites who had never seen an Indian. The red men of the plains were now buried on reservations. Even though they walked around and breathed, they might as well be under the ground.

She wanted to cry, and cry until she fell asleep and then awoke to find herself standing on a hill, the wind blowing her hair, Tohave riding toward her. But that would not happen now. She looked out the window again. It all would be so much more bearable if she just could have seen Tohave once more before he'd died, could have held and comforted him. Tohave. The prairie would be silent now. The song was ended.

The army doctor sewed the last stitches in Tohave's back, while Rosebud held the lamp in just the right position. Tohave lay in a sedated sleep as the doctor breathed a deep sigh and straightened, dropping the needle and catgut into a bowl of alcohol.

"That's all I can do, Rosebud. Remember, I made no guarantees."

"Guarantees?"

"Promises. I did not promise this would make Tohave a whole man again. I said I would do what I could. How

349

much nerve damage has been done by now no one can tell. Sometimes nerves heal. Sometimes they don't. But if they do, it takes a lot of time. Tohave won't just wake up in the morning and get up and walk. Do you understand that?"

She nodded, setting the lamp down and looking around the room at the doctor's strange objects. She felt uncomfortable here. She had wanted the doctor to operate inside her own tipi, but he had insisted that to do it properly Tohave would have to be carried to his office.

"What should we do?"

"Leave him here a couple of days and let me keep an eye on him. He'll probably throw up anything he eats for a while so I want to watch that, and his temperature and such. Then you can take him back to the reservation and hope for the best. It wouldn't hurt if you helped him do a few light exercises after a couple of weeks—picked up his arms and legs and bent them, things like that. When he wakes up, I'll see if he has any feeling in his extremities. If he does, that's a sign that there's hope he'll regain some motion, perhaps speech and arm movements at least. These things are very unpredictable. The human body has a way of doing what it wants. A lot depends on his will to live."

"He has that will. Tohave was a strong man, full of life. He enjoyed freedom, the wind, horses, the hunt. He liked playing games on people; he laughed. And he was a stubborn man sometimes, loving freedom so much that he refused to stay on the reservation. That was what got him wounded."

"Well, I kept my promise. I lied about the identity of my patient, so you shouldn't fear for him. I don't know how he got this way, but if the soldiers still wanted him, they'd have come for him by now. Don't worry."

"I do not trust them. I did not bring Tohave here to be hung. You must not tell."

350

The doctor began to wash his hands. "He wouldn't be hung. I don't really care what happened. My job is to make people well. What happens to them after that is their problem. And I draw no lines on race." He began to dry his hands. "Tohave must have been big and strong at one time. Even in the sorry condition he's in now, one can see that. If this operation improves his appetite, I would start shoving food down him as much as possible. He'll never move or walk if he doesn't get better nourishment and gain some weight. He needs to get some strength back. And if he does get well, Rosebud, my guess is it will take six months to a year. Maybe longer. So don't expect instant success."

"I understand, doctor, and I thank you. Our people thank you. Tohave was loved. Our people are grateful."

"Well, if I can do anything at all to mend the differences between us, I'm willing to try. Just don't come after me with lances if Tohave doesn't get better."

He smiled and she returned the smile. "Thank you." She looked lovingly at the sleeping Tohave. "I will go now, but I will return soon. I should be here when he wakes up. He will think perhaps he is a prisoner if I am not here, and I want to see if he has any feeling in his feet and hands."

"You're welcome to come in any time."

She touched Tohave's head lovingly, then left.

The doctor studied Tohave for a moment, visualizing the grand specimen he must have once been. It made no sense to him that Indians should be considered less than human. Tohave was a man just like any soldier he might operate on. It was too bad that white migration into this land had brought disaster to the people who belonged here. But that was history. Since the beginning of time, certain people had been overtaken by others; those with the greatest numbers and with superior weapons always were victorious. And so it was with the white man, despite the Indian's superb skill as a warrior and his amazing strength and resilience. Still, since the Indians had been driven onto reservations, the least the whites could do was make sure they had a decent life. The doctor had been to the reservation, and he'd found the conditions there inexcusable. If he hadn't promised the next two years to the Army, he'd go work at the reservation.

He stepped closer to Tohave, putting a hand on the man's arm. "Well, my red friend, here's hoping my knife didn't do more damage. Don't die on me. You're my greatest experiment." He patted the Indian's arm and then called for two men to come and help him get Tohave into a bed.

Katie did not enjoy being in Illinois, not that she ever had. She remembered how she'd hated leaving; now she hated being back. Her father and brothers expected her to cook and clean for them as she always had, and she had the baby to care for. Her only aunt, her mother's sister, offered to let her and Ezra live with her so she could be around the baby more, and after much begging on Katie's part, Ezra agreed to the arrangement, which was a great relief to Katie. She was with someone she liked, someone she could talk to, and someone who understood that she was not just a slave. Her father and brothers had no more respect for her than when she'd left, but with her Aunt Jessica, she could enjoy some peace, the first she'd ever really known.

Ezra worked long hours in a factory, sometimes sixteen hours, in order to save up all the money he could. He intended to go back to Nebraska, but Katie wasn't certain whether she could take this roller-coaster life, getting used to one place, loving it, leaving it, going back to it again. She had said her good-byes to Nebraska—to

Tohave—and it would be hard to go back to that land again.

His long hours of work made Ezra too tired to bother her in the night, except on his one day of rest, when he embarrassed her by keeping her in bed long after Aunt Jessica was up. There was still nothing passionate or gentle about him, but at least he did not leave bruises on her.

Little Ben, Katie's only pride and comfort had grown into a fat, giggling baby. She spent the summer sitting under the huge oak in Aunt Jessica's back yard playing with him, gleaning what pleasure and rest she could before they went back to the killing task of farming in Nebraska next spring. She wasn't sure she could bear to face the loneliness again. At least in Illinois she was around people, and there were big trees for shade. She could take Aunt Jessica's buggy to the store and could visit with ladies on the street. Yet in some ways she missed the lonely prairie. It seemed to call to her, and she often found herself standing and looking westward, hearing a strange music. It was as though someone was calling to her, and sometimes, deep in the night, she could swear she heard Tohave whisper her name.

Was she losing her mind? How could she miss such a land, and why did Tohave continue to haunt her? She had never been able to face the fact that he was dead. She could not really believe that so much life suddenly was no more. Yet he was only human. He was not indestructible. Still, despite everything Rosebud told of Tohave's death and McBain's statement that Tohave could not possibly survive his wounds, she could not imagine him dead. She attributed her gnawing doubt to the fact that she had not seen him again, had never been allowed a last good-bye, had not seen where he was buried.

She was rocking little Ben under the oak tree on a late-summer afternoon, thinking again of Tohave, when Aunt

Jessica brought some coffee to her. The woman lived in a small house not far from Katie's father's farm, and she made her living by taking in sewing, raising flowers, and sometimes cleaning for the wealthier people in town. She was plain and she lived in a plain house, an "old maid" Katie's brothers called her. She had lived alone for many years. Katie often wondered why her aunt had never married. She was attractive, even in her later years. She must have been pretty once. She had Katie's blue eyes, and there was only a little gray in her auburn hair. Strangers who saw Katie and her Aunt Jessica together would have thought them mother and daughter.

"Have some coffee, dear," Jessica told Katie now. "I'm so glad you've been able to stay with me. I always wanted you to before you married, but your father wanted to use you like a little slave." She set the tray down on a sawed-off stump and then eased herself onto a bench near Katie.

"Thank you, Aunt Jessica. I'm glad we could stay here, too. Things haven't changed at home."

The older woman frowned as she reached for Ben and took him from Katie. "I never agreed with the way your father treated you. He killed your mother, you know. Not outright, but he worked her to death, and kept her pregnant to boot. She wasn't made for it."

Katie poured herself some coffee. "I think I know what she went through," she said quietly. She poured another cup for her aunt.

Jessica grunted. "That father of yours shouldn't have made you marry that man. How does Ezra treat you? Does he beat you? He's got no right to do that, you know. You poor thing . . . so young. You should have been allowed to marry a man of your own choosing."

Katie sighed. "It's done. It was bad at first. He beat me whenever he . . . wanted his pleasure." She stared into the distance. "Then one day I told him if he beat me again

354

I'd kill him, and I meant it. I told him he'd better beat me to death or I'd shoot him the next chance I got." She turned to her aunt, who gave her a surprised look.

"What did he do?"

"I guess he believed me. He hasn't been really kind since, but he's stopped beating me. I don't love him, Aunt Jessica, and I don't pretend to. I didn't choose him. But little Ben is his son, and Ezra is my husband—legally. I'm trying to make it work. At least he's been civil these past few months. The baby changed him so he's bearable, and he's told me a few things, in the rare moments he bothers to open up to me, things that have helped me understand him enough to tolerate him."

Jessica laid the baby against her shoulder. "I don't care what he's told you. I never liked that man. He and your father are just alike, you know. Your father killed your mother, and Ezra Russell will kill you eventually. Imagine, him taking you back out to that desolate place next year. The man is crazy. Now that you're back in Illinois, you should stay here. You'll probably be having more babies, and you shouldn't be having them out there. It's a miracle that Indian woman happened to come when you needed her." She frowned. "You never did explain how she happened to be around, Katie."

Katie stared at her coffee cup for several seconds. "Were you ever in love, Aunt Jessica? I mean so in love that thinking of a man made you feel sick and excited, on fire and joyful, all at the same time?"

The older woman patted Ben's bottom and studied the girl. "Yes. Once." She swallowed. "I never told anyone about him because I was very young, and I knew my parents would be angry. Then he got thrown from a horse and died." She sighed deeply. "I'm not sure I ever got over it. I guess that's why I never could love again, why I never married." She was quiet for a moment. "You're the only person I've ever told that to."

355

Katie turned and looked at her. "Did you make love with him?"

Jessica reddened a little and turned away. "It isn't nice to ask such questions, Katie."

"I need to know."

"Why?"

"I just do, that's all. Please, Aunt Jessica, I need to talk to someone."

Her aunt frowned. "What's wrong, Katie?"

"Did you make love with him?"

They stared at each other for several seconds. "Yes," Jessica finally answered. "And after he was killed I was glad I had done it."

Katie burst into tears, then, set down her coffee cup and held her head in her hands.

"Katie!" Jessica placed Ben in his cradle before pulling her chair closer to Katie's and putting a hand on her niece's shoulder. "Whatever is wrong, child?"

The girl wept for several minutes before wiping her eyes and straightening to stare at her lap. "What if I told you I was in love like that, Aunt Jessica . . . while we were in Nebraska?"

The older woman stroked Katie's hair. "Now how on earth did you get a chance to meet anyone out there? The way Ezra talks, you were alone all the time, except when you went to the fort."

"He thought I was alone, but sometimes in the night, when Ezra was gone to the fort or to cut wood, someone came . . . someone who was just a friend at first. He was the kindest, most gentle, most wonderful man. He watched over me, came to my rescue once when I collapsed from sunstroke, rescued me again when traders intended to rape and kill me."

"Katie!"

"Yes. Ezra left out those parts, and so did I." She looked at her aunt proudly. "He was killed, just like the boy you loved, and he was the reason the Indian woman came to see me . . . to tell me he was dead."

As their eyes held, Jessica's suddenly widened. "Katie! He was an Indian?"

Katie shuddered on a sob. "I loved him, Aunt Jessica, as much as any woman can love a man. And he made love to me."

The woman's mouth dropped open for a second. "I . . . I can't blame you, child, knowing Ezra," she finally told her. "But an Indian? I thought they were savages, dirty and wild and—"

"They aren't, Aunt Jessica! If you had known him—" She choked back another sob and blew her nose. "He was tall and beautiful, clean and strong and brave—and so handsome, Aunt Jessica! And he was a man full of life and love. He saw beauty in everything. I have some things he made. I'll get them. I'll show you what a beautiful man he was."

She dashed into the house, returning moments later with the carvings of the eagle and the horse. "I've kept them hidden from Ezra. I can't bear to destroy them. He gave me the eagle, and the woman who came to tell me he was dead brought me the horse. Aren't they beautiful?"

Jessica held up the objects and studied them intently. "They are indeed. To carve like this you must see the true beauty in what you are carving. It's like . . . like he's caught the very spirit of these creatures."

Katie smiled through her tears. "He did. That's the kind of man he was. White people bought his carvings. He was even contacted once by a dealer from the East. The man wanted to buy all his carvings and he wanted Tohave to make even more for him . . . but he was killed." She wiped at her eyes and then sat down. "He killed a couple of the traders who attacked me. He was going to the fort to turn himself in, but soldiers shot at him before he could explain himself. Indians are judged before they're tried, Aunt Jessica. He was shot in the back, and he died. And just like the boy you loved, I don't know if I'll ever get over him."

Jessica laid the objects in her lap. "I'm so sorry, Katie. It must be very hard holding all that inside." She glanced at Ben. "He isn't . . . he isn't Ben's father, is he?"

Katie shook her head. "No. I was already pregnant when Tohave—" She sighed deeply. "Sometimes I think I'll go crazy, Aunt Jessica. I never got to see him after the rescue. I should have been with him when he died. He was such a virile man, so full of life, that I have trouble imagining him dead and buried. When he was killed, I knew I'd never love that way again so I decided I had to try to make it work with Ezra. Little Ben was all I had left, and Ezra is his father. I had no choice but to try to make my marriage better." She wiped at her eyes and blew her nose. "Don't tell anyone, Aunt Jessica, not ever. Promise me."

The woman blinked back tears. "Of course I won't. I understand better than anyone how you feel, and if you ever find you can't bear to live with Ezra Russell a moment longer, you're free to come here and live with me, Katie. You remember that."

Katie brushed away her tears. "Thank you, Aunt Jessica. I will remember."

The older woman leaned back in her chair. "An Indian! I can't imagine! Was he . . . I mean . . . was he like any other man?"

Katie had to smile. "A man is a man, Aunt Jessica. I didn't look at him as an Indian. He was just a man—a sweet, wonderful, gentle man, but one who would die for his woman. He could fight bravely and skillfully, and he loved with great passion and joy. When I was with him . . ."

She could not go on, and Jessica put a hand on her arm.

358

"I understand, child. There is no way to describe it."

Katie swallowed back more tears. "He said . . . I was his wife . . . and he was my husband. He said the piece of paper making me Ezra's wife meant nothing, that only love and the sharing of spirits and bodies made a man and woman husband and wife. He believed that two people who came together because the Gods wanted it were truly married, and I felt that way, too. When Tohave took me for the first time, it was as though he was my first man. I'd never felt the things with Ezra that I felt with Tohave."

"That is because you never loved Ezra. Love makes all the difference."

Katie sniffed and blew her nose. "At least I found that out. I discovered that being with a man can be joyful and beautiful. Before Tohave, I never thought it could. I'll never know that kind of joy again."

Jessica patted her hair. "You're young, Katie. It might come again for you. Who knows what will happen over the years? Anyway you have known love for a little while. You have a memory—a secret—no one can take from you, not even Ezra."

Katie could not stop tears from coming again, and this time she wept bitterly. She needed to cry this way, needed to let go of her grief and to face reality. Tohave was dead. It was over.

Summer ended. Autumn came, and then winter. When the snow fell, Katie thought of the little earthen house and of how she and Ezra had huddled inside it while snow buried them like prairie dogs. At least this winter she was not so lonely and frightened. Little Ben, ten months old in January, was crawling everywhere. Ezra worked long hours, and the money was accumulat-

359

ing. He still talked of going back to Nebraska, but to Katie Nebraska was a memory, something she would rather leave in the past, much as she missed the land. Here she had company, and Ezra was more civil than he'd been any other time in their marriage. Medical help was available when needed, and she didn't have to slave away in the fields. But having a farm in Nebraska was Ezra's dream. He was determined to try again.

By the end of March Ezra was having his way. Their bags were being packed for the return trip. It seemed the months had gone by too quickly. Little Ben's first birthday was celebrated, and he walked on that day. Then, three days later, they were boarding a train to go through it all again—the long trip, the planting, the earthen home, the hot prairie sun. Katie's heart was heavy. She loved Nebraska. It had been painful to leave it, but now it was even more painful to go back. And she hated leaving Aunt Jessica behind.

"I'll write," she told her aunt, hugging Jessica tightly at the train station.

"You do that, child. And you remember what I said about coming to live with me if things get too bad."

"I will, Aunt Jessica. I'll miss you so! It hurts to go back."

"I know child. Be brave, for him, and I don't mean Ezra."

Katie smiled through her tears. "Thank you," she whispered. She looked around. Neither her father nor any of her brothers had come to bid her farewell. She quickly boarded the train then, for she hated good-byes. They brought the memory of her last good-bye to Tohave, of sharing that last night with him. As Katie sat down next to a window and held Ben up to it so he could wave to Jessica, her heart ached for her aunt, who stood on the platform, crying and waving. How lonely her life must have been, always carrying the secret of her young love. Still, it was comforting to Katie that she was not the only one who carried such a secret.

The train puffed out a cloud of steam and was underway. They were going west again. She was not a frightened young bride this time. She was a woman who had known brutality and sorrow. She had delivered a child, and she had loved. She had been through more than some women suffered in a lifetime, yet she was only twenty. If Tohave were still alive he would be only twenty-seven. But what was the use of thinking of that now? Tohave was dead. If she were not going back to the land that breathed his name, it would be easier to accept.

The lonely March winds howled down from the Rockies and swept across the prairie with a haunting groan. The door to the Russell dugout had come open, and it creaked and banged in a ghostly manner. A lone rider came to see for himself that the woman who once lived there had truly gone back to her homeland, never to return, as Rosebud had told him.

He rode his black Appaloosa down the ridge to the vacant farm, and his heart shuddered with the same loneliness that penetrated the empty dugout. Had any of it been real? Had a pretty young woman with auburn hair and sky-blue eyes really lived here once, a white woman he had loved with his whole being? Two winters had passed since that last night he had spent with her in his tipi. Two winters. Yes. It was over. Even if he could see her again, what was the use? She had a son. She had long been with her white husband and they could never pick up the pieces again. Their dream of running away was gone. And how could he run away now, with one useless arm and a stiff leg, unable to stay on a horse for long without extreme pain? He could not be the man he once was. It was true that he got better and better all the time, but it had taken months to get this far, and it would take many more months before he was whole again, if he ever was.

He rode closer to the door and stared, picturing her coming out of it, running to him with open arms. How he missed her! How he ached to hold her once more, smell the white woman's soapy scent, touch her lips with his, be one with her. But he could not even make love to a woman yet, and even if he could, how could he come back into her life after all this time, start the pain all over again? It would be unfair to her.

Besides, she was gone, probably forever. He must say his last good-bye right here, whispering it into the wind. He would leave this place now and never come back. He had made his last visit to Katie Russell.

"Come, Tohave," Stiff Leg called. "I told you she was gone. It is over now. Let it be."

A tear slipped down Tohave's cheek. *"Nemehotatse, Hemene,"* he whispered. He turned his horse and headed back to Stiff Leg, who had come with him to help him on and off his horse.

It was ended. Many things were ended for him: the great days of the warrior, of the roving buffalo herds . . . of freedom. Now Katie was gone, and his virility was gone, too. He could not even carve his animals. Without Katie and without his carvings, what was there left to live for? Yet something in him would not let him take his life. The land was inside him, the wind and the song of the prairie had not quite died in his soul. He could not forget his dream of riding away with Katie, his vision that she belonged with him. And the Spirits had blessed him with this much recovery. In time he would recover more. A certain stubbornness within him ordered him not to give up.

But he must give up on Katie Russell. That much he had to face. She was a beautiful memory, but only that. A memory. He would have to think about his dream. Perhaps it had not meant what he'd thought. As he rode away, the door kept opening and closing, as though to wave good-bye.

Chapter Twenty-One

It began all over again: the plowing, the planting, the backbreaking work. But this time there was no Tohave on the horizon to occupy Katie's thoughts and give her something to hope for. This time the prairie was even lonelier and harder to accept.

She spent the first day home chasing prairie dogs out of the dugout and cleaning it out, as well as one could clean a dirt home. Animals had taken over, and it was damp inside from sitting all winter without the cookstove having been used. In spite of the warm day, she got a fire going in the stove to help dry out the interior.

Some of the food in the storage dugout was no longer edible, but most of the canned foods were still good. They had picked up their wagon and belongings from the Hembres, and while they were away their cow had delivered a second calf. Elizabeth Hembre was overjoyed to see them coming; Katie well knew the feeling of seeing someone after a long, lonely winter. The woman's spirits were not quite as uplifted as they had been when Katie and Ezra left. The prairie had a way of stealing a person's spirit, and soul, Katie thought. The Hembres had hung on and would try another summer—both couples prayed there would be no grasshoppers this time—and they were already having a well dug and a windmill erected to pump the water. Ezra hoped to do the same.

Katie shivered at how quickly they had gotten back into their routine after returning. It was as though they had never left. Here she was, back in this land that had taken so much from her, but it had also given her something—love, strength, a new outlook on the land. It now seemed that their first experience here had been only a dream. Tohave was more and more distant, a part of a past she could never get back. He had ridden into her life on the wind and had left that way, though there still were times when she was sure he was watching her. She would straighten and look about, but see no one. In spite of her acceptance of his death, and of her present feeling that it was unreality that he had ever held her in his arms and slept beside her, she often felt his presence. She attributed it to the fact that he had been so much a part of the land. Hearing the call of the wolf and the singing of the crickets, feeling the wind on her face, all made her feel as though he were near. She knew she must stop thinking about him, but how could she when the wind and the dancing grass and the singing insects all reminded her of him? If she and Ezra had stayed in Illinois, it would have been easier. To say good-bye to Tohave, one also had to say good-bye to the land. It was the only way to forget.

But she had been thrown right back into the very land she'd decided to forget. She had not wanted to leave it, but once she had, she'd realized that was the best way to get over Tohave. Now she had returned, and so had all the memories, the heartache, the longing for a lost love.

Little Ben toddled around in the fields, a healthy boy full of laughter and playfulness. His skin being darker than Katie's he was better able to take the sun, and soon turned brown. He was Katie's only joy, her only link to beauty and love. His free spirit reminded her of Tohave.

The child enjoyed everything, touched everything, explored everything. He was curious and full of life and love, not caring if his hands and feet were dirty, or if the crops would be good this year. He cared only for his freedom to run and play and enjoy the sun. Tohave had not been much different. He had been a bundle of energy, just like Ben—smiling and teasing, a free spirit. In happier times the two would have been very much alike. But little Ben, unlike Tohave, had not yet learned about bad times, about evil men. He had not killed or made war. He knew love, but he did not know hate. Hate and prejudice had killed Tohave, and before that it had been breaking his spirit. She prayed that little Ben's happy spirit—the love and joy in his heart—would never be destroyed. Tohave must have been much like little Ben once, a playful young boy running freely with the wind, until the white men changed his world, until the Little Big Horn, until the cruel and hideous death of his mother. How sad that there were such evils in the world: prejudice and war, things that destroyed a man's spirits; and cruel men who destroyed a woman's. Her only joy was Ben.

And then one night, when the wind came out of the north, a new sound came to Katie's ears, one she had not heard before. It was not a wolf or a coyote, not insects or moving animals. This was different, eerie, almost ghostly as it came and went on the spitting wind. She sat up, straining her ears, then walked outside, while Ezra slept soundly. Little Ben was also sleeping, on a small homemade bed beside their own.

Katie shivered in the dark night. Though it was warm, she felt an ominous chill in the air. What was bothering her? Why did she feel so restless, and why was Tohave still so strong on her mind? There! There it was again, the strange sound. Voices, drums. Drums! That was it. Drums and chanting from far, far to the north, carried on the wind in tiny bits and pieces of sound that she could not completely make out.

Indians? Her chest tightened. What was happening? Were the Sioux preparing to make war? Then it came again, an eerie cry on the night wind. Was it singing? Or was it a woman crying? She heard the drums again, rhythmic, loud when the wind blew hard, fading away when it did not.

Again she felt a ghostly presence. Was she losing her mind? She looked around her, half expecting to see Tohave appear. But no one was there. Then she gazed up. The sky was black and peppered with millions of sparkling stars. Did he ride up there somewhere, from cloud to cloud, star to star, on his grand black stallion? She could envision him high and free, sailing through the sky. She was perched in front of him as they rode through the heavens.

Little did she know that her vision was much like Tohave's own. She could see him clearly, for the night was dark and the stars were so abundant that they almost seemed to run together in places. It was the kind of night that evoked dreams and wonder, and it was made more mysterious by the strange chanting and the distant drums.

Katie trembled in the chill night. Something was definitely wrong. The drumming could only be coming from the Indians. She was suddenly frightened, for she realized that not even the crickets were singing this night. She hurried back inside, but could not sleep so she picked up little Ben and carried him to her own bed, holding him in her arms and feeling somehow that she needed to protect him.

The Hembres pulled into the Russell farm the next morning, James looking upset and Elizabeth sitting nervously on the wagon seat as her husband climbed down and walked toward Ezra, who was milking the cow.

"Ezra, did you hear the drums last night?" James asked loudly.

Katie came from inside the dugout, little Ben toddling behind.

"What drums?" Ezra was asking.

Katie looked up at Elizabeth. "You heard them, too?"

The woman nodded, looking frightened. "What do you think it is, Katie? I'm so scared of Indians!"

"I'm sure there's nothing to be afraid of," she tried to sound reassuring.

Ezra came toward them then, James walking beside him carrying on about the drums and chanting and going to the fort to find out what was going on. Ezra looked angry because they had come and interrupted his chores.

"You hear anything last night, Katie?" he asked, setting down a bucket of milk.

"I did," she answered. "But it was very far away and hearing it depended on the wind. I didn't think it was worth waking you just to have you listen."

"You think it was Indians?"

She bent down and picked up Ben. "It could have been nothing else."

"Oh, my!" Elizabeth put a hand to her chest.

"It was probably just some kind of ceremonial gathering," Katie assured her. "They sing and beat drums for those as well as for going to war, Elizabeth."

"Well, I don't care!" James climbed back onto his wagon. "I don't like it. Since last summer there hasn't been a sign of an Indian, and certainly there's been no chanting and drumming in the night. I'm going to Fort Robinson to find out what it's all about. Besides, we need some supplies. You two want to bring little Ben and come along?"

Katie looked at Ezra. "We do need supplies. The

planting is done and we've had a good rain, Ezra, and I'm in bad need of material to make Ben some clothes. He's outgrown everything. We haven't been to the fort since we returned. It would be fun for Ben."

Ezra sighed, still looking disgruntled. "I've got tools that need sharpening and mending, but the calf is still ailing and needs watching. You take Ben and go if you want, long as the Hembres don't intend to stay more than a day. I need you back here."

She stared at him in surprise. Never had he offered to let her go anywhere alone. It had taken a son who needed clothes to bring her such a privilege. The boy had saved her from her brutal husband. He was the only reason Ezra Russell was civil to her.

"Thank you, Ezra," she told him.

He only scowled. "Go get your things. Don't be making the Hembres wait too long." She hurried toward the house. "And see what you can find out about that chanting or whatever it was you heard," he called after her. "Use that money in the canning jar I said you could spend on woman things."

"I will Ezra."

She hurriedly changed into a better dress and put combs into her hair, brushing it back from her face first. Then she packed a carpetbag with things for herself and Ben, and, picking up the child she put on his best pants, jacket, and shoes. Finally she dumped the money out of the jar and put it in her handbag. It wasn't much. She would have to spend it carefully.

She went outside and lifted Ben and the carpetbag into the back of the wagon. Ezra was checking a shoe on one of the horses several yards away.

"We're leaving, Ezra," she called. He just nodded and looked back at the shoe. She reddened slightly, embarrassed that he had not come to give her a kiss and a hug as most husbands would. She had not expected him to, but

370

she'd thought he might put on a show for the Hembres. And in spite of the better state of their marriage now, she realized how painfully she missed sharing true love, true compassion. How long could she go on being starved for affection and tenderness? Could she really live out her life this way?

She climbed into the back of the wagon and sat down on some blankets, pulling Ben down beside her. James Hembre whipped the horses into motion and they were off. Katie watched Ezra until she could see him no more. He never looked up or waved. He had his chores to do.

Katie and the Hembres were not the only ones to come to the fort to inquire about the chanting and the drums. Several wagons belonging to farmers and settlers were hitched outside, and settlers stood about them talking, some loudly. Katie noticed that unlike the other times she had been here, there were no Indian tipis outside. No Indians had come to trade.

James hitched the wagon and helped Elizabeth down; then he came around to help Katie alight and lift Ben down to her. Carrying the boy and her handbag, she followed the Hembres into the fort's supply store, where more people were gathered. They were talking about the Indians as they stocked up on things they needed. Several men were buying extra ammunition.

"If those red bastards come for us, I'll be ready," one of them muttered.

Katie frowned. What was happening? Was it more serious than she thought?

"Just wait till we talk to the commander," another man told the first. "Maybe it's nothing, Hugh."

"It's never nothing when it involves the Sioux. Maybe they've been peaceful, but you don't want to see what they can be like when riled. You'd be better off to kill your woman and kids yourself than to let them Sioux get their hands on them."

Katie held Ben closer. The Tohave she had known would not hurt her little Ben. Surely the other Indians were not so different from him. And they had been at peace. Still, she could vividly remember the day Tohave and his friends had killed the trappers. McBain had once told her the Indians had a savage side, able to show itself quickly in a moment of anger and misunderstanding, but she could not imagine men like Tohave riding down on a farm and murdering women and children. Still, that day at the fort when she'd been studying Tohave's carvings, Two Moons had looked at her with so much hatred. Yes. Perhaps some Indians thought the only way to. rid themselves of the troubles the whites brought them was to rid themselves of the whites. But if they were on the warpath, whose fault was it? The Indians were here first. The whites were the intruders. They'd brought disease, poverty, and near extinction to the Indian.

"They'll keep their butts on the reservation once they feel my buckshot in their rears," the first man told the second, laying boxes of shells on the counter.

"Did you hear? They think the Indians are preparing to make war again," a woman near Katie said to her. Elizabeth Hembre turned, wringing her hands.

"Are you sure?" she asked the woman.

"Yes! They're even sending more troops here from Fort Laramie."

Katie frowned. "Who is 'they'? Where did you get your information?"

The woman sniffed indignantly. "From the other settlers. Everyone is talking about it. My husband already learned about the soldiers coming from Laramie."

"Has anyone actually talked to the commander to find out what is going on?" Katie asked.

"A meeting will be held in just a few minutes," the woman replied, indignantly looking Katie over. "And I would not be so casual about this, young lady. Those filthy Indians cannot be trusted. Do you have any idea what they would do to a pretty young thing like you if they went on the warpath again?"

Katie could only think of Tohave, but she forced herself not to smile. She was fully aware it would be quite another situation if the Indians were going to make war, but this woman made her angry.

"It is your kind of attitude that keeps us from having a lasting peace," she told the woman. "The Indians are not filthy. They are quite clean, for the most part, and they can be very friendly. They're dying, ma'am. I don't believe they want to make war again. There aren't enough of them left to fight us and they know it. And have you ever considered what we have done to them, how all this got started? We brought them disease, we killed off their buffalo and shoved them off their land, we robbed their sacred grounds of gold, raped their women—"

"I beg your pardon! How can you stand there and defend those . . . those filthy heathen! They should all be dead! All of them! They should line them up and shoot them down—men, women and children. And if those savages go on the warpath, I hope your place is the first one they visit!"

The woman stormed out, and several people stared at Katie, including Elizabeth Hembre. "Katie, you shouldn't have defended them."

Katie held her ground and spoke loudly enough for the others to hear. "I think a lot of people here are jumping to conclusions. Wars have often been started by misunderstandings. Why don't we just wait and see what the commander tells us? The Indians are only people, like us. They're just as afraid, and they have families they love and don't want to lose, feelings and—"

"You shut your mouth, woman!" one of the men said angrily. "You're young and foolish and don't know what you're talking about. Therefore we'll forgive you for defending those redskinned bastards. You probably don't know what they can do. You're too young to understand that some people can't be trusted. Young people have big dreams about peace, but the world doesn't work that way, little lady. I hope you don't find that out the hard way. If them white-woman lovers come after you, you'll wonder why you ever defended them, because they'll slit open your little boy's hide and stretch it out on the ground to dry."

The man stormed out and people mumbled. But Katie stared after him, her face red with anger. Elizabeth looked around nervously, but just then James came in to get them both.

"We can get supplies later. The commander is outside, wanting to talk to everybody. Come on."

Katie followed quietly. It was the first time she realized the depth of the white man's hatred for the Indian. It was her neighbors who wanted blood, not the Sioux. To men like the one who had just talked to her, the Indian was no more than a wild dog and should be shot down just as easily. Indeed, to most of these people, the Indian was not even human. But Katie knew better. She'd known an Indian who was more man than any of those standing here today. And he'd had more gentleness and goodness than any of those about her. Yet she remembered that there was much about the white man Tohave did not understand, and she decided that that was the whole problem. Neither group understood the other, and neither was really willing to try to understand. Would there ever be peace then? Perhaps Tohave's dream that they would learn together and then help others to understand was not so impossible. But he was dead now—there was no hope for such a dream—and after this morning she wasn't sure she would have been strong enough to marry an Indian and stand up to the prejudice she would suffer for it. To do so would have taken tremendous love and courage.

She followed the others out. "I'm sorry if I embarrassed you," she said quietly to Elizabeth, "but I've known some Indians. I told you that once. They aren't that terrible, Elizabeth. I think some of these people are making something out of nothing."

"I hope you're right, Katie."

They joined the crowd, and to Katie's surprise it was Lieutenant Rogers who stood on a crate motioning for the settlers to gather around him. He had not been around the last time she and Ezra had been here, the day they'd left the fort and returned to Illinois. That had been months ago, and they'd been told he'd been reassigned. Now he was back at Fort Robinson. He glanced down at her, and when she smiled and nodded, he frowned for a moment, then broke into a wide smile himself, recognizing her. She thought him quite handsome. His gray eyes were framed by dark lashes, his thick sandy hair spilled from beneath his Army hat, his smile was pleasant, and his neat blue uniform revealed a fine physique.

Katie was surprised at herself. She had never thought about another man this way since . . . no. She had resigned herself to her marriage now. Nothing could be done about that, and there could never be another Tohave in her life. A woman loved that way only once. Besides, she had no particular sensations when looking at Lieutenant Rogers. She merely found him handsome and pleasant, the kind of young man who was probably respectful to women and kind to them. Perhaps he was even married.

"May I have your attention!" Rogers yelled, waving

his arm to still the crowd.

"We want to know what the Indians are up to, and what you and your men are doing about it!" someone shouted.

"Be still and I will tell you!" Rogers waited for them to quiet down. "I am Colonel William Rogers, the new commander here at Fort Robinson." He glanced at Katie, whose eyebrows arched in surprise. So, the lieutenant was now a colonel.

"You don't look old enough to be in command of anything," a grizzly settler grumbled.

Rogers frowned. "I assure you that I am. I've had several years experience here in the West, and with Indian fighting. I know why you're here. You've been hearing drums and chanting in the night, and you're all afraid the Sioux are preparing for war. I can assure you they are not."

"What do you know about it? Do they tell you their war plans?" someone shouted. There was a round of nervous laughter, and Rogers smiled.

"Of course not. But what is going on is that the Sioux have found a new religion. It's called the Ghost Dance religion, and it's harmless. In fact, its teachings are very similar to our own Christian beliefs—peace, love of fellow man, that sort of things. We're told it came from the Paiutes in Nevada. This thing has spread like wildfire through the Indian camps, and the Indians believe that the more they dance and sing and celebrate this new religion, the sooner the buffalo will return and their ancestors will rise from the dead to rejoin them, and they'll all be happy again. It's quite harmless and will remain that way if you folks don't go making something more out of it. There is no talk of war or killing among the Sioux."

"It's a cover!" shouted a man. It was the same man who had yelled at Katie in the supply store. "They're up

376

to something, you can bet on it. And Sitting Bull is behind it. So is Red Cloud! You shut them two up, and the rest will shut up."

"You are imagining things, sir," Rogers shot back. "People like you make our job harder. Believe me, it's all perfectly harmless. We're close to the Indians at all times. We keep in touch with the agents at Standing Rock, where Sitting Bull is now, and with Big Foot's people at Cheyenne River, with the agents at Rosebud Reservation, where Short Bull is the leader, and with Red Cloud and the agents at Pine Ridge. There is no talk of war at any of these reservations."

"Then why all the singing and drumming?" another settler asked.

"When you went to church back east, wasn't there singing and music—a piano or organ?" Rogers asked. "This is no different. This is their way of worshipping. I don't know everything about this new religion, but there is even talk of a Christ who will return as an Indian."

There was general laughter again, and Katie's chest ached. Surely the Sioux were sincere about this religion and it was not something to be laughed at. How would these people feel if someone laughed at their own beliefs? Rogers apparently felt as she did. He scowled at the crowd and then glanced at Katie, who looked away.

"I'm telling all of you to go home and tend to your fields," he said firmly. "Let us handle this thing with the Indians. It's our affair and we know what we're doing. We're here to protect you, and that is what we will do. Right now it's simply something to be watched but not interfered with. Word has been dispatched to General Miles in Chicago, and he'll tell us what to do next. Some extra men have been brought in from Fort Laramie so for the moment there is absolutely nothing to be concerned about. Everything is under control."

"Is that what Custer told his men before they rode into

the Little Big Horn?" someone shouted.

There was more laughter, but Rogers kept a straight face. For a moment Katie could see Tohave, free, wild, riding as a young boy with the other warriors, circling Custer and his men, striving to become a man, a warrior.

"You people just leave the Indians to us," Rogers repeated. "If there is any cause for alarm, I assure you men will be sent out to warn you. If you want to come camp near the fort for protection, you are welcome to do so. But I doubt that will be necessary. Please believe me, we're keeping a very close watch on this thing, and at the present time there is no cause for alarm, no war talk among the Sioux, only talk of peace. Their dancing and drumming are simply a celebration. They're a demonstrative people, and they have a lot of pent-up energy to release. They're releasing it in a harmless way. Even their young warriors are getting caught up in this new religion. It's keeping them out of trouble, and that's good. You should be grateful this came along. The Indians are actually in better spirits, not worse."

"Better because they plan to kill a lot of white people!" The man near Katie spoke up again. "Say and believe what you want, Colonel, but I'm keeping my guns loaded and if the Indians come to my land they'll die. Then I'm coming after you."

Rogers shot the man a hard look, and Katie knew he wanted to jump off the crate and hit the man. But he was a soldier. Soldiers did not hit civilians unless civilians attacked them.

"You, too, may believe what you wish, sir," he told the man. "But your attitude is the very thing that starts wars unnecessarily. I want all of you to get your supplies and then go home to your farms. If there is going to be trouble, you'll be warned in plenty of time. And don't let the chanting and drumming bother you. It's just a celebration, nothing more."

378

Rogers got down from the crate and the crowd began to disperse, still mumbling about a Sioux uprising.

"We'll write the governor and make damned sure he does something about this," a man growled. "I say troops should go onto the reservations and put a stop to this new religion. It will only get the Indians all wound up. It sounds dangerous to me."

Katie wondered how the man would feel if soldiers came to his church and ordered him to stop worshipping. But things were always different for the Indians. The white man applied different rules to them. As she turned to leave with Elizabeth and James, Colonel Rogers called out her name, and she turned, holding little Ben in her arms.

Rogers removed his hat and came closer, smiling. "Hello! I heard you and your husband had gone back to Illinois. I'm surprised to see you here."

She smiled in return. "We came back. I'm also surprised to see you. When we left, you had been transferred. And congratulations on your promotion, Colonel Rogers. You're a fine replacement for Mr. McBain."

He blushed a little. "Thank you, ma'am."

Katie frowned. "How did you know we had left? Were you asking about us?"

The man blushed even more. "Well, I . . . when I was sent back here I rode out on a patrol and we went to your place. I thought I'd check on you. I knew you were pregnant and all . . . we like to keep an eye on people."

She knew he meant he was wondering how her husband was treating her, so she gave him a reassuring smile. "Thank you, Colonel Rogers. As you can see I delivered our baby. This is my son, Benjamin. He's fifteen months old now."

Rogers looked the boy over approvingly. "He's a fine-looking little boy."

"He's my only joy. I don't know what I'd do without him."

Their eyes met. How much did he know about Tohave, or about her unhappy marriage? Her smile faded. "May I ask you something without it going any farther, Colonel?"

He nodded. "If it's about Tohave, I've heard he's dead, ma'am."

She looked away. "I . . . I knew that. A woman called Rosebud came and told me . . . over a year ago. It happened that I went into labor while she was there, so she helped deliver Benjamin. I might have died without her help. I was going to ask about her. She was a good friend to Tohave, and she was good to me. I was wondering if you know anything about her . . . if there is any way I could see her again."

He sighed and shook his head. "I doubt it, ma'am. I think I know who you mean. She went clear up to the Standing Rock Reservation, and as you can see, this is a real bad time for whites to venture onto reservation land. I remember the circumstances under which Tohave was shot. I don't think your presence would help, ma'am, no matter how good your intentions."

Katie nodded. "I'm sure you're right. But if you ever see her, tell her I send greetings, will you? And tell her she is welcome to come to my home at any time."

"I'll tell her." Rogers took a moment to scan her lovely form as she turned away, the full breasts beneath the nicely fitted dress, the slim waist that didn't reveal that she'd ever been swollen with child, her beautiful complexion and cascading auburn hair. What a waste that she was still married to Ezra Russell. "Is your husband here, ma'am?"

"No. He had too much to do. I came with neighbors, to get a few supplies."

He put his hat back on, and started to walk with her.

"Ma'am, I'd be happy to carry that son of yours for a while. He might run off and get hurt by a horse or wagon if you put him down, and he looks like he's getting heavy. I could carry him to the supply house for you."

She studied him a moment. What a kind and thoughtful man he was. But what would people think? "I'm not—"

"Nonsense! We're here to help." He reached for the boy, and Ben took to him right away, not putting up a fuss at all. Then Rogers started walking toward the supply store. "Don't you be worrying about this Indian problem, ma'am. It's like I said. There really isn't any. It's just that folks get nervous when they hear Indians chanting and drumming. They don't understand the Indians at all. If they did, they wouldn't be alarmed."

"That's what I tried to explain to a man awhile ago. He got very angry, and very rude. I quickly discovered it isn't a good idea to defend Indians around here."

Rogers laughed. "I could have told you that." He sighed and shook his head. "Maybe someday by some miracle there won't be so much misunderstanding and hatred."

"I like to think so. But to be realistic, I don't think that day will come, Colonel Rogers."

"Well, we can always hope. You going back today?"

"I believe so. I'm with the Hembres. We all heard the drums last night, and I think they frightened Elizabeth. They didn't really frighten me that much. I can't quite explain how I felt . . . sort of like I was receiving a warning of some tragedy." She stopped walking and looked up at Rogers. "I feel that something terrible is going to happen, Colonel Rogers, and as though . . . as though it will affect me in some way. Yet I'm not afraid of it. I'm almost curious. It gives me chills. Do you know anything more about this new religion the Indians are celebrating?"

"Not much more than what I told you. It seems to be intertwined with Christianity. An Indian prophet had a vision, something like that. In it, Christ returned to earth as an Indian, and soon he will make everything the way it once was for them, even bring back their dead ancestors. They sincerely believe this is going to happen, but I'm afraid that when reality hits them, they'll know it won't and there will be even more drinking and depression among the Sioux. Many of their young men commit suicide, you know."

Her eyes clouded with concern. "No, I didn't. How sad."

"It is. Of course most of the people around here wouldn't care if they all killed themselves." He handed Ben back to her. "We're at the store. I'm glad to see you had a healthy son and you're looking well, Mrs. Russell. I hope you have success with your farm this time. I remember what a dry, hot summer you had the first year out here."

"Yes. We've had more rain this year, and thank God, the grasshoppers didn't come. My husband is working very hard to make the farm prosper."

"I'm sure he is." Rogers looked her over carefully. "Is he . . . treating you well?"

She reddened a little. "He's been much better since Ben was born, and I think going back to Illinois for the winter was good for both of us."

"Good. I'm glad for you then." He tipped his hat. "I'll be saying good-bye to you now, and good luck. I'll probably see you at the autumn gathering, and don't you worry about this Indian thing."

"I won't. Thank you, Colonel Rogers."

He smiled warmly. "My pleasure."

She walked into the supply store and he watched her go. She was a pretty woman, but he felt sorry for her. It was sad to see such a lovely girl buried on the prairie, with a man she did not love, one who had no appreciation for a good woman. Katie Russell would make a deserving man a fine wife. She was different, stronger somehow, prettier, more womanly. Perhaps she would make it out here after all. He sighed deeply. If she were not a married woman, he would most certainly make a vigorous effort to court her. He cursed his luck and turned away, heading for his own quarters.

Chapter Twenty-Two

The Ghost Dance religion spread like wildfire among the Sioux. Kicking Bear and Short Bull, of the Cheyenne River Agency, had traveled with nine other Sioux by hitching a ride on the Union Pacific all the way across the shining Mountains into Nevada, to learn from the Paiutes, the Fish Eaters as the Sioux called them, about this wonderful new religion which proclaimed that Christ had returned to earth, but was an Indian. Kicking Bear and his friends walked many miles to the Paiute agency at Walker Lake, there joining hundreds of other Indians speaking many different languages. All had come to see the Messiah.

What happened then could have been real, but more likely it was just something the Indians wanted to be real. They were desperate and heartbroken. They needed new hope, some assurance that their days of freedom and power were not over. When a people are desperate and hopeless, they will cling to anything that gives them hope. At any rate, the Indians who had gathered that night saw a man who proclaimed to be Christ returned. He taught them the movements of the special dance that would someday bring back their dead ancestors, bury all white men, and bring back green grass and water and trees. It would also cause great herds of buffalo and wild horses to return. The land would be brand new; its only inhabitants would be Indians.

Throughout the night the Christ taught them this dance, and throughout the next day he preached the new belief. He taught that in the beginning God had made the earth and had sent Christ to teach people. But the white men had been cruel to the Christ and so He had gone back to heaven. Now He had returned, but He was Indian, because white men had been bad. He would renew the earth, and God had determined that all white men should be buried forever. But this must not be done through violence.

That was the key to this new religion. If white men had understood it, they would not have been alarmed when Kicking Bear and the others returned to tell of this new belief and when the Sioux began to do the special Ghost Dance. The new Christ had taught that they must harm no one, that they must not fight and must always do right. His only requirement was that they do the special Ghost Dance and sing certain songs. The new Christ would then bring back their loved ones.

If the whites had not been so biased against the red man, had not been so sure that he was always ready to wage war, the new religion would have led to nothing. The Indians would have danced and danced until they could no longer walk; then, finally, they would have realized that they were clinging to a false hope. But as they had done so many other times, the white men began to panic at the mere sound of singing and drums.

So an outcry arose from the Dakotas to Arizona, from Nevada to Oklahoma. The Ghost Dance religion would surely lead to every Indian tribe in the West joining in an effort to slaughter all white men. The new religion must be stopped. No one recognized that the Indians' new religion was actually Christianity, the only difference being their point of view. They could only imagine the new Christ as Indian, just as the white man imagined him to be white.

The Indians danced, many women dancing until they fainted in order to bring back their dead warrior husbands, and Kicking Bear explained the new religion to Sitting Bull. The old chief did not fully believe in it, but he knew his people needed to cling to this new hope. He allowed the Ghost Dance religion to spread, though he knew the whites were becoming restless and afraid. He heard rumors that soldiers would come and try to stop the dancing and his people might be hurt. But Kicking Bear assured him that if his people wore sacred garments as directed by the Messiah, they could not be harmed. Ghost Shirts painted with magic symbols would protect them, even from bullets. And so the dancers donned the Ghost Shirts and danced, day and night, hoping, praying, believing that their dancing would make the Messiah look favorably upon them and bring them all the wonderful things He had promised, and that they would see their dead loved ones again.

The religious fervor became frenzied, but still the believers continued to practice no violence. They must love, they must cooperate, they must do right and harm no one. At no time did they preach that they should make war. A more peaceful religion could not have come to the Sioux or to the other tribes. It was their last great hope.

But the white man turned the new religion into a disaster. He was afraid, suspicious, perhaps even jealous of this new religion that said the Messiah was an Indian. Blasphemy! The new religion must end!

So in the late summer and early autumn of 1890, there was increasing uneasiness in the West, on the Sioux reservations and the area surrounding them. The government and Army were in a quandary. What should be done? More soldiers were sent to forts near Indian agencies, and meetings were held. The settlers and townspeople in these areas were crying out for action. Someone must put a stop to this religion. It was all the Indians thought about now. As for the Sioux, their children no longer came to the schoolhouses. No Indians came to trade and their farms were not being worked. In the eyes of the white man, the Indians were going crazy and must be stopped. Preparations were made to do just that.

"It will bring us much trouble," Stiff Leg declared quietly to Rosebud.

Rosebud stood watching, her eyes teared. "I suppose it will. But look at the hope in their eyes, the joy in their hearts." Before them those who could still stand danced. Others, mostly women who wanted their dead husbands to return, lay exhausted on the ground, resting only a little while before rising to dance again. "How can such a thing be stopped, Stiff Leg? Even our young men dance now, instead of drinking or taking their lives. Sitting Bull himself says this is good for our people."

She glanced over at Tohave, watching also and seriously considering joining in the dancing. Would it bring back his mother? Would it bring back Two Moons and Short Arrow? He, too, needed some kind of hope. Katie Russell was gone, but his love for her still stabbed fiercely at him. He had been drinking too much lately, and yes, he had considered ending his life as Short Arrow had done. For it seemed all hope had gone with Katie Russell. It hurt too much to lose her and to watch his people lose their freedom and die. He had traveled north, to the Standing Rock Reservation where Sitting Bull lived, where he could be far from Katie Russell's land.

Now there was this new hope, this new religion. Even without Katie, he could go on if the people could be strong again, if his mother and friends and the buffalo would come back and the white man would disappear. He raised a bottle of whiskey to his lips and swallowed. During his months of painful recovery, firewater was the only thing that had killed the pain and raised his spirits.

He lowered the bottle. Then someone knocked it from his hand, startling him. He whirled to see Rosebud glaring at him.

"You will kill yourself with the firewater!" she hissed. "The Tohave I once knew would not touch it!"

He grasped her hair painfully, jerking her forward. "This is not the Tohave you once knew!" He sneered. "And if you ever break another bottle of Tohave's whiskey, Tohave will never come to your bed again!" He pushed her away then.

She looked at him scathingly. "So. You are strong now, huh, warrior? You are strong enough to grab me and bring me pain." She spat at him. "I do not care if you are strong enough to lift a mountain! It is inner strength you no longer have! You are like a weak woman on the inside! You need the firewater to make you strong. You lean on it, just like the cane you used when you were learning to walk again! The firewater is your cane now, Tohave!" Her eyes teared. "And when you are out there lifting your mountain, remember that if it were not for Rosebud, you would be dead now. It is Rosebud who nursed you and cleaned up after you and talked the white doctor into helping you. It is Rosebud you leaned on when first you walked again. Life is not always good to any of us. You are not the only Indian man who has suffered losses. Look out there at those who dance. Look at all the broken hearts and bodies. But they will go on living, just as you will. And they do not all need the firewater to do it."

She whirled and went inside her tipi, and Tohave stared after her, hating himself for hurting her.

Wondering what had happened to him, he kicked at the bottle and followed her inside. She sat on a bed of robes, removing her moccasins. Then she pulled off her tunic and sat there naked, glaring at him. "I am going to sleep. Why don't you go out there and dance, now that you can walk and run again. Maybe the new religion will give you strength, not in body, but in mind and heart." She pulled a robe over herself and curled up.

Tohave sighed, then removed his shirt and moccasins and leggings. He walked over to her and untied his loincloth, crawling in beside her and pulling her close, her back to him.

"Forgive me, Rosebud. You stayed with me through the bad times." He kissed her hair, gently massaging her breasts as he did so and shifting his mouth to her cheek and neck. Only two weeks earlier he had learned he could still do this. It was the last thing he'd relearned after his injury, something he had put off because he was afraid he would fail, afraid that his injury had left him a lesser man. But in one wonderful, wild night he had learned otherwise, although in his mind then and every time since, it was not Rosebud in his arms. It was Katie. Would he ever be able to face not seeing her again, not being able to explain why he had not come for her? What had happened to her? Was she still with Ezra Russell, or had she finally rid herself of the man and found another?

Rosebud turned, and he kissed her savagely, hungrily, like a man who is sorry and wants to make up for it through lovemaking. But she was a wise woman, and as he moved over her, touching, tasting, shuddering with need, she knew it was not Rosebud he held. She did not mind, if it made him feel better.

Outside the singing and drumming continued, and inside the warm, dimly lit tipi, Tohave drove himself into Rosebud for he was consumed by an aching need for someone else. He moved rhythmically but almost savagely, feeling joy because he was again able to do this, and sorrow because the woman beneath him was not Katie Russell, his Mourning Dove.

Rosebud took him gladly, as she had always done, for Tohave was a handsome man, still thinner than he'd been but again strong and virile. He was a man whose smile made women long for his touch, but he had changed on the inside. He was pining away for something he could never have, and it was killing him. How many times had they fought over the whiskey? So far she had managed to keep him from being drunk every day, but she was not sure how long that would last. He was depending on the firewater to get him through his sorrow. It started when he was in terrible pain, learning to move again after the operation. Some days were worse than others, and he used the whiskey to ease the pain. Soon he had become dependent on it, and Rosebud struggled to ease him away from it. The old Tohave she had known had always preached against the firewater, scorning his friends who used it and turned into worthless men who sometimes could not even stay on a horse.

Tohave raised himself now, a grand specimen of a man again, grasping her hips and looking down at her like a conquerer as he invaded her over and over until she felt the pleasant explosion his movements brought. He came down on her then and rolled over, and she rhythmically shifted on top of him. He reached up and gently fingered her breasts, but when he opened his eyes to look at her, her skin was white, her breasts pink, her hair auburn, and her eyes blue. She was Katie, sitting there and taking her man in this daring way, making him wild with desire.

He groaned and rolled Rosebud back over, and moments later his seed poured into her. He lay still then, breathing deeply, his face buried in her neck. She could feel the wetness of his tears.

Rosebud stroked his hair soothingly. "The whiskey is

391

not the answer, Tohave. You know this. Do not lower yourself be letting it rule you. Once you were strong and spoke against it. The woman is gone. She thinks you are dead. I told you that, and we agreed it was best. We did not know whether you would get well, and even if you did, to try to run away with her would only have brought heartache and pain to both of you. This way is best, but she would not want to see you this way, Tohave, strong in body but weak in spirit. She would rather have you strong in spirit and weak in body. Be the Tohave she loved, and do not forget the gift the Gods have given you, to capture the spirit of animals in wood. This is a great gift. You should start carving again, Tohave.''

He sighed deeply and rolled off her, rubbing at his eyes. "It has been two winters since I carved the wood. I am afraid to try. My hands do not always do what I command. Sometimes they shake.''

"You must try, Tohave. Perhaps if you use them more, you will learn to control them better. If you carve again, you will be stronger. It will pass the time, help you to stop drinking the whiskey. And it will help you to remember the beauty in life, in the land, and in animals. We must face the fact that the old ways are gone. Your carving gives you something to turn to, instead of the farming the white man wants us to do. White people pay money for your carvings. Let them. Take their money and we can live well.''

He stared up at the smoke hole. "I will think about it. And I am thinking about this new religion, wondering if dancing the Ghost Dance, would make me stronger inside, whether it would help me find some kind of answer to my life. Perhaps my mother will return, my friends. What do you think of this thing, Rosebud? Do you think the white men will all be buried and the buffalo will return like they say?''

She turned and nestled into his shoulder. "I do not

know what to think. I want to believe, but I am afraid to do so. Because if these things do not come true, the people will be more disheartened than ever. It will be bad then."

"I have thought the same thing. But when I watch them, I get excited. I want to dance. I want to believe."

"Then you should dance, Tohave. And when you are not dancing, you should carve your animals again."

He lay quietly for several seconds, still staring at the smoke hole. "Do you think she will ever come back?"

Rosebud sighed deeply. "I think not. You said you went to her home once, even though I told you it would be a bad thing to do. She was not there, and you came home with such a heavy heart that you drank the firewater until you collapsed. You must stop thinking about her, Tohave. She is gone. To her, you are dead. It is done. She has a son now, perhaps even another. She belongs to someone else."

He swallowed and blinked, then wiped at his eyes before he rose and quickly washed himself before tying on his loincloth. Moving to the side of the tipi where his belongings were kept, he reached for a bottle of whiskey.

"Tohave!" Rosebud said sharply.

He didn't move for a moment, only stared at the bottle. Inside it was a pleasant dulling of his pain, physical and emotional. But what about his pride, the old pride that had made him the kind of man a woman like Katie could love. He thought about Ezra Russell, and how Katie had hated it when he drank. What would she think of him now when he had a whiskey bottle in his hand most of the time?

He put the bottle back and turned. "I am going to dance and pray," he told her quietly. He left then, without another word.

*   *   *

393

It was hot, as always, but the people new to this land were learning to live with the heat and the absence of shade trees. The crops were good, the rain was unusually plentiful, but for people like Katie and Ezra, this summer brought a hardship different from that usually brought by the land.

This summer it was not the land that wore them down. They were used to the hard work of farming here. This time the hardship came from emotional strain. They wondered if the Indians would attack, if they were preparing for a grand slaughter. Katie could not believe they were planning such a thing, but the majority of the settlers did and they did not sleep well at night. For it was at night, when all was quiet, that sounds carried on the winds from the north, and they could hear the sounds of chanting and drumming from the Pine Ridge Reservation.

Some settlers had fled at the mere mention of Indian trouble, gone back to safer places. Ezra chose to stay, muttering that no goddamned Indians were going to chase him off his land. Katie was not afraid. She did not believe the Indians would attack, but she was confident that Colonel Rogers would give them plenty of warning if trouble arose.

She thought about Rogers often. If there had not been a Tohave in her life, if she were free and unattached, she could be attracted to someone like the colonel. But the days were gone when she could have been courted like other young women. She was married, and she had known love only once, with a man who was not her husband. She had vowed to stay with her husband. Loveless as her marriage might be, Ezra was little Ben's father. She was resigned to living with a man she could never love, a man who knew nothing of love himself.

Her worry this summer wasn't due to the Indians, but to Ezra. He seemed harsher again. Did his head wound cause him to experience periodic moods, to sometimes become savage? He was becoming more demanding in the night, which was difficult for her, for she felt like a harlot, lying with a man she did not love. And his lovemaking was more brutal, reviving old memories in her and waves of renewed terror. It seemed that sometimes he was on the verge of hitting her or pinching her or asking her to perform some sexual act that she would hate. So far he had not touched any whiskey, and she was certain that had saved her from another beating. It frightened her to realize that Ezra might beat her in front of little Ben and terrify the child, though she didn't doubt that Ben's presence had probably kept him from doing so. He would not want to look bad in front of his son.

During the summer she lived with her inner terror. She was prepared to threaten him with a gun again if necessary, and to remind him of his promise that if she gave him a son and if she loved the boy, he would not harm her. But he seemed to, again, be slipping into that mental realm she could not reach, a place removed from the rest of the world. Sometimes she felt sorry for him, but she had to think of her own safety. She had to keep her health for little Ben's sake. One punch might put an end to her life, and who would take care of little Ben then? She could not leave him in the care of Ezra. The man was too unpredictable, despite his love for his son. And Ben was still so small. He needed his mother.

She worked hard that summer, trying her best to please Ezra, and she wept often. When would she be delivered from this hell? If she was not, how would she bear years of living this way? The moments when Ezra talked to her were few and far between, and even then he would not let her get close to him. They just set up a fleeting hope that faded fast.

When the potatoes were dug and the corn was picked,

Ezra announced that he would take wagon loads of them to the fort to sell, and that Katie must stay home and keep digging and picking. The crops were good this year. More than one trip would be necessary. Katie wanted to protest. Going to the fort in the fall was her only opportunity to see people before the long, lonely winter. She would miss the festival, but she had a suspicion that if she protested too much Ezra would become angry. Perhaps when he took the last load he would let her go. She calmly hinted that she would be left alone, and there was Indian trouble. He glowered at her then.

"James Hembre told me how you defended the Indians when I let you go to the fort alone," he told her. "You always did defend them. If you're so all-fired sure there's no danger and they're our friends, then you shouldn't be worried about staying here alone, should you?"

There was a threat in his voice, a threat she did not care to challenge. So, that was it. Hembre had told him she had spoken in defense of the Sioux, and it had angered him.

"I was only trying to calm Elizabeth," she answered. "She was upset. People were saying things that weren't even true, making trouble where there was none. If we don't stay calm, Ezra, there will be a war, and it will be our fault, not theirs."

He grabbed her around the throat, startling her. "No more Indian talk, understand? I feel like the rest feel, that we're better off if they're all dead, and you'd better back me up!" He shoved her a little when he let go of her, and Ben stared and blinked. Ezra acted like he wanted to do more to her, but he caught the boy watching him and suddenly changed. Smiling, he picked the boy up to hug him. "See you in a few days, son." He set the boy down and gave Katie a warning look before leaving.

She sat down after he left, shaking and rubbing at her throat. Was he going to turn cruel again? She did not know how to control his moods. She had been the best wife she could since their agreement about the baby, but he was returning to his old ways. When Katie put her head down and wept bitterly, little Ben came and put his head in her lap, hugging her around the hips and feeling afraid. Why was mama crying?

Ezra made three more trips to the fort, saying little when he was home. Each time Katie longed to go but did not ask. On his last trip back, to her horror, he was drunk when he returned. What had set him off this time? What triggered these moods? She could tell from where she stood by the horse stall that he was drunk because he half fell from the wagon seat. He had a bottle in each hand.

She picked up little Ben and held him close, ducking inside the stall. But he had seen her. She had no gun with her, and even if she had, could she shoot little Ben's father right in front of the boy?

"Come out here, woman!" Ezra called. "Come out, or I'll come in after you, get inside your ass right there in the horse manure with Ben watching!"

Slowly she emerged, trembling, clinging to Ben. "I told you what would happen if you drank again!" she said, trying to make her voice sound firm.

"That so?" He swallowed the last bit of whiskey and threw the bottle aside. "That Colonel Rogers was asking about you when I went to the fort. How come he was asking about you?"

She blinked, her heart pounding. "I . . . I don't know. He asks about all the settlers. That's his job."

"It's none of his business how my wife is doing. Did you see that man when you went to the fort alone? Did you cry on his shoulder about your ugly husband and how you want a better man between your legs?"

Her eyes widened in horror. "Ezra! I've done no such

thing! Why are you doing this! You told me if I gave you a son . . . if I loved little Ben—"

"To hell with Ben!" He leaped at her, his eyes wide like a madman's. Had his mind slipped completely? She had never seen him this wild looking. To her horror he grabbed little Ben from her arms and tossed him aside like a sack of potatoes. The boy started to cry. Katie turned to run, but he grabbed her hair and jerked her around. His big hand slammed across her face so hard that the blows that came after were hardly felt, for she was almost unconscious. After the third or fourth punch, she felt nothing.

When she awoke, Katie found herself in bed, naked. She remembered absolutely nothing. When she moved, pain erupted throughout her entire body. She opened swollen eyes to see Ezra sitting at the table feeding Ben. She only watched a moment, trying to get her thoughts together. She sensed her nakedness, and knew that Ezra had raped her, even though she remembered none of it. Was he insane? He had beaten her into unconsciousness and had still taken his pleasure from her limp, half-dead body.

She watched Ben a moment. There were tear stains on his dirty little face, but no signs that he had been abused. How much had he seen? Had he screamed and cried while his mother was being abused?

Ezra caught her looking at him, and he quickly looked away. "I'm sorry," he told her. "It was the whiskey. I was celebrating the harvest . . . got carried away."

She turned her battered body away from him. "It's too late to be sorry. Go away, Ezra. Please just go away. I think I'm going to be sick."

He sighed and rose from the table. "I'm going to the

woods along the river and cut some wood for our winter supply."

"We won't need a winter supply," she answered coldly. "Ben and I won't be here. Cut the wood for yourself, if you want, but I'll not spend another winter with you, not out here alone."

She didn't care what he thought of her decision or if he killed her for it. She could take no more. The next thing she heard was the door closing and the wagon rolling away.

Four days later Katie was able to walk around, but with a great deal of pain. She had no idea how extensive her injuries might be. Her lower lip was cut, and her left eye was swollen nearly shut. In the mirror she hardly recognized herself for all the bruises. Her ribs ached, her insides ached, even her breasts were bruised. Little Ben followed her everywhere, crying often and clinging to her skirts. She wanted to leave, but was physically unable to consider making the journey to the fort. She would have to wait, but she would go.

When she heard the dreaded sound of the wagon returning, she hurried to the handgun and made sure it was loaded. If Ezra was drunk again, she would shoot him. She ordered Ben to stay inside and she went to the door, determined not to let the man inside.

She stepped outside and glared at Ezra, but he looked pale. He halted the wagon and looked at her strangely. "I'm . . . not drunk, Katie," he told her, turning and clinging to the seat as though he might fall off. "I . . . was chopping . . . axe slipped. I tried to stop . . . the bleeding . . ."

She frowned and lowered the gun as he literally fell out of the wagon onto the ground. Then she gasped and felt

399

ill. His right foot was missing. "Ezra!" She hurried to him and knelt down, cradling his head in her lap. "Help me get you inside. I'll tie it off!"

"No," he said, his voice weak. "No . . . time left. I hung on . . . to get this far . . . to tell you . . . ask you . . . forgive me . . . before I die, Katie. Something . . . happens . . . inside . . . can't stop it."

She burst into tears and bent over, cradling his head against her breast. "My God, Ezra!" She choked back a sob. "Yes. Yes, I forgive you," she told him, her lips close to his ear. "Ezra, I tried—"

She felt his hand on her arm. "I know. Take care of . . . my Ben. Only thing . . . I did right."

"Ezra! Ezra! I could have loved you, if you just would have let me."

His hand fell from her arm and she straightened. His eyes were open but looked glazed. "Ezra!" Too much blood had left his body. He was dead. "Ezra!" She screamed his name then, bending over and weeping bitterly. Whether for him or herself or Tohave she wasn't sure. She really could have learned to love him, if only he had been kind to her from the beginning. She rocked him against her tired, bruised body, as she sat alone under the big Nebraska sky.

Chapter Twenty-Three

Colonel Rogers rode toward the Russell farm, accompanied by seven men. He called out, but there was no reply and apparently no one around. The horses and cows wandered loose, grazing at random, and the door to the earthen home stood open.

"Mrs. Russell. Mr. Russell," he called out again. When no one answered, he started to dismount.

"Sir . . . up there." One of his men pointed, and Rogers looked toward a distant ridge, where someone sat alone.

"You men stay here," he told the others, heading toward the lone figure. "I see no sign of violence, but something is wrong." He glanced at the load of wood in the wagon nearby, the horses still hitched to it. "Someone unhitch that team. It looks worn out." Then he saw the blood near the wagon and in front of the wagon seat. "I take that back about the violence. Unhitch the team and keep an eye out." He headed up the ridge.

As he came closer, Rogers saw that the figure was that of a woman. He was relieved, for he'd feared something had happened to Katie Russell. Little Ben wandered near her, chasing a butterfly, but Rogers' heart tightened with concern as, drawing closer, he found Katie sitting beside a fresh grave, staring down at the palms of her hands. They were bleeding. A shovel lay nearby, as well as a piece of rope.

"Mrs. Russell?"

She turned and looked up at him with a blank expression. Startled to see her face so badly bruised and swollen, he immediately dismounted and came close, kneeling beside her.

"What the hell happened to you, Katie?" He used her first name naturally, for he had thought of her often, and now she was hurt. It tore at his heart to see her this way.

"I . . . don't think I dug it . . . deep enough. Do you think it's deep enough?"

"What?" He glanced at the grave, then back at her oddly staring eyes. "Who is in the grave, Katie? Is it your husband?"

She blinked, and her eyes teared. "I dug . . . deep as I could. See my hands? It was hard . . . all that shoveling. I dragged him up here myself . . . all by myself. It took me a long time. He's . . . so heavy."

Rogers glanced at the rope and shovel, then her hands. He took them gently in his own. "Katie, what happened?"

"His . . . foot . . . he . . . chopped it off . . . bled to death. I tried . . . to help, but it was . . . too late. His foot was gone . . . when he came home." Her eyes widened and she sucked in her breath. "Gone! It was . . . gone!" Her voice rose to a near scream at the words, and Rogers grasped her arms.

"It's all right, Katie. Everything will be all right."

She smiled and touched his face. "Tohave," she whispered.

He frowned, unable to quell a slight tinge of jealousy. Perhaps his suspicions about her and Tohave had been true. Now, in her sorry state, she was reaching out for someone who had loved her.

"Tohave is dead, Katie." He shook her slightly.

"Katie, it's me—Colonel Rogers. Remember me?"

She blinked again, then hung her head and started crying. "My God!" she wept. "I . . . tried to love him . . . tried to make it work. If he just . . . would have been kind . . ."

He could not resist pulling her close. She needed to be held. "What happened to you, Katie? Did Ezra beat you?"

She sucked in a sob and cried harder. "I told him . . . to get out. I was . . . going to shoot him . . . if he came home drunk again . . . but his foot . . . he died. I was bad! I was bad!"

"No. You weren't bad, Katie. No man has a right to do this to a woman. Come on, now. Come away from here and let me help you. I'll help you gather your things. You're coming to the fort so the doctor can have a look at you. God only knows what that man did to you."

"I . . . have to stay . . . the crops . . . the animals—"

"Never mind them. We'll herd the animals back to the fort with us and I'll send men back to get your stored food, to keep or sell, whatever you want. We'll just take your necessities for now. We can't take your wagon. The horses look too tired, and it's full of wood. I'll have men unload the wood and we'll take care of the other things later. Right now you're coming to the fort, and no arguments."

"The grave . . . it's not deep enough . . ."

"We'll take care of that, too." He couldn't help wondering if she might have killed her husband herself. He would have his men dig up the grave and verify that Ezra Russell had a missing foot but no bullet wounds. He didn't like to think the worst, but from the looks of Katie Russell, he would not blame her if she had shot her husband in self-defense. He helped her up, keeping a supportive arm around her. "Come along, Ben," he told the boy. "Follow your mama back to the house."

Ben hurried up to them, taking Rogers' hand, and the three of them walked down the hill as one of his men rode up it. The young soldier stopped before them and stared at Katie's face.

"Her husband is dead," Rogers told him. "He had an accident chopping wood, from what I can get out of Mrs. Russell. Apparently he bled to death. Take care of my horse, and get a couple more men up here to dig up the grave and make sure it's deep enough. She's worried that it isn't."

"Yes, sir. What happened to her face, sir?"

Rogers sighed. "Her husband beat her. From the looks of her bruises, it was a few days ago. I fear she's suffered injuries that should have been tended to right away. I'm taking her to the fort. We'll see to any other details later. Right now I want to get her to the house. Bring my horse down."

"Right, sir."

The young man headed up the hill to get the horse, and Rogers slowly walked Katie to the house, supporting her.

"Why did you drag him up there, Katie? Why didn't you use a horse?"

"I . . . had to do it myself . . . I was a bad wife . . . my punishment . . ."

"Nonsense! No man alive would call you a bad wife. The first time I saw you over two years ago I could see what was going on. Considering the circumstances, it's amazing you accomplished what you did and kept your sanity."

He led her inside and made her sit on the bed while he poured water from a kettle into a pan and looked around for clean washclothes. He wet one and pressed it against her palms. "I have some salve I can put on these blisters. It will help. You lie down, and I'll get you some water."

She winced as she lay back, grasping at her side. Rogers frowned. "Lie still, Katie." He pulled her hand away and

404

felt along her ribs, and she jumped with pain. "Bastard!" he muttered. He was glad Ezra Russell was dead. Now this poor young woman was free to live a normal life.

He walked to the doorway and ordered two men to make up a travois. Two others were already digging the grave again and three men had begun to unload wood from the wagon.

Then Rogers brought a cup of water to Katie. While she sipped it, still looking blank and confused, he hunted around in the dresser, picking up a carpetbag and stuffing it with things that seemed most necessary. He picked up an undergarment and saw the objects that had lain beneath it—two carvings, a Sioux hair ornament. He frowned, picking them up and studying them in the light. The carvings were Tohave's work, and he did not doubt who had owned the hair ornament. There could be only one reason why she had kept these items hidden in her drawer. They were special to her, as Tohave had been. It made sense now, her defense of the Indians, but he still could not blame her. He put the items into the carpetbag. She might want to have them with her.

As he packed a few of little Ben's things, he looked at the boy, who had been watching him curiously, saying nothing. The child clung to a stuffed bear Katie had purchased for him at the fort during a long-ago visit.

"You hungry, Ben?" Rogers asked.

The boy stared at him, then nodded and he pointed to the cup Rogers had just used to give Katie some water.

"Of course! You're thirsty," Rogers said with a smile. "I should have known. God knows how long you've been wandering around while your mother was half out of her mind." He took the boy a cup of water and Ben grabbed it, holding it in chubby hands and drinking it down.

"Big boy!" Ben said, before handing the tin cup back to Rogers.

The colonel laughed lightly. "I guess you are!" He

405

then went to the doorway and ordered one of his men to milk the cow and bring the milk inside for Ben. Poking about, he found some bread in a wooden box, and there was stew on the stove, now getting cold. He rekindled the fire to heat it. "We'll get you something to eat now, son, and then we're all going for a little ride. Would you like to go for a ride on a horse? You can sit in front of me."

The boy toddled toward him. "Horse? Ride horse?"

Rogers grinned. "Yes. Ride horse. You sure say a lot of words for such a little thing. You must be a very smart boy, Ben."

He walked over to check on Katie again, and Ben followed, staring at his mother. Rogers wasn't sure if she slept, or if she had passed out.

"Daddy hurt," Ben said quietly, puckering his lips. When he reached out with a dimpled hand and patted his mother's face, Rogers' heart tightened with anger and sympathy.

"Mommy is okay now, Ben. She's just sleeping. She won't cry anymore, and daddy can't hurt her anymore. I'll take you back to the fort with me, and you can be around all the soldiers."

The boy looked the man over, reaching out and fingering the buttons on the front of Rogers' uniform. "Pitty," he said with a grin. He tried to pull one off but could not.

"Yes, they're pretty. Come along now and eat something." He picked Ben up and plunked him into one of the homemade chairs. The stew was beginning to heat up. Suddenly Rogers realized that by the time they were ready to go and little Ben was fed, it would be too late in the day to leave for the fort. Considering Katie's condition, he decided it would be better to let her rest for now. She had apparently dragged her husband up the hill to bury him, in spite of her bruises and very likely one or more cracked ribs. How she had done it, he couldn't imagine, for she was a small woman to begin with. He walked over to look at her again, then sighed.

"I wanted to start back today, Ben, but I suppose the morning will be soon enough. Then you can have a good sleep before we go." He looked over at the boy. "You be real quiet tonight for your mother, all right? No rough play and no screaming and laughing. And don't touch your mommy or jump on her. Do you understand, Ben?"

The boy nodded. "Mommy sick."

Rogers looked at her again, a lump forming in his throat. "Yes. Mommy is sick."

By the next morning Katie, utterly exhausted, had slipped into depression. She tried to rise but could not. Hopelessness swept over her. Ezra was dead. Was she to blame in some way? And what would she do now? She opened her eyes and stared around the room to see Colonel Rogers sleeping on his bedroll on the floor.

Colonel Rogers. She vaguely remembered he'd come the day before, talked to her, said something about going to the fort and seeing a doctor. What did he know? How terrible she must look now, all bruised and swollen, and how sick inside she was over Ezra. Ezra! He had asked her to forgive him, at the very last moment. In all their stormy married life he had never said he was sorry for anything; then, dying, he had said it.

She choked back a sob, then cried out because of the pain in her ribs, which seemed to be worse. Within a second Colonel Rogers was at her side.

"Mrs. Russell. Are you awake?"

She looked up at him with tear-filled eyes. "My side . . . hurts. I have to go . . . to the bathroom. I can't . . . get up. I try and try . . ."

"It's all right." He picked her up and carefully carried her outside to the outhouse Ezra had built at Katie's insistence. Then he gingerly set her on her feet. "Do you need some help, Katie? It's all right, you know. I'm here to help you."

She grasped the wall. "I'm . . . all right. Wait for me. I don't think . . . I can walk back."

He moved back and closed the door. Minutes later it opened and she half fell outside. Rogers picked her up again.

"All modesty aside," he said sternly. "I'm going to get these clothes off you and bathe you and wrap those ribs. I'll put something more comfortable on you before we leave, a gown or something, then wrap you in blankets."

"Don't let . . . the men see . . ."

"No one will see. Just me. You trust me, don't you, Katie?"

She looked into his soft gray eyes then. What choice did she have? But he was a kind man, and yes, she did trust him. She was sick. She wanted to get better, for Ben's sake. "Don't . . . look at me."

"Don't talk foolish. I'm not that kind of man. I just want to get you as comfortable as I can and then get you to the fort and turn you over to the doctor. He's good, but not as good as the one we had here a year ago. That one was only at the fort for a little while, to train this new one they sent us. I'm told the doctor who's gone was an expert at removing bullets, but you'll like this new one. He's young, but he's good. He'll fix you right up and you'll feel better in no time."

"I have to . . . get better . . . for Ben."

"Of course you do."

He carried her inside and laid her back down, then put a kettle of water on the stove to heat before carefully removing all her clothing except her bloomers. His men were still working outside, feeding the animals, stacking wood, building a cross for the grave. To Rogers' relief, one of them had reported that Ezra Russell had, indeed, lost a foot, and that there were no signs of any other wounds. Fearing Katie might have shot her husband, Rogers had asked them to check.

Now, although he longed to let his eyes linger on Katie's full, firm breasts, he checked his baser needs. He was a moral man, and this was not a situation in which he had the right to let his eyes linger on her. Katie Russell trusted him, and she was injured. He pulled a sheet over her and poured water into a pan, then wet a cloth and sponged her off, getting angrier by the minute as he saw the bruises on her body, even on her breasts, which he could not help but notice as he washed her. If Ezra Russell were still alive, he would consider killing the man himself. He took gauze from his saddle bag and began to wrap it around Katie's middle, hoping the support would ease her pain. Then he found a flannel gown and slipped it over her head.

How tempting and beautiful she was, even in her condition, as she lay there on the bed, her figure lithe and curved. What a waste for a man to abuse such a treasure. If he had the right, Rogers would hold her, kiss her, touch her tenderly and soothingly. But he did not. He pulled the gown over her and covered her, then searched around for whiskey, finding a bottle and bringing it to her.

"Sip some of this," he told her. "It will ease the pain. Then we'll leave."

Her eyes widened at the sight of the whiskey bottle, and she let out a little squeal, pushing at it weakly. "No! No, take it away! Don't . . . drink it! Don't drink it! You'll hurt me!"

He frowned and quickly set the whiskey aside. "Katie, I just wanted you to sip a little for pain, that's all. I'm not drinking any."

"No! I don't want to look at it! Take it away, please!"

"All right." He rolled it under the bed, then gently

stroked the hair back from her face. "It's all right, Katie. I'm here to help you, not hurt you. The men are putting together a travois. The wagon is unloaded but it has a bad wheel. We'll take you to the fort and leave you with the doctor, then come back here, fix the wagon, and fill it with your belongings. We'll bring them to the fort, and you're welcome to stay there until you are well and can decide what you want to do."

She studied Rogers' gray eyes again. He was a good man. "I need my things . . . clothes . . ."

"I've taken care of all that."

"And there's something in the drawer I want to take."

Their eyes held. "The eagle and horse? The hair ornament?"

Her eyes teared again. "How did you know?"

"I already found them. They belonged to Tohave, didn't they?"

A tear slipped down the side of her face and she turned away. He wiped at the tear. "It's all right, Katie. I understand. You've been through hell, but it's over now. We're going to the fort. I'll help you. Everything will be fine now."

She closed her eyes, enjoying the gentle touch of his hand as he stroked her hair. It reminded her of Tohave and the way he had touched her. Tohave. She was free now. But he was dead. How cruel fate could be sometimes.

Katie lay in the infirmary, recovering from Ezra's cruel beating, her emotions mixed. She grieved for her husband, not because she had loved him or would miss him, but because of his own lost soul. Ezra Russell had never been a happy man, and his kind of unhappiness was not anything she could have done anything about. If he had lived, he would only have destroyed her as well as himself, and perhaps little Ben, too. She knew that now. The most understanding woman in the world could not have gotten along with Ezra Russell, let alone the young girl who'd known nothing about life and love or men and sex when she'd married him.

What was she to do now? Perhaps she should go back to Illinois and Aunt Jessica, but it hurt to think of leaving Nebraska again. Something was pulling at her, yet she could not name what it was. She still clung to her love of this land because of the love she had had for Tohave. After all she had been through, Tohave seemed to be the only sweet and wonderful thing she had known, and the only way she could cling to the memory of him was to stay in the land that he'd loved.

But what did a lone young woman with a son do in this land? There seemed to be little choice but to sell Ezra's acreage and go back East. But she had been through so much. Her blood was in this land and perhaps her heart, too. She would write Aunt Jessica and tell her about Ezra. Her aunt would tell her father and her brothers. They were one of the reasons she didn't want to go back. Perhaps her father would find a way to force her to care for him and her brothers again, now that Ezra was dead. He had a way of dominating her, and she was afraid to be under his thumb.

She felt lost and alone, with nowhere to turn. She had not seen Colonel Rogers since he'd first brought her here. The doctor had told her there was a lot of trouble on the reservations. Patrols were sent out constantly. Rogers was a busy man. As she lay there healing, she could hear the drums and singing clearly, especially at night. Fort Robinson was much closer to the reservation than her farm had been. They were eerie sounds. At night, when she lay listening, she could picture Tohave, standing tall amid the dancers, his powerful arms raised in prayer. If he were alive, would he be taking part in this

411

new religion? She could not help but wonder what he would think of it, of what his people were doing, of the problems this new faith was creating. Sometimes she longed to be able to talk to him. His simple outlook on life would make her smile, as would his practicality and his sweet sense of humor. How she missed him!

It had been two years now since he had ridden out of her life, to die and never return. Yet even now, after all this time and all the proof of his death, she could not get over the feeling that a man like Tohave did not die. To envision him lifeless was impossible. Yet he was, and now Ezra was dead. For the first time in her entire life she was on her own. She was free to choose what she wanted, but what was there to choose from? Once she would have chosen Tohave, but that choice had been taken from her. She now had the freedom she should have had before she'd married Ezra. She was no longer the innocent virgin she'd been then, a young girl with dreams of how marriage should be. Those dreams had been shattered, and all the beauty had gone out of her life. All she had left was little Ben, and her love for her son overcame the ugliness of the act that had conceived him. The boy could not be blamed for that. He was sweet and beautiful and good. Perhaps all the goodness Ezra could not seem to pull from his own being had been transferred to Ben. The boy would be good whereas his father had not. Ben would not be an unloved, tormented soul.

Watching over the boy had been no problem. He was a popular character around the fort now, seen to by one man or another and given horseback rides and all the food he wanted to eat. Katie feared that her son was being spoiled, that she would never get him back to a normal routine once she was able to go home, wherever that would be. She really didn't have a home anymore. She could not bear going back to the farm. There were simply too many bad memories there. She had never been happy

412

on it, except for one precious night. No. Going back to the farm would be too painful. But going back to Illinois didn't seem right either, in spite of her affection for Aunt Jessica. She was afraid of her father, afraid he would gain control of her. Besides, she didn't belong in Illinois anymore. She really didn't belong anywhere.

Depression swept over her, as it had many times during her recovery; and she found herself crying confusedly. When Colonel Rogers entered Katie's room he caught her in one of her low moments, and he frowned as he walked briskly to her bedside.

"What's this? You're getting better, and you're all safe and cared for here, but you're crying. We can't have this."

She put a hand to her eyes. "I'm sorry. I . . . didn't know anyone was coming. I haven't seen you since you brought me here." She pushed back a piece of hair self-consciously. "I must look a mess."

He grasped her hand, squeezing it lightly. "You look beautiful. You always look beautiful."

She met his eyes and reddened. "Colonel Rogers, I don't know how to thank you."

"You can start by calling me Will—short for William, my first name. I've been calling you Katie since the day I came for you. It just seemed natural. I hope that doesn't offend you." He continued to hold her hand, his grip gentle and reassuring.

"I'm not offended," she replied, and their eyes held again. "I'm . . . glad you came. I've thought about you."

"Have you truly?"

She smiled a little through her tears. "I have. I was worried, what with all the trouble they say is going on. What is happening with the Indians?"

He sighed deeply, let go of her hand, and pulled a chair up to her bed. "Plenty. General Miles is working on his own strategy. I'm afraid we're going to get orders to put

413

an end to the dancing and singing. It's scaring the citizens to death, harmless though it is, but I personally do not care to go in there and stop it. There is bound to be trouble. It's only October. I'm afraid there is a long winter ahead for all of us, which brings me to you. I've been thinking about you, too, you know."

She wiped at her eyes again. "You have?"

"Almost constantly, while I've been out on patrol." When he hesitated, his eyes scanning her lovely form beneath the sheet, she reddened again, for she realized he had seen her nearly naked the morning he had bathed her and wrapped her ribs. It had been necessary, yet she could not help but be embarrassed now. She looked away, but he took her hand again. "I only helped you, Katie," he told her, reading her thoughts. "And I've been thinking about you because . . ."—he sighed—"I've always worried about you, since the first time I met you and saw you with Ezra Russell, saw how he acted toward you, saw the sadness in your pretty eyes. I admire your courage and strength, your determination to keep going."

She closed her eyes, and her chest shook in a sob. "I'm not so courageous," she said. "When I was forced to marry Ezra . . . I didn't know any better. I'd only known brutality. I thought that was how it was supposed to be for a woman. I didn't find courage or strength or beauty until I . . . met someone. He's gone now, and I think all my courage went with him."

Rogers felt a pang of jealousy. "Courage comes from inside, Katie. You're much stronger than you think. The woman I saw on the hill a couple of weeks ago had dragged her husband up there and had buried him, and she'd wept for him in spite of the beast he'd been. That took courage."

A tear slipped down her cheek. "Well, I don't have any left now. I don't know what to do . . . where to go."

"That's why I came to see you. I was afraid you would leave before I could talk to you." He kept hold of her hand. "Katie, if you have no place to go, why don't you just stay right here?"

She turned to look at him. "Here? What would I do here?"

"Our men could stand a woman's cooking now and then. We have our own cooks, of course, but no one would mind if you baked a few pies and such. And some of the men would gladly pay you to do their mending. God knows none of us are very good at that. There are a number of things you could do. You could live in one of the small houses on the post reserved for married couples, and while you're here, I could help you put ads in the Denver and Chicago papers if you choose to sell your land. Your livestock can be sold right here at the fort to other farmers. You can't handle the sale of the land very well if you're back in Illinois. You almost have to stay here, at least until that is taken care of."

She sniffed and wiped at her eyes again. "You're very kind, Colonel—I mean, Will. You've given me something to think about."

"The men all like little Ben. He's having a picnic."

"I'm afraid he'll be spoiled," Katie said, smiling now.

"It's good for him. He's surrounded by soldiers and horses—all good things for a boy to grow up with."

She sniffed again. "I suppose."

Rogers pulled a clean handkerchief from an inside pocket and handed it to her. "Here. No more crying."

She took it gratefully and blew her nose. "That won't be easy."

He glanced at the horse and the eagle she kept on the little stand beside her bed, and when his eyes met hers again, she sobered. What was the use in hiding it now? Perhaps he should know. It might change his opinion of her. He might not even want her to stay.

415

"They were Tohave's," she told him. "He gave me the eagle. The woman who came to tell me he was dead gave me the horse."

He picked up the eagle and studied it. "Tohave had a way of capturing the very spirit of an animal."

"That's because he was close to the animals in spirit." She looked away. "He was as wild and graceful as a wild creature. He was a beautiful person."

Rogers ran a finger over the eagle. "I found a Sioux hairpiece with your things, too." He looked at her, but her face was turned away. "Somehow the two of you became close. I don't know how Tohave managed it, but if anyone could do it, Tohave could. He must have been very clever to find ways to see you without your husband knowing. You loved him, didn't you?"

She met his eyes then, her own proud and unflinching. "Yes."

He wanted to ask her how far they had gone, but he had no right. Not yet. And perhaps it was best he never knew. If she had become as involved with Tohave as he feared, he could not fully blame her. Tohave had been bright and handsome, and probably gentle with women. Still, Katie's relationship was difficult for him to accept. Tohave was an Indian. But he was dead now, and this woman had suffered enough.

He patted her hand. "Love is something that knows no bounds," he told her. "I suspected all of this a long time ago. My God, Katie, you needed a friend, some kind of hope. I'm sure Tohave gave that to you." He rose then. "I want you to stay, and I hope you and I can be friends. When you're well, and you've made your decision . . . if you decide to stay here, I'd like to feel free to call on you when I'm not out on patrol." He smiled nervously. "God knows there isn't much a man can do out here for a woman. There are no nice places to go. But I can take you

416

riding, or walk you from one side of the fort to the other."

They both smiled then. "Thank you, Will, for understanding. If I stay, I'd love to see you as often as you choose. I do need a friend, and you've been a good friend already." Her eyes teared a little. "I'm so lonely. The last two and a half years have been ... like a nightmare."

He leaned closer, pressing her shoulders reassuringly. "Don't think about it anymore. Look ahead, Katie. Just look ahead." He leaned down and kissed her forehead, then quickly straightened, looking nervous again. "I have to go. If you feel like getting up tomorrow, the doctor said it would be all right if I took you for a walk. Would you like that?"

She smiled. "I'd love it."

He nodded. "Fine. I'll come after lunch."

Their eyes held a moment longer. "Good-bye," he said quietly. Then he turned and left.

Katie watched him go. "Good-bye," she whispered.

Chapter Twenty-Four

Katie accepted Colonel Rogers' offer and stayed on at Fort Robinson. He was indeed right about the mending. She had almost more than she could keep up with, and the money this work brought in enabled her to buy the few things she needed until her land could be sold. Her wants were few because she ate at the mess hall with Colonel Rogers whenever he was there, and with an appointed escort if he was not. All the soldiers found themselves hoping to be Katie Russell's appointed escort for she was a very pretty young woman, a rare sight in this territory, and her son provided entertainment for all of them.

For Katie her days at the fort were a time of healing, inside and out. She had friends among the soldiers and among the settlers who came and went. For the first time, she was free to talk to other women openly, to be her own person. Sometimes at night she awoke, shivering with fear, thinking this was all a dream and that she was back in the earthen dugout being mauled by Ezra Russell. She always breathed a sigh of relief when she came fully awake and realized she was still at the fort in her little whitewashed wooden house. There were even rosebushes by the steps, although they were dying off now, as

October moved into November.

Colonel Rogers often came to visit her. Sometimes she cooked a meal for him, and sometimes they just went for a ride or a walk. He was a kind and pleasant man, and she knew he had more than friendly interest in her. She was aware that she would be wise to nourish his interest. She was a widow with a son, and no finer man could be found than William Rogers, a colonel, no less. But something prevented her from allowing her friendship with Will to move toward something more serious. There was a restlessness inside of her, and at night when she heard the Indians singing, heard their rhythmic drums, it increased.

She knew the why. Tohave. She could not get him off her mind, no matter how hard she tried. He was in her blood, haunting her like a ghost. If he was dead, why, then, couldn't she bury him? She was angry with herself. She should be looking ahead, as Will had told her to do. She should be thinking about Will, letting herself love again. To cling to a memory was fruitless. She was only twenty-one. She must forget about Tohave. Yes. That was what she would do.

By late November, Colonel Rogers was visiting almost nightly, so Katie prepared a grand Thanksgiving meal for him and his aids. Will stayed after the others left, and helped Katie clean up the table. Little Ben had fallen asleep in the stuffed chair in the corner of the room.

"You needn't do this, Will," Katie declared. "Go and sit by the fire. I'll be through soon."

He took her arm and turned her to face him, holding her eyes. "Come sit by the fire with me. Leave this until later. I want to talk to you, Katie."

She swallowed and looked down, her heart racing. She knew what he wanted, but she was not sure that she wanted it too. Will led her to the old sofa in front of the fireplace setting her down and sitting beside her. Then he took a deep breath.

"Katie, I—" He stopped a moment, meeting her eyes again. What pretty blue eyes they were. She watched him carefully, seeing the love in his gray eyes and telling herself not to draw away as his face came closer and his lips touched her own. He kissed her tenderly at first, then more demandingly as he pulled her into his arms. Katie returned his kiss, not out of passion, but out of curiosity. She had to know. Could she love this man? Could she feel passion for him? He was kind, good, intelligent, handsome, successful. She wanted to love him. She should love him.

Rogers was trembling now, his lips moving over her cheek and throat as he started to lay her down on the sofa, but she stiffened and pushed at him. "No, Will." She moved away, putting her hands to her flushed cheeks and looking at her lap. "I'm sorry."

He sighed deeply. "I'm the one who should be sorry. Forgive me, Katie. I had no right. It's just that . . . that I think I love you. I mean, I do love you. But I know your husband has only been gone for two months, and—"

"I didn't love him, Will. I don't pretend to be in deep mourning. It isn't that, really. It's just . . ."—she sighed deeply, wanting to cry—"I've been through so much these last two years. I guess I'm just . . . tired. Ezra was so brutal, our marriage so loveless, I'm afraid of something like that happening again." She stood up and walked to a window, looked out at the lightly falling snow. "You're kind and wonderful, Will, but I don't know if I want any man right now. I've loved, truly loved, only once, yet I almost feel that I have no love left in me."

He rose and came up behind her, putting a hand on her shoulder. "You have plenty of love in you. It's just been buried under ugly memories, that's all. You're afraid to feel anything, afraid to let go."

421

She put her face in her hand and cried quietly. "Ezra made me feel like a harlot," she said in a near whisper. "I felt so dirty and used."

"Katie! That's foolish talk." He turned her and held her close. "He was your husband, and a forceful man. You've got to rid yourself of those thoughts, Katie."

She rested her head against his chest. "I don't think I can give myself to a man again without being completely certain that I love him, that I feel passion for him. I'm frightened of giving myself to someone out of loneliness, or just to find a father for Ben."

"Look at me, Katie." She raised her eyes to meet his. "Are you trying to tell me you feel no passion for me?"

She swallowed. "I don't even know. I'm so afraid to feel anything."

He bent down and his lips met hers, searching, teasing, sparking a little flame deep inside her, the flame that had died out when Tohave had ridden out of her life. But it was not the same. With Will the flame only flickered. With Tohave it had roared up into a hot fire that could not be put out. So much had died with him, never to be reawakened.

Will broke off the kiss, pain in his eyes. "It's Tohave, isn't it?"

Her eyes teared and she pulled away.

"He's dead, Katie."

"Is he? Has anyone ever seen his grave, his burial site? We only know what we were told. Perhaps he's crippled and doesn't want anyone to know it. Perhaps he's afraid that if the soldiers know he's alive, they'll come for him to punish him for killing those traders. We have no real proof of his death, and I just can't accept it, Will."

"You must!" he said, his voice sharp. "He was just a man, not superhuman, Katie. He got shot. He died. It's as simple as that. And if you don't accept it, you're going to die a shriveled old widow who never knew love and happiness except for one brief encounter with an Indian."

She reddened and turned away, folding her arms and shivering. "I'm sorry, Will."

He sighed deeply, trying to control his jealousy. She had been to young, too brutalized. He could not possibly blame her. "Katie, I love you. I want to marry you. And I think I have a right to know how far . . . what happened between you and Tohave. Were you more than just friends?"

She stood turned away for several long, silent moments. "He brought beauty into my life where there was none," she replied. "With him, for the first time I realized not all men were beasts. My father beat me as far back as I can remember. My wedding night with Ezra was . . ." She shivered, and Will came closer, putting his hands on her shoulders.

"Katie, I didn't mean to make you remember all that."

"It's all right." She took a deep breath. "Tohave made me feel warm and alive and loved—pretty, appreciated, respected. He taught me that a woman can enjoy giving herself to a man when it's done out of true love, genuine desire." She stepped away from Will, her back still to him. "Yes, we were more than friends, Will. In our hearts we were man and wife, even though a piece of paper said I belonged to Ezra Russell. I had never belonged to Ezra, not in my mind. When Ezra touched me I felt I was being raped. But Tohave didn't just take me. I took him in return. There aren't many whites who would understand why, not many who would appreciate the kind of man he was. If you hate me now, you're free to go. I wouldn't blame you."

He forced back his jealousy, telling himself not to be biased. He didn't want to lose her to a memory. "Tohave was an intelligent, likable young man," he replied. "He was exceedingly handsome, skilled and talented. If he'd

423

had any sense, he could have made a lot of money selling his carvings to that art dealer who came through here a couple of years ago. But he wasn't ready to settle down. His wild blood kept getting him into trouble. It made him dare to love a white woman and to claim her, and that ended in his death. I liked Tohave, Katie. I'm not out here to kill Indians. I'm out here to keep the peace. I'll fight if I have to, but I'm not against Indians in general like most whites. I know what you went through, and I don't hate you for turning to someone who helped you forget the ugliness in your life, someone who gave you hope for something better. God knows what any woman would do in such a situation."

She turned to face him, a tear slipping down her cheek. "I appreciate your understanding, Will. But you must understand it didn't happen because my marriage was so horrible. I truly loved Tohave. He wasn't just a way out. And he loved me. He didn't see me as white anymore, and I didn't see him as an Indian. We were good friends, natural together, happy; and if I should love you and marry you, can you honestly say that knowing I was with him wouldn't bother you? Are you sure you wouldn't harbor some resentment that might come out later? And if we were in a big city, like St. Louis, where there are many young women, untouched women, isn't it possible you'd find yourself wishing you had married one like that? Maybe you think you love me because I'm the only available young woman around here and you're lonely."

His eyes ran over her shapely body. He wanted her, but was she right? Was it because he was lonely? Katie was indeed beautiful. Of that there was no question. He smiled sadly.

"You do have a way of making a man think, don't you?"

She came closer, hugging him around the middle. "Oh, Will, I just don't want to marry for the wrong reasons. It

424

has to be right, completely right. It would be so easy to tell myself that I love you, to give myself to you just to be a woman again. But I want my heart to belong to you totally, and yours to belong to me in return. There can be no jealousy, no harbored resentment. I guess maybe it's still too soon. I often wake up with nightmares about Ezra, and this is the first time I've ever been free and on my own. I need more time, Will, time to think, to know my own heart. If I didn't care so much for you, it wouldn't matter. But you're a good man. You deserve the best."

"Hey." He took hold of her chin and forced her to look up at him. "You are the best. Don't underestimate yourself, Katie. Your problem is brutal, thoughtless men have told you that you aren't important, that you're only good for washing floors and making babies. I don't look at a woman that way, Katie—surely you know that—and I would never be cruel to you."

She turned her face and kissed his hand. "I know." She sighed and pulled away. "Will you do something for me, Will? It might help me to think about the future instead of living in the past."

"What's that?" When he came closer and stroked her hair, she turned and met his eyes boldly.

"Will you inquire about Tohave, ask where he's buried? You'll be riding onto the reservations soon to order the Ghost Dancing stopped."

He sighed and frowned. "I'm afraid so. It's a job I don't care to do, but orders are coming down to put an end to it." He studied her eyes. "I wish I could hate you, Katie. That would be easier than loving you and knowing your heart still bleeds for someone else."

"I'm so sorry, Will. I'm not saying I don't love you. I do. But I don't know if I love you enough to marry you. I don't want to be unfair to you, and it would be easier for me if I could just settle this thing in my heart about

425

Tohave. Rosebud came and told me he was dead, but that's all the proof I have. When he left me, he was still alive. Then McBain left, and you left, and new men came in, and he was just . . . forgotten. The rumor spread that he was dead, and that was the end of it. Perhaps it was circulated to make sure there would be no more trouble. Isn't it possible he's hiding, perhaps on another reservation, because he's afraid the soldiers will arrest him? Rosebud might have been protecting him. And maybe Tohave thinks I went away for good and never came back. I don't know, Will. I just can't believe that a man like Tohave is really dead."

He shook his head. "Katie, I saw him when they brought him in. The army doctor said there was no way to take out the bullet—to remove it would have killed him—and if it was left in him he couldn't possibly live. There has been no word of Tohave ever since. I'll ask around, but I'm warning you that you've got to stop hoping for something that cannot be. It isn't good for you, and it's bad for Ben. Your son needs a father, Katie, and you need a husband, someone to look after you. And surely you want more children."

She blushed and looked away. "Yes. I don't want Ben to grow up an only child."

"Then you're going to have to make up your mind. Ben will be two years old come spring, and you'll have been out here three years then. By spring I'll make damned sure we have proof Tohave is dead, and I'll know what I still want. It will be up to you then, Katie. I'll let you be during the winter, so you can get your strength back and look into your heart. God knows you deserve to be left entirely alone for a while. Perhaps I spoke too soon. But I would like an answer by spring, and I'll have an answer for you then, about Tohave. Agreed?"

She met his gaze. "Agreed." She sighed deeply. "Will, I'm deeply honored that you want to marry me. I don't take it lightly. That's why I want to be sure. You're a fine man, and you've been a good friend when I needed one. And there aren't many men who would understand about Tohave."

His cheeks colored a little with repressed jealousy. "I'm not that understanding, Katie, but I care about you. God knows you don't need someone hammering at you over Tohave."

The wind picked up then, making the little house creak, and Katie looked up at the ceiling, remembering how the wind had picked up whenever Tohave was near. She could not get over the feeling. She looked back at Will.

"I have to risk losing you, Will, in order to know if we really could work out as a pair. I had to tell you the truth about Tohave. You will have to weigh it. And what about you? You say you're from Colorado. Isn't there, or wasn't there, some young lady who interested you, one who may think she loves you?"

He smiled nervously. "Not really. Oh, I saw McBain's daughter a couple of times when I visited him in Denver, but it was just a friendly thing."

Her eyebrows arched. "Oh? She came to your mind. Does that mean you think about her now and then?"

He studied her eyes. "Now and then."

She smiled and walked to him. "You see? I'm not the only one who has some thinking to do before spring."

She looked up at him, and their lips met again. It would be so easy to surrender to him out of pure need and sweet friendship. But that was not enough. When he pressed her close, awakening buried feelings, she found herself wishing it was Tohave holding her. Tohave. She pulled away then. Why couldn't she forget?

"You'd better go, Will, before we both do something foolish."

He sighed deeply, his whole body aching. But Katie

was right. This was not the time. And she had stirred up memories of Lisa McBain whom he hadn't thought of in quite some time.

"You're a fine woman, Katie, a wise woman." He picked up his hat. Remember what I said—I love you and want to marry you. We'll still see each other, won't we?"

She nodded. "Of course. And remember your promise to ask about Tohave."

"I will. I'll be riding out tomorrow morning to Pine Ridge. I'll see you in a couple of weeks."

"You'll be here for Christmas?"

"I hope to be. We celebrate big around here. Ben will have a good time."

She smiled. "Bring me a tree when you come back."

He nodded and winked. "Done."

Their eyes held a moment longer.

"Good night, Katie. Tell Ben good-bye for me."

"I will."

He turned then. If he kissed her again he knew he might not leave, so he hurried out, closing the door behind him. Katie walked to a window. Though it was down, she could hear the drums.

In Chicago, General Miles was convinced Sitting Bull was the primary instigator of the Ghost Dance religion, and he believed the Indians were planning an uprising. To remove Sitting Bull from Standing Rock and imprison him would not be an easy task. Only a few years earlier, Sitting Bull had spent one year traveling with Buffalo Bill's Wild West Show, in the hope of gaining white sympathy for the Indian. Cody, a friend to Sitting Bull, was therefore commissioned to go to Standing Rock to try to convince the Indian leader to come to Chicago for a conference. Whether or not Cody knew that in doing so, Sitting Bull would be made a prisoner, history has never revealed. But when he arrived at Standing Rock, the agent there turned him away and requested an order from Washington prohibiting Cody from talking to Sitting Bull. Buffalo Bill left in an angry huff, without being granted the chance to talk to his old friend Sitting Bull. Why agent McLaughlin refused Bill Cody permission to see Sitting Bull is another historical mystery, but he was not an agent who was well liked by the Indians. Like many agents, perhaps he would rather have trouble, just to make the Indians look bad, than peace. Or perhaps he was a jealous man, angry that Cody, who had more authority than McLaughlin himself, had come to the reservation.

In the meantime, Colonel Rogers proceeded with troops to the Pine Ridge Reservation. Deep inside he knew the presence of soldiers would only make the situation more tense. It would become a stick of dynamite just waiting for the fuse to be lit. When orders were given for the Indians to desist their new religious practices, some of the dancing stopped, but there was much praying inside the tipis and the Indians were very frightened. Would the soldiers open fire on them and shoot them down just for practicing their religion? What were they doing wrong? The white man worshipped his God. Were not their Saviors the same? Did soldiers ride in on the white men's churches and order them to stop worshipping?

While his men surrounded Pine Ridge and kept watch, Rogers received word by wire that General Miles had ordered more troops to Standing Rock from Fort Yates, for the purpose of taking Sitting Bull prisoner. Rogers checked his anger. It was a ridiculous order, but he could do nothing about it. He could only wait. If big trouble broke out, it would be wise to pull his troops away from the reservation and go back to Fort Robinson to await orders. The presence of soldiers only frightened the

Indians at Pine Ridge. Most of the Ghost Dancing had stopped, for the Indians knew that resuming their celebrations would bring more soldiers. The presence of troops had accomplished its purpose, for the time being. But there could be big trouble at Standing Rock.

It was mid-December when troops from Fort Yates, under Lieutenant-Colonel William F. Drum, moved in to take over Standing Rock. Tohave and other young men gathered in an angry circle.

"We had better arm ourselves!" Tohave warned.

"There are too many soldiers," the man next to him replied. "You know what they will do if we fire one shot! Our women and children and our old ones will be slaughtered! They only want Sitting Bull."

"And should we just let them take him without a fight?" Tohave growled.

"We no longer have a choice," a third man put in. "Sitting Bull warned us that if something like this happened we should not resist."

"Women! We are all women!" Tohave spat to the side in disgust.

"You know better than some of us what resisting can bring, Tohave. You are lucky to be alive," a friend told him. "Do you wish to take another bullet like the last one?"

"If it means I keep my pride, I will gladly take it!"

"Do as our leader asks, Tohave," an older Indian urged. "Sitting Bull says we must remain peaceful. Our new religion teaches this. We do not have to fight. All we have to do is wait for the Savior to come and renew the land, bring back our buffalo, and awaken our ancestors from the dead. Soon, Tohave. Soon all will be as it once was, and the white man will be gone."

Tohave whirled, throwing down his rifle and walking

away, to sit in the trees near Sitting Bull's cabin. Their leader lived in a white man's house now, as did many Indians. Tohave still preferred a tipi, but tonight he would sleep under the stars. He would watch over the beloved and wise Sitting Bull, a great man who had traveled all over the country and even into Canada, speaking to white people, showing white audiences the skills and the wisdom of the Indian. Surely he should be treated with great respect by the white leaders. But Tohave did not trust the soldiers. He had never trusted them. He would keep watch.

In the wee hours of the morning soft voices woke Tohave. He shivered under his thin blanket. It was December fifteenth and it was snowing. Sensing the presence of many men, he threw off the blanket and then peered through the trees to see forty or fifty of their own Indian police approaching Sitting Bull's cabin.

"So," he muttered to himself. "The soldiers were too much cowardly to come for you, Sitting Bull. They send our own men, thinking you will not resist them." He watched the Indians quietly come closer. "Traitors!" he hissed. He prayed Sitting Bull would go quietly.

He recognized Bull Head, a lieutenant in the Indian police. As that man approached the door of the cabin, Tohave looked around. He could not see the soldiers, but he knew that somewhere on the outer boundaries of the reservation they waited, ready to ride in and slaughter everyone in sight if there was trouble. His eyes quickly shifted back to Bull Head, who kicked in the door of Sitting Bull's cabin.

To Tohave's delight he saw that he was not the only one who had come to watch over Sitting Bull. Many of his friends, most of them Ghost Dancers, emerged now from hiding places and moved up behind the Indian police.

431

"You are my prisoner, Sitting Bull!" he heard Bull Head shout. "You must come to the agency with me."

Sitting Bull answered in a quiet voice that Tohave could not hear. He seemed to be offering no resistance. Tohave moved out of the trees and went to join his friends, one hand on his knife. More and more of them had gathered, and they now outnumbered the Indian police. From everywhere they came, one hundred, two hundred! Tohave smiled.

Bull Head emerged with Sitting Bull. From then on it all happened quickly. Catch-the-Bear, a Ghost Dancer, stepped forward, telling Bull Head he could not take Sitting Bull away. The confrontation made Sitting Bull hesitate to go. Bull Head urged the old chief not to listen to the others, that it would only make trouble, and he began to push Sitting Bull. Catch-the-Bear then pulled the blanket from around his shoulders, revealing a rifle. He fired at Bull Head and wounded him in the side. Bull Head fired back, missing Catch-the-Bear and hitting Sitting Bull instead, while at the same time another Indian policeman shot Sitting Bull in the head, killing him.

All hell broke loose then, and Tohave gladly joined in the fighting. He had not seen action in a long time. Now he would find out if he was still strong. As he drove his knife into one of the Indian police, another jumped him from behind. Tohave rose up, throwing the man off and then turning and kicking yet another policeman in the groin. How many men he killed or wounded before the soldiers rode in to stop the melee, he wasn't sure, but thinking the soldiers might still be looking for him because of the trappers, he ran off.

He quickly disappeared into the woods before he could be caught, as did some others. Behind him lay dead and wounded on both sides, including their beloved leader, Sitting Bull. The dead chief's old show horse, a gift from

Buffalo Bill during the days of Sitting Bull's appearance in the Wild West Shows, was standing near the bodies, but Sitting Bull would be seen and heard no more. Tohave looked back once, then down at his bloody knife. He was glad he'd sunk it into the heart of a traitor. He stabbed it over and over into a tree, in anger and sorrow, tears streaming down his face. It was over. Over! Over! Over! With Sitting Bull dead, what was left? And Katie . . . He felt a bit insane for always wondering what was happening to her. He ran through the woods to his tipi, shoving the knife into its sheath on the way. Rosebud looked up in alarm when she saw him coming.

"What is it?"

"Sitting Bull is dead!" He groaned. "I was there. I killed some men. I am leaving, Rosebud."

"Where will you go?"

"I do not know! I just want to go away, to ride. I will go to some of the other reservations, tell them the news, and see what is happening there. I am afraid my vision of more of our people being slaughtered will come true."

He quickly gathered some things and shoved them into his parfleche, then picked up his rifle.

"But what happened! How did Sitting Bull die?"

He whirled, glaring at her. "He was shot by one of us! The Indian police! Our own men killed him! Do you understand what that means? Divided we can never be strong again! Never! It is over. I see it now, Rosebud. This new religion will not save us! Nothing will save us! Nothing!" He walked out and threw his gear onto his black Appaloosa, which already carried a small, flat Indian saddle. "You stay here," he told Rosebud. "Once the soldiers stop the fighting over there by Sitting Bull's cabin, there will be no trouble for you. Stay here and do not resist if the soldiers make you move in closer to the agency. Stiff Leg will protect you. I must go. The soldiers might recognize me."

"Tohave, will you return?"

"I will see you again." Effortlessly he eased himself up onto his horse. "Tell Stiff Leg I said to watch over you. He has always been fond of you, Rosebud. I think he would like you to be his wife, for he needs no more sons. You have cared for me long enough. I am strong now. Stay with Stiff Leg. Marry him if you choose. I know that sometimes you look at him with desire. My heart is too full of someone else, and I no longer know what I want. Rosebud, Tohave is no good for you."

She grabbed his leg. "Tohave! I love you."

He sighed, reaching down and grasping her hand. "It is time for you to have peace in your life. Lie with Stiff Leg and let him love you, as I know he has silently for many moons. Let us just be the good friends we have always been. If nothing happens to Tohave, he will often bring you meat, and I will catch wild horses and bring them to you so you can trade them for things you need. Tohave can never repay you for what you have done for me, Rosebud. I will spend the rest of my life repaying you, but for now I must go. Stay with Stiff Leg. Take him to your bed and be a happy woman."

He turned his horse then and rode off. With an aching heart, Rosebud watched him go. Since he'd met Katie Russell he'd been a different man, and he probably never would be happy. Was he riding off to try to die in battle?

Word came quickly by wire that many Hunkpapas were fleeing Standing Rock in fear, most of them headed directly for Red Cloud's reservation at Pine Ridge. Colonel Rogers' anger knew no bounds. Sitting Bull had been killed. What had gone wrong? He left some of his men at Pine Ridge and headed into the hills, hoping to intercept some of the fleeing Hunkpapas and reassure them, perhaps escort them to Pine Ridge until things quieted down. At the same time a Major Samuel Whitside of the Seventh U.S. Cavalry was in the process of doing the same, but with orders from General Miles to disarm and dismount all Indians he found fleeing, and make them prisoners and escort them as such to Pine Ridge.

Rogers knew that in such confusion there could only be more disaster. The Hunkpapas had been frightened by charging soldiers at Standing Rock, by the death of their leader, Sitting Bull. They were running, sure that the soldiers would hunt them down to slaughter them, as had happened so many times in the past when they were simply trying to run to a safe place. He hoped the other soldiers realized that the new religion among the red men forbade them to fight. So far there had been no further apparent retaliation for Sitting Bull's death, only flight. If the Indians could be kept calm, if no white man did something stupid out of panic, the entire situation might be saved. But he knew how such events had, too often, ended in the past. He headed for Standing Rock, thinking about Katie. He wondered what she would think of all this, and if she was safe. He had not even had a chance to ask about Tohave. There was no time now. Besides, it was useless. Tohave was dead. A lot of good people were dead, and there would be more deaths before this was over.

Chapter Twenty-Five

Katie's anxiety grew when more troops arrived at Fort Robinson. There had been no word from Will yet, and he had been gone over two weeks. She stood at the doorway of the supply store, holding little Ben's hand, when the new troops rode in. It was a cold, windy day, and she pulled her coat closer around her neck. She decided she would go to command headquarters, where a lieutenant had been left in charge, and see if there was any word about Colonel Rogers. She had almost reached the door when a sergeant came out to greet the commander of the new troops. The men saluted quickly.

"Did you hear sir?" the sergeant spoke up. "Sitting Bull was shot. He's dead."

Katie's eyes widened, and she put a hand to her chest. What had happened?

"I heard," the major who had just arrived replied. "I'd like to go inside and talk to Lieutenant Dobson."

"Yes, sir."

The sergeant stepped aside, then noticed Katie standing nearby and listening. He nodded to her.

"Sergeant!" she spoke up, hurrying closer. "Is it true? About Sitting Bull?"

"Yes, ma'am. I'm afraid so. There was some kind of

skirmish up at Standing Rock. The soldiers sent in Indian police to arrest Sitting Bull for instigating the spread of the Ghost Dance. The way we heard quite a few of Sitting Bull's followers ganged up on the Indian police. A fight broke out and Sitting Bull was shot by the Indian police." He shook his head. "Shot by his own people. It's ironic, isn't it?"

She felt a chill, but from the inside, not the wind. "Yes. What will happen now?"

"I don't know, ma'am. I expect that's why the major just arrived from Fort Sully. Troops have been ordered to ride through Indian country and round up prisoners and keep guard until this thing quiets down. I'm told a lot of Indians broke loose from Standing Rock after the fight, running scared, I expect. The soldiers have to round them up, keep them from leaving reservation property and possibly attacking outlying farmers in retaliation. Some say they won't do any such thing—their new religion prohibits fighting and killing—but most don't believe they'll stick to that now. Sounds like a real mess."

She picked up little Ben and held him close. "I don't know who to feel sorry for, Sergeant. The Indians haven't really done anything wrong. Why was the government so insistent on stopping their worshipping?"

He shook his head. "You know how it goes, ma'am. The Indians raise their little finger, and the settlers think they're ready to go out and slaughter people. They scream for action, so the government gives it to them."

She closed her eyes and sighed. "What about Colonel Rogers. Have you heard from him?"

"Last we heard he'd left Pine Ridge and was heading north to Standing Rock to intercept fleeing Indians. Most seem to be headed toward Big Foot's Minneconjou camp near Cherry Creek. Now orders have been given to arrest Big Foot, too. That can only mean more trouble."

"Dear God." She turned away, hugging Ben close.

"Don't you worry about Colonel Rogers, ma'am. He's got plenty of men with him. He'll be fine. Most of the fleeing Indians don't even have weapons. Those who do have rifles that are outdated and little ammunition, and they can't move very fast in this cold weather. They're heading south, right into the arms of the soldiers."

As she looked back at him, her eyes teared. "They're just scared, Sergeant. What will the soldiers do to them?"

He sighed deeply. "Hard to say, ma'am. They're excited, out for blood, convinced the Indians are on the break to kill white people."

She shook her head. "I've got to get Ben home where it's warm. Please let me know if you hear anything from Colonel Rogers, will you?"

"Yes, ma'am. I'll do that."

"Thank you, Sergeant." She turned to walk back to the house. The wind whipped at her face, stinging her with a fine sleet. She felt sorry for Will, being out on patrol in such weather. But she could not help but feel equally sorry for the fleeing Indians. She thought about Tohave's stories of slaughter, of how the Indians hated the sight of bluecoats and sometimes panicked when they saw soldiers coming. She could not help but believe all of this could have been avoided, including Sitting Bull's death. How sad. Sitting Bull, a great leader, who had traveled all over the country with Buffalo Bill Cody. Now he was dead, shot by his own people. It seemed impossible.

Perhaps it was best that Tohave was dead and did not know about any of this. It would make him very sad, she was sure. She wondered about Rosebud. Was the woman safe and well?

"Cold, mommy," Ben spoke up.

"I know, dear. We're going to the house."

She reached her home and hurried inside, closing the

439

door and then stirring the coals in the fireplace and putting on more wood. After she took off Ben's coat and hat, the boy ran to a corner to play with big wooden blocks the soldiers had made for him, and setting aside her own coat and woolen scarf Katie went to stand by the fire to warm her hands. Outside, the winter wind continued to whip around the house. Winters in this land could be merciless, she well knew. She pictured the poor Indians, running in the snow—old ones, little children, women, warriors trying to protect them. How terrible to be running, alone and afraid, in such weather, unsure where to go, whom to trust. But at least they were headed for Pine Ridge, or so the soldiers thought. Rogers had told her once that Rosebud had gone up to Standing Rock. Was she among those fleeing south? If so, perhaps Katie could find her at Pine Ridge and see her again, once everything settled down. She would like that. She prayed nothing would happen to Rosebud, and if she saw the woman again, she wanted to look her straight in the eyes and ask her if Tohave really was dead. If he was, Katie vowed to go and see his burial site, so that she could put her own mind and heart to rest and make a decision about Will.

She glanced at a ticking clock on the mantel. The next few days of waiting and wondering would be difficult, the nights sleepless. She hoped Will was all right, and she was fearful about what would happen to the Indians.

"God help them," she whispered. "For Tohave's sake, help them."

It was almost Christmas Eve, and it was now obvious Will would not return for Christmas, or bring the tree he had promised.

Rosebud and Stiff Leg joined the fleeing Hunkpapas. Like the rest, they felt their only safety now lay in reaching their only remaining great leader, Red Cloud, at the Pine Ridge Agency.

They fled into the cold, stinging wind—women, children, old people—most of them on foot. Some of the old people had to be carried by others, for most of their horses had been scattered by the soldiers at Standing Rock. Those who had horses shared them with others who were weak and sick. They fled through the Black Hills, hiding in cold, hard rocks, moving ever southward and soon joining up with Big Foot and his Minneconjous, all headed for Pine Ridge and safety. Big Foot was old and sick, but although he knew it might kill him, he led his people, who looked to him for guidance. The soldiers were coming to arrest him, he had heard. Would he be shot down like Sitting Bull? He would take his people to Pine Ridge. It was safer there. But the coughing he had been suffering from grew worse due to his exposure to the cold winds. It became so bad that the old man began to hemorrhage from the lungs and throat whenever he coughed. He could no longer walk or even ride a horse. He was put into one of the few wagons his people had managed to keep their hands on.

"They will come! They will come and kill us!" Rosebud told Stiff Leg in the night, as they huddled together inside a dark, cold tipi, afraid to make a fire lest they be spotted.

"We will make it to Pine Ridge and Red Cloud. You will see. But Big Foot is a sick, old man. I am afraid he will die before we get there. He should not be doing this. Damn them! Damn them all!"

Rosebud shivered. "I am afraid for Tohave. Where did he go?"

"It is hard to say. He can be like a shadow. I would not be surprised if he is watching us right now but not showing himself. He does not want the soldiers to see him. He is afraid they will come for him if they know he is alive."

Rosebud's eyes teared. "What will happen to us, Stiff Leg? I miss Standing Rock. Do you think we can go back there?"

"Who knows? Perhaps after this they will herd us onto even less land. We now know how it feels to be hunted. Men are closing in all around us."

His words were truer than he knew. Major Whitside was only a few miles from them. Big Foot and his followers had been struggling for over ten days to reach Pine Ridge, most of them on foot. On December twenty-eighth their efforts to reach Pine Ridge before the soldiers reached them had failed, and Whitside's four troops of cavalry were upon them.

Big Foot ordered a white flag to be raised over his wagon. As the troops moved in among the shivering, half-starved Indians who watched them suspiciously. Whitside approached Big Foot's wagon and was greeted by the leader, whose blankets were stained with blood he'd coughed up, and whose nose dripped drops of blood into the snow, where they froze. Whitside announced to the dying old chief that he had come to take him and his people prisoner. They would be marched to the army camp at Wounded Knee, there to give up their arms and what remaining horses they had.

In the timber above, a lone Indian watched, sitting on a black Appaloosa. He had spotted Rosebud's horse earlier in the day. She must be with Big Foot. He also could see Stiff Leg's mount, but he did not see his own pinto. The soldiers must have run his horse off up at Standing Rock. At least he still had his black.

Tohave watched the soldiers below. He did not trust them. An army ambulance was brought up and someone was put into it. He did not know then that it was for Big Foot, or that the chief was dying of pneumonia. To Tohave's surprise, the soldiers then herded the Indians

442

into a tight group and the cavalry moved forward again, followed by the ambulance and the Indians' wagons, those soldiers on foot bringing up the rear. Behind them mules pulled two Hotchkiss guns, the hated guns that had killed so many Indians.

Tohave followed quietly, angry that the soldiers had compelled the Indians to make a forced march. Some of the old ones could barely walk.

It was a tired, beaten, quiet group of Indians that arrived at *Chankpe Opi Wakpala*, the creek called Wounded Knee. It was rumored that the bones of Crazy Horse were buried somewhere in this area, but no one knew for sure. Tohave figured by eye count that the women and children outnumbered the men two to one. Why were the soldiers being so careful? The Indians were watched constantly as everyone bedded down for the night. At least from what Tohave could tell, the prisoners were being fed, and some were given shelter in Army tents. But a heavy guard was placed around the tipis and tents, and Tohave's heart tightened when the hated Hotchkiss guns were placed on a rise above the campsite, in a position from which they could rake the entire village if necessary, splattering explosive charges into the defenseless Indians.

Before the night was fully dark, more troops came in. Tohave had seen the leader before, Colonel James Forsyth, the man who had taken over Custer's regiment. He smiled at the memory of defeating Custer. Those were the good days, the wild, free days. The Indians he watched now were a far cry from the proud people they once were. He had no way of knowing that Forsyth had orders to take all of Big Foot's people to the railroad and herd them to a military prison in Oklahoma. He thought the soldiers would help them the rest of the way to Pine Ridge the next morning. But when Forsyth's troops positioned two more Hotchkiss guns above the camp, Tohave became alarmed. He waited for full darkness, then tied his horse and crept into the village, the snow making a carpet that hid his footsteps. He recognized Rosebud's tipi and crawled on his belly to the back of it. A soldier stood in front of it unaware of Tohave's presence, as Tohave shoved his head under the bottom hem of the buffalo-skin wall. Rosebud turned and gasped. Tohave put a finger to his lips. Stiff Leg was there also, and several others who had huddled together for warmth. None of them made a sound, not even the two small children present.

Tohave shimmied all the way inside and crawled over to Rosebud, hugging her.

"You should not be here!" she whispered. "There are soldiers everywhere!"

"I know." He looked at Stiff Leg. "You are all right?"

The man nodded. "I do not trust these soldiers, though."

"Nor do I."

"Big Foot is very sick, Tohave. Blood comes up when he coughs, and he bleeds from his nose. I do not think he has long to live, and I fear we will not be allowed to go to Pine Ridge."

"What should we do, Tohave?" Rosebud asked.

"I don't know. We can only hope the soldiers let you through."

"Some of our men have weapons hidden in their clothing, as do some of the women," Stiff Leg told him. "The soldiers will surely try to disarm us in the morning. They only waited to get us here where they could surround us, in case there is trouble. They will not find all of our weapons. We will have something to fight with, if necessary."

"There are too many, Stiff Leg." Tohave touched

Rosebud's arm. "Do not be afraid if those animals search your person. You know how the soldiers can be. Do not fight them, Rosebud, or they will put a bayonet right through your middle. They cannot rape you. There are too many of them present."

She stared at him with frightened eyes. "Tohave—"

"I am going back. Perhaps I can be of more help that way if something happens. I still have my horse. If you have to run, I will ride down and gather you up, you and Stiff Leg. I only wish I could take everyone. But I urge you not to fight." He looked around at all of them. "Four of the big guns look down on you from above. It would be bad if there was a fight. All of us know what the big guns can do. Do what the soldiers tell you, and perhaps you will get to Pine Ridge peacefully."

He looked at Stiff Leg, then put a hand on the man's shoulder. "Take care of her." He turned to Rosebud and they touched cheeks. "*Nemehotatse*, Rosebud."

He left quickly then, not wanting them to see the tears in his eyes, unable to look any longer at the little children inside the tipi. He slipped back up into the timber to wait for morning, and whatever it would bring to his people.

Tohave awoke to a bugle call. By the time he threw off his blanket and shook the snow from it, soldiers had surrounded the camp, most of them mounted. Someone shouted a command, and all the Indian men began to move to the center. Tohave's anger built when Big Foot was brought out of the warm tent where he had been kept and was set outside with the others, though he was obviously dying.

"Soldier scum!" he hissed to himself.

Something was passed around that the Indians chewed on, apparently an excuse for breakfast. Then another order was shouted, and the Indian men began to stack their rifles in a heap. That done, soldiers were were ordered to go and search the tipis for more weapons. Tohave stiffened. The women would be very afraid of soldiers coming into their tents and tipis. He mounted his Appaloosa, ready to ride. There were a couple of screams. He knew there would be no raping, but he also knew how white soldiers sometimes "searched" Indian women. He rode daringly closer, hardly able to check himself. Soldiers emerged from the dwellings carrying every kind of weapons—axes, knives, even tent stakes—bringing out bundles of possessions and ripping them open and spilling out the contents. Tohave heard the faint sound of women crying. Still, the soldiers were not satisfied. The men were ordered to strip to their loincloths, in spite of the bitter cold.

It was then that Yellow Bird, a medicine man, began to do the Ghost Dance and chant a holy song which assured the others, in their own tongue, that they should not be afraid for the soldiers' bullets could not harm them. A rifle was found on one young Minneconjou called Black Coyote, a new Winchester that the young man did not want to give up. It was his prize possession.

What happened then will never be clear. Black Coyote raised his rifle over his head, protesting its confiscation. He did not fire it, but somewhere, someone did fire a shot, and it was followed by a ripping sound. Had the soldiers fired a Hotchkiss, its shrapnel ripping a tent? What followed was total confusion. The air exploded with gunfire, the firing of soldiers' carbines being so rapid and heavy that it hurt Tohave's ears. This was it! There would be another massacre. Tohave stripped off his shirt. Bullet wounds were cleaner and not as dangerous if no clothing was worn. He headed his horse down toward the melee in which he could already see

Rosebud running with Stiff Leg. He charged blindly into the camp, ducking bullets all the way. His heart ached at the sight of Big Foot lying sprawled on the ground, shot dead, probably one of the first to die.

Some of the firing had stopped, and soldiers on foot grappled with the Indian men who'd stayed behind to keep the soldiers busy while the women and children ran. The Indian men used anything they could get their hands on for clubs, and some had managed to hide knives on their persons, which they now used on the soldiers.

Tohave saw a soldier taking aim with his rifle, his target a fleeing Rosebud. Tohave rode down on the man, swinging his warclub and smashing it into the soldier's head, sending the trooper flying, his skull cracked open.

"Get him!" someone shouted. Tohave whirled, his rifle already out of its scabbard and cocked. Tohave fired, instantly killing the one holding the gun. He charged the second one then, who turned and ran, but Tohave rode up beside him, kicking out and knocking the man down, then firing at him point-blank.

It was then the loud booming of the Hotchkiss guns began. Tohave's horse reared in alarm, and he reined the animal in, turning, searching. Where was Rosebud? Shrapnel rained around him, for the big guns fired rapidly now, almost a shell a second ripping into tents and tipis—and bodies. All around him there was screaming and fighting and blood. His eyes teared at the sight of little children lying sprawled and bloody on the ground, others wandering about and crying or shaking their bloody mothers in attempts to wake them. Tohave ducked down and rode in the direction Rosebud had taken. The ground thundered around him as he headed into the underbrush where she might be trying to hide. He suddenly reined to a quick halt, just before riding over someone. His eyes widened. Rosebud lay sprawled on her

447

stomach, her back ripped open. Stiff Leg sat beside her, a hole in his chest. The man stared up at Tohave.

"Go. Go quickly!" he managed to groan to Tohave. "Do not . . . let them catch you. I am dying . . . and she is already dead."

Tohave could not move. He just stared, unable to stop tears from brimming in his eyes and making their way down his face.

"Go, Tohave! Get away! She would want you . . . to get away!" Stiff Leg slumped over Rosebud's body then. Tohave stared a moment longer, then threw his head back and screamed a long, "No!" that came up from his guts and reached the heavens. He took out his knife and slashed it all the way down his left arm, making a blood sacrifice for lost loved ones. Shrapnel ripped through the underbrush around him then, and his horse whinnied and jerked when a small piece cut his rump. "Bastards!" Tohave yelled. "Coward bluecoat bastards! You shoot your big guns at women and babies—at men without weapons! You are brave men!" He charged up the hill into the safety of the timber, blood streaming from his arm, and tears streaming from his eyes.

When Rogers and his men arrived on the scene late that afternoon, he stared in shock at the bloody mess, bodies strewn in the reddened snow as far as he could see. Soldiers were loading some groaning, crying people into wagons, a few of them soldiers, most of them Indians. Rogers charged his mount up to a lieutenant.

"I'm Colonel Rogers from Fort Robinson. What the hell happened here!" he demanded.

The lieutenant shook his head. "I don't even know, sir. It just happened so fast. We were disarming the Indians . . . someone fired a shot and all hell broke loose."

Rogers could not believe how many dead bodies he was staring at. He rode forward, searching, seeing none alive. Tents and tipis were in shreds, as were most of the bodies. Women lay in the snow still clinging to dead children, and the white landscape was peppered with red blood everywhere he looked. The wind was kicking up a new storm, and it stung his face. The skies were black with the on-coming snows that would bury the already stiff, frozen bodies of dead Indians.

He turned his horse, forcing back an urge to cry. This could not possibly have been necessary. Who was responsible? That would probably never be known. But these were certainly not warring Indians. Big Foot was an old man. Women and children had been along. They were only trying to get to safety; they'd had no thought of making war. Rogers raged silently as he rode back toward the lieutenant, who was directing the placement of the wounded into the wagons. It was then he noticed old Big Foot, lying on his back in the snow, frozen into an almost lifelike form, his head raised and his hands reaching up as though he had been pleading with someone.

"Good God!" he groaned. He turned to the lieutenant and rode closer. "How the hell many do you think were killed, Lieutenant?"

"It's hard to say, sir. There were about three hundred and fifty of them. So far we've only found about forty alive. I think some of the wounded ones crawled away to die alone. We can't find them all."

Rogers rubbed at his eyes. "Where are those who were in charge?"

"Colonel Forsyth and Major Whitside have gone on to Pine Ridge, sir. They left a few of us behind to gather up the wounded. We're taking them to Pine Ridge."

"Why weren't they just walked there in the first place? That's where they were headed. All they wanted to do was get to Pine Ridge."

"I don't knfow about that, sir. Forsyth had orders to arrest them all and ship them to Oklahoma. He was disarming them when the fight broke out."

Rogers gripped his reins tighter. "It was all unnecessary. There was no reason to ship these people to Oklahoma. All they had to do was let them get to Pine Ridge. They were afraid, running."

"Maybe so, sir. I can only follow orders."

Rogers stared at him sadly. "How true for all of us." He turned to his men, ordering them to do what they could to help the others. "I'll go with you to Pine Ridge," he told them. "Get this done as fast as you can, Lieutenant," he added, turning to the man. "There's a blizzard on its way. I feel it in the air. It's getting colder by the minute and the wind is picking up."

"Yes, sir."

Rogers turned his horse and walked it slowly through the bodies, searching for any sign of movement. He well knew how Indians sometimes crawled away to die. Perhaps there were some in the underbrush who needed help. He rode up and down the creek. Some bodies floated in the icy water. As he passed a woman lying on her stomach, a blanket covering her, he thought he heard a sound. He frowned and halted, then dismounted, knelt down, and touched her arm. It was stiff and cold, frozen hard. Again he heard a whimpering sound, almost like the mewing of a kitten. He rolled the woman over, exposing the tiny baby that appeared to be practically newborn. The baby was still alive. The woman had lain over it for protection and warmth.

Rogers could not keep back tears then. He cleared his throat and swallowed, breathing deeply to control his emotions as he took his own blanket from his horse—it was dryer than the Indian blanket—and wrapped it around the baby. Then he picked the infant up, remounted, and rode back to the wagons. He handed the baby to the lieutenant.

"You take damned good care of this infant," he told him. "See that he or she gets some milk as soon as you get to Pine Ridge. Wash the baby and keep it dry and warm. Understand?"

The lieutenant looked at the tiny bundle in surprise, then back up at Rogers. "Yes, sir."

"I know someone who might take that baby and care for it," Rogers added, thinking of Katie. Perhaps the Indian baby would help ease her grief over Tohave, as well as the sorrow she would feel when she learned what had happened here today. He realized then that Christmas had already passed. He'd missed it. He'd never brought her the tree he had promised.

He sighed. Christmas. He had not seen much Christian love today at Wounded Knee—just another bloody massacre. How would the government and those in charge make themselves look good this time? They would probably find a way. They always did.

He turned his horse and began the search again, huddling under the cape he wore over his woolen coat. The wind was getting nastier by the minute as he rode farther out, into places where the soldiers had given up searching. Hoof and boot prints were everywhere, evidence that men had already searched. Rogers followed trails of blood to places where bodies had fallen. One led into thick underbrush far downstream.

He dismounted and walked into the thicket, literally stumbling over a body as he did so. His footsteps were muffled by the thick snow, and the body lay just beneath a rocky ledge so that he did not see it until the last minute. He leaned forward, and as he did so, he thought he heard a strange gasp and a movement. He whirled, drawing his pistol.

451

A chilly wave swept through him then, as he stared into an Indian's face. The man had been kneeling beside not just one dead body but two. For a moment both men did nothing but stare.

"Tohave!" Rogers finally whispered. "My God!"

Tohave backed up like a cornered wildcat. He remembered Rogers from Fort Robinson. "Do not shoot," he said. His face was drawn and tear-stained, and a long, ugly red scar was forming on his left arm. He was still shirtless in spite of the cold. "I only came to get my friends. I want to bury them myself."

Rogers hesitated, speechless. Katie's suspicions had been right. Tohave interpreted his hesitation as a sign that Rogers intended to shoot him or arrest him, but he remembered that Rogers was a good white man, a rarity. He did not want to kill him. He leaped at Rogers then, grabbing the man's wrist and pushing. The gun went off before Tohave slammed Rogers' hand against a rock, making him drop the gun. Tohave picked up the gun then and ran for soldiers were coming, drawn by the sound of the shot. Rogers got to his feet and ran for his horse. From somewhere in the underbrush Tohave emerged, now mounted on the black Appaloosa. He headed into the timber.

Troopers were already coming closer. "Don't shoot! For God's sake don't shoot!" Rogers called to them. "Leave him to me!" He rode out after Tohave then, while the bewildered soldiers watched.

Rogers' heart pounded. If anything happened to Tohave now, after he'd found him alive, Katie would never forgive him. He rode hard, but he realized his horse could not catch the black Appaloosa. He did not want to shoot Tohave from the saddle, yet he had to stop him. He pulled out his rifle, cocked it, and then lowered it, halting his horse and resting the rifle on his lap.

He cupped his hands around his mouth. "Tohave! Katie's back!" he screamed as loud as he could. The words echoed against the forested hills, carried by the winter winds. He saw Tohave's horse slow, and he screamed the words again. "Katie's back! She needs you!"

Tohave's horse slowed more and turned, then stood still. The Indian stared at Rogers from a distance, and Rogers gripped his rifle in his right hand and slowly rode forward. Tohave did not move.

As Rogers came closer, Tohave sat rigid, seemingly unaffected by the wicked wind that whipped against his bare skin. his jaw was flexed in distrust, his dark eyes were menacing. He looked ready to dart away at any moment.

"I speak the truth, Tohave," Rogers told him carefully. "Katie is back. Her husband is dead and she's living at Fort Robinson."

Tohave seemed to tremble then. "If you lie, Tohave will find a way to kill you! Do not trick me, white eyes!"

"It's not a trick. I speak the truth. I always have, Tohave. You know that."

Tohave backed his horse. "The soldiers search for Tohave . . . to hang him because of the traders."

"That's not true. That matter is over. No thought was given to arresting or hanging you once we heard the story from Katie. What happened to you, Tohave? We were told you were dead, so was Katie."

"I was badly wounded. I could not move or speak for many months, until one of your white doctors took out the bullet in my spine. Then I learned to walk again."

Rogers' eyebrows arched. "An Army doctor?"

Tohave nodded. "He swore himself to secrecy for the chance to see if he could remove a bullet from such a dangerous place. When they brought me to him, they

453

covered me. No one knew or cared who I was. As a man, I was already dead. I was no use to anyone. I knew Katie would try to come to me, if she knew. It would have been bad for her. It was best she thought me dead, for I never thought I would walk again. When I did, she was gone, and my heart stopped singing."

Rogers felt pain at the look of love in Tohave's eyes, though he would rather have found proof of Tohave's death. "She came back, Tohave," he said. "Her husband died after accidentally severing his foot while chopping wood, so she decided to stay at Fort Robinson for the winter." He smiled sadly. "If I let you get away, she'll be a very upset lady. Come with me, and you can see her."

Tohave's breathing quickened and he swallowed. "It is true?"

Rogers nodded. "Give me your weapons, Tohave. Just come with us peacefully. I'll take you to Pine Ridge with the others and then I'll send for Katie. You won't be arrested, and you won't be harmed. I promise. You can live at Pine Ridge again."

Tohave tensed, then backed away as soldiers started to come up behind Rogers. The officer turned to them. "Stay back, damn it!" he ordered. "Get the hell back to the wagons!"

The men frowned curiously, then turned their horses and retreated. Rogers met Tohave's eyes again. "I only need your weapons to show the others you don't intend to put up a fuss, Tohave. They're all trigger-happy right now. When things settle down, you can have your weapons back. I give you my word."

Their eyes held.

"I can see her? It is true?"

Rogers nodded. "It is true."

"And she is free? Her husband is dead?"

Rogers fought to control his jealousy. He could shoot

454

Tohave right now, shoot him dead and get away with it, rid himself of the barrier that kept him from Katie. But he loved her too much to do that. She had known little enough happiness. She deserved to have whatever life she chose. "He's dead."

Tohave's eyes brightened. He handed his pistol and rifle over, but when his hand rested on his knife, he hesitated. After a moment, he pulled it out and handed it over also. "I wish to bury my friends first," he told Rogers. "The others will be pushed into a common grave like dead cattle. I know the soldiers and how they bury the Indians after something like this. I do not want my friends in that grave. They stayed with me when I was like a vegetable, nursed me, cleaned up after me. I must bury them properly before I go."

Rogers nodded. "I'll help you. We'll have to work fast, Tohave. There's a storm coming."

Tohave's eyes teared. "There is always a storm coming, for my people. What I have seen today will live in my mind for many winters, Lieutenant Rogers."

Rogers sighed. "I'm a colonel now." He looked out over the bodies strewn for hundreds of yards. "This won't live just in your memory, Tohave. It will live in the memory of a lot of white men, too, and will bring them shame in years to come. If you think I'm proud of this, think again. I guarantee that those who participated in this massacre will be doing a lot of thinking from now on."

"I told them," Tohave said brokenly, his voice husky. "I told them it was not true that the Ghost Shirts would protect them. I wanted to believe . . . but deep inside I knew. No Savior is going to come for us and bring back the buffalo and our loved ones and the good days."

He stared vacantly at the bloody mess below. Katie! Katie was back, and she was free. After all of this, if she did not still want him, he decided he would end his life. She was his only hope of finding some happiness. But perhaps she had changed. After all this time she might not want him anymore, other than as a friend. He rode forward, his emotions mixed, telling himself not to hope for too much. He would see Katie, but first he must bury Rosebud and Stiff Leg. Gone! So much was gone! Katie was all that was left.

Katie answered the knock at the door to find a sergeant standing there with a telegraph message. The man removed his hat and held out the note. "This came for you, ma'am, from Pine Ridge."

She took it quickly. "Has there been any more word about that terrible massacre? Have you heard from Colonel Rogers?" she asked quickly.

"I think that message is from him, ma'am."

"Oh, thank God! Come in, Sergeant. It's cold out there. I'll fix you a cup of coffee."

The man hesitated. "Well, maybe for just a minute. I have to get back."

He stepped inside and closed the door, and Katie quickly opened the message.

Safe at Pine Ridge. Must stay a few days, make reports, etc. Terrible massacre at Wounded Knee. Have an escort bring you here right away. Have found Tohave alive and well. After every storm comes the sun.

Love, Will

Katie grabbed the back of a chair and stumbled.

"Ma'am?" The sergeant quickly walked over and took her arm. "What is it?"

She read the telegram again, then hunched over, in

456

tears. The sergeant helped her to the sofa. "Mrs. Russell? What is it? Is something wrong with Colonel Rogers?"

She shook her head. How could she explain that her tears were tears of joy? Tohave! Could it really be true? "Get some men together," she said brokenly. "Colonel Rogers wants me to go to Pine Ridge right away."

Chapter Twenty-Six

Rogers entered the log house at Pine Ridge where Tohave was staying with two Indian men and the wife of one of them. The additional Indians at Pine Ridge meant doubling and tripling the numbers in each house, and tipis were springing up around the agency. The tipi Tohave had once shared with Rosebud had been blown to pieces. It was Tohave who had answered Will's knock, looking ready to fight if necessary. Will could see fear on the faces of the Indians who shared the house.

"Come ride with me, Tohave. We have to talk," he said.

"You promised I would get my weapons back. Show them to me, and I will go with you."

Will sighed and went out to his horse. Taking from it a rifle, a handgun, and a knife, he carried them back to the door. "Now will you come with me?"

Tohave took the weapons and looked them over. Then he nodded, shoving the knife into an empty sheath and sticking the handgun into the front of his weapons belt. He left his rifle inside the cabin and put on a heavy buffalo skin coat, then left with Rogers. He walked out to a stall, pushing snow in front of his winter moccasins as he walked. Quickly, he slipped an Indian-style rope bridle

459

onto his Appaloosa and then slid up onto the animal's bare back, guiding it out to Rogers, who rode until he was nearly a mile from the main buildings before halting his horse and turning to Tohave. He just stared at the man for several seconds.

"I sent the telegram," he finally said. "Someone will bring her here. You said you didn't trust the soldiers at Fort Robinson, and right now I don't blame you, so she's coming here. You don't have to go to the fort. I'll wait till she arrives, then I'll be going back to the fort, with or without her, whichever she chooses."

Tohave studied the white man's gray eyes. "You hardly spoke of her on the way here, but I see in your eyes that she is more than just another white woman to you."

Will swallowed, repressing his jealousy of the handsome warrior. He realized the man had made love to Katie Russell, and he suddenly knew that he would never have her.

"I love her, Tohave."

Tohave looked defensive again, and a bit jealous himself. Had the soldier brought him out here to kill him because he did not want Katie to see him after all?

"Don't go resting your hand on that knife," Will told him, reading Tohave's thoughts. "She told me about you—all of it."

"She is not bad!" Tohave spoke up sharply, defensively. "She is a good woman who had a cruel husband. He was not her husband at all, just a man she was forced to live with. Tohave was her true husband!"

Rogers sighed and rubbed at his eyes. He took a cigarette from an inside pocket and offered one to Tohave, who took it carefully, watching Will's every move as a hunted creature would. Will lit his own cigarette, taking a deep puff before lighting Tohave's.

"I'll tell you something, Tohave. When I first realized

you had bedded Katie Russell, I had murder in my heart, but I've watched Katie since the first time I saw her at the fort. I know what she's been through." He puffed the cigarette again. "I never blamed her for turning to you. God knows she needed someone to hold her and be her friend, show her the gentler side of man. I would have liked to do that myself . . ." He looked Tohave over almost chidingly. "But I didn't have the opportunity to ride all over the prairie free as a bird and fly down on her nest whenever I felt like it."

Tohave grinned a little at the sarcastic remark. "There is something you are trying to tell Tohave?"

"Yes, there is something I'm trying to tell you," Rogers answered. "I'm trying to tell you that if Katie still wants you, I'll not stand in the way. But it will be a damned hard life for her, and you are going to have to settle down and make some kind of a decent living, try to live at least a little bit like a white man. She should have a cabin, and her husband should be with her, not off wandering the land like a wild animal."

Tohave looked out across the prairie. "Tohave wandered the land because he had nothing better to do. There was nothing he cared about anymore." He looked back at Will. "I have thought of these things, Colonel. Tohave is no fool. He knows how it is with white women, needing a house with four walls, a man at their side. I have a card, see?" He reached into a pocket on the inside of his weapons belt and pulled out a small card, handing it over to Rogers. "See? There is a name on there. It is the name of the man who wants to buy Tohave's carvings. All I have to do is write to him and he will come and see me. He will pay Tohave well for his carvings—white man's money that can buy the things a white woman needs. Tohave will carve, and sometimes hunt for meat. But he will not wander." He puffed his cigarette and took the card back from Will. "Tohave will have Katie write to this man. And perhaps the white man's government would pay Katie Russell to work for the agency, teach the Indian children white man's words and ways, writing and numbers. Tohave thinks of these things. You see?"

Will took a long drag on his cigarette. "I see." He sighed deeply, throwing the cigarette down into the snow. "Where will you live? It can't be at the fort—too many whites there who might make trouble for Katie—and I'm not so sure she'd be entirely welcome here."

"Tohave will build a cabin close to here, but not too close. My people will slowly accept her. You know Katie. Do you not think they would soon learn to love her, when they see she does not look at them as Indians but only as people?"

Will nodded and smiled sadly. "I suppose."

Tohave sobered then, throwing down his own cigarette stub. "*Ai.* But what if she does not want Tohave? A fine soldier man loves her, a white man who can give her everything. She would have no more problems." He looked Will over. "And what about her feelings for you, Colonel? Does she love you back?" He suddenly stiffened. "Have you claimed her?"

Will looked away, shifting in his saddle. "If you mean have I bedded her, the answer is no. I don't think she felt the same . . ."—the word was bitter in his mouth—". . . passion with me that she did for you." He met Tohave's dark eyes then. "She'll want you, Tohave. When she told me about you, the look in her eyes told me she'd never love me like that. She refused to believe you were dead. When I came out here I was supposed to look for proof of your death, a grave, anything. She said she couldn't rest easy until she knew for certain. I guess that's what love is. You get certain feelings. You sense things that no one else senses. She begged me to get her some kind of proof before she would give me an answer."

462

"An answer? You asked her to be your wife?"

Will nodded. "I did. That's when she decided it was only fair to tell me everything about you."

Their eyes held for several seconds. "You are an unusual white man, Colonel Rogers. Most would have rid themselves of the problem by just shooting me. You could have done so easily, but you did not. I will remind her of this, that it might be better to stay with Colonel Rogers. It would be an easier life for her. I, too, love her, Colonel, but it is not up to us to choose. It is up to Katie."

Will looked him over. "Personally I don't think I have a chance. She loved you first, and when a man beds a woman, she feels she belongs to him. You've already captured something I'll never have. Don't think I haven't thought about shooting you. I've considered doing so more than once. But then I'd lose her for good, wouldn't I? She'd know it was deliberate, and she'd never love me. She'd hate me. I'd rather we part friends than lose her that way. And she's suffered enough, Tohave. If she still wants you, it's her right to have that little bit of happiness. But your worlds are very different, and that will make things hard sometimes. I just want your promise that if she stays with you you'll always be good to her, provide for her—and no whiskey. She went through enough hell with her husband and his whiskey."

Tohave shook his head. "Tohave is against the firewater. When I was in pain I drank it until I could not be without it. Rosebud helped me stop. I do not touch it now." His eyes saddened. "I have lost much, Colonel Rogers. If I had not learned Katie is alive, I might have ended my own life, and this thing at Wounded Knee will burn in Tohave's heart for many winters to come, probably until he dies. Most of my friends are dead. My family is dead. Tohave has nothing now, nothing but Katie, if she still wants me. I would not betray her, would not harm her. And I would not drink the firewater."

"She has a fine son, Tohave. His name is Ben. You can teach him many things about being a man, but you must love him as if he were your own."

Tohave nodded. "You know how important sons are to the Indian, even adopted ones. The son cannot be blamed for the father's evils. He will be his own man. Tohave can teach him to hunt, to ride. And we will have more sons. We will—" He stopped then and sighed. "But perhaps she will not even stay with Tohave." He eyed Will. "Tohave will not bring you harm if she chooses you, as she would be wise to do. It will simply be ended."

Will turned his horse and moved closer, his mount facing in the opposite direction from Tohave's so that he could look straight at the Indian. "Don't do something stupid if she does choose me, Tohave. You have too much potential. You're intelligent and talented. You could do a lot for your people, be a good representative. Don't waste your gifts by killing yourself over a woman. Promise me you'll think about what you could do for the Sioux and the Northern Cheyenne. They need strong leaders right now. They need hope. With or without Katie, you can help them."

Tohave's eyes teared. "I will think on these things. It is not easy to watch your people die slowly, Colonel. It brings rage to my heart, yet I can no longer fight back. There is nothing left to fight for, no place else to run."

Will put out his hand and they grasped wrists. "A pact then. It's up to Katie, and no revenge on either side once she chooses."

Tohave nodded. "Agreed."

Will smiled sadly. "I'm afraid I have no doubt what she'll do. You take damned good care of her or I'll have your ass."

A faint smile passed over Tohave's lips. They held

wrists for several seconds, firmly, lightly testing each other out, wondering as men do how they would fare in a fight together, wanting that fight but knowing it would be foolish. The answer lay in Katie, not in each other. Tohave swallowed then.

"In battle, Tohave has never been afraid," he told Will. "Now for the first time Tohave is afraid . . . afraid of losing one tiny woman. I lost her once. To lose her twice would be very hard, and Tohave shakes like a child."

Will squeezed his arm. "You're a good man, Tohave. If I didn't think so, I'd never have given Katie the chance to choose. You'd be lying back there at Wounded Knee."

Tohave looked in the direction of the terrible slaughter. Out there in the cold snow lay frozen Indians, half-buried in the blizzard of the day before. Soon soldiers would go back to dig a large hole and bury them in a common grave, men, women, children, old ones, all shoved in together like diseased cattle. The few Indians remaining were at Pine Ridge now, most of them wounded, some grotesquely, limbs missing, open, painful wounds gaping. This was what the new religion had brought them, disaster rather than hope, death rather than life.

Tohave released his grip and turned his horse. "You go back now. Tohave has much to think about," he told Rogers. "Tohave wishes to stay out here alone and pray."

Will backed off. "All right. I'll send word when she arrives. You ride out to this spot when you hear. I want to talk to her first. Then I'll send her out. It will be a couple of days yet."

Tohave nodded. "The blessings of *Maheo* be upon you, Colonel William Rogers."

Will sighed. He could not help but like Tohave. "And upon you, Tohave. But most of all on Katie Russell."

465

Tohave turned, a tear on his cheek, and rode off into the timber. Will headed back to camp. There was nothing he could do now but wait for Katie.

Katie rode in on an Army horse, surrounded by four men, one of whom held little Ben in front of him. The snows were deep but not impassable, and the blizzard had moved east, leaving the air still, with a few snowflakes drifting down now and then. The men led her to Colonel Rogers' tent, and he came out just as they were dismounting.

"Katie! You got here fast." Rogers reached up to help her down.

"We came by horse. It's faster than a wagon." She turned and looked up at him as soon as she was on her feet. "Where is he? What happened?"

His eyes saddened at the joy in her own. He had his answer. He looked over at one of the men who had been guarding his tent. "Go to Tohave's cabin and tell him Katie Russell is here," he told the private. "Tell him to go to the place where we rode. He'll know what I mean."

"Yes, sir."

The young man left right away and Will took Katie's arm, urging her inside his tent. He looked back at the man who still held Ben. "Keep the boy occupied for a while, will you? Mrs. Russell has some things to tend to."

The man nodded and turned his horse, riding toward the agency supply store. Will led Katie inside and closed the tent flap. A heating stove was set up inside, and the interior was warm enough to permit Katie to remove her gloves and her coat.

"Is something wrong with Tohave? she asked anxiously. "Why didn't I hear from him? My God, Will, is he really alive?"

He laughed lightly and shook his head. "Will you calm

down?" He urged her to a chair. "Sit."

She did as he'd bid, never removing her eyes from his face, and Will sat down across from her, studying her a moment. "You look prettier than ever. Must be love."

Her eyes teared. "I'm sorry, Will. Are you all right? I heard about that awful massacre."

He rolled and lit a cigarette. "It was over when I got there." He took a deep drag on the cigarette. "It was pretty horrible, Katie. I'm afraid Rosebud was killed, and Tohave's friend Stiff Leg."

"Oh, no!" She swallowed back tears. "Tohave wasn't wounded, I hope!"

"No. I was riding through the mess of bodies, searching for anyone still alive. I stumbled through some underbrush and practically fell over Rosebud and Stiff Leg. And there he was—Tohave—staring right at me. He apparently had been there during the fighting and I don't doubt he killed his share of soldiers, although he won't say, of course. He'd come back for Rosebud's and Stiff Leg's bodies. He didn't want them buried in a common grave with the others. I very nearly shot him, he startled me so." He held her eyes. "And then I was tempted to shoot him anyway. Doing so would have saved me a lot of heartache."

"Will," Katie said softly. She reached out and took his hand. "How can I thank you? And how in God's name did he happen to be there? He was supposed to be dead."

He pulled his hand away and went to the stove, pouring coffee into two cups. "The wounds he received after that business with the traders left him totally paralyzed. The way he tells it, he couldn't even talk. How he lived as long as he did, no one will ever know. I suppose he survived because he's a tough, strong, stubborn man. The condition he was in, you being married and pregnant and all, Rosebud and Stiff Leg decided it was better for both of you if you thought Tohave was dead. It would have been

467

impossible for you to go to him, and you would have pined away for him if you'd known he was alive. And then, Tohave wouldn't have wanted you to see him that way, no longer a man, just a vegetable."

He handed her a cup of coffee. "Warm yourself up. You're going back out in the cold soon." He sat down again, taking another puff on his cigarette. "Then you and Ezra left for Illinois. Not long after, one of our Army doctors operated on Tohave as sort of an experiment. From what I can determine, he kept Tohave's identity a secret. He was probably afraid the officers would refuse to let him operate if he didn't because Tohave was considered a troublemaker and they would have preferred to let him die. I think I know which doctor it was. He's an expert surgeon. I'm sure Tohave was a great challenge for him. The bullet was lodged right beside the spine. It had come close to severing the spine, in fact." He sipped some coffee. "Obviously the operation was successful. Tohave says it took many long, painful months for recovery, and during them he used whiskey for a pain killer. But he says he doesn't touch it now. You make sure he sticks to that. Whiskey and Indians don't mix well."

She thought about Ezra. "It isn't just Indians who don't mix well with whiskey," she said absently.

Will put out his cigarette and took her hand. "Well, Tohave is not like Ezra Russell, and I really don't think it will be a problem for him now. At any rate, he says he went to your farm once, but it was deserted and he figured you were gone for good. At that time he was living clear up at Standing Rock on Sitting Bull's reservation and feeling pretty low, still struggling with the whiskey. You know what happened then: Sitting Bull killed, and I suspect Tohave was in on the skirmish that followed. Afterward, most of the Hunkpapas and Minneconjous fled, trying to get here, to Red Cloud and the Oglala. God only knows what really happened at Wounded Knee. It was totally unnecessary, I can tell you that, but it probably won't be reported that way. At any rate, I saw Tohave. He wrestled my gun from me and took off running, got to his horse. There was no way I could catch that black Appaloosa of his, and I didn't want to shoot him. So I just called out to him that you were back." He grinned, but his eyes were sad. "That stopped him faster than a bullet."

She smiled, squeezing his hand. "Oh, Will, what can I say? I have to go to him. I have to!" She leaned forward and kissed his cheek. "I'm so sorry."

He shrugged. "Well, I tried. I guess I'll have to pay a few more visits to Colonel McBain's daughter, won't I?"

She pressed her lips together, struggling not to cry, then put down her cup and flung her arms around his neck. "Am I crazy, Will? Maybe he doesn't even want me anymore."

He set aside his cup, stood, and pulled her into his arms. "You aren't crazy. You're just in love. What the hell difference should it make that he's Indian? Of course he still wants you. The man's been going crazy waiting and wondering if you still want him. You just keep in mind that it won't be easy, Katie. You're choosing a hard road."

"Compared to living with Ezra, it won't be hard at all. I'll be loved, Will. That's all I care about."

He held her tightly and kissed her hair. "I would have loved you, too. But I guess if feeling doesn't go both ways, it's not the same, is it?"

When she leaned back and looked up at him, his lips met hers, firmly, hungrily. He released her mouth then and hugged her tightly. "Good-bye, Katie. I'll say it now, and you remember it. If anything goes wrong, if something happens to Tohave—anything—you get hold of me, even if I'm stationed someplace else, understand?

469

No matter what happens, don't be afraid to come to me or contact me. Promise me, Katie."

"I promise." She hugged him tighter. "Oh, Will, I'm so scared and excited and happy and—" She looked up at him then. "How can I thank you? How can I ever, ever thank you? You could have killed him and never told me. God bless you, Colonel William Rogers."

He smiled bashfully. "Maybe I'm a bigger fool than either you or Tohave."

She smiled and kissed him lightly. "Will, I'm so scared."

He let go of her, squeezing her arms gently. "Well, that's interesting. Tohave told me the same thing. He's nervous as a caged bear about seeing you again. He's probably already at the place I arranged for you to meet. It's about a mile from the agency. I thought you'd want to be alone."

She hurriedly put on her coat. "Show me where!"

He smiled and shook his head. In many ways she was still like a little girl. She'd never really known young, passionate love. She deserved this chance.

"Katie, I'd like you to consider something, once you've talked with Tohave."

She pulled on her gloves and looked up at him. "What is it?"

"I found a baby under the body of its dead mother at Wounded Knee, practically a newborn. It's a beautiful little girl child. I thought maybe you'd consider taking it. The few Indian women left around here have a big load to carry, but I'm sure one of them will take the child if you can't."

Her eyes softened. "I'll be glad to see her when I come back. And if Tohave is the same man I once loved, he'll let me take her in a minute."

He nodded. "She couldn't be in better hands. Let's go then." He led her outside, to where his own horse stood saddled, and he helped her mount. Then he got on his own horse and rode off with her. He would take her most of the way and then let her go on alone. She would be riding to Tohave, and out of his life, but for once Katie Russell would have what she wanted. She would be a happy woman.

Katie's heart pounded so hard she felt she could hardly get her breath. They rode far beyond the agency's main buildings, toward a forested hill. Suddenly in the distance the black Appaloosa emerged. Katie reined her horse to a halt, staring, shaking. Tohave! Will pulled up beside her, pressing her arm.

"You go on alone."

She looked at him a moment. "I'm sorry, Will. I do love you . . . but it just isn't the same."

He touched her cheek gently, then turned his horse and rode off.

Katie's eyes returned to the lone figure on the black horse, and her heart raced. She was painfully aware of every nerve and muscle in her body as she urged her horse forward. Tohave! He had seen so much loss, so much death. They both had suffered, in different ways. She rode closer, ever closer, as he headed toward her. Finally he halted his horse and stared at her with tear-filled eyes. When he dismounted, she quickly did the same. What was there to say? They only had to look at each other to know. She ran to him. He opened the thick buffalo-skin coat he wore, and in the next moment she was enveloped by his arms and the coat, wrapped in love and joy. He lifted her, both of them laughing and crying at the same time. Then he swung her around and around, as she breathed in the sweet scent of man and buckskins, the familiar, wonderful scent that was Tohave.

Could this be real? Could God truly be this good to her? He muttered something softly in the Cheyenne tongue, then fell into the deep snow with her, rolling her onto her

471

back and hovering over her.

"Hemene! Nemehotatse, Hemene!"

She looked up into his handsome face. Behind his brilliant smile and dark, dancing eyes, she saw his pain.

"Tohave!" she whispered.

Their eyes held for a moment as he studied her lovingly. Then he pulled the woolen scarf from her head and fingered her thick, auburn hair.

"I did not dream the Spirits could be this good to Tohave again. He will spend the rest of his life thanking them. Tohave not only walks, but he has found his Mourning Dove, and she is free."

He came closer, his lips covering her mouth then, searching hungrily in the old, familiar way, softly stirring her innermost passions and awakening all the love she had kept hidden for so long. Teasing her with his tongue, he made her whimper and return his kiss with so much passion she wondered if she would burst with love for him. She was lost beneath him, his broad shoulders made broader by the big fur coat, his thick, shining hair shrouding her.

When his lips left hers and moved over her cheek and throat, they were both crying openly, his tears mingling with her own. He gathered her into his arms and held her close, as they lay in a deep indentation in the snow, neither feeling cold for their blood was too warm.

He kissed her over and over—her eyes, her cheeks, her throat—slipping a hand under her coat and running it over her stomach as he finally raised up on one elbow to study her.

"You are more beautiful than ever, Katie Russell."

She sniffed and reached up to touch his face. "My sweet, beautiful Tohave."

He grinned. "A man cannot be beautiful."

"But you are."

He kissed her fingers, his smile fading. "It will be hard

472

for you, if you stay with me."

"I don't care."

"The colonel loves you. He would give you a good life."

She traced a finger over his lips. "And what if ten years from now I saw you, Tohave? I would feel no differently. If we could be alone together, I might be untrue to my husband. I married once for reasons other than love, and even though Will is a good man, I will not do that again, not just to have a husband and a father for Ben. If I can't marry for love, I don't want to marry at all, Tohave. I'll not lie with one man while my heart longs for another."

He smiled. "And what about this land that you once hated so much? Tohave must live here for he loves it."

"It was never the land, I hated. I've grown to love it. I hated the man who brought me here, but I love the man who would keep me here. This land is you, Tohave, wild and open and free. And I'm not afraid of what others will think. I will never hang my head or speak softly when I tell others that you are my husband, Tohave. You are my beautiful, proud, brave warrior."

He met her lips again, softly, lovingly. "There are Christian missionaries on the reservation. We will be married your Christian way so they cannot speak against us, and Tohave will build you a cabin, then carve the animals for money. I will love your son as my own, and—"

"When, Tohave? When can we marry?"

He laughed, nuzzling her neck. "Today. Why not today?"

He ran a hand over her breast beneath the coat, and she kissed his hair. "Yes. Why not today?" She smoothed some hair back from his face. "You are completely well, Tohave? You have no pain?"

"Sometimes a little. But I can bear it. I am a whole man again, and now I have found my woman."

He laughed and rolled her over so that she was on top of him. She met his mouth again, and they kissed in joy and passion. Then he turned her over onto her back, snuggling over her to keep her warm, and they lay together for several minutes, enjoying being close, and drinking in the reality that he was alive and she was free to go to him. How long they lay there, quietly loving, sometimes crying, they were not sure. The wind blew, but they did not feel it. Snow wisped over them, but they were unaware of the cold. At last he raised up, his dark eyes searching her blue ones.

"There is much to talk about. You do not have to marry Tohave today if you are not sure."

She reached up and ran her fingers over his lips. "From the moment I received word that you were still alive I was sure what I wanted, Tohave. I don't want to wait. Let others think what they will. I want to be your wife. Just promise me you will love my son."

"The Indian loves all children."

She smiled the smile he had missed for so long. "Will found an Indian baby with its dead mother at Wounded Knee—a little girl. He asked me to take her."

Tohave gently ran a hand over her forehead and pressed it to the side of her face. "You think Tohave would turn away a homeless child of his own blood? But we will have more . . . our own sons and daughters."

She felt hot passion rise at the words, and her eyes shone with love. "Yes. We will have our own."

He grinned, and getting up and lifting her into his arms, he swung her around, laughing.

"You make Tohave's heart sing, Hemene. The whole prairie sings for Tohave when he thinks of you, even in the winter when the insects sleep. You are my prairie love song."

He put her on his black Appaloosa and leaped up behind her, and picking up the reins of her horse, he headed back toward the reservation. The Nebraska wind she had once hated stung her face, but it didn't bother her. She was hearing the most beautiful music of all—the music in her own heart.

And so out of sorrow came a spark of joy, at least for two people, one white, one Indian, in a big country where it was possible whites and Indians would never abide peacefully. But the Indian no longer had any choice in the matter. Soon soldiers would leave for Wounded Knee, to gather the dead bodies frozen into the grotesque positions in which they had fallen. They would shove them all into a mass grave, and another chapter in history would be closed. At Pine Ridge were the few Indians left alive, most of them badly wounded, only four of them men. The others, forty-seven women and children, all lay on beds of hay on the floor of an Episcopal mission. The year was 1890, and Christmas was just past. A banner hung inside the mission, reading "PEACE ON EARTH, GOOD WILL TO MEN," a sad and ironic contrast to the white man's attitude toward the Indians who lay bleeding and dying on the floor. Few could rise above such differences. Two now rode toward the agency, a white woman called Katie, and an Indian called Tohave. His vision had come true. His people had suffered again, but Tohave rode free on his Appaloosa, his Katie in front of him.

GLOSSARY OF CHEYENNE TERMS

Ai—Yes, agreed
Hahkotaho—Grasshoppers
Hekonoestse—Buffalo grass
Hemene—Mourning Dove
Heyoka—Fool
Hoshuh—Be still, be calm
Katum!—Damn!
Maoestse—Prairie grass
Nemehotatse—I love you
Pave-voonao—Good morning!
Vehoe—White Man

Taylor—made Romance From Zebra Books

Whispered Kisses   (2912, $4.95/5.95)
Beautiful Texas heiress Laura Leigh Webster never imagined that her biggest worry on her African safari would be the handsome Jace Elliot, her tour guide. Laura's guardian, Lord Chadwick Hamilton, warns her of Jace's dangerous past; she simply cannot resist the lure of his strong arms and the passion of his *Whispered Kisses*.

Kiss of the Night Wind   (2699, $4.50/$5.50)
Carrie Sue Strover thought she was leaving trouble behind her when she deserted her brother's outlaw gang to live her life as schoolmarm Carolyn Starns. On her journey, her stagecoach was attacked and she was rescued by handsome T.J. Rogue. T.J. plots to have Carrie lead him to her brother's cohorts who murdered his family. T.J., however, soon succumbs to the beautiful runaway's charms and loving caresses.

Fortune's Flames   (2944, $4.50/$5.50)
Impatient to begin her journey back home to New Orleans, beautiful Maren James was furious when Captain Hawk delayed the voyage by searching for stowaways. Impatience gave way to uncontrollable desire once the handsome captain searched *her* cabin. He was looking for illegal passengers; what he found was wild passion with a woman he knew was unlike all those he had known before!

Passions Wild and Free   (3017, $4.50/$5.50)
After seeing her family and home destroyed by the cruel and hateful Epson gang, Randee Hollis swore revenge. She knew she found the perfect man to help her—gunslinger Marsh Logan. Not only strong and brave, Marsh had the ebony hair and light blue eyes to make Randee forget her hate and seek the love and passion that only he could give her.

Available wherever paperbacks are sold, or order direct from the Publisher. Send cover price plus 50¢ per copy for mailing and handling to Zebra Books, Dept. 3160, 475 Park Avenue South, New York, N.Y. 10016. Residents of New York, New Jersey and Pennsylvania must include sales tax. DO NOT SEND CASH.